# BEN HUR

...hrist

...than ...storical ...ma of the whole Roman world at the time of Christ, and it tells, in marvelous detail, the story of Christ and His followers.

Its hero, Judah Ben Hur, scion of an old and eminent Jewish family, is a patriot—a proud representative of a splendid culture. His adventures take him from Jerusalem to Rome, back to Antioch and to a life sentence in the Roman galleys. His escape, his revenge, his search for his lost mother and sister, all lead to his meeting with Christ. The awesome and sublime spectacle of the Crucifixion itself becomes the climax of this extraordinary novel.

BEN HUR is a rich reading experience—one of the classics of all time.

# BEN HUR

### A Tale of the Christ

by

## LEW WALLACE

BANTAM BOOKS  NEW YORK

BEN HUR

A BANTAM BOOK

PUBLISHED APRIL 1956

Bantam Books are published by Bantam Books, Inc.
Its trade mark, consisting of the words "BANTAM BOOKS"
and the portrayal of a bantam, is registered in the U. S.
Patent Office and in other countries. *Marca Registrada.*

PRINTED IN THE UNITED STATES OF AMERICA

BANTAM BOOKS, 25 West 45th Street, New York 36, N. Y.

TO THE WIFE OF MY YOUTH
WHO STILL ABIDES WITH ME

*"But this repetition of the old story is just the fairest charm of domestic discourse. If we can often repeat to ourselves sweet thoughts without ennui, why shall not another be suffered to awaken them within us still oftener."*—*Hesp*: JEAN PAUL F. RICHTER.

----

"See how from far upon the eastern road
  The star-led wisards haste with odours sweet
\*   \*   \*   \*   \*   \*   \*   \*   \*
But peaceful was the night
Wherein the Prince of Light
  His reign of peace upon the earth began,
The winds with wonder whist
Smoothly the waters kist,
    Whispering new joys to the mild ocean—
Who now hath quite forgot to rave,
While birds of calm sit brooding on the charmed wave."
              *Christ's Nativity; The Hymn*—MILTON

# BEN-HUR:
## A Tale of the Christ

## BOOK FIRST

### CHAPTER I.

OUT OF one of the innumerable wadies running from the base of the narrow mountain called the Jebel es Zubleh which intersect the Roman road, a lone traveller mounted on a great white dromedary emerged, going toward the table-lands of the Desert of Arabia. It was winter, the dry season, and months since the wadies had passed their torrents into the Jordan or the Dead Sea. Now, as the camel and its passenger lifted from the final break of the gulley, before them spread the semi-arid desert-edge, strewn with boulders of granite and gray and brown stones, interspersed with languishing acacias and tufts of camel-grass. And before them also was the end of the road.

Of this, the traveller, raising his large dark eyes, seemed unaware. He was a man of middle years, his flowing black beard streaked with white, his face brown as a parched coffee berry and all but hidden by a red *kufiyeh* or head kerchief. He reclined beneath a small green awning stretched over the carpeted and cushioned space on the camel's back, between two wooden boxes, balanced so that they hung on either side.

The dromedary itself was remarkable for its height, its breadth of foot, its long, slender neck of swanlike curvature, its head, wide between the eyes and tapering to a muzzle which a lady's bracelet might have almost clasped; its step long and elastic, tread sure and soundless—all certified its Syrian blood, old as the days of Cyrus, and absolutely priceless. There was the usual bridle, covering the forehead with scarlet fringe and garnishing the throat with pendent brazen

1

chains, each ending with a tinkling silver bell. But, strangely, there was neither rein for the rider nor strap for a driver.

More than ever now did the camel seem insensibly driven; it lengthened and quickened its pace, its head pointing straight toward the horizon; through the wide nostrils it drank the wind in great draughts as the litter swayed and rose and fell like a boat in the waves.

Off to the right rose the hills of the Jebel, and over their highest peak a vulture sailed, its broad wings carrying it in ever-widening circles. Still the tenant under the green tent gave no sign of recognition; his eyes were fixed as in a dream. The going of the man, like that of the animal, was as one being led.

The dromedary swung forward, keeping the trot steadily and the line due east. In that time the traveller never changed position, nor looked to the right or the left. Four hours passed without rest or deviation from the course. Vegetation ceased. The sand, so crusted on the surface that it broke into rattling flakes at every step, held undisputed sway. The shadow that before followed had now shifted to the north, and was keeping even race with the objects which cast it.

Then exactly at noon the dromedary, of its own will, stooped, and uttered the cry, peculiarly piteous, by which its kind sometimes craves attention and rest. The master bestirred himself, waking, as it were, from sleep. He threw the curtains of the *houdah* up, looked at the sun, surveyed the country on every side long and carefully, as if to identify an appointed place. Satisfied with the inspection, he drew a deep breath and nodded, much as to say, "At last, at last!" A moment after, he crossed his hands upon his breast, bowed his head, and prayed silently. The pious duty done, he prepared to dismount. He spoke the command heard doubtless by the favorite camels of Job—*Ikh! ikh!*—the signal to kneel. Slowly the animal obeyed, grunting the while. The rider then put his foot upon the slender neck, and stepped upon the sand.

## Chapter II.

THE MAN, loosening the silken rope which held the *kufiyeh* on his head, brushed the fringed folds back until his face was bare—a strong face, the low, broad forehead, aquiline nose, the outer corners of the eyes turned slightly upward, the straight hair falling to the shoulder in many plaits, were signs of origin impossible to disguise. So looked the Pharaohs and later Ptolemies; so looked Mizraim, father of the Egyptian race. He wore the *kamis*, a white cotton shirt, tight-sleeved, open in front, extending to the ankles and embroidered down

2

the collar and breast, over which was thrown a brown woollen cloak, edged with a margin of yellow. His feet were protected by sandals, attached by thongs of soft leather. A sash held the *kamis* to his waist. What was very noticeable, considering he was alone, and that the desert was the haunt of leopards and lions, and men quite as wild, he carried no arms, not even the crooked stick used for guiding camels.

The traveller's limbs were numb for the ride had been long and wearisome; so he rubbed his hands and stamped his feet, and walked round the camel, now content with the cud he had already found. Shading his eyes with his hands, he examined the horizon; and when the survey was ended, his face clouded enough to show that he was expecting company. He went first to the litter, and produced a sponge and a small skin of water, with which he washed the eyes, face, and nostrils of the camel; that done, he drew out a circular cloth, red-and-white-striped, a bundle of rods, and a stout cane. The latter was a device of lesser joints, one within another, which formed a centre pole higher than his head. When the pole was planted, and the rods set around it, he spread the cloth over them, and was at home. From the litter he brought a square rug, and covered the floor of the tent on the side from the sun. That done, he went out, and once more, and with greater care and more eager eyes, swept the encircling country.

"They will come," he said calmly. "He that led me is leading them. I will make ready."

From the pouches which lined the interior of the cot, and from a willow basket which was part of its furniture, he brought forth materials for a meal: platters close-woven of the fibres of palms; skins of wine, mutton dried and smoked; Syrian pomegranates; dates of El Shelebi; cheese, like David's "slices of milk"; and leavened bread from the city bakery— all of which he had carried and set upon the carpet under the tent. As the final preparation, about the provisions he laid three pieces of silk cloth, used among people of the East to cover the knees of guests while at table.

All was now ready. He stepped out: lo! in the east a dark speck on the face of the desert. He stood as if rooted to the ground; his eyes dilated; his flesh crept chilly. The speck grew; became large as a hand; at length assumed defined proportions. A little later, full into view swung a duplication of his own dromedary, tall and white, and bearing a houdah, the travelling litter of Hindostan. Then the Egyptian crossed his hands upon his breast, and looked to heaven.

"God only is great!" he exclaimed.

The stranger drew nigh—at last stopped. Then he, too, seemed just waking. He beheld the kneeling camel, the tent, and the man standing prayerfully at the door. He crossed his

3

hands, bent his head, and prayed silently; after which, in a little while, he stepped from his camel's neck to the sand, and advanced towards the Egyptian, as did the Egyptian towards him. A moment they looked at each other; then they embraced according to the custom of the East.

"Peace be with thee, O servant of the true God!" the stranger said.

"And to thee, O brother of the true faith!—to thee peace and welcome," the Egyptian replied, with fervor.

The new-comer was tall and gaunt, with lean bronze face, sunken eyes, white hair and beard. He, too, was unarmed. His costume was Hindostani; over the skull-cap a shawl was wound in great folds, forming a turban; his body garments were in the style of the Egyptian's, except that the *aba,* or cloak, was shorter, exposing wide flowing breeches gathered at the ankles. In place of sandals, his feet were clad in half-slippers of red leather, pointed at the toes. Save the slippers, the costume from head to foot was of white linen. The air of the man was stately, severe. Only in his eyes was there proof of humanity; when he lifted his face from the Egyptian's breast, they were glistening with tears.

They looked to the north, where already plain to view, a third camel, of the whiteness of the others, came careening like a ship. They waited, standing together—waited until the new-comer arrived, dismounted, and advanced towards them.

"Peace to you, O my brother!" he said, while embracing the Hindoo.

And the Hindoo answered, "God's will be done!"

The last comer was unlike his friends: his frame was slighter; his complexion white; a mass of waving light hair was a perfect crown for his well-shaped head. He was also unarmed. Under the folds of the Tyrian blanket appeared a tunic, short-sleeved and low-necked, gathered to the waist by a band, and reaching nearly to the knee; leaving the neck, arms, and legs bare. Sandals guarded his feet. Fifty years, probably more, had spent themselves upon him, with no other effect, apparently, than to tinge his demeanor with gravity and temper his words with forethought.

When his arms fell from the Egyptian, the latter said, with a tremulous voice, "The Spirit brought me first; wherefore I know myself chosen to be the servant of my brethren. The tent is set, and the bread is ready for the breaking. Let me perform my office."

Taking each by the hand, he led them within, and removed their sandals and washed their feet, and he poured water upon their hands, and dried them with napkins.

Then, when he had laved his own hands, he said, "Let us eat, that we may be strong for what remains of the day's

4

duty. While we eat, we will each learn who the others are, and whence they come, and how they are called."

He took them to the repast, and seated them so that they faced each other. Simultaneously their heads bent forward, their hands crossed upon their breasts, and, speaking together, they said aloud this simple grace:

"Father of all—God!—what we have here is of thee; take our thanks and bless us, that we may continue to do thy will."

With the last word they raised their eyes, and looked at each other in wonder. Each had spoken in a language never before heard by the others; yet each understood perfectly what was said.


## CHAPTER III.

THE MEETING took place in the year of Rome 747. The month was December, and winter reigned over all the regions east of the Mediterranean. The company under the little tent ate heartily; and after the wine they talked.

"To a wayfarer in a strange land nothing is so sweet as to hear his name on the tongue of a friend," said the Egyptian. "Before us lie many days of companionship. It is time we knew each other. So, if it be agreeable, he who came last shall be first to speak."

Then, slowly at first, like one watchful of himself, the Greek began:

"Far to the west of this there is a land which may never be forgotten; if only because the world is too much its debtor, and because the indebtedness is for things that bring to men their purest pleasures. O my brethren, hers is the glory which must shine forever in perfected letters, by which He whom we seek and proclaim will be made known to all the earth. The land I speak of is Greece. I am Gaspar, son of Cleanthes the Athenian.

"In the northern part of my country, in Thessaly, there is a mountain famous as the home of the gods; Olympus is its name. There I found a cave in a hill near the mountain, and there I dwelt, waiting for revelation. Believing in God, invisible yet supreme, I also believed it possible so to yearn for him with all my soul that he would take compassion and give me answer.

"The door of my heritage looks over an arm of the sea, the Thermaic Gulf. One day I saw a man flung overboard from a ship sailing by. He swam ashore. I received and took care of him. He was a Jew, learned in the history and laws of his people; and from him I came to know that the God of my prayers did indeed exist, and had been for ages their lawmaker, ruler, and king. What was that but the revelation I dreamed of? My faith had not been fruitless; God answered me!

"That was not all," the Greek continued. "The man told me more. He said the prophets who, in the ages which followed the first revelation, walked and talked with God, declared he would come again. He told me, further, that the second coming was at hand—was looked for momentarily in Jerusalem.

"When the Jew was gone, and I was alone again, I chastened my soul with a new prayer—that I might be permitted to see the King when he was come, and worship him. One night I sat by the door of my cave when suddenly, on the sea below me, I saw a star begin to burn; I raised my eyes and slowly it arose and drew nigh, and stood over the hill and above my door, so that its light shone full upon me. I fell down, and was silent, and I heard a voice say:

"'O Gaspar! Thy faith hath conquered! Blessed art thou! With two others, come from the uttermost parts of the earth, thou shalt see Him that is promised, and be a witness for him, and the occasion of testimony in his behalf. In the morning arise, and go meet them, and keep trust in the Spirit that shall guide thee.'

"And in the morning I put off my hermit's garb, and dressed myself as of old. From a hiding-place I took the treasure which I had brought from the city. A ship went sailing past. I hailed it, was taken aboard, and landed at Antioch. There I bought the camel and his furniture. Thus I journeyed to Emesa, Damascus, Bostra, and Philadelphia; thence hither. And so, O brethren, you have my story. Let me now listen to you."


CHAPTER IV.


THE EGYPTIAN and the Hindoo looked at each other; the former waved his hand; the latter bowed, and began:

"You may know me, brethren, by the name of Melchior. I speak to you in a language which, if not the oldest in the world, was at least the soonest to be reduced to letters—I mean the Sanscrit of India. My people were the first to walk in the fields of knowledge, first to divide them, first to make them beautiful according to the Great Shastras, or books of sacred ordinances. In further explanation, let me say that Brahm is taught, by the same sacred books, as a Triad— Brahma, Vishnu, and Shiva. Of these, Brahma is said to have been the author of our race; which, in course of creation, he divided into four castes. From his mouth proceeded the Brahman caste, nearest in likeness to himself, highest and noblest, sole teachers of the Vedas, which at the same time flowed from his lips in finished state, perfect in all useful knowledge. From his arms next issued the Kshatriya, or warriors; from his breast, the seat of life, came the Vaisya, or producers— shepherds, farmers, merchants; from his foot, in sign of degre- dation, sprang the Sudra, or serviles, doomed to menial duties for the other classes—serfs, domestics, laborers, artisans. Take notice, further, that the law, so born with them, forbade a man of one caste becoming a member of another; the Brahman could not enter a lower order; if he violated the laws of his own grade, he became an outcast, lost to all but outcasts like himself."

The brows of the Hindoo knit painfully. "I was born a Brahman. My life, consequently, was ordered down to its least act, its last hour. I might not walk, eat, drink, or sleep without danger of violating a rule. And the penalty, O breth- ren, the penalty was to my soul! According to the degrees of omission, my soul went to one of the heavens—Indra's the lowest, Brahma's the highest; or it was driven back to become the life of a worm, a fly, a fish, or a brute. The reward for perfect observance was Beatitude, or absorption into the being of Brahm, which was not existence as much as absolute rest."

The Hindoo gave himself a moment's thought. "When I was ready to marry and become a householder—I questioned everything, even Brahm; I was a heretic. At last I beheld the principle of life, the element of religion, the link between the soul and God—Love!"

The shrunken face of the good man kindled visibly, and he clasped his hands with force. "The happiness of love is in action; its test is what one is willing to do for others. I could not rest. Brahm had filled the world with so much wretched- ness. The Sudra appealed to me; so did the countless devotees and victims. In the shade of the temple built to the sage Kapila, I thought to find rest. But twice every year came pil- grimages of Hindoos seeking the purification in the waters of the sacred Ganges. Their misery strengthened my love. Against its impulse to speak I clenched my jaws; for one word, one act of kindness to the outcast Brahmans who dragged themselves to die on the burning sands—a blessing said, a cup of water given—and I became one of them, lost to family, country, privileges, caste. Then love conquered! I spoke to the disciples in the temple; they drove me out. I spoke to the pilgrims; they stoned me from the island. On the high- ways I attempted to preach; my hearers fled from me, or sought my life. In all India, finally, there was not a place in which I could find peace or safety—not even among the out- casts, for, though fallen, they were still believers in Brahm. In my extremity, I looked for a solitude in which to hide from all but God. I followed the Ganges to its source, far up in the Himalayas. Through gorges, over cliffs, across glaciers, by peaks that seemed star-high, I made my way to the Lang Tso, a lake of marvelous beauty, asleep at the feet of the mountains which flaunt their crowns of snow everlastingly in the face of the sun. There, in the centre of the earth, where the Indus, Ganges, and Brahmapootra rise to run their different courses; where man took up his first abode, there I went to abide alone with God, praying, fasting, waiting for death.

"One night I walked by the shores of the lake, and spoke to the listening silence. 'When will God come and claim his own? Is there to be no redemption?' Suddenly a light began to glow tremulously out on the water; soon a star arose, and moved towards me, and stood overhead. The brightness stunned me. While I lay upon the ground, I heard a voice of infinite sweetness say, 'Thy love hath conquered. Blessed art thou, O son of India! The redemption is at hand. With two others, from far quarters of the earth, thou shalt see the Redeemer, and be a witness that he hath come. In the morning arise, and go meet them; and put all thy trust in the Spirit which shall guide thee.'

"In the morning I started to the world by the way I had come. In a cleft of the mountain I found a stone of vast worth, which I sold in Hurdwar. In Ispahan I bought the camel, and thence was led to Bagdad, not waiting for caravans. Alone I travelled, fearless, for the Spirit was with me, and is with me yet. What glory is ours, O brethren! We are to see the Redeemer—to worship him! I am done."


## Chapter V.

The Egyptian said, with characteristic gravity:

"I salute you, my brother. You have suffered much, and I rejoice in your triumph. If you are both pleased to hear me, let me first speak of myself and my people. I am Balthasar the Egyptian."

Both listeners bowed to the speaker.

"There are many distinctions I might claim for my race," he continued; "but I will content myself with one. History began with us. We were the first to perpetuate events by records kept. So we have no traditions; instead of poetry, we offer you certainty. On the façades of palaces and temples, on obelisks, on the inner walls of tombs, we wrote the names of our kings, and what they did; and to the delicate papyri we intrusted the wisdom of our philosophers and the secrets of our religion—all the secrets but one, whereof I will presently speak. Older than the Vedas of Para-Brahm, O Melchior; older than the songs of Homer or the metaphysics of Plato, O my Gaspar; older than the sacred books or kings of the people of China, or those of Siddârtha, son of the beautiful Maya; older than the Genesis of Mosché the Hebrew—oldest of human records are the writings of Menes, our first king.

"By those records," Balthasar continued, "we know that when the fathers came from the far East, from the region of the birth of the three sacred rivers, from the centre of the earth—the Old Iran of which you spoke, O Melchior—they came bringing with them the history of the world before the Flood, and of the Flood itself, as given to the Aryans by the sons of Noah, they taught God, the Creator and the Beginning, and the Soul, deathless as God. The ideas—God and the Immortal Soul—were borne to Mizraim over the desert, and by him to the banks of the Nile.

"Many nations have loved the sweet waters of the Nile," he next said; "the Ethiopian, the Pali-Putra, the Hebrew, the Assyrian, the Persian, the Macedonian, the Roman—of whom all, except the Hebrew, have at one time or another been its masters. So much coming and going of peoples corrupted the old Mizraimic faith. The Valley of Palms became a Valley of Gods. The Supreme One was divided into eight, each personating a creative principle in nature, with Ammon-Re at the head. Then Isis and Osiris, and their circle, representing water, fire, air, and others forces, were invented. Still the multiplication went on until we had another order, suggested by human qualities, such as strength, knowledge, love, and the like.

"The records show that Mizraim found the Nile in possession of the Ethiopian, who, without writing, without books, quieted his soul by the worship of animals, birds, and insects, holding the cat sacred to Re, the bull to Isis, the beetle to Pthah. A long struggle against their rude faith ended in its adoption as the religion of the new empire. Then rose the mighty monuments that cumber the river-bank and the desert —obelisk, labyrinth, pyramid, and tomb of king, blended with tomb of crocodile.

"I said awhile ago that to papyri we intrusted all the secrets of our religion except one; of that I will now tell you. We had as king once a certain Pharaoh who, to establish the new system, strove to drive the old entirely out of mind. The Hebrews then dwelt with us as slaves. They clung to their God; and when the persecution became intolerable, they were delivered in a manner never to be forgotten. I speak from the records now. Mosché, himself a Hebrew, came to the palace, and demanded permission for the slaves, then millions in number, to leave the country. The demand was in the name of the Lord God of Israel. Pharaoh refused. Hear what followed: First, all the water, that in the lakes and rivers, like that in the wells and vessels, turned to blood. Yet the monarch refused. Then frogs came up and covered all the land. Still he was firm. Then Moshé threw ashes in the air, and a plague attacked the Egyptians. Next, all the cattle, except of the Hebrews, were struck dead. Locusts devoured the green things of the valley. At noon the day was turned into a darkness so thick that lamps would not burn. Finally, in the night all the first-born of the Egyptians died; not even Pharaoh's escaped. Then he yielded. But when the Hebrews were gone he followed them with his army. At the last moment the sea was divided, so that the fugitives passed through it dry-shod. When the pursuers drove in after them, the waves rushed back and drowned horse, foot, charioteer, and king.

"The priests of that time wrote what they witnessed, and the revelation has lived. So I come to the one unrecorded secret: In my country, brethren, we have, from the day of the unfortunate Pharaoh, always had two religions—one private, the other public; one of many gods, practised by the people; the other of one God, cherished only by the priesthood. Rejoice with me, ⌣ brothers! Like a seed under the mountains waiting its hour, the glorious Truth has lived; and this—this is its day!"

From a gurglet of water near-by the Egyptian took a draught, and proceeded: "I was born at Alexandria, a prince and a priest, and had the education usual to my class. But very early I became discontented. Part of the faith imposed was that after death the soul at once began its former progression from the lowest up to humanity, the highest and last existence; and that without reference to conduct in the mortal life. When I heard of the Persian's Realm of Light, his Paradise across the bridge Chinevat, where only the good go, the thought haunted me and I brooded over the ideas of Eternal Transmigration and Eternal Life in Heaven. If, as my teacher taught, God was just, why was there no distinction between the good and the bad? At length it became clear that death was only the point of separation at which the wicked are left or lost, and the faithful rise to a higher life; life active, joyous, everlasting—life with God! The discovery led to another inquiry. Why should the Truth be longer kept a secret for the selfish solace of the priesthood? The reason for the suppression was gone. In Egypt we had Rome instead of Rameses. One day, in the most splendid and crowded quarter of Alexandria, I arose and preached. The East and West contributed to my audience. I preached God, the Soul, Right and Wrong, and Heaven, the reward of a virtuous life. You, O Melchior, were stoned; my auditors pelted me with epigrams, covered

10

my God with ridicule, and darkened my Heaven with mockery.

"I gave much thought to finding the cause of my failure, and at last succeeded. Up the river there is a village of herdsmen and gardeners. I went there. In the evening I called the people together, men and women, the poorest of the poor. I preached to them exactly as I had preached in the Brucheium. They did not laugh. Next evening I spoke again, and they believed and rejoiced, and carried the news abroad. At the third meeting a society was formed for prayer. I returned to the city then and evolved this lesson: To begin a reform, go not into the places of the great and rich; go rather to those whose cups of happiness are empty—to the poor and humble. And then I laid a plan and devoted my life. From that day, O brethren, I travelled up and down the Nile, in the villages, and to all the tribes, preaching One God, a righteous life, and reward in Heaven."

A flush suffused the swarthy cheek of the speaker.

"The years so given, O my brothers, were troubled by one thought—When I was gone, what would become of the cause I had started? Was it to end with me? Brethren, the world is now in the condition that one must not merely come in God's name, he must demonstrate all he says, even God. So much do false deities crowd every place, converts must be willing to die rather than recant. And who in this age can carry the faith of men to such a point but God himself? To redeem the race he must make himself once more manifest; He must come in person.

"Like you, my brethren, I went out of the beaten ways, I went where man had not been, where only God was. Above the fifth cataract, above the meeting of rivers in Sennar, up the Bahr el Abiad, into the far unknown of Africa, I went. There, by a lake which is the mother of the great river, for a year and more I lived. One night I walked in the orchard close by the little sea. 'The world is dying. When wilt thou come?' So I prayed. The glassy water was sparkling with stars. One of them seemed to leave its place, and rise to the surface, where it became a brilliancy burning to the eyes. Then it moved towards me, and stood over my head, apparently in hand's reach. I fell down and hid my face. A voice, not of the earth, said, 'Thy good works have conquered. Blessed art thou, O son of Mizraim! With two others, from the remotenesses of the world, thou shalt see the Saviour, and testify for him. In the morning arise, and go meet them. And when ye have all come to the holy city of Jerusalem, ask of the people, Where is he that is born King of the Jews? For we have seen his star in the East, and are sent to worship him. Put all thy trust in the Spirit which will guide thee.'

11

"I bought my camel, and came hither without rest, by way of Suez and Kufileh, and up through the lands of Moab and Ammon. God is with us, O my brethren!"

He paused, and thereupon, with a prompting not their own, they all arose, and looked at each other. Then, by a simultaneous impulse, the three joined hands.

Presently they went out of the tent. The desert was still as the sky. The sun was sinking fast. The camels slept.

A little while after, the tent was struck, and, with the remains of the repast restored to the cot, the friends mounted and set out single file, led by the Egyptian. The camels swung forward in steady trot, keeping the line and the intervals so exactly that those following seemed to tread in the tracks of the leader. The riders spoke not once.

And as the three tall white figures sped, with soundless tread, through the opalescent light, suddenly before them, not farther up than a low hill-top, flared a lambent flame; as they looked at it, the apparition contracted into a focus of dazzling lustre. Their hearts beat fast; and they shouted as with one voice, "The Star! the Star! God is with us!"

## Chapter VI.

IT WAS the third hour of the day, and the press of people at the market of the Joppa Gate of Jerusalem, vendors hawking their wares, travellers, Romans, Jews, Arabs, had continued without apparent abatement since dawn. Over by the south wall, a man, a woman, and a donkey, stood apart from the teeming, busy throng.

The man stood by the animal's head, holding a leading-strap, and leaning upon a stick which seemed to have been chosen for the double purpose of goad and staff. His dress was like that of the ordinary Jews around him, except that it had an appearance of newness. His features told of fifty years of life, a surmise confirmed by the gray that streaked his otherwise black beard. He looked around him with the half curious, half-vacant stare of a stranger and provincial.

The donkey ate leisurely from an armful of green grass in sleepy content, unmindful of the woman sitting upon its back in a cushioned pillion. An outer robe of dull woollen stuff completely covered her person, while a white wimple veiled her head and neck. Once in a while, impelled by curiosity to see or hear something passing, she drew the wimple aside, but so slightly that the face remained invisible.

"Are you not Joseph of Nazareth?" The speaker was standing close by.

12

"I am," answered Joseph, turning gravely around. "And you—ah, peace be unto you: my friend Rabbi Samuel!"

"The same give I back to you." The Rabbi paused looking at the woman, then added, "To you and unto your house and all your helpers, be peace."

With the last word, he placed one hand upon his breast and inclined his head to the woman, who, to see him, had by this time withdrawn the wimple enough to show the face of one but a short time out of girlhood. Thereupon the acquaintances grasped right hands, as if to carry them to their lips; at the last moment, however, the clasp was let go, and each kissed his own hand, then put its palm upon his forehead.

"You passed the night in this city of our fathers?"

"No," Joseph replied, "as we could only make Bethany before the night came, we stayed in the khan there, and took the road again at daybreak."

"The journey before you is long then—not to Joppa, I hope."

"Only to Bethlehem."

The countenance of the Rabbi became lowering and sinister, and he cleared his throat with a growl.

"Yes, yes—I see," he said. "You were born in Bethlehem, and go thither now, with your daughter, to be counted for taxation as ordered by Cæsar. The children of Jacob are as the tribes in Egypt were—only they have neither a Moses nor a Joshua. How are the mighty fallen!"

Joseph answered, "The woman is not my daughter."

But the Rabbi clung to the political idea; and he went on, without noticing the explanation, "What are the Zealots doing down in Galilee?"

"I am a carpenter, and Nazareth is a village," said Joseph cautiously. "The street on which my bench stands is not a road leading to any city. Hewing wood and sawing plank leave me no time to take part in the disputes of parties."

"But you are a Jew," said the Rabbi earnestly, "and of the line of David. It is not possible you can find pleasure in the payment of any tax except the shekel given by ancient custom to Jehovah."

Joseph held his peace.

"I do not complain," his friend continued, "of the amount of the tax—a denarius is a trifle. Oh, no! The imposition is the offence. And, besides, what is paying it but submission to tyranny? Tell me, is it true that Judas claims to be the Messiah? You live in the midst of his followers."

"I have heard his followers say he was the Messiah."

At this point the wimple was drawn aside, and for an instant the whole face of the woman was exposed. The Rabbi

13

had time to see a countenance of rare beauty, kindled by a look of intense interest; then a blush overspread her cheeks and the veil was returned to its place.

The politician forgot his subject. "Your daughter is comely," he said, speaking lower.

"She is not my daughter," Joseph repeated.

The curiosity of the Rabbi was aroused; seeing which, the Nazarene hastened to say further, "She is the child of Joachim and Anna of Bethlehem, of whom you have at least heard; for they were of great repute—"

"Yes," remarked the Rabbi, deferentially, "I know them. They were lineally descended from David. I knew them well."

"Well, they are dead now," the Nazarene proceeded. "Joachim was not rich, yet he left a house and garden to be divided between his daughters Marian and Mary. This is one of them; and to save her portion of the property, the law required her to marry her next of kin. I am her uncle, and she is now my wife."

The Rabbi clasped his hands, and looked indignantly to heaven, exclaiming, "The God of Israel still lives! The vengeance is his!"

With that he turned and abruptly departed. A stranger near by, observing Joseph's amazement, said quietly, "Rabbi Samuel is a zealot. Judas himself is not more fierce."

In another hour the couple passed out the gate, and, turning to the left, took the road to Bethlehem. Carefully, tenderly, the Nazarene walked by the woman's side, leading-strap in hand. On their left, reaching to the south and east round Mount Zion, rose the city wall, and on their right the steep prominences which form the western boundary of the valley.

The sun streamed down and Mary, daughter of Joachim, dropped the wimple entirely, and bared her head.

She was not more than fifteen. Her form, voice, and manner belonged to the period of transition from girlhood. Her face was perfectly oval, her complexion more pale than fair. The nose was faultless; the lips, slightly parted, were full and ripe, giving to the lines of the mouth warmth, tenderness, and trust; the eyes were blue and large, and shaded by drooping lids and long lashes; and, in harmony with all, a flood of golden hair, in the style permitted to Jewish brides, fell unconfined down her back to the pillion on which she sat. Often, with trembling lips, she raised her eyes to heaven, often she crossed her hands upon her breast, as in adoration and prayer; often she raised her head like one listening eagerly for a calling voice. Now and then Joseph turned to look at her, and, catching the expression kindling her face as with light, with bowed head, wondering, plodded on.

So at length, across a valley, they beheld Bethlehem, the

old, old House of Bread, its white walls crowning a ridge, and shining above the brown scumbling of leafless orchards. They paused there, and went down into the valley to the well. The narrow space was crowded with people and animals. A fear came upon Joseph—a fear lest, if the town were so thronged, there might not be house-room for Mary. Without delay, he hurried on, past the pillar of stone marking the tomb of Rachel, up the gardened slope, saluting none of the many persons he met on the way, until he stopped before the portal of the khan that stood outside the village gates, near a junction of roads.

## CHAPTER VII.

AT THE khan, or inn, there was no host or hostess; no clerk, cook, or kitchen; a steward at the gate was all the assertion of government or proprietorship anywhere visible. Strangers arriving stayed at will without rendering account. A consequence of the system was that whoever came had to bring his food and culinary outfit with him, or buy them of dealers in the khan. The same held good as to his bed and bedding, and forage for his beasts. Water, rest, shelter, and protection were all he looked for from the proprietor, and they were gratuities. The peace of synagogues was sometimes broken by brawling disputants, but that of the khans never. The houses and all their appurtenances were sacred: a well was not more so.

The khan at Bethlehem, before which Joseph and his wife stopped, was a quadrangular block of rough stones, one story high, flat-roofed, the wall unbroken by a window, and with but one principal entrance—a gateway on the front. The road ran by the door so near that the chalk dust half covered the lintel. A stone fence extended down the slope to a limestone bluff; making what was the first essential to a khan—a safe enclosure for animals.

In a village like Bethlehem, there was but one khan; and though born in the place, the Nazarene, from long residence elsewhere, had no claim to hospitality in the town. Moreover, the enumeration for which he was coming might be the work of weeks or months; Roman deputies in the provinces were proverbially slow; and to impose himself and wife for a period so uncertain upon acquaintances or relations was out of the question. So, while he was yet climbing the slope, in the steep places toiling to hasten the donkey, the fear that he might not find accommodations in the khan became a painful anxiety; for he found the road thronged with men and boys. And when he was close by, his alarm increased at the discovery of a crowd investing the door of the establishment, while the enclosure adjoining, broad as it was, seemed already full.

"We cannot reach the door," Joseph said, in his slow way. "Let us stop here, and learn, if we can, what has happened."

The wife, without answering, quietly drew the wimple aside. The look of fatigue at first upon her face changed to one of interest. She found herself at the edge of an assemblage that could not be other than a matter of curiosity to her. There were men on foot, running hither and thither, talking shrilly and in all the tongues of Syria; men on horseback screaming to men on camels; men struggling doubtfully with fractious cows and frightened sheep; men peddling bread and wine; and among the mass a herd of boys apparently in chase of a herd of dogs. Everybody and everything seemed to be in motion at the same time. She sighed, and settled down on the pillion, looking off to the tall cliffs of the Mount of Paradise.

While she was thus looking, a man pushed his way out of the press, and, stopping close by the donkey, faced about with an angry brow. The Nazarene spoke to him.

"As I am what I take you to be, good friend—a son of Judah—may I ask the cause of this multitude?"

The stranger turned fiercely; but, seeing the solemn countenance of Joseph, so in keeping with his deep, slow voice and speech, he raised his hand in half-salutation, and replied,

"Peace be to you, Rabbi! When the proclamation went abroad requiring all Hebrews to be numbered at the cities of their birth— That is my business here, Rabbi."

Joseph's face remained stolid. "I have come for that also— I and my wife."

The stranger glanced at Mary and kept silence. She was looking up at the bald top of Gedor. The sun touched her upturned face, and filled the violet depths of her eyes, and upon her parted lips trembled an aspiration which could not have been to a mortal.

"Of what was I speaking? Ah! I remember—the multitude here." He turned to Joseph and spoke positively: "I tell you the khan is full. It is useless to ask at the gate."

Joseph hesitated, but at length replied, "Let me speak to the gate-keeper myself. I will return quickly."

The keeper sat on a great cedar block outside the gate. Against the wall behind him leaned a javelin. A dog squatted on the block by his side.

"The peace of Jehovah be with you," said Joseph at last confronting the keeper. "I am a Bethlehemite. Is there not room for—"

"There is not."

"You may have heard of me—Joseph of Nazareth. This is

the house of my fathers. I am of the line of David."

These words held the Nazarene's hope. If they failed him, further appeal was idle, even that of the offer of many shekels. To be a son of Judah was one thing—in the tribal opinion a great thing; to be of the house of David was yet another; on the tongue of a Hebrew there could be no higher boast. A thousand years and more had passed since the boyish shepherd became the successor of Saul and founded a royal family. Wars, calamities, other kings, and the abrasions of time might have impoverished many of his descendents; yet they had the benefit of history and genealogy sacredly kept; they could not become unknown, while, wherever they went in Israel, acquaintance drew after it a respect almost amounting to reverence.

If this were so in Jerusalem and elsewhere, certainly one of the sacred line might reasonably rely upon it at the door of the khan of Bethlehem.

The keeper of the gate slid down from the cedar block, and, laying his hand upon his beard, said, respectfully, "Rabbi, I cannot tell you when this door first opened in welcome to the traveller, but it was more than a thousand years ago; and in all that time there is no known instance of a good man turned away save when there was no room to rest him in. If it had been so with the stranger just cause must the steward have who says No to one of the line of David. Wherefore, I salute you again; and, if you care to go with me, I will show you that there is not a lodging-place left in the house; neither in the chambers, nor in the lewens, nor in the court—not even on the roof. May I ask when you came?"

"But now."

The keeper smiled. "'The stranger that dwelleth with you shall be as one born among you, and thou shalt love him as thyself.' Is not that the law, Rabbi? Or can I say to one a long time come, 'Go thy way; another is here to take thy place?'"

Still Joseph quietly persisted: "I do not care for myself, but I have with me my wife, and the night is cold—colder on these heights than in Nazareth. She cannot live in the open air. Is there not room in the town?"

"These people"—the keeper waved his hand to the throng before the door—"have all besought the town, and they report no more accommodations."

Again Joseph studied the ground, saying, half to himself. "She is so young! if I make her bed on the hill, the frosts will kill her."

Then he spoke to the keeper again. "It may be you knew her parents, Joachim and Anna once of Bethlehem, and, like myself, of the line of David."

17

"Yes, I knew them. They were good people. That was in my youth."

This time the keeper's eyes sought the ground in thought. Suddenly he raised his head. "If I cannot make room for you," he said, "I cannot turn you away. Rabbi, I will do the best I can for you. You shall not lie out on the ridge. Bring your wife, and hasten; for, when the sun goes down behind the mountain, you know the night comes quickly."

"I give you the blessing of the houseless traveller; that of the sojourner will follow."

So saying, the Nazarene went back joyfully to Mary and he put her again on the donkey. Mary's veil was raised.

"Blue eyes and hair of gold," muttered the steward to himself, seeing but her. "So looked the young king when he went to sing before Saul."

Then he took the leading-strap from Joseph and said to Mary, "Peace to you, O daughter of David!"

The party were conducted into a wide passage paved with stone, from which they entered the court of the khan. By a lane reserved in the stowage of the cargoes, they emerged into the enclosure adjoining the house, and came upon camels, horses, and donkeys, tethered and dozing in close groups; among them were the keepers, men of many lands; and they, too, slept or kept silent watch. They went down the slope of the crowded yard and at length turned into a path running towards the gray limestone bluff overlooking the khan on the west.

"We are going to the cave," said Joseph, laconically.

The guide lingered till Mary came to his side.

"The cave to which we are going," he said to her, "must have been a resort of your ancestor David. From the field below us, and from the well down in the valley, he used to drive his flocks to it for safety; and afterwards when he was king, he came back to the old house here for rest and health, bringing great trains of animals. The mangers yet remain as they were in his day. Better a bed upon the floor where he has slept than one in the court-yard or out by the roadside. Ah, here is the house before the cave!"

The building was low and narrow, projecting but a little from the rock to which it was joined at the rear, and wholly without a window. In its blank front there was a door, swung on enormous hinges, and thickly daubed with ochreous clay. Upon the opening of the door, the keeper called out, "Come in!"

The guests entered, and stared about them. It became apparent immediately that the house was but a mask or covering for the mouth of a natural cave, probably forty feet long, nine or ten high, and twelve or fifteen in width. The light streamed through the doorway, over an uneven floor, falling upon piles of grain and fodder, and earthenware and household property, occupying the centre of the chamber. Along the sides were mangers, low enough for sheep, and built of stones laid in cement. Dust and chaff yellowed the floor, filled all the crevices and hollows, and thickened the spider-webs, which dropped from the ceiling like bits of dirty linen; otherwise the place was clean, and as comfortable as any of the arched lewens of the khan proper. In fact, a cave was the model and first suggestion of the lewen.

"Come in!" said the guide. "These piles upon the floor are for travellers like yourselves. Take what of them you need."

Then he spoke to Mary. "Can you rest here?"

"The place is sanctified," she answered.

When he was gone, they busied themselves making the cave habitable.

## Chapter VIII.

A NUMBER of shepherds, seeking fresh graze for their flocks, led them up to a sheltered, fertile plain, about two miles southeast of Bethlehem; and from early morning the groves had rung with calls, and the blows of axes, the bleating of sheep and goats, the tinkling of bells, the lowing of cattle, and the barking of dogs. When the sun went down, they led the way to the *mârâh,* or sheepcot, and by nightfall had everything safe in the field; then they kindled a fire down by the gate, partook of their supper, and sat down to rest and talk, leaving one on watch.

There were six of these men, omitting the watchman; and afterwhile they assembled in a group near the fire, some sitting, some lying prone. As they went bareheaded habitually, their hair stood out in thick, coarse, sunburnt shocks; their beard covered their throats, and fell in mats down the breast; mantles of the skin of kids and lambs, with the fleece on, wrapped them from neck to knee, leaving the arms exposed; broad belts girthed the rude garments to their waists; their sandals were of the coarest quality; from their right shoulders hung scrips containing food and selected stones for slings, with which they were armed; on the ground near each one lay his crook, a symbol of his calling and a weapon of offence.

They rested and talked; and their talk was all about their flocks. Yet these men, rude and simple as they were, had a knowledge and a wisdom of their own. On Sabbaths they were accustomed to purify themselves, and go up into the synagogues, and sit on the benches farthest from the ark. When the chazzan bore the *Torah* round, none kissed it with greater zest; when the sheliach read the text, none listened to the interpreter with more absolute faith. In a verse of the Shema they found all the learning and all the law of their simple lives—that their Lord was One God, and that they must love him with all their souls. And they loved him, and such was their wisdom, surpassing that of kings.

The night, like most nights of the winter season in the hill country, was clear, crisp, and sparkling with stars. There was no wind. The atmosphere seemed never so pure, and the stillness was more than silence; it was a holy hush, a warning that heaven was stooping low to whisper good things to the listening earth.

By the gate, hugging his mantle close, the watchman walked; at times he stopped, attracted by a stir among the sleeping herds, or by a jackal's cry off on the mountain-side. The midnight was slow coming to him; but at last it came. He moved towards the fire, but paused; a light was breaking around him, soft and white, like the moon's. He waited breathlessly. The light deepened; things before invisible came to view; he saw the whole field, and all it sheltered. A chill of fear smote him. He looked up; the stars were gone; the light was dropping as from a window in the sky; as he looked, it became a splendor; then, in terror he cried, "Awake, awake!"

Up sprang the dogs, and, howling, ran away.

The herds rushed together bewildered.

The men clambered to their feet, weapons in hand.

"See!" cried the watchman, "the sky is on fire!"

Suddenly the light became intolerably bright, and they covered their eyes, and dropped upon their knees; then, as their souls shrank with fear, they fell upon their faces blind and fainting, and a voice said to them,

"Fear not: for behold, I will bring you good tidings of great joy, which shall be to all people."

The voice, low and clear, filled them with assurance. They rose upon their knees, and, looking worshipfully, beheld in the centre of a great glory the appearance of a man, clad in a robe intensely white; above its shoulders towered the tops of wings shining and folded; a star over its forehead glowed with steady lustre, brilliant as Hesperus; its hands were stretched towards them in blessing; its face was serene.

They had often heard of, and, in their simple way, talked of angels; and they doubted not now, but said, in their hearts, The glory of God is about us, and this is he who of old came to the prophet by the river of Ulai.

The angel continued: "For unto you is born this day, in the city of David, a Saviour, which is Christ the Lord! And

20

this shall be a sign unto you: Ye shall find the babe, wrapped in swaddling-clothes, lying in a manger."

The herald spoke not again. Suddenly the light, of which he seemed the centre, turned roseate and began to tremble; then up, far as the men could see, there was flashing of white wings, and coming and going of radiant forms, and voices as of a multitude chanting in unison,

"Glory to God in the highest, and on earth peace, good-will towards men!"

Then the herald rose lightly, and, without effort, floated out of view, taking the light up with him. Long after he was gone, down from the sky fell the refrain in measure mellowed by distance, "Glory to God in the highest, and on earth peace, good-will towards men."

When the shepherds came fully to their senses, they stared at each other stupidly, until one of them said, "It was Gabriel, the Lord's messenger unto men." He gazed into the fire thoughtfully. "There is but one place in Bethlehem where there are mangers and that is in the cave near the old khan. Brethren, let us go see this thing which has come to pass. The priests and doctors have been a long time looking for the Christ. Now he is born, and the Lord has given us a sign by which to know him. Let us go up and worship him."

So they all arose and left the *mârâh.*

Around the mountain and through the town they passed, and came to the khan, where there was a man on watch.

"What would you have?" he asked.

"We have seen and heard great things to-night," they replied.

"Well, we, too, have seen great things, but heard nothing. What did you hear?"

"Let us go down to the cave in the enclosure, that we may be sure; then we will tell you all. Come with us and see for yourself; the Christ is born."

The man laughed scornfully. "The Christ indeed! How are you to know him?"

"He was born this night, and is now lying in a manger, so we were told; and there is but one place in Bethlehem with mangers. Come with us."

The door of the cavern was open. A lantern was burning within, and they entered at once.

"I give you peace," the watchman said to Joseph. "Here are people looking for a child born this night, whom they are to know by finding him in swaddling-clothes and lying in a manger."

For a moment the face of the stolid Nazarene was moved; turning away, he said, "The child is here."

They were led to one of the mangers, and there the child was. The lantern was brought, and the shepherds stood by mute. The little one made no sign; it was as others just born.

"Where is the mother?" asked the watchman.

A woman took the baby, and went to Mary, lying near, and put it in her arms. Then the bystanders collected about the two.

"It is the Christ!" said a shepherd, at last.

"The Christ!" they all repeated, falling upon their knees in worship.

"It is the Lord, and his glory is above the earth and heaven."

And the simple men, never doubting, kissed the hem of the mother's robe, and with joyful faces departed. In the khan, to all the people aroused and pressing about them, they told their story.

The story went abroad, confirmed by the light so generally seen; and for days thereafter the cave was visited by curious crowds, of whom some believed, though the greater part laughed and mocked.

## Chapter IX.

The eleventh day after the birth of the child in the cave, about mid-afternoon, the three wise men approached Jerusalem by the road from Shechem.

Judea was of necessity an international thoroughfare, and that was her wealth. The riches of Jerusalmen were the tolls she levied on passing commerce. Nowhere else, consequently, unless in Rome, was there such constant assemblage of so many people of so many different nations; in no other city was a stranger less strange to the residents than within her walls. And yet these three men excited the wonder of all whom they met on the way to the gates.

The bells were silver; the camels of unusual size and whiteness, and moved with singular stateliness; the trappings told of long desert journeys, and also of ample means of the owners, who sat under the little canopies. Yet it was not the bells or the camels, or their furniture, or the demeanor of the riders, that were so wonderful; it was the question put by the man who rode foremost of the three.

The approach of Jerusalem from the north is across a plain which dips southward, leaving the Damascus Gate in a vale or hollow. The road is narrow, but deeply cut by long use, and in this road the three stopped before a party in front of the Tombs.

"Good people," said Balthasar, stroking his plaited beard, and bending from his cot, "is not Jerusalem close by?"

22

"Yes," answered one of the women. "If the trees were a little lower you could see the towers on the market-place."

Balthasar gave the Greek and the Hindoo a look, then asked,

"Where is he that is born King of the Jews?"

The women gazed at each other without reply.

"You have not heard of him?"

"No."

"Well, tell everybody that we have seen his star in the east, and are come to worship him."

Thereupon the friends rode on. Of others they asked the same question, with like result. A large company whom they met going to the Grotto of Jeremiah were so astonished by the inquiry and the appearance of the travellers that they turned about and followed them into the city.


## Chapter X.

THAT EVENING, before sunset, some women were washing clothes on the upper step of the flight that led down into the basin of the Pool of Siloam. A girl at the foot of the steps kept them supplied with water, and sang while she filled the jar.

While they plied their hands, rubbing and wringing the clothes in the bowls, two other women came to them, each with an empty jar upon her shoulder.

"Peace to you," one of the new-comers said. "Have you heard the news?"

The women paused, sat up, wrung the water from their hands. "What news have you?"

"They say the Christ is born," said the newsmonger, eagerly plunging into her story.

The faces of the women brightened with interest; on the other side down came the jars, which in a moment were turned into seats for their owners.

"The Christ!" the listeners cried. "Who says so?"

"Everybody; it is common talk."

"Does anybody believe it?"

"This afternoon three men came on the road from Shechem," the speaker replied, intending to smother doubt. "Each one of them rode a camel spotless white, and larger than any ever before seen in Jerusalem."

The eyes of the auditors opened wide.

"To prove how great and rich the men were," the narrator continued, "they sat under awnings of silk; the buckles of their saddles were of gold, as was the fringe of their bridles. They looked as if they had come from the ends of the world.

23

Only one of them spoke, and of everybody on the road, even the women and children, he asked this question—'Where is he that is born King of the Jews?' No one understood what they meant. So then they asked the Roman guard at the gate; and he sent them up to Herod."

"Where are they now?"

"At the khan. Hundreds have been to look at them already, and hundreds more are going."

"Who are they?"

"Nobody knows. They are said to be Persians—wise men who talk with the stars—prophets, it may be, like Elijah."

"What do they mean, 'King of the Jews'?"

"The Christ, and that he is just born."

One of the women laughed, and resumed her work, saying, "Well, when I see him I will believe."

Another followed her example: "When I see him raise the dead, then I will believe."

A third said quietly, "He has been a long time promised. It will be enough for me to see him heal one leper."

And the party sat talking until the night came, and, with the help of the frosty air, drove them home.

Later in the evening, there was an assemblage in the inner court-yard of the palace on Mount Zion, of probably fifty persons, who never came there except by order of Herod, and then only when he had demanded to know some one or more of the deeper mysteries of the Jewish law and history. The company were mostly men advanced in years; immense beards covered their faces; to their large noses were added the effects of large black eyes, deeply shaded by bold brows, their demeanor was grave, dignified, patriarchal. Their session was that of the Sanhedrim.

He who sat before the immense bronze tripod, having his associates on his right and left, had been cast in large mould, but was now shrunken and stooped to ghastliness; his white robe dropped from his shoulders in folds that gave no hint of anything but an angular skeleton. His hands, half-concealed by sleeves of silk, white and crimson striped, were clasped upon his knees. When he spoke, sometimes the first finger of the right hand extended tremulously. His eyes were wan and dim; the nose was pinched; and all the lower face was muffled in a beard flowing and venerable as Aaron's. Such was Hillel the Babylonian. The line of prophets, long extinct in Israel, was now succeeded by a line of scholars, of whom he was first in learning—a prophet in all but the divine inspiration. At the age of one hundred and six, he was still Rector of the Great College.

On the table before him lay outspread a roll of parchment

inscribed with Hebrew characters; behind him, in waiting, stood a page.

There had been discussion, but at this moment of introduction the company had reached a conclusion; each one was in an attitude of rest, and the venerable Hillel, without moving, called the page.

"Go tell the king we are ready to give him answer."

The boy hurried away.

After a time two officers entered and stopped, one on each side of the door; after them slowly followed a most striking personage—an old man clad in a purple robe bordered with scarlet, and girt to his waist by a band of gold linked so fine that it was pliable as leather; the latchets of his shoes sparkled with precious stones; a narrow crown wrought in filigree shone outside a *trabooshe* of softest wrought plush. He walked with a halting step, leaning heavily upon a staff. Then, as for the first time conscious of the company, he raised himself, and looked haughtily round, like one startled and searching for an enemy—so dark, suspicious, and threatening was the glance. Such was Herod the Great—a body broken by disease, a conscience seared with crimes, a mind magnificently capable, a soul fit for brotherhood with the Cæsars; now seven-and-sixty years old, but guarding his throne with a jealousy never so vigilant, a power never so despotic, and a cruelty never so inexorable.

There was a general movement on the part of the assemblage—a bending forward in salaam by the more aged, a rising-up by the more courtly, followed by low genuflections, hands upon beard or breast.

His observations taken, Herod moved on until at the tripod opposite the venerable Hillel, who met his cold glance with an inclination of the head, and a slight lifting of the hands.

"The answer!" said the king, addressing Hillel, and planting his staff before him with both hands. "The answer!"

The eyes of the patriarch glowed, and, raising his head, he looked the inquisitor full in the face. "Thou hast demanded of us where the Christ should be born."

The king bowed, though the eyes remained fixed upon the sage's face. "That is the question."

"Then, O king, speaking for myself, and all my brethren here, not one dissenting, I say, in Bethlehem of Judea."

Hillel glanced at the parchment on the tripod; and, pointing with his tremulous finger, continued, "In Bethlehem of Judea, for thus is it written by the prophet, 'And thou, Bethlehem, in the land of Judea, art not the least among the princes of Judah; for out of thee shall come a governor that shall rule my people Israel.'"

Herod's face was troubled, and his eyes fell upon the parchment while he thought. Those beholding him scarcely breathed; they spoke not, nor did he. At length he turned about and left the chamber.

"Brethren," said Hillel, "we are dismissed."

The company then arose, and in groups departed.

Later in the evening the wise men were lying awake in a lewen of the khan. The stones which served them as pillows raised their heads so they could look out of the open arch into the depths of the sky; and as they watched the twinkling of the stars, they thought of the next manifestation. How would it come? What would it be? They were in Jerusalem at last; they had asked at the gate for Him they sought; they had borne witness of his birth; it remained only to find him; and so to that, they placed all trust in the Spirit.

While they were speculating, a man stepped inside the arch. "Awake!" he said to them. "I bring you a message from King Herod."

"What would the king with us?"

"His messenger is without; let him answer."

"Tell him, then, to abide our coming."

They arose, put on their sandals, girt their mantles about them, and went out to meet the messenger.

"My master, the king, has sent me to invite you to the palace, where he would have speech with you privately."

A lamp hung in the entrance, and by its light they looked at each other, and knew the Spirit was upon them. Then the Egyptian stepped to the steward, and said, so as not to be heard by the others, "You know where our goods are stored in the court, and where our camels are resting. While we are gone, make all things ready for our departure, if it should be needful."

The streets of the Holy City were narrow then as now, but not so rough and foul; for the great builder, not content with beauty, enforced cleanliness and convenience also. Following their guide, the brethren proceeded without a word. At last they came to a portal reared across the way. Then by passages and arched halls; through courts, and under colonnades, they were conducted into a tower of great height. Suddenly the guide halted.

"Enter. The king is there."

The air of the chamber was heavy with sandal-wood, and upon the floor a tufted rug was spread, and upon that a throne was set. Herod, sitting upon the throne to receive them, clad as when at the conference with the doctors and lawyers, claimed all their minds.

At the edge of the rug, to which they advanced uninvited, they prostrated themselves.

26

"Seat yourselves," said the monarch.

"From the North Gate," he continued, "I had this afternoon report of the arrival of three strangers, curiously mounted, and appearing as if from far countries. Are you the men?"

The Egyptian took the sign from the Greek and the Hindoo, and answered, with the profoundest salaam, "Were we other than we are, the mighty Herod, whose fame is an incense to the whole world, would not have sent for us. We may not doubt that we are the strangers."

Herod acknowledged the speech with a wave of the hand. "Who are you? Whence do you come?" he asked. "Let each speak for himself."

In turn they gave him account, referring simply to the cities and lands of their birth, and the routes by which they came to Jerusalem.

"What was the question you put to the officer at the gate?"

"We asked him, 'Where is he that is born King of the Jews.'"

"I see now why the people were so curious. You excite me no less. Is there another King of the Jews?"

"There is one newly born."

An expression of pain knit the dark face of the monarch. "Not to me, not to me!" he exclaimed then: "Where is this new king?"

"That, O king, is what we would ask."

"You bring me a wonder—a riddle surpassing any of Solomon's. As you see, I am in the time of life when curiosity is as ungovernable as it was in childhood, when to trifle with it is cruelty. Tell me further, and I will honor you as kings honor each other. Give me all you know about the newly-born, and I will join you in the search for him; and when we have found him, I will do what you wish, I will bring him to Jerusalem, and train him in kingcraft; I will use my grace with Cæsar for his promotion and glory. Jealousy shall not come between us, so I swear. But tell me first how, so widely separated by seas and deserts, you all came to hear of him."

Balthasar raised himself erect, and said, solemnly, "There is an Almighty God. He bade us come hither, promising that we should find the Redeemer of the World; that we should see and worship him, and bear witness that he was come; and, as a sign, we were each given to see a star. His Spirit stayed with us. O king, his spirit is with us now!"

Herod's gaze darted quickly from one to the other; he was more suspicious and dissatisfied than before. "You are mocking me," he said. "If not, tell me more. What is to follow the coming of the new king?"

"The salvation of men from their wickedness."

27

"How?"

"By the divine agencies—Faith, Love, and Good Works."

"Then you are the heralds of the Christ. Is that all?"

Balthasar bowed low. "We are your servants, O king."

The monarch touched a bell, and the attendant appeared. "Bring the gifts," the master said.

The attendant went out, but in a little while returned, and kneeling before the guests, gave to each one a mantle of scarlet and blue, and a girdle of gold.

"A word further," said Herod. "To the officer of the gate, and but now to me, you spoke of seeing a star in the east. What time did it appear?"

"When we were bidden come hither."

Herod arose, signifying the audience was over. Stepping from the throne towards them, he said, with all graciousness,

"If, as I believe, O illustrious men, you are indeed the heralds of the Christ just born, know that I have this night consulted those wisest in things Jewish, and they say with one voice he should be born in Bethlehem of Judea. I say to you, go thither; go and search diligently for the young child; and when you have found him bring me word again, that I may come and worship him. To your going there shall be no let or hindrance. Peace be with you!"

And, folding his robe about him, he left the chamber.

Directly the guide came, and led them back to the street, and thence to the khan, at the portal of which the Greek said, impulsively, "Let us to Bethlehem, O brethren, as the king has advised."

They gave gifts to the steward, received directions to the Joppa Gate, and departed. At their approach the great doors were unbarred, and they passed out into the open country, taking the road so lately travelled by Joseph and Mary. As they came up on the plain of Rephaim, the star appeared, perfect as any in the heavens, but low down and moving slowly before them. And they folded their hands, and shouted, rejoicing.

They watched the star rise out of the valley beyond Mar Elias, and then stand still over a house up on the slope of the hill near the town.


CHAPTER XI.

AT BETHLEHEM, the watchman on the roof of the old khan, shivering in the chilly dawn, first thought it a torch in some one's hand; next moment he thought it a meteor; the brilliance grew, however, until it became a star. Afraid, he cried out, and brought everybody within the walls to the roof. Its brightness became blinding. The more timid of the beholders fell upon their knees, and prayed, with their faces hidden; the boldest covering their eyes, crouched, and now and then snatched glances fearfully. The khan lay under the intolerable radiance. Such as dared look beheld the star standing still directly over the house in front of the cave where the Child had been born.

In the height of this scene, the wise men came up, dismounted from their camels, and shouted for admission.

"Is this Bethlehem of Judea?" they asked the steward.

"No, this is but the khan; the town lies farther on."

"Is there not here a child newly born?"

The bystanders turned to each other marvelling, and some of them answered, "Yes, yes."

"Show us to him!" cried Balthasar, "for we have seen his star, even that which ye behold over the house, and are come to worship him."

The people from the roof came down and followed the strangers as they were taken through the court and out into the enclosure. When the door before the cave was opened, they crowded in. A lantern enabled the strangers to find the mother, and the child awake in her lap.

"Is the child thine?" asked Balthasar of Mary.

She held it up in the light, saying, "He is my son!"

Kneeling before him, they saw the child was as other children: about its head was neither nimbus nor material crown; its lips opened not in speech; if it heard their expressions of joy, their invocations, their prayers, it made no sign whatever, but, baby-like, looked longer at the flame in the lantern than at them.

In a little while they arose, and, returning to the camels, brought gifts of gold, frankincense, and myrrh, and laid them before the child.

This was the Saviour they had come so far to find! And they worshipped without an instant's doubt.

29

# BOOK SECOND

## CHAPTER I.

TWENTY-ONE years later, the beginning of the administration of Valerius Gratus, fourth imperial governor of Judea, was a period which was rent by political agitations in Jerusalem, and marked the opening of the final quarrel between the Jew and the Roman.

Judea had been subjected to many changes, but nothing so grave as her political status. Herod the Great died within one year after the birth of the Child—died miserably.

Augustus Cæsar struck the people of Jerusalem in a manner that touched their pride, and keenly wounded the sensibilities of the haughty habitués of the Temple. He reduced Judea to a Roman province, and annexed it to the prefecture of Syria. So, instead of a king ruling royally from the palace left by Herod on Mount Zion, the city fell into the hands of an officer of the second grade, an appointee called procurator, who communicated with the court in Rome through the Legate of Syria, residing in Antioch. To make the hurt more painful, the procurator was not permitted to establish himself in Jerusalem; Cæsarea was his seat of government. Most humiliating, however, most exasperating, most studied, Samaria, of all the world the most despised—Samaria was joined to Judea as a part of the same province.

In this rain of sorrows, one consolation, and one only, remained to the fallen people: the high-priest occupied the Herodian palace in the market-place, and kept the semblance of a court there. Judgment of life and death was retained by the procurator. Justice was administered in the name and according to the decretals of Rome. Yet more significant, the royal house was jointly occupied by the imperial exciseman, and all his corps of assistants, registrars, collectors, publicans, informers, and spies. Still, to the dreamers of liberty to come, there was a certain satisfaction in the fact that the chief ruler in the palace was a Jew. His mere presence there kept them reminded of the covenants of the prophets; it was to them a certain sign that Jehovah had not abandoned them: so their hopes lived, and served their patience, and helped them wait grimly the son of Judah who was to rule Israel.

Judea had been a Roman province eighty years and more—ample time for the Cæsars to learn that the Jew, with all his pride, could be quietly governed if his religion were respected. Proceeding upon that policy, the predecessors of Gratus had carefully abstained from interfering with any of the sacred observances. But almost his first official act was to expel Hannas from the high-priesthood, and give the place to Ishmael, son of Fabus.

Whether the act was directed by Augustus, or proceeded from Gratus himself, its impolicy became speedily apparent.

Hannas, the idol of his party, had used his power faithfully in the interest of his imperial patron. A Roman garrison held the Tower of Antonia; a Roman guard kept the gates of the palace; a Roman judge dispensed justice civil and criminal; a Roman system of taxation, mercilessly executed, crushed both city and country; daily, hourly, and in a thousand ways, the people were bruised and galled, and taught the difference between a life of independence and a life of subjection; yet Hannas kept them in comparative quiet. Rome had no truer friend; and he made his loss instantly felt. Delivering his vestments to Ishmael, the new appointee, he walked from the courts of the Temple into the councils of the Separatists, and became the head of a new political combination.

Gratus, the procurator, left thus without a Judean party to support him, now saw the fires of discontent and rebellion which, in the fifteen years, had sunk into sodden smoke, begin to glow with returning life. A month after Ishmael took the office, the Roman found it necessary to visit him in Jerusalem. When from the walls, hooting and hissing him, the Jews beheld his guard enter the north gate of the city and march to the Tower of Antonia, they understood the real purpose of the visit—a full cohort of legionaries was added to the former garrison, and the keys of their yoke could now be tightened with impunity. If the procurator deemed it important to make an example, alas for the first offender!

IN THE enclosed garden of the palace on Mount Zion, unmindful of the mid-July sun, two boys, one about nineteen, the other seventeen, sat engaged in earnest conversation.

They were both handsome, and, at first glance, could have been pronounced brothers. Both had black hair and eyes; their faces were deeply browned; and sitting, they seemed of a size proper for the difference in their ages.

The elder was bareheaded. A loose tunic, dropping to the knees, was his attire complete, except sandals and a light-blue mantle spread under him on the seat. The tunic, of softest woollen, gray-tinted, at the neck, sleeves, and edge of the skirt bordered with red, and bound to the waist by a tasselled silken cord, certified him the Roman he was. And if in speech he now and then gazed haughtily at his companion and addressed him as an inferior, he might almost be excused, for he was of a family noble even in Rome—a circumstance which in that age justified any assumption. Octavius, as the Emperor Augustus, sent the son of an old retainer, Messala, to Jerusalem, charged with the management of the taxes levied in that region; and in that service the son had since remained, sharing the palace with the high-priest. The youth in the garden was his son.

The associate of the Messala, a Judean, was slighter in form, and his garments were of fine white linen; a cloth covered his head, held by a yellow cord, and arranged so as to fall away from the forehead down low over the back of the neck.

"Did you not say the new procurator is to arrive to-morrow?"

The question proceeded from the younger of the friends and was asked in Greek, at the time, singularly enough, the language everywhere prevalent in the politer circles of Judea.

"Yes," Messala answered. "I heard Ishmael, the new governor in the palace—you call him high-priest—tell my father so last night. The news had been more credible, I grant you, coming from an Egyptian, who is of a race that has forgotten what truth is, or even from an Idumæan, whose people never knew what truth was; but, to make quite certain, I saw a centurion from the Tower this morning, and he told me preparations were going on for the reception."

The other remained silent.

"Our farewell took place in this garden. 'The peace of the Lord go with you!'—your last words. 'The gods keep you!' I said. Do you remember? How many years have passed since then?"

"Five," answered the Jew, gazing into the water.

"Well, you have reason to be thankful to—whom shall I say? The gods? No matter. You have grown handsome; the Greeks would call you beautiful—happy achievement of the years! Tell me, my Judah, how the coming of the procurator is of such interest to you."

Judah turned his large eyes, grave and thoughtful, and caught the Roman's gaze and held it while he replied, "Yes, five years. I remember the parting; you went to Rome; I saw you start, and cried, for I loved you. The years are gone, and you have come back to me accomplished and princely—I do not jest; and yet—yet—I wish you were the same Messala you went away."

The young Roman put on a longer drawl as he said, "What an oracle you would make, my Judah. A few lessons from my teacher of rhetoric—a little practice of the art of mystery, and Delphi will receive you as Apollo himself. . . . Seriously, O my friend, in what am I not the Messala I went away?"

The lad reddened under the cynical look. "You have availed yourself, I see, of your opportunities. You talk with the ease of a master; yet your speech carries a satirist's sting. My Messala, when he went away, had no poison in his nature; not for the world would he have hurt the feelings of a friend."

The Roman smiled as if complimented. "O my solemn Judah, be plain. Wherein have I hurt you?"

The other drew a long breath. "I know the space that lies between an independent kingdom and the petty province Judea is. I were meaner than a Samaritan not to resent the degradation of my country. Ishmael is not lawfully high-priest, and he cannot be while the noble Hannas lives; yet he is a Levite; one of the devoted who for thousands of years have acceptably served the Lord God of our faith and worship. His—"

Messala broke in upon him with a biting laugh. "Oh, I understand you now. Ishmael, you say, is a usurper, yet to believe an Idumæan sooner than Ishmael is to sting like an adder. By the drunken son of Semele, what it is to be a Jew! To him there is no backward, no forward; he is what his ancestor was in the beginning. In this sand I draw you a circle—there! Now tell me what more a Jew's life is? Round and round, Abraham here, Isaac and Jacob yonder, God in the middle. And outside the circle's little space, is there nothing of value? Painting, sculpture? To look upon them is sin. Poetry you make fast to your altars. Except in the synagogue, who of you attempts eloquence? In war all that you conquer in the six days you lose on the seventh. Satisfied with the worship of such a people, what is your God to

33

our Roman love, who lends us his eagles that we may compass the universe with our arms?"

The Jew arose, his face flushed.

"No, no; keep your place, my Judah, keep your place," Messala cried, extending his hand.

"You mock me."

"Listen a little further. I am mindful of your goodness in walking from the old house of your fathers to welcome me back and renew the friendship of our childhood—if we can. 'Go,' said my teacher, in his last lecture—'Go, and, to make your lives great, remember Mars reigns and Eros has found his eyes.' He meant love is nothing, war everything. It is so in Rome. Marriage is the first step to divorce. Virtue is a tradesman's jewel. Cleopatra, dying, bequeathed her arts, and is avenged; she has a successor in every Roman's house. The world is going the same way; so, as to our future, down Eros, up Mars! I am to be a soldier; and you, O my Judah, I pity you; what can you be?"

The Jew moved nearer the pool; Messala's drawl deepened. "See what possibilities lie before a Roman: A campaign into Africa; another after the Scythian; then—a legion! Most careers end there; but not mine. I—by Jupiter, what a conception!—I will give up my legion for a prefecture. Think of life in Rome with money—money, wine, women, games— poets at the banquet, intrigues in the court, dice all the year round. Such a rounding of life may really be—a fat prefecture, and it is mine. O my Judah, here is Syria! Judea is rich; Antioch a capital for the gods. I will succeed Cyrenius, and you—shall share my fortune."

To the young Jew these sayings were unlike the solemn conversation to which he was accustomed. The superior airs that Messala had assumed had been offensive to him in the beginning; soon they became irritating, and at last an acute smart. To him, furthermore, patriotism was a savage passion that responded instantly to derision, and Messala's progress down to the last drawling pause was exquisite torture to his hearer. At that point the latter said, with a forced smile,

"There are a few, I have heard, who can afford to make a jest of their future; you convince me, O my Messala, that I am not one of them."

The Roman studied him; then replied, "Why not the truth in a jest as well as a parable? The great Fulvia went fishing the other day; she caught more than all the company besides. They said it was because the barb of her hook was covered with gold.

"Then you were not merely jesting?"

"My Judah, I see I did not offer you enough," the Roman

answered, quickly, his eyes sparkling. "When I am prefect, with Judea to enrich me, I—will make you high-priest."

The Jew turned off angrily.

"Do not leave me," said Messala.

Judah answered, coldly, "I wish I had not come. I sought a friend and find a—"

"—Roman," said Messala quickly.

The hands of the Jew clenched, but controlling himself again, he started off. Messala arose, and, taking the mantle from the bench, flung it over his shoulder, and followed after; when he gained his side, he put his hand upon his shoulder and walked with him.

"This is the way—my hand thus—we used to walk when we were children. Let us keep it as far as the gate."

Apparently Messala was trying to be serious and kind, though he could not rid his countenance of the habitual satirical expression. Judah permitted the familiarity.

"You are a boy; I am a man; let me talk like one." The complacency of the Roman was superb. "My Judah, why did you get angry when I spoke of succeeding old Cyrenius? You thought I meant to enrich myself plundering your Judea. Suppose so; some Roman will do it. Why not I?"

Judah shortened his step. "There have been strangers in mastery of Judea before the Roman," he said, with lifted hand. "Where are they, Messala? She has outlived them all."

When they had gone a few yards, the Roman spoke again. "I told you I meant to be a soldier. Why not you also? Why not you step out of the narrow circle which, as I have shown, is all of noble life your laws and customs allow?"

Judah made no reply.

"Who are the wise men of our day?" Messala continued. "Not they who exhaust their years quarrelling about dead philosophies and religions. Give me one great name, O Judah; I care not where you go to find it—to Rome, Egypt, the East, or here in Jerusalem—Pluto take me if it belong not to a man who wrought his fame by holding nothing sacred that did not contribute to the end, scorning nothing that did! How was it with Herod? How with the Maccabees? How with the first and second Cæsars? Imitate them. At hand see—Rome, as ready to help you as she was the Idumæan Antipater."

The Jewish lad trembled with rage; and, as the garden gate was close by, he quickened his steps, eager to escape.

"O Rome, Rome!" he muttered.

"Be wise," continued Messala. "See the situation as it is. Dare look the Fates in the face, and they will tell you that Rome is the world. Ask them of Judea, and they will answer that she is only what Rome wills."

They were now at the gate. Judah stopped, and took the hand from his shoulder, and confronted Messala, tears in his eyes.

"I understand you, because you are a Roman; you cannot understand me—I am an Israelite. You have given me suffering to-day by convincing me that we can never be the friends we have been—never! Here we part. The peace of the God of my fathers abide with you!"

When he was gone, the Roman was silent awhile; then he, too, passed through, saying to himself with a toss of the head, "Be it so. Eros is dead, Mars reigns!"

## CHAPTER III.

NOT LONG after the young Jew parted from the Roman at the palace up on the Market-place he stopped before the western gate of a large stone house and knocked. The wicket, a door hung in one of the leaves of the gate, was opened to admit him. He stepped in hastily, and failed to acknowledge the low salaam of the porter.

The passage into which he was admitted appeared not unlike a narrow tunnel with panelled walls and pitted ceiling. There were benches of stone on both sides, stained and polished by long use. The servants coming and going along the terraces; the noise of millstones grinding; the garments fluttering from ropes stretched in the court; the chickens and pigeons in full enjoyment of the place; the goats, cows, donkeys and horses stabled in the lewens; a massive trough of water, apparently for the common use, showed this court as part of the domestic arrangement of the house.

The young man entered a second court, spacious, square, and set with shrubbery and vines, kept fresh and beautiful by water from a basin erected near a porch on the north side. Here was observable a scrupulous neatness which allowed no dust in the angles, not even a yellowed leaf upon a shrub; all contributed to the impression that the owner was a person of privilege, power and taste.

The young man ascended to the terrace—a broad pavement of white and brown flags closely laid, and making his way under the awning to a doorway, he entered an apartment which the dropping of the screen behind him returned to darkness. He proceeded to a divan, upon which he flung himself, face downwards, and lay at rest, his forehead upon his crossed arms.

About nightfall a woman came to the door and called; he answered, and she went in.

"Supper is over, and it is night. Is not my son hungry?"

"No," he replied. "I am sleepy."

"Your mother has asked for you."

He stirred himself, and sat up.

"Very well. Bring me something to eat. Anything you please, Amrah."

The woman laid her hand upon his forehead; then, as satisfied, went out, saying, "I will see."

After a while she returned, bearing on a wooden platter a bowl of milk, some thin cakes of white bread broken, a delicate paste of brayed wheat, a bird broiled, and honey and salt. On one end of the platter there was a silver goblet full of wine, on the other a lighted brazen hand-lamp. Drawing a stool to the divan, she placed the platter upon it, then knelt close by ready to serve him. A white turban covered her head, leaving the lobes of the ear exposed, and in them the sign that settled her condition—an orifice bored by a thick awl. She was a slave, of Egyptian origin, to whom not even the sacred fiftieth year could have brought freedom; nor would she have accepted it, for the boy she was attending was her life. She had nursed him through babyhood, tended him as a child, and could not break t' ...rvice.

"You remember, O my Amrah," he said, "the Messala who used to visit me here days at a time."

"I remember him."

"He went to Rome some years ago, and is now back. I called upon him to-day. . . . He is much changed, and I shall have nothing more to do with him."

When Amrah took the platter away, he also went out, and up from the terrace to the roof which served as a playground, sleeping-chamber, boudoir, rendezvous for the family, place of music, dance, conversation, reverie, and prayer.

The lad walked slowly across the house-top to a tower built over the northwest corner of the palace. He entered, passing under a half-raised curtain. In one of the openings, reclining against a cushion from a divan, he saw the figure of a woman, indistinct even in white floating drapery. At the sound of his steps upon the floor, the fan in her hand stopped, glistening where the starlight struck the jewels with which it was sprinkled, and she sat up, and called his name.

"Judah, my son!"

Going to her, he knelt, and she put her arms around him and with kisses pressed him to her bosom.

## CHAPTER IV.

THE MOTHER resumed her easy position against the cushion, while the son took a place on the divan beside her. The city was still. Only the winds stirred.

37

"Amrah tells me something has happened to you," she said, caressing his cheek. She spoke in the language almost lost in the land, but which a few—and they were always as rich in blood as in possessions—cherished in its purity, that they might be more certainly distinguished from Gentile peoples—the language in which the loved Rebekah and Rachel sang to Benjamin.

The words appeared to set him thinking anew; after a while, however, he caught the hand with which she fanned him, and said, "To-day, O my mother, I have been made to think of many things that never had place in my mind before. Tell me, first, what am I to be? You know the law—every son of Israel must have some occupation. I am not exempt, and ask now, shall I tend the herds? or till the soil? or drive the saw? or be a clerk or a lawyer? What shall I be? Dear mother, help me to an answer."

"Gamaliel has been lecturing to-day?" she asked.

"No, I did not hear him. I have been up on the Market-place, not to the Temple. I visited the young Messala."

A certain change in his voice attracted the mother's attention. A presentiment quickened the beating of her heart; the fan became motionless again. "The Messala has come back—a Roman?"

"Yes."

"Roman," she continued, half to herself, "to all the world the word means master. How long has he been away?"

"Five years."

She raised her head, and looked off into the night. "The airs of the Via Sacra are well enough in the streets of the Egyptian and in Babylon; but in Jerusalem—our Jerusalem—the covenant abides."

"What Messala said, my mother, was sharp enough in itself; but, taken with the manner, some of the sayings were intolerable. I suppose all great peoples are proud," he went on, "but the pride of the Roman is so grown the gods barely escape it."

"The gods escape!" said the mother quickly. "More than one Roman has accepted worship as his divine right."

"Well, Messala always had his share of arrogance. For the first time, in conversation with me to-day, he trifled with our customs and God. As you would have had me do, I parted with him finally. And now, O my dear mother, I would know with more certainty if there be just ground for the Roman's contempt. In what am I his inferior? Is ours a lower order of people? Why should I, even in Cæsar's presence, feel the shrinking of a slave? Tell me especially why, if I have the soul, and so choose, I may not hunt the honors of the world in all its fields? Why may not I become a soldier? As a poet,

38

why may not I sing of all themes? I can be a worker in metals, a keeper of flocks, a merchant, why not an artist like the Greek? Tell me, O my mother—and this is the sum of my trouble—why may not a son of Israel do all a Roman may?"

She sat up, and in a voice quick and sharp as his own, replied, "I see, I see! From association Messala, in boyhood, was almost a Jew; had he remained here, he might have become a proselyte, but the years in Rome have been too much for him. I do not wonder at the change; yet"—her voice fell—"he might have dealt tenderly at least with you, his oldest friend."

Her hand dropped lightly upon his forehead. "Take heart, O my son. The Messala is nobly descended; his family has been illustrious through many generations. In the days of Republican Rome they were famous, some as soldiers, some as civilians. I can recall but one consul of the name; their rank was senatorial, and their patronage always sought because they were always rich. Yet if to-day your friend boasted of his ancestry, you might have shamed him by recounting yours. If he referred to the ages through which the line is traceable, or to deeds, rank, or wealth—such allusions, except when great occasion demands them, are tokens of small minds.

"One of the ideas now is that time has much to do with the nobility of races and families. A Roman boasting his superiority on that account over a son of Israel will always fail when put to the proof. The founding of Rome was his beginning; the very best of them cannot trace their descent beyond that period; few of them pretend to do so; and of such as do, I say not one could make good his claim except by resort to tradition. Messala certainly could not. Let us look now to ourselves.

"Your father, O my Judah, is at rest with his fathers; yet I remember, as though it were this evening, the day he and I, with many rejoicing friends, went up into the Temple to present you to the Lord. We sacrificed the doves, and to the priest I gave your name, which he wrote in my presence—'Judah, son of Ithamar, of the House of Hur.' The name was then carried away, and written in a book of the division of records devoted to the saintly family.

"I cannot tell you when the custom of registration in this mode began. We know it prevailed before the flight from Egypt. I have heard Hillel say Abraham caused the record to be first opened with his own name, and the names of his sons, moved by the promises of the Lord which separated him and them from all other races, and made them the highest and noblest, the very chosen of the earth. . . . So the record was required to be kept with absolute certainty."

"And I, mother—by the Books, who am I?"

"We have absolute assurance that you are lineally sprung from Hur, the associate of Joshua. Take the Torah, and search the Book of Numbers, and of the seventy-two generations after Adam you can find the very progenitor of your house."

"But in the years since Father Abraham, what has our family achieved? What have they done? What great things to lift them above the level of their fellows?"

She hesitated, thinking she might all this time have mistaken his object. The information he sought might have been for more than satisfaction of wounded vanity.

"I have a feeling, O my Judah," she said, "that all I have said has been in strife with an antagonist more real than imaginary. If Messala is the enemy, let not me fight him in the dark. Tell me all he said."

## CHAPTER V.

THE YOUNG Israelite rehearsed his conversation with Messala, dwelling with particularity upon the latter's speeches in contempt of the Jews, their customs, and confined round of life.

Afraid to speak, the mother listened, discerning the matter plainly. Unconscious of the effect, her son had come away hurt in pride, yet touched with a natural ambition; but she, the jealous mother, saw it, and, not knowing the turn the aspiration might take, became at once Jewish in her fear. What if it lured him away from the patriarchal faith? In her view, that consequence was more dreadful than any of all others. She could discover but one way to avert it, and she set about the task.

"When the Roman looks down upon Israel and laughs, he merely repeats the folly of the Egyptian, the Assyrian, and the Macedonian; and as the laugh is against God, the result will be the same."

Her voice became firmer. "Your friend—or your former friend—charged that we have no poets, artists, or warriors; by which he meant, I suppose, to deny that we have had great men, the next most certain of the signs.

"There is an idea that war is the most noble occupation of men, and that the most exalted greatness is the growth of battle-fields. Because the world had adopted the idea, be not deceived. That we must worship something is a law which will continue as long as there is anything we cannot understand. The prayer of the barbarian is a wail of fear addressed to Strength, the only divine quality he can clearly conceive; hence his faith in heroes. The Greeks have their great glory because they were the first to set Mind above Strength. In Athens the orator and philosopher were more revered than

40

the warrior. But was the Hellene the first to deny the old barbaric faith? No. My son, that glory is ours; against brutalism our fathers erected God; in our worship, the wail of fear gave place to the Hosanna and the Psalm. So the Hebrew and the Greek would have carried all humanity forward and upward. But, alas! the government of the world presumes war as an eternal condition; wherefore, over Mind and above God, the Roman has enthroned his Cæsar, the prohibition of any other greatness.

"In nothing but war has Rome a claim to originality. Her games and spectacles are Greek inventions, dashed with blood to gratify the ferocity of her rabble; her religion, if such it may be called, is made up of contributions from the faiths of all other peoples; her most venerated gods are from Olympus —even her Mars, and, for that matter, the Jove she much magnifies. So it happens, O my son, that of the whole world our Israel alone can dispute the superiority of the Greek, and with him contest the palm of original genius.

"To the excellences of other peoples the egotism of a Roman is impenetrable as his breastplate. Under their trampling the earth trembles like a floor beaten with flails. They have our highest places, and the holiest, and the end no man can tell; but this I know—they may reduce Judea as an almond broken with hammers, and devour Jerusalem, yet the glory of the men of Israel will remain a light in the heavens out of their reach: for their history is the history of God, who dwelt with them, a Lawgiver on Sinai, a Guide in the wilderness, in war a Captain, in government a King."

For a time the rustling of the fan was all the sound heard in the chamber.

"I claim for our Hebrew fathers the first statues," the mother resumed, "in the cherubim of beaten gold above the ark in the first tabernacle. Yet the trick of the sculpture, Judah, is not all there is of art any more than art is all there is of greatness. I always think of a great man marching down the centuries; here the Indian, there the Egyptian, yonder the Assyrian; above them the music of trumpets and the beauty of banners; and on their right hand and left, as reverent spectators, the generations from the beginning, numberless. As they go, I think of the Greek, saying, 'Lo! the Hellene leads the way.' Then the Roman replies, 'Silence! what was your place is ours now; we have left you behind as dust trodden on.' And all the time, from the far front back over the line of march, as well as forward into the farthest future, streams a light of which the wranglers know nothing, except that is it forever leading them on—the Light of Revelation! Who are they that carry it? None but our fathers, servants of God, keepers of the convenants! Ye are the leaders of

41

men, the living and the dead. The front is thine; and though every Roman were a Cæsar, ye shall not lose it!"

"As for what you shall do, my Judah—serve the Lord, the Lord God of Israel, not Rome."

"I may be a soldier then?" Judah asked.

"Why not? Did not Moses call God a man of war? You have my permission, if only you serve the Lord instead of Cæsar."

He was content, and by-and-by fell asleep. She arose then, and put the cushion under his head, and, throwing a shawl over him and kissing him tenderly, went away.

## CHAPTER VI.

THE luxurious mansion of the Hurs—it was in truth a palace, as its owner had been accounted a Prince of Jerusalem—was not the only heritage he had left to his widow, his son and his daughter. A man of vast estate, coupled with his proud blood-line going back directly to the famous son of his tribe, Judah, he had enjoyed the favor of Herod, the homage of his countrymen, and the esteem and respect of Gentiles. At home and abroad he had served the king faithfully and, his affairs having taken him to Rome, he soon attracted the attention of Augustus, who strove to engage his friendship. In the house of Hur, accordingly, were many presents—purple togas, ivory chairs, golden *paterae*—all chiefly valuable because of the imperial hand which had honorably conferred them. Yet his wealth was by no means entirely the largess of royal patrons. He had welcomed the Hebraic Law that had bound him to some pursuit; but instead of one, he had entered into many and had prospered in them all. In faith, he was a servant of the Law and of every essential rite; his place in the synagogue and Temple knew him well; he carried his reverence for Hillel almost to the point of worship. Yet his hospitality took in strangers from every land; the carping Pharisees even accused him of having more than once entertained Samaritans at his table. Had he lived, the world might have heard of him as a rival of Herodes Atticus; as it was, he perished at sea some ten years before, in the prime of life, and was lamented in both Judea and in lands beyond its borders.

When Judah awoke, he was vaguely conscious of the sun over the mountains, the flocks of pigeons filling the air with the gleams of their white wings, and the distant temple, an apparition of gold against the blue of the sky. But his wakening attention was concerned with the young girl seated on the edge of the divan; a girl scarcely fifteen, Tirzah, his sister, who sat singing to the accompaniament of a *nebel* which she rested upon her knee and touched with graceful fingers.

A chemise, buttoned upon her right shoulder, passing loosely over her breast and back under the left arm, but half concealed her body above the waist, while it left her arms entirely nude. Her coiffure was a simple silken cap, Tyrian-dyed, and over that a striped scarf of the same material. She wore rings, ear and finger; anklets and bracelets all of gold; and around her neck was a golden collar, curiously garnished with a network of delicate chains, on which were pendants of pearl.

The song finished, she set down the instrument, and turned, smiling, to her brother.

"Very pretty, my Tirzah, very pretty!" he said, with animation.

"The song?"

"Yes—and the singer, too. I am proud of my little sister. Have you another song as good?"

"Very many. But Amrah sent me to tell you she will bring you your breakfast, and that you need not come down. She thinks you sick—that a dreadful accident happened you yesterday. What was it? Tell me, and I will help Amrah ____tor you. She knows the cures of the Egyptians, but I have many recipes of the Arabs who—"

"—are even more stupid than the Egyptians," he finished, grinning.

"Do you think so? Very well, then," she replied, almost without pause, and putting her hands to her left ear. "We will have nothing to do with any of them. I have here what is much surer and better—the amulet which was given to some of our people—I cannot tell when, it was so far back—by a Persian magician. See, the inscription is almost worn out."

She offered him the earring, which he took, looked at, and handed back, laughing.

"If I were dying, Tirzah, I could not use the charm. I have no faith in amulets. So you wear it, my little sister. It becomes you—it helps make you beautiful, though I think you that without help."

Satisfied, she returned the amulet to her ear just as Amrah entered the summer chamber, bearing a platter, with wash-bowl, water, and napkins.

The servant then went out, leaving Tirzah to dress his hair. When a lock was disposed to her satisfaction, she took the small metallic mirror which, as was the fashion, she wore at her girdle, and gave it to him, that he might see the triumph, and how handsome it made him.

"What do you think, Tirzah?—I am going away."

She dropped her hands with amazement. "Going away! When? Where? For what?"

He laughed. "Three questions, all in a breath! What a girl you are!" Next instant he became serious. "You know the law requires me to follow some occupation. Even you would despise me if I spent in idleness the results of our father's industry. I am going to Rome."

"Oh, I will go with you!"

"You must stay with mother. If both of us leave her she would die."

The brightness faded from her face. "Ah, yes, yes! But—must you go? Here in Jerusalem you can learn all that is needed to be a merchant—if that is what you are thinking of."

"But that is not what I am thinking of. I am going to be a soldier," he said, with unconscious pride in his voice.

Tears came into her eyes. "You will be killed!"

He smiled, patting her hand. "Tirzah, the soldiers are not all killed."

She threw her arms around his neck, as if to hold him back. "We are so happy! Stay at home, my brother."

"War is a trade," he continued. "To excel at it one mus. go to school, and there is no school like a Roman camp."

"You would not not fight for Rome?" She held her breath.

"And you—even you hate her. The whole world hates her. Yes, I will fight for her, if, in return, she will teach me how one day to fight against her."

"When will you go?"

Amrah's steps were returning.

"Hush," he cautioned. "Do not let her know."

The faithful slave came in with breakfast, and placed the waiter holding it upon a stool before them; then, with white napkins upon her arm, she remained to serve them. They dipped their fingers in a bowl of water, and were rinsing them, when a noise arrested their attention. They listened, and distinguished martial music in the street on the north side of the house.

"Soldiers from the Prætorium! I must see them," he cried, springing from the divan, and running out.

In a moment more he was leaning over the parapet of tiles which guarded the roof, so absorbed that he did not notice Tirzah by his side, resting one hand upon his shoulder.

The street below, not more than ten feet wide, was spanned here and there by bridges, open and covered, which, like the roofs along the way, were occupied by men, women, and children, called out by the uproar of trumpets and the shriller *litui,* so delightful to the soldiers.

First came a vanguard of the light-armed—mostly slingers

44

and bowmen—marching with wide intervals between their ranks and files; next a body of heavy-armed infantry, bearing large shields, and spears identical with those in the duels before Ilium; then the musicians; and then an officer riding alone, but followed closely by a guard of cavalry; after them again, a column of infantry also heavy-armed, which, moving in close order, crowded the street from wall to wall, and appeared to be without end.

The brawny limbs of the men; the cadenced motion from right to left of the shields; the sparkle of scales, buckles, and breastplates and helmets, all perfectly burnished; the plumes nodding above the tall crests; the sway of ensigns and iron-shod spears; the bold, confident step, exactly timed and measured; the demeanor, so grave, yet so watchful; the machine-like unity of the whole moving mass, all made an impression upon Judah as something felt rather than seen. Two objects fixed his attention; the eagle of the legion first—a gilded effigy perched on a tall shaft, with wings outspread until they met above its head.

The officer riding alone in the midst of the column was the other attraction. His head was bare; otherwise he was in full armor. At his left hip he wore a short sword; in his hand, however, he carried a truncheon, which looked like a roll of white paper. He sat upon a purple cloth instead of a saddle, and that, and a bridle with a forestall of gold and reins of yellow silk broadly fringed at the lower edge, completed the housings of the horse.

While the man was yet in the distance, Judah observed that his presence was sufficient to throw the people looking at him into angry excitement. They would lean over the parapets or stand boldly out, and shake their fists at him; they followed him with loud cries, and spit at him as he passed under the bridges; the women even flung their sandals, sometimes with such good effect as to hit him. When he was nearer, the yells became distinguishable—"Robber, tyrant, dog of a Roman! Away with Ishmael! Give us back our Hannas!"

When quite near, Judah could see that the man did not share the indifference shown by the soldiers; his face was dark and sullen, and the glances he cast at his persecutors were full of menace; the timid shrank from them.

Judah had heard of the custom, borrowed from a habit of the first Cæsar, by which chief commanders, to indicate their rank, appeared with only a laurel vine upon their heads. By that sign he knew that this officer was Valerius Gratus, the new Procurator of Judea!

To say the truth, the Roman under the unprovoked storm had the young Jew's sympathy; so that when he reached the corner of the house, the latter leaned yet farther over the parapet to see him go by, and in the act rested a hand upon a tile which had been a long time cracked and allowed to go unnoticed. The pressure was strong enough to displace the outer piece, which started to fall. A thrill of horror shot through the youth. He reached out to catch the missile. In appearance the motion was exactly that of one pitching something from him. The effort only served to push the descending fragment farther out over the wall. He shouted with all his might. The soldiers of the guard looked up; so did the great man, and that moment the missile struck him, and he fell from his horse.

The cohort halted; the guards leaped from their horses, and hastened to cover the chief with their shields. On the other hand, the people who witnessed the affair, never doubting that the blow had been purposely dealt, cheered the lad as he yet stooped in full view over the parapet, transfixed by what he beheld.

A mischievous spirit flew with incredible speed from roof to roof along the line of march, seizing the people, and urging them all alike. They laid hands upon the parapets and tore up the tiling and the sunburnt mud of which the housetops were for the most part made, and with blind fury began to fling them upon the legionaries halted below. A battle then ensued. Discipline, of course, prevailed, with the struggle, the slaughter, the skill of one side, the desperation of the other.

Judah arose from the parapet shaken, his face very pale. "O Tirzah, Tirzah! What will become of us?"

She had not seen the occurrence below, but was listening to the shouting and watching the mad activity of the people in view of the houses. Something terrible was going on, she knew; but what it was, or the cause, or that she or any of those dear to her were in danger, she did not know.

"What has happened? What does it all mean?" she asked in sudden alarm.

"I have killed the Roman governor. The tile fell upon him."

Her face grew white instantly. She put her arm around him, and looked without a word into his eyes. His fears had passed to her, and the sight gave him strength.

"I did not do it purposely, Tirzah—it was an accident," he said, more calmly.

"What will they do?" she asked.

He looked off over the tumult momentarily deepening in the street and on the roofs, and thought of the sullen countenance of Gratus. If he were not dead, where would his vengeance stop? And if he were dead, to what height of fury would not the violence of the people lash the legionaries? To evade an answer, he peered over the parapet again, just as the guard were assisting the Roman to remount his horse.

"He lives, he lives, Tirzah! Blessed be the Lord God of our fathers! Be not afraid, I will explain how it happened, and they will remember our father and his services, and not hurt us."

He was leading her to the summer-house, when the roof jarred under their feet, and a crash of strong timbers, followed by a cry of surprise and agony from the court-yard below. He stopped and listened. The cry was repeated; then came a rush of many feet, and voices lifted in rage blent with voices in prayer; and then the screams of women in mortal terror. The soldiers had beaten in the north gate, and were in possession of the house. The terrible sense of being hunted smote him. He looked wildly about, instinctively seeking a refuge. Then Tirzah, her eyes wild with fear, caught his arm.

"O Judah, what does it mean?"

The servants were being butchered—and his mother! Was not one of the voices he heard hers? With all the will left him, he said, "Stay here, and wait for me, Tirzah. I will go down and see what is the matter, and come back to you."

Clearer, shriller, no longer a fancy, his mother's cry arose. He hesitated no longer. "Come, then, let us go."

The terrace or gallery at the foot of the steps was crowded with soldiers. Other soldiers with drawn swords ran in and out of the chambers. At one place a number of women on their knees clung to each other or prayed for mercy. Apart from them, one with torn garments, and long hair streaming over her face, struggled to tear loose from a man all whose strength was tasked to keep his hold. Her cries were shrillest of all; cutting through the clamor, they had risen distinguishably to the roof. To her Judah sprang—his steps were long and swift—"Mother, mother!" he shouted. She stretched her hands towards him; but when almost touching them he was seized and forced aside. Then he heard some one say, speaking loudly.

"That is he!"

Judah looked, and saw Messala.

"What, the assassin—that?" said a tall man, in legionary armor. "Why, he is but a boy."

"Gods!" drawled Messala. "A new philosophy! What would Seneca say to the proposition that a man must be old before he can hate enough to kill? You have him; and that is his mother; yonder his sister. You have the whole family."

For love of them, Judah forgot his quarrel, forgot his pride.

"Help them, O my Messala! Remember our childhood and help them. I—Judah—pray you"

Messala affected not to hear. "I cannot be of further use to you," he said to the officer. "There is richer entertainment in the street. Down Eros, up Mars!"

With the last words he turned and left. Judah understood him, and, in the bitterness of his soul, prayed to Heaven. "In the hour of thy vengeance, O·Lord," he said, "be mine the hand to put it upon him!" By great exertion, he drew nearer the officer. "O sir, the woman you hear is my mother. Spare her, spare my sister yonder. God is just, he will give you mercy for mercy."

The man appeared moved. "To the Tower with the women!" he shouted, "but do them no harm. I will demand them of you." Then to those holding Judah, he said, "Get cords, and bind his hands, and take him to the street. His punishment is reserved."

The mother was carried away. The little Tirzah, in her home attire, stupefied with fear, went passively with her keepers. Judah gave each of them a last look, and covered his face wtih his hands, as if to possess himself of the scene for all his days.

There was no sign that he had undergone a change when he raised his head and held his arms out to be bound, but in that instant he had put off childhood and become a man.

A trumpet sounded in the court-yard. With the cessation of the call, the gallery was cleared of the soldiery; many of whom, as they dared not appear in the ranks with visible plunder in their hands, flung what they had upon the floor, until it was strewn with articles of richest artistry. When Judah descended, the formation was complete, and the officer waiting to see his last order executed.

The mother, daughter, and entire household were led out of the north gate, the ruins of which choked the passage-way. When, finally, the horses and other animals were driven past him, Judah began to comprehend the scope of the procurator's vengeance. The very structure was doomed. Nothing living was to be left within its walls. If in Judea there were others desperate enough to think of assassinating a Roman governor, the story of what befell the princely family of Hur would be a warning to them, while the ruin of the habitation would keep the story alive.

The officer waited outside while a detail of men temporarily restored the gate.

In the street the fighting had almost ceased. Upon the houses here and there clouds of dust told where the struggle was yet prolonged. The cohort was, for the most part, standing at rest, its splendor, like its ranks, in nowise diminished. Borne past the point of care for himself, Judah had heart for nothing in view but the prisoners, among whom he looked in vain for his mother and Tirzah.

Suddenly, from the earth where she had been lying, a woman arose and started swiftly back to the gate. Some of the

48

guards reached out to seize her, and a great shout followed their failure. She ran to Judah, and, dropping down, clasped his knees, the coarse black hair powdered with dust veiling her eyes.

"O Amrah, good Amrah," he said to her, "God help you; I cannot." He bent down, and whispered, "Live, Amrah, for Tirzah and my mother. They will come back, and—"

A soldier drew her away; whereupon she sprang up and rushed through the gateway and passage into the vacant court-yard.

"Let her go," the officer shouted. "We will seal the house, and she will starve."

The men resumed their work, and, when it was finished there, passed round to the west side. That gate was also secured, after which the palace of the Hurs was lost to use.

The cohort at length marched back to the Tower, where he procurator stayed to recover from his hurts and dispose of his prisoners.

Next day a detachment of legionaries went to the desolated palace, and, closing the gates permanently, sealed the corners with wax, and at the sides mailed a notice in Latin.

In the haughty Roman idea, the sententious announcement was thought sufficient for the purpose—and it was. It said:

THIS IS THE PROPERTY OF
THE EMPEROR.

## CHAPTER VII.

ABOUT NOON of the day following, a decurion with his command of ten horsemen approached Nazareth from the direction of Jerusalem. The place was then a straggling village, perched on a hill-side, and so insignificant that its one street was little more than a path well beaten by the coming and going of flocks and herds.

A trumpet, sounded when the cavalcade drew near the village, had a magical effect upon the inhabitants. The gates and front doors cast forth groups eager to be the first to catch the meaning of so unusual a visitation.

Nazareth was not only far from any great highway, but within the sway of Judas of Gamala; wherefore the feelings with which the townsfolk received the legionaries was an admixture of hostility and fear. But when the mounted men were up and traversing the street, the duty that occupied them became apparent, and then fear and hatred were lost in curiosity. The people, knowing there must be a halt at the well in the northeastern part of the town, quit their gates and doors, and closed in after the procession.

A prisoner whom the horsemen were guarding was the object of curiosity. He was afoot, bareheaded, half naked, his hands bound behind him. A thong fixed to his wrists was looped over the neck of a horse. The dust went with the party when in movement, wrapping him in yellow fog. He dropped forward, foot-sore and faint. The villagers could see he was young.

At the well the decurion halted, and, with most of the men, dismounted. The prisoner sank down in the dust of the road, stupefied, asking nothing: apparently he was in the last stage of exhaustion. The villagers would have helped him had they dared.

In the midst of their perplexity, and while the pitchers were passing among the soldiers, a man was descried coming down the road from Sepphoris. At sight of him a woman cried out, "Look! Yonder comes the carpenter. Now we will hear something."

The person spoken of was quite venerable in appearance. Thin white locks fell below the edge of his full turban, and a mass of still whiter beard flowed down the front of his coarse gray gown. He came slowly, for, in addition to his age, he carried an axe, a saw and a drawing-knife, all very rude and heavy—and had evidently travelled some distance without rest.

He stopped close by to survey the assemblage.

"O Rabbi, good Rabbi Joseph!" cried a woman, running to him. "Here is a prisoner; come ask the soldiers about him, that we may know who he is, and what he has done, and what they are going to do with him."

The rabbi's face remained stolid; he glanced at the prisoner, however, and presently went to the officer.

"The peace of the Lord be with you!" he said, with unbending gravity.

"And that of the gods with you," the decurion replied.

"May I ask what your young prisoner has done?"

"He is an assassin."

The people repeated the word in astonishment, but Rabbi Joseph pursued his inquest.

"Is he a son of Israel?"

"He is a Jew," said the Roman dryly. "You may have heard of a prince of Jerusalem named Hur—Ben-Hur, they called him. He lived in Herod's day. This is his son."

Exclamations became general, and the decurion hastened to stop them.

"In the streets of Jerusalem, day before yesterday, he nearly killed the noble Gratus by flinging a tile upon his head from the roof of a palace—his father's I believe."

"He is under sentence?"

"Yes—the galleys for life."

"The Lord help him!" said Joseph, for once moved out of his stolidity.

Thereupon a youth who came up with Joseph, but had stood behind him unobserved, laid down an axe he had been carrying, and, going to the great stone standing by the well, took from it a pitcher of water. The action was so quiet that before the guard could interfere he was stooping over the prisoner, and offering him drink.

The kindly hand laid upon his shoulder awoke Judah, and, looking up, he saw a face he never forgot—the face of a boy about his own age, shaded by locks of yellowish bright chestnut hair; a face lighted by dark-blue eyes, so full of sympathy and holy purpose, that they had all the power of command and will. The spirit of the Jew, hardened though it was by days and nights of suffering, and so embittered by wrong that its dreams of revenge took in all the world, melted under the stranger's look. He put his lips to the pitcher, and drank long and deep. Not a word was said to him, nor did he say a word.

When the draught was finished, the hand that had been resting upon the sufferer's shoulder was placed upon his head, and stayed there in the dusty locks time enough to say a blessing; the stranger then returned the pitcher to its place on the stone, and, taking his axe again, went back to Rabbi Joseph.

When the men had drunk, and the horses, the march was resumed. But the temper of the decurion was not as it had been: he himself raised the prisoner from the dust, and helped him to a horse behind a soldier. The Nazarenes went to their homes—among them Rabbi Joseph and his apprentice.

And so, for the first time, Judah and the Son of Mary met and parted.

# BOOK THIRD

## CHAPTER I.

THE CITY of Misenum gave name to the promontory which it crowned, a few miles southwest of Naples. An account of ruins is all that remains of it now; yet in the year of our Lord 24 the place was one of the most important on the western coast of Italy.*

A traveller coming to the promontory to regale himself with the view, would have mounted a wall, and, with the city at his back, looked over the bay of Neapolis, the matchless shore, the smoking cone, the sky and waves so softly, deeply blue, Ischia here and Capri yonder; and half the reserve navy of Rome astir or at anchor below him. Thus regarded, Misenum was a very proper place for three captains to meet, and at leisure parcel the world among them.

There was a gateway in the wall fronting the sea—an empty gateway forming the outlet of a street which, after the exit, stretched itself, in the form of a broad mole, out many stadia into the waves.

The watchman on the wall above the gateway was disturbed, one cool September morning, by a party coming down the street in noisy conversation. He gave one look, then settled into his drowse again.

There were twenty or thirty persons in the party, of whom the greater number were slaves with torches, which flamed little and smoked much. The masters walked in advance arm-

* The Roman government had two harbors in which great fleets were constantly kept—Ravenna and Misenum.

in-arm. One of them, apparently fifty years old, slightly bald, and wearing over his scant locks a crown of laurel, seemed, from the attentions paid him, the central object of some affectionate ceremony. They all sported ample togas of white wool broadly bordered with purple. A glance had sufficed the watchman. He knew, without question, they were of high rank, and escorting a friend to ship after a night of festivity.

"No, my Quintus," said one, speaking to the wearer of the crown, "it is ill of Fortune to take thee from us so soon. Only yesterday thou didst return from the seas beyond the Pillars. Why, thou hast not even got back thy land legs."

Another said, somewhat worse of wine, "Let us not lament. Our Quintus is but going to find what he lost last night. Dice on a rolling ship is not dice on shore—eh, Quintus?"

"The Greeks are taking him away," a third broke in. "Let us abuse them, not the gods. In learning to trade they forgot how to fight."

With these words, the party passed the gateway, and came upon the mole, with the bay before them beautiful in the morning light. To the veteran sailor the plash of the waves was like a greeting. He drew a long breath. The slaves waved their torches.

"She comes—yonder!" he said, pointing to a galley outside the mole. "What need has a sailor for other mistress? Is your Lucree more graceful, my Caius?"

He gazed at the coming ship, and justified his pride. A white sail was bent to the low mast, and the oars dipped, arose, poised a moment, then dipped again, with wing-like action, and in perfect time.

"Yes, spare the gods," he said soberly, his eyes fixed upon the vessel. "They send us opportunities. Ours the fault if we fail. And as for the Greeks, you forget, O my Lentulus, the pirates I am going to punish are Greeks. One victory over them is of more account than a hundred over the Africans."

"Then thy way is to the Aegean?"

The sailor's eyes were full of his ship. "See!" he said, but almost immediately added, "Thy pardon, my Lentulus. Yes, the Aegean; and as my departure is so near, I will tell the occasion—only keep it under the rose. The trade between Greece and Alexandria, as ye may have heard, is so grown that it will not brook interruption a day. Ye may also have heard that the Cheronesan pirates, nested up in the Euxine, had rowed their fleet down the Bosphorus, sunk the galleys off Byzantium and Chalcedon, swept the Propontis, and then burst through into the Aegean. The corn-merchants who have ships in the East Mediterranean are frightened. They had audience with the Emperor himself, and from Ravenna there go to-day a hundred galleys, and from Misenum"—he paused as if to pique the curiosity of his friends, and ended with an emphatic—"one."

"Happy Quintus! We congratulate thee!"

"The preferment forerunneth promotion. We salute thee duumvir; nothing less."

"Quintus Arrius, duumvir, hath a better sound than Quintus Arrius, tribune."

"Thanks, many thanks!" Arrius replied, speaking to them collectively. "Had ye but lanterns, I would say ye were augurs. *Perpol!* I will go further, and show what master diviners ye are! See—and read."

From the folds of his toga he drew a roll of paper, and passed it to them, saying, "Received while at table last night from—Sejanus."

*Sejanus to C. Cæcilius Rufus, Duumvir.*

ROME, *XIX. Kal. Sept.*

Cæsar hath good report of Quintus Arrius, the tribune. In particular he hath heard of his valor, manifested in the western seas, insomuch that it is his will that the said Quintus be transferred instantly to the East.

It is our Cæsar's will, further, that you cause a hundred triremes, of the first class, and full appointment, to be despatched without delay against the pirates who have appeared in the Aegean, and that Quintus be sent to command the fleet so despatched.

Details are thine, my Cæcilius.

The necessity is urgent, as thou wilt be advised by the reports enclosed for thy perusal and the information of the said Quintus.

SEJANUS.

Arrius gave little heed to the reading. As the ship drew closer, she became more and more an attraction to him. At length he tossed the loosened folds of his toga in the air; in reply to the signal, over the fan-like fixture at the stern of the vessel, a scarlet flag was displayed; while several sailors appeared upon the bulwarks, and swung themselves hand over hand up the ropes to the yard, and furled the sail. The bow was put round, and the time of the oars increased one half; so that at racing speed she bore down directly towards him and his friends. He observed the manœuvre with a brightening of the eyes.

"By the Nymphæ!" said one of the friends, giving back the roll, "we may not longer say our friend will be great; he is already great. Our love will now have famous things to feed upon."

The vessel was long, narrow, low in the water, and modelled for speed and quick manœuvre. Below the bow, fixed to the keel, and projecting forward under the water-line, was a device of solid wood, reinforced and armed with iron, used as a ram. A stout moulding extended from the bow the full length of the ship's sides; below the moulding, in three rows, each covered with a cap or shield of bullhide, were the holes in which the oars were worked—sixty on the right, sixty on the left. Two immense ropes passing across the bow marked the number of anchors stowed on the foredeck.

The simplicity of the upper works declared the oars the chief dependence of the crew. A mast, set a little forward of midship, was held by fore and back stays and shrouds fixed to rings on the inner side of the bulwarks. The tackle was that required for the management of one great square sail and the yard to which it was hung. Above the bulwarks the deck was visible.

Save the sailors who had reefed the sail, but one man was to be seen by the party on the mole, and he stood by the prow helmeted and with a shield.

The hundred and twenty oaken blades, kept white and shining by pumice and the constant wash of the waves, rose and fell as if operated by the same hand, and drove the galley forward.

So rapidly, and apparently so rashly, did she come that the landsmen of the tribune's party were alarmed. Suddenly the man by the prow raised his hand with a peculiar gesture; whereupon all the oars flew up, poised a moment in the air, then fell straight down. The water boiled and bubbled about them; the galley shook in every timber, and stopped as if scared. Another gesture of the hand, and again the oars rose, feathered, and fell; but this time those on the right, dropping towards the stern, pushed forward; while those of the left, dropping towards the bow, pulled backwards. Three times the oars thus pushed and pulled against each other. Round to the right the ship swing as upon a pivot; then, caught by the wind, she settled gently broadside to the mole.

In the midst of the rounding-to, a trumpet was blown brief and shrill, and from the hatchways out poured the marines, all in superb equipment, brazen helms, burnished shields and javelins. While the fighting-men thus went to quarters as for action, the sailors proper climbed the shrouds and perched themselves along the yard. The officers and musicians took their posts. There was no shouting or needless noise. When the oars touched the mole, a bridge was sent out from the helmsman's deck. Then the tribune took the chaplet from his head and gave it to the dice-player.

"Take thou the myrtle, O favorite of the tesseræ!" he said. "If I return, I will seek my sestertii again; if I am not victor, I will not return. Hang the crown in thy atrium."

Then he turned to the waiting ship. As he stepped upon the

bridge, the trumpets sounded, and over the aplustre rose the pennant of a commander of a fleet.


## CHAPTER II.

THE TRIBUNE, standing upon the helmsman's deck with the order of the duumvir open in his hand, spoke to the hortator, or chief of the rowers.

"What force hast thou?"

"Of oarsmen, two hundred and fifty-two; ten supernumeraries."

"Making reliefs of—"

"Eighty-four. We change every two hours."

The tribune mused a moment. "The division is hard, and I will reform it, but not now. The oars may not rest day or night."

Then to the sailing-master he said, "The wind is fair. Let the sail help the oars."

When the two thus addressed were gone, he turned to the chief pilot.

"What service hast thou had?"

"Two-and-thirty years between Rome and the East."

"Thou art the man I would have chosen," said the tribune, and set the course. "The gods willing, I will not anchor until the Bay of Antemona. The duty is urgent. I rely upon thee."

All night as master of the feast Arrius had sat at table drinking and playing; yet he would not rest until he knew his ship. Nothing escaped his inspection. When he was through, he alone knew perfectly all there was of material preparation for the voyage and its possible incidents; and, finding the preparation complete, there was left him but one thing further —thorough knowledge of the personnel of his command.

At noon that day the galley was skimming the sea off Pæstum. The wind was yet from the west, filling the sail to the master's content. The watches had been established. On the foredeck the altar had been set and sprinkled with salt and barley, and before it the tribune had offered solemn prayers to Jove and Neptune and all the Oceanidæ, and, with vows, poured the wine and burned the incense. And now the better to study his men, he was seated below in the great cabin.

The cabin was the central compartment of the galley, sixty-five by thirty feet and lighted by three broad hatchways. A row of stanchions ran from end to end, supporting the deck which served here as the ceiling, and near the centre the foot of the mast was visible, bristling with axes and spears and javelins. To each hatchway there were double stairs descending right and left, with a pivotal arrangement at the top to allow the lower ends to be hitched to the ceiling; and, as these were now raised, the compartment had the appearance of a skylighted hall.

At the after-end of the cabin there was a platform, reached by several steps. Upon it the chief of the rowers sat; in front of him a sounding-table, upon which, with a gavel, he beat time for the oarsmen; at his right a water-clock, to measure the reliefs and watches. Above him, on a higher platform, well guarded by gilded railing, the tribune had his quarters, overlooking everything, and furnished with a couch, a table, and a cushioned chair.

Thus at ease, lounging in the great chair, swaying with the motion of the vessel, the military cloak half draping his tunic, sword in belt, Arrius kept watchful eye over his command. He saw critically everything in view, but dwelt longest upon the rowers.

Along the sides of the cabin, fixed to the ship's timbers, were three rows of benches arranged in a succession of rising ranks, in each of which the second bench was behind and above the first one, and the third above and behind the second, to accommodate the sixty rowers on a side.

As to the rowers, those upon the first and second benches sat, while those upon the third, having longer oars to work, were suffered to stand. The oars were loaded with lead in the handles, and near the point of balance hung to pliable thongs, making feathering possible, but, at the same time, increasing the need of skill, since an eccentric wave might at any moment catch a heedless fellow and hurl him from his seat. Light streamed upon the oarsmen from the grating which formed the floor of the passage between the deck and the bulwark overhead. Communication between them was not allowed. Day after day they filled their places without speech; in hours of labor they could not see each other's faces; their short respites were given to sleep and the snatching of food. They never laughed; no one ever heard one of them sing.

Nearly all the nations had sons there, mostly prisoners of war, chosen for their brawn and endurance. In one place a Briton; before him a Libyan; behind him a Crimean. Elsewhere a Scythian, a Gaul, and a Thebasite. Roman convicts cast down to consort with Goths and Longobardi, Jews, Ethiopians, and barbarians.

The reach forward, the pull, the feathering the blade, the dip, were motions most perfect when most automatic. So, as the result of long service, the poor wretches became patient, spiritless, obedient—creatures of vast muscle and exhausted intellects, at last lowered into the semi-conscious state wherein misery turns to habit, and the soul takes on incredible endurance.

From right to left, hour after hour, the tribune, swaying in his easy chair, amused himself singling out individuals. With his stylus he made note of objections, thinking, if all went well, he would find among the pirates better men for the places.

For convenience, the slaves were usually identified by the numerals painted upon the benches to which they were assigned. As the sharp eyes of the great man moved from seat to seat on either hand, they came at last to number sixty, which had been fixed above the first bench of the first bank. There they rested.

The light glinting through the overhead grating showed the rower like all his fellows, naked, except a cincture above the loins. He was very young, not more than twenty. Furthermore, Arrius was not merely given to dice; he was a connoisseur of men physically, and when ashore visited the gymnasia to see and admire the most famous athlete. He had caught the idea that strength was as much of the quality as the quantity of the muscle, while superiority in performance required a certain mind as well as strength. Having adopted the doctrine, like most men with a hobby, he was always looking for illustrations to support it.

Arrius observed that the rower seemed of good height, and that his limbs, upper and nether, were singularly perfect. Altogether there was in the man's action a certain harmony which, besides addressing itself to the tribune's theory, stimulated both his curiosity and general interest.

"By the gods," he said to himself, "the fellow impresses me! He promises well. I will know more of him."

Suddenly the rower turned and looked at him.

"A Jew! And a boy!"

Under the tribune's gaze, the large eyes of the slave grew larger, the blade lingered in his hands. But instantly, with an angry crash, down fell the gavel of the hortator. The rower started, withdrew his face from the inquisitor. When he glanced again at the tribune, he was vastly more astonished —he was met with a kindly smile.

Meantime the galley entered the Straits of Messina, and, skimming past the city, turned eastward, leaving the cloud over Ætna in the sky astern.

Often as Arrius returned to his platform in the cabin he returned to study the rower, and he kept saying to himself, "The fellow hath a spirit. A Jew is not a barbarian. I will know more of him."

# Chapter III.

The fourth day out, and the *Astræa* was speeding through the Ionian Sea. The sky was clear, and the wind blew as if bearing the good-will of all the gods.

As it was possible to overtake the fleet before reaching the bay east of the island of Cythera, designated for assemblage, Arrius, somewhat impatient, spent much time on deck. He took note diligently of matters pertaining to his ship, and as a rule was well pleased. In the cabin, swinging in the great chair, his thought continually reverted to the rower.

A relief was going on at the moment.

"Knowest thou the man just come from yon bench?" he asked the hortator.

"As thou knowest," he replied, "the ship is but a month from the maker's, and the men are as new to me as the ship."

"He is a Jew," Arrius remarked, thoughtfully.

"And our best rower," said the other. "I have seen his oar bend almost to breaking."

"Of what disposition is he?"

"He is obedient; further I know not. Once he made request of me to change him alternately from the right to the left."

"Did he give a reason?"

"He had observed that the men who are confined to one side become misshapen. He also said that some day of storm or battle there might be sudden need to change him, and he might then be unserviceable."

"*Perpol!* The idea is new. Have you nothing of his history?"

"Not a word."

"If I should be on deck when his time is up, send him to me. Let him come alone."

About two hours later Arrius stood in the stern; the pilot sat with a hand upon the rope by which the rudder paddles, one on each side of the vessel, were managed. In the shade of the sail some sailors lay asleep, and up on the yard there was a lookout. Lifting his eyes, Arrius beheld the rower approaching.

"The chief called thee the noble Arrius, and said it was thy will that I should seek thee here. I have come."

Arrius surveyed the figure, tall, sinewy, glistening in the sun, and tinted by the rich red blood within—surveyed it admiringly, and with a thought of the arena; yet the manner was not without effect upon him; there was in the voice a suggestion of life at least partly spent under refining influences; the eyes were clear and open, and more curious than defiant.

"The hortator tells me thou art his best rower."

"The hortator is kind," the rower answered.

"Hast thou seen much service?"

"About three years. I cannot recall a day of rest from them."

"The labor is hard; few men bear it a year without breaking, and thou—thou art but a boy."

"The noble Arrius forgets that the spirit hath much to do with endurance. By its help the weak sometimes thrive, when the strong perish."

"From thy speech, thou art a Jew."

"My ancestors further back than the first Roman were Hebrews."

"The stubborn pride of thy race is not lost in thee," said Arrius, obs        a flush upon the rower's face.

"Pride            loud as when in chains."

"I have      en to Jerusalem," Arrius said; "but I have heard of      rinces. I knew one of them. He was a merchant and sailed the seas. He was fit to have been a king. Of what degree art thou?"

"I must answer thee from the bench of a galley. I am of the degree of slaves. My father was a prince of Jerusalem, and, as a merchant, he sailed the seas. He was known and honored in the guest-chamber of the great Augustus."

"His name?"

"Ithamar, of the house of Hur."

The tribune raised his hand in astonishment.

"A son of Hur— ou? What brought thee here?"

Judah looke     : tribune in the face. "I was accused of attempting to    ssassinate Valerius Gratus, the procurator."

"Thou!" c ed Arrius, yet more amazed, and retreating a step. "Thou that assassin! All Rome rang with the story. I thought the family of Hur blotted from the earth."

Judah drew nearer Arrius, so near that his hands touched the cloak where it dropped from the latter's folded arms.

"The horrible day is three years gone," he continued, "and every hour a whole lifetime in a bottomless pit with death, and no relief but in labor. And in all that time not a word from my mother or my sister, not a whisper. I have felt the plague's breath, and the shock of ships in battle; I have heard the tempest lashing the sea, and laughed, though others prayed: death would have been a riddance. Tell me they are dead, if no more. I have heard them call me in the night; I have seen them walking on the water. And Tirzah—she came and went in music. And mine was the hand that laid them low! I—"

"Dost thou admit thy guilt?" asked Arrius, sternly.

The change that came upon Ben-Hur was instant and extreme. The voice sharpened; the hands arose tight-clenched. "Thou has heard of the God of my fathers," he said. "By his truth and almightiness, and by the love with which he hath followed Israel from the beginning, I swear I am innocent."

The tribune was moved. "Didst thou not have a trial?"

"No!"

The Roman raised his head, surprised. "No trial—no witnesses! Who passed judgment upon thee?"

"They bound me with cords, and dragged me to a vault in the Tower. I saw no one. No one spoke to me. Next day soldiers took me to the seaside. I have been a galley-slave ever since."

"Who was with thee when the blow was struck?"

"Tirzah was at my side. . . ." And Judah went on to recount the fateful accident and its results.

Arrius brought all his experience with slaves to his aid. If the feeling shown by this one were assumed, the acting was perfect; on the other hand, if it were real, the Jew's innocence might not be doubted. A whole family blotted out to atone an accident! The thought shocked him.

The tribune could be inexorable, else he had not been fit for his calling; he could also be just; and to excite his sense of wrong was to put him in the way to right the wrong. The crews of the ships in which he served came after a time to speak of him as the good tribune.

For once the tribune hesitated. He was monarch of the ship. His prepossessions all moved him to mercy. His faith was won. Yet, in the haste to Cythera the best rower could not be spared; Arrius would at least be sure this was the prince Ben-Hur, and that he was of a right disposition. Ordinarily, slaves were liars.

"It is enough," he said aloud. "Go back to thy place."

Ben-Hur bowed; looked once more into the master's face, but saw nothing for hope. He turned away slowly, looked back, and said,

"If thou dost think of me again, O tribune, let it not be lost in thy mind that I prayed thee only for word of my mother and sister."

He moved on and Arrius followed him with admiring eyes. *"Perpol!"* he thought. "With teaching, what a man for the arena! What a runner! Ye gods! what an arm for the sword or the cestus!—Stay!" he said aloud.

Ben-Hur stopped, and the tribune went to him. "If thou wert free, what wouldst thou do?"

"The noble Arrius mocks me!" Judah said.

"No; by the gods, no!"

"Then I will answer gladly. I would give myself to duty the first of life. I would know no other. I would know no

61

rest until my mother and Tirzah were restored to home. I would give every day and hour to their happiness. They have lost much, but, by the God of my fathers, I would find them more!"

The answer was unexpected by the Roman. "I spoke to thy ambition. If thy mother and sister were dead, or not to be found, what wouldst thou do?"

A distinct pallor overspread Ben-Hur's face, and he looked over the sea. There was a struggle with some strong feeling; when it was conquered, he turned to the tribune.

"Tribune, only the night before the dreadful day of which I have spoken, I obtained permission to be a soldier. I am of the same mind yet; and, as there is but one school of war, thither I would go."

"The palæstra!" exclaimed Arrius.

"No; a Roman camp."

"But thou must first acquaint thyself with the use of arms."

Now a master may never safely advise a slave. Arrius saw his indiscretion, and, in a breath, chilled his voice and manner. "Go now," he said, "and do not build upon what has passed between us. If thou dost think of it with any hope, choose between the renown of a gladiator and the service of a soldier. The former may come of the favor of the emperor; there is no reward for thee in the latter. Thou art not a Roman. Go!"

A short while after Ben-Hur was upon his bench again.


## CHAPTER IV.

IN THE Bay of Antemona, east of Cythera, the hundred galleys assembled. There the tribune gave one day to inspection. He sailed then to Naxos, the largest of the Cyclades, midway between Greece and Asia, like a great stone planted in the centre of a highway, from which he could challenge everything that passed; at the same time, he would be in position to go after the pirates instantly, whether they were in the Aegean or out on the Mediterranean.

As the fleet, in order, rowed in towards the mountain shores of the island, a galley was sighted coming from the north. She proved to be a transport just from Byzantium, and from her commander he learned the particulars of which he stood in most need.

The pirates were from all the farther shores of the Euxine. Their preparations had been with the greatest secrecy. The first known of them was their appearance off the entrance to the Thracian Bosphorus, followed by the destruction of the fleet in station there. Thence to the outlet of the Hellespont everything afloat had fallen their prey. There were sixty galleys in the squadron, all well manned and supplied. A few were biremes, the rest stout triremes. A Greek was in command, and the pilots, said to be familiar with all the Eastern seas, were Greek. The plunder had been incalculable. The panic, consequently, was not on the sea alone; cities, with closed gates, sent their people nightly to the walls. Traffic had almost ceased.

Where were the pirates now?

After sacking Hephæstia, on the island of Lemnos, they had coursed across to the Thessalian group, and, by last account, disappeared in the gulfs between Eubœa and Hellas.

Such were the tidings.

The island of Eubœa lay along the classic coast like a rampart against Asia, leaving a channel between it and the continent a hundred and twenty miles in length, and scarcely an average of eight in width. The inlet on the north received the old raiders from the Euxine. All things considered, therefore, Arrius judged that the robbers might be found somewhere below Thermopylæ. He resolved to enclose them north and south, to do which not an hour could be lost; even the fruits and wines and women of Naxos must be left behind. So he sailed away without stop or tack until, a little before nightfall, Mount Ocha was seen upreared against the sky, and the pilot reported the Eubœan coast.

At a signal the fleet rested upon its oars. When the movement was resumed, Arrius led a division of fifty of the galleys, intending to take them up the channel, while another division, equally strong, turned their prows to the outer or seaward side of the island, with orders to make all haste to the upper inlet, and descend sweeping the waters.

To be sure, neither division was equal in number to the pirates; but each had compensation, among them a discipline impossible to a lawless horde, however brave. Besides, it was a shrewd count on the tribune's side: if one should be defeated, the other would find the enemy shattered by his victory, and in condition to be easily overwhelmed.

Meantime Ben-Hur kept his bench, relieved every six hours. The rest in the Bay of Antemona had freshened him, so that the oar was not troublesome, and the chief on the platform found no fault.

In his long service, by watching the shifting of the meagre sunbeams upon the cabin floor when the ship was under way, he had come to know, generally, the quarter into which she was sailing. This, of course, was only of clear days.

He had no idea that, following the vessel he was helping to drive, there was a great squadron close at hand and in

63

beautiful order; no more did he know the object of which it was in pursuit. Night fell, and the smell of incense floated down the gangways from the deck.

"The tribune is at the altar," he thought. "Can it be we are going into battle?"

A battle possessed for him and his fellow-slaves an interest unlike that of the sailor and marine; it came, not of the danger encountered but of the fact that defeat, if survived, might bring freedom—at least a change of masters, which might be for the better.

In good time the lanterns were lighted and hung by the stairs, and the tribune came down from the deck. At his word the marines put on their armor. At his word again, the machines were looked to, and spears, javelins, and arrows, in great sheaves, brought and laid upon the floor, together with jars of inflammable oil, and baskets of cotton balls wound loose like the wicking of candles. And when, finally, Ben-Hur saw the tribune mount his platform and don his armor, and get his helmet and shield out, he made ready for the last ignominy of his service.

To every bench, as a fixture, there was a chain with heavy anklets. These the hortator proceeded to lock upon the oarsmen, going from number to number, leaving no choice but to obey, and, in event of disaster, no possibility of escape.

In the cabin, then, a silence fell, broken, at first, only by the sough of the oars turning in the leathern cases. Every man upon the benches felt the shame, Ben-Hur more keenly than his companions. Soon the clanking of the fetters notified him of the progress the chief was making in his round. He would come to him in turn; but would not the tribune interpose for him?

Ben-Hur waited anxiously. The interval seemed like an age. At every turn of the oar he looked towards the tribune, who, his simple preparations made, lay down upon the couch and composed himself to rest; whereupon Ben-Hur laughed grimly, and resolved not to look that way again.

The hortator approached. Now he was at number one—the rattle of the iron links sounded horribly. At last number sixty! Calm from despair, Ben-Hur held his oar at poise, and gave his foot to the officer. Then the tribune stirred—sat up —beckoned to the chief.

A strong revulsion seized the Jew. From the hortator, the great man glanced at him; and when he dropped his oar all the section of the ship on his side seemed aglow. He heard nothing of what was said; enough that the chain hung idly from its staple in the bench, and that the chief, going to his seat, began to beat the sounding-board. The notes of the gavel were never so like music. With his breast against the leaded handle, he pushed with all his might—pushed until the shaft bent as if about to break.

The chief went to the tribune, and, smiling, pointed to number sixty.

"What strength!" he said.

"And what spirit!" the tribune answered. *"Perpol!* He is better without the irons. Put them on him no more."

So saying, he stretched himself upon the couch again.

The ship sailed on hour after hour under the oars in water scarcely rippled by the wind. And the people not on duty slept, Arrius in his place, the marines on the floor.

Once—twice—Ben-Hur was relieved; but he could not sleep. Three years of night, and through the darkness a sunbeam at last! At sea adrift and lost, and now land! Dead so long, and lo! the thrill and stir of resurrection. Sleep was not for such an hour. Sorrows assuaged; home and the fortunes of his house restored; mother and sister in his arms once more—such were the central ideas which made him happier that moment than he had ever been. That he was rushing, as on wings, into deadly battle had, for the time, nothing to do with his thoughts. Messala, Gratus, Rome, and all the bitter, passionate memories connected with them, were as dead plagues—miasms of the earth above which he floated, far and safe, listening to singing stars.

The deeper darkness before the dawn was upon the waters, and all things going well with the *Astræa,* when a man, descending from the deck, walked swiftly to the platform where the tribune slept, and awoke him. Arrius arose, put on his helmet, sword, and shield, and went to the commander of the marines.

"The pirates are close by. Up and ready!" he said, and passed to the stairs, calm and confident.


CHAPTER V.

EVERY SOUL aboard, even the ship, awoke. Officers went to their quarters. The marines took arms, and were led out, looking in all respects like legionaries. Sheaves of arrows and armfuls of javelins were carried on deck. By the central stairs the oil-tanks and fire-balls were set ready for use. Additional lanterns were lighted. Buckets were filled with water. The rowers in relief assembled under guard in front of the chief. Ben-Hur was one of the latter. Overhead he heard the muffled noise of the final preparations—of the sailors furling sail, spreading the nettings, unslinging the machines, and hanging the armor of bullhide over the side. Presently quiet settled about the galley again; a stillness filled with vague dread and expectation, which means *ready*.

At a signal passed down from the deck, all at once the oars stopped.

What did it mean?

Of the hundred and twenty slaves chained to the benches, not one but asked himself the question. They were without incentive. Patriotism, love of honor, sense of duty, brought them no inspiration. They felt the thrill common to men rushed helpless and blind into danger. Victory would only rivet their chains the firmer, while the chances of the ship were theirs; sinking or on fire, they were doomed to her fate. Of the situation on deck they might not ask. And who were the enemy? And what if they were friends, brethren, countrymen?

A sound like the rowing of galleys astern attracted Ben Hur, and the *Astræa* rocked as if in the midst of counter ing waves. The idea of a fleet at hand broke upon him—a fleet in manœuvre—forming probably for attack.

Another order was relayed down from the deck. The oars dipped, and the galley started imperceptibly. No sound from without, none from within, yet each man instinctively poised himself for a shock; the very ship seemed to hold its breath and go crouched tiger-like.

At last there was a sound of trumpets on deck, full, clear, long blown. The chief beat the sounding-board until it rang; the rowers reached forward full length, and, deepening the dip of their oars, pulled suddenly with all their united force. The galley, quivering in every timber, answered with a leap. Other trumpets joined in the clamor—all from the rear, none forward—from the latter quarter only a rising sound of voices in tumult. There was a mighty blow; the rowers in front of the chief's platform reeled, some of them fell; the ship bounded back, recovered, and rushed on more irresistibly than before. Shrill and high arose shrieks of terror; over the blare of trumpets, and the grind and crash of the collision, they arose; then under his feet, under the keel, pounding, rumbling, breaking to pieces, drowning, Ben-Hur felt something overridden. The men about him looked at each other afraid. A shout of triumph from the deck—the beak of the Roman had won! But who were they whom the sea had drunk? Of what tongue, from what land were they?

Forward rushed the *Astræa;* and, as it went, some sailors ran down, and, plunging the cotton balls into the oil-tanks, tossed them dripping to comrades at the head of the stairs: fire was to be added to other horrors of the combat.

Directly the galley heeled over so far that the oarsmen on

the uppermost side barely kept their benches. An opposing vessel, caught by the grappling-hooks of the great crane swinging from the prow, was being lifted into the air that it might be dropped and sunk.

The shouting increased on the right hand and on the left; before, behind, swelled an indescribable clamor. Occasionally there was a crash, followed by sudden peals of fright, telling of the ships ridden down, and their crews drowned in the vortexes.

Nor was the fight all on one side. Now and then a Roman in armor was borne down the hatchway, and laid bleeding, sometimes dying, on the floor.

Sometimes, also, puffs of smoke, blended with steam, and foul with the scent of roasting human flesh, poured into the cabin, turning the dimming light into yellow murk. Gasping for breath the while, Ben-Hur knew they were passing through the cloud of a ship on fire, and burning up with the rowers chained to the benches.

The *Astræa* all this time was in motion. Suddenly she stopped. The oars forward were dashed from the hands of the rowers, and the rowers from their benches. On deck, then, a furious trampling, and on the sides a grinding of ships afoul of each other. For the first time the beating of the gavel was lost in the uproar. Men sank on the floor in fear. In the midst of the panic a body was pitched headlong down the hatchway, falling near Ben-Hur. He beheld the half-naked carcass, a mass of hair blackening the face, and under it a shield of bull-hide and wicker-work—a barbarian from the white-skinned nations of the North whom death had robbed of plunder and revenge. The *Astræa* had been boarded? If so, the Romans must be fighting on their own deck! A chill smote the young Jew: Arrius was hard pressed—he might be defending his own life. If he should be slain! God of Abraham forefend! The hopes and dreams so lately come, were they only hopes and dreams? The tumult thundered above him; he looked around; in the cabin all was confusion—the rowers on the benches paralyzed; men running blindly hither and thither; only the chief on his seat imperturbable, vainly beating the sounding-board, and waiting the order of the tribune—in the red murk illustrating the matchless discipline which had won the world.

The example had a good effect upon Ben-Hur. He controlled himself enough to think. Honor and duty bound the Roman to the platform; but what had Ben-Hur to do with such motives then? The bench was a thing to run from; while, if he were to die a slave, who would be the better of the sacrifice? With him living was duty, if not honor. His life belonged to his mother and sister. He saw them, their arms outstretched; he heard them imploring him. And he would go to them. But a Roman judgment held him in doom. While it endured, escape would be profitless. In all the earth there was no place in which he would be safe from the imperial demand. Whereas he required freedom according to the forms of law, so only could he abide in Judea and execute the purpose to which he would devote himself. But what if his benefactor should now be killed?

Once more Ben-Hur looked around. Upon the deck above the battle still beat; against the sides the hostile vessels crushed and grided. On the benches, the slaves struggled to tear loose from their chains, and, finding their efforts vain, howled like madmen; the guards had gone above; discipline was out, panic in. No, the chief kept his chair, unchanged, calm as ever—except the gavel, weaponless. Vainly with his clangor he filled the lulls in the din. Ben-Hur gave him a last look, then broke away to seek the tribune.

He took it with a leap, and was half-way up the comᵢ way—up far enough to glimpse the sky blood-red the ships alongside, the sea covered with ships an wrecks, the fight closed in about the pilot's quarter, the assailants many, the defenders few—when suddenly his foothold was knocked away, and he pitched backward. The deck, when he reached it, seemed to be lifting itself and breaking to pieces; then, in a twinkling, the whole after-part of the hull broke asunder, and the sea, hissing and foaming, leaped in. All became darkness and surging water.

The influx of the flood tossed him like a log forward into the cabin, then, fathoms under the surface, the hollow mass vomited him forth, and he arose along with the loosed debris. In the act of rising, he clutched something, and held to it. The time he was under seemed an age longer than it really was; at last he gained the top; with a great gasp he filled his lungs afresh, and climbed higher up the plank he held, and looked about him.

Smoke lay upon the sea like a semitransparent fog, through which here and there shone cores of intense brilliance of ships on fire. The battle was yet on; nor could he say who was victor. Within the radius of his vision now and then ships passed, shooting shadows athwart lights. Out of the dun clouds farther on he caught the crash of other ships colliding.

About that time he heard oars in quickest movement, and beheld a galley coming down upon him. The tall prow seemed doubly tall, and the red light playing upon its gilt and carving gave it an appearance of snaky life. Under its foot the water churned to flying foam.

He struck out, pushing the plank, which was very broad and unmanageable. Seconds were precious—half a second might save or lose him. In the crisis of the effort, up from the sea, within arm's reach, a helmet shot like a gleam of gold. Next came two hands with fingers extended—large hands were they, and strong—their hold once fixed, might not be loosed. Ben-Hur swerved from them appalled. Up rose the helmet and the head it encased—then two arms, which began to beat the water wildly—the head turned back, and gave the face to the light. The mouth gaping wide; the eyes open, but sightless, and the bloodless pallor of a drowning man. Yet he gave a cry of joy at the sight, and as the face was going under again, he caught the sufferer by the chain chinstrap and drew him to the plank.

The man was Arrius, the tribune.

The water foamed and eddied violently about Ben-Hur, taxing all his strength to hold to the support and at the same time keep the Roman's head above the surface. The galley had passed right through the floating men; over heads helmeted as well as heads bare, she drove, in her wake nothing but the sea sparkling with fire. A muffled crash, succeeded by a great outcry, made the rescuer look again from his charge. A certain savage pleasure touched his heart—the *Astræa* was avenged.

After that, the battle moved on. Resistance turned to flight. But who were the victors? He pushed the plank under the tribune until it floated him, after which all his care was to keep him there. Would the dawn bring Romans or pirates?

At last morning broke in full, the air without a breath. Off to the left he saw the land, too far to think of attempting to make it. Here and there men were adrift like himself. In spots the sea was blackened by charred and smoking fragments. A galley up a long way was lying to with a torn sail hanging from the tilted yard, and the oars all idle. Still farther away he could discern moving specks, which he thought might be ships in flight or pursuit, or they might be white birds a-wing.

An hour passed. His anxiety increased. If relief came not speedily, Arrius would die. Sometimes Arrius seemed already dead, he lay so still. He took the helmet off, and then, with greater difficulty, the cuirass; the heart he found fluttering. He took hope at the sign, and held on. There was nothing to do but wait, and, after the manner of his people, pray.

## Chapter VI.

GRADUALLY, PAINFULLY, Arrius recovered consciousness. From incoherent questions as to where he was, and by whom and how he had been saved, he reverted to the battle.

"Our rescue, I see, depends upon the result of the fight. I see also what thou hast done for me. To speak fairly thou has saved my life at the risk of thy own. More than that, if we get out of this peril, I will do thee such favor as becometh a Roman to prove his gratitude. Yet, yet it is to be seen if, with thy good intent, thou hast really done me a kindness; or, rather, I would exact of thee a promise to do me, in a certain event, the greatest favor one man can do another—and of that let me have thy pledge now."

"If the thing be not forbidden, I will do it."

Arrius rested again. "Art thou, indeed, a son of Hur?" he next asked.

"It is as I have said."

"I knew thy father. I knew him, and loved him," Arrius continued.

There was another pause, during which something diverted the spea⸳ ⸳'s thought.

"It ⸳ t be," he proceeded, "that thou, a son of his, ha not he⸳ Cato and Brutus. They were very great men, and never a ⸳t as in death. In their dying, they left this law— a Roman ⸳ y not survive his good-fortune. There is a heavy ring on my ⸳an⸳ ⸳ke it now and put it on thine own finger."

Ben-Hur did

"The trinket ha⸳ ⸳ s uses," said Arrius next. "I have property and money. I a⸳ accounted rich even in Rome. I have no family. Show the ring to my freedman, who hath control in my absence; you will find him in a villa near Misenum. Tell him how it came to thee, and ask anything, or all he may have; he will not refuse the demand. If I live, I will do better by thee. I will make thee free, and restore thee to thy home and people; or thou mayst give thyself to the pursuit that pleaseth thee most. Pledge me to do what I tell thee now, and as I tell thee; I am waiting, let me have thy promise."

"Noble Arrius, I am warned by thy manner to expect something of gravest concern. Tell me thy wish first."

"Wilt thou promise then?"

"That were to give the pledge, and— Blessed be the God of my fathers! Yonder cometh a ship from the north."

"Hath she a flag?"

"I cannot see one."

Arrius remained quiet, apparently in deep reflection. "Nor any other sign?"

"She hath a sail set, and is of three banks, and cometh swiftly—that is all I can say of her."

"A Roman in triumph would have out many flags. She must be an enemy. Hear now," said Arrius, "while yet I may speak. If the galley be a pirate, thy life is safe; they may not give thee freedom; they may put thee to the oar again; but they will not kill thee. On the other hand, I—" The tribune faltered.

"This is what I would have thee do," he continued resolutely. "If the galley prove a pirate, push me from the plank and drown me. Dost thou hear? Swear thou wilt do it."

"I will not swear," said Ben-Hur firmly, "neither will I do the deed. The Law, O tribune, would make me answerable for thy life. Take back the ring"—he took the seal from his finger—"take it back, and all thy promises of favor in the event of delivery from this peril. The judgment which sent me to the oar for life made me a slave, yet I am not a slave; no more am I thy freedman. I am a son of Israel, and this moment my own master. Take back the ring."

Arrius remained silent.

"Thou wilt not?" Judah continued. "Then, to free myself from a hateful obligation, I give thy gift to the sea. See, O tribune!"

Arrius heard the splash where the ring struck and sank.

"Thou hast done a foolish thing," he said. "Life is a thread I can break without thy help; and, if I do, what will become of thee? If the ship be a pirate, I will escape from the world. I am a Roman. Success and honor are all in all. Yet I would have served thee; thou wouldst not. The ring was the only witness of my will available in this situation. We are both lost. I will die regretting the victory and glory wrested from me; thou wilt live to die a little later, mourning the pious duties undone because of your own folly. I pity thee."

Ben-Hur did not falter. "In all my servitude, O tribune, thou wert the first to look upon me kindly. No, there was another." And he saw plainly the face of the boy who helped him to a drink by the old well at Nazareth.        "ast," he proceeded, "thou wert the first to ask me who . was; and if, when I reached out and caught thee, blind and sinking the last time, I, too, had thought how thou couldst be useful to me in my wretchedness, still the act was not all selfish; this I pray you to believe. Moreover, as a thing of conscience, I would rather die with thee than be thy slayer."

Both became silent, waiting, and Ben-Hur looked at the coming ship, watchful of the actions of the strangers. "Now the ship stops. Now she moves off," he said.

"Whither?"

"On our right there is a galley I take to be abandoned. The new-comer heads towards it. Now she is alongside. Now she is sending men aboard."

Then Arrius opened his eyes. "Thank thou thy God," he said to Ben-Hur, after a look at the galleys, "thank thou thy God, as I do my many gods. A pirate would sink, not save,

71

yon ship. The victory is mine. We are saved. Wave thy hand—call to them—bring them quickly. I shall be duumvir, and thou—I knew thy father, and loved him. He was a prince indeed. He taught me a Jew was not a barbarian. I will take thee with me. Give thy God thanks, and call the sailors. Haste!"

Judah raised himself upon the plank; at last he drew the attention of the sailors in the small boat, and they were speedily taken up.

When the survivors afloat were all saved and the prize secured, Arrius spread his flag of commandant anew, and sailed swiftly northward to rejoin the fleet. In due time the fifty vessels coming down the channel closed in upon the fugitive pirates, and not one escaped. To swell the tribune's glory, twenty galleys of the enemy were captured.

Upon his return, Arrius had warm welcome on the mole at Misenum. The young man attending him very early attracted the attention of his friends and the tribune told the story of his rescue and introduced the stranger, omitting carefully the latter's previous history. At the end, he called Ben-Hur to him.

"Good friends, this is my son and heir, who, as he is to take my property—if it be the will of the gods that I leave any—shall be known to you by my name. I pray you all to love him as you love me."

The adoption was legally perfected. And in such manner the newly-appointed Roman duumvir kept his faith with Ben-Hur, giving him happy introduction into the imperial world of Rome.

# BOOK FOURTH

CHAPTER I.

THAT THE extravagance and dissoluteness of the age had their origin in Rome, and spread thence throughout the empire; that the great cities but reflected the manners of their mistress on the Tiber, may be doubted. In Greece she found a spring of corruption; so also in Egypt; the flow of the demoralizing river was from the East westwardly, and now, in the year of our Lord 29, this very city of Antioch, one of the oldest seats of Assyrian power and splendor, was a principal source of the deadly stream.

A transport galley entered the mouth of the river Orontes from the blue waters of the sea. It was in the forenoon. The July heat was great, yet the passengers crowded the deck—Ben-Hur among others.

Five years had brought the young Jew to perfect manhood. For an hour and more he had occupied a seat in the shade of the sail, and in that time several fellow-passengers of his own nationality had tried to engage him in conversation, but without avail. His replies to their questions had been brief, though gravely courteous, and in the Latin tongue. The purity of his speech, his cultivated manners, his reticence, served to stimulate their curiosity the more. Yet, at odds with his patrician demeanor, his arms were disproportionately long; and the size and evident power of his hands compelled remark; so the wonder of who and what he was mixed continually with a wish to know the particulars of his life. This man had a story to tell.

The galley, in coming, had stopped at one of the ports of

Cyprus, and picked up a Hebrew merchant of most venerable appearance, quiet, reserved, paternal. Ben-Hur ventured to ask him some questions; the replies won his confidence, and resulted finally in an extended conversation.

It chanced also that as the galley from Cyprus entered the bay of the Orontes, two other vessels passed into the river at the same time; and as they did so both the strangers broke out flags of bright yellow. There was much conjecture as to the meaning of the signals. At length a passenger addressed himself to the merchant for information.

"Yes, I know the meaning of the flags," he replied. "They do not signify nationality—they are merely identifying marks of the owner—a vastly rich man of Antioch, a trusted friend of a late Jerusalem prince of very ancient family named Hur."

Judah strove to be composed, yet his heart beat quicker.

"The prince was a merchant, with a genius for business. He set on foot many enterprises, some reaching far East, others West. In the great cities he had branch houses. The one in Antioch was in charge of a man said to have been a family servant, a slave, called Simonides, Greek in name, yet an Israelite. After the master was drowned at sea his business still prospered. But misfortune overtook the family. The prince's only son, nearly grown, tried to kill the procurator Gratus in one of the streets of Jerusalem, and has not since been heard of. In fact, not one of the name was left alive. Their palace was sealed up, and is now a rookery for pigeons; the estate was confiscated; everything that could be traced to the ownership of the Hurs was confiscated. The procurator cured his b⸱ ⸱ with a golden salve."

The pa⸱ ⸱ ⸱gers laughed.

The Hebrew continued, "I am only telling the story as I received it. This man Simonides, who had been the prince's agent here in Antioch, opened trade on his own account, and in an incredibly brief time became the master merchant of the city. They say nothing goes amiss with him. His camels do not die except of old age; his ships never founder; if he throw a chip into the river, it will come back to him gold."

"How long has he been going on thus?"

"Less than ten years."

"He must have had a good start."

"Yes, they say the procurator took only the prince's property ready at hand—his horses, cattle, houses, land, vessels, goods. But the money could not be found, though there must have been vast sums of it. That it furnished old Simonides his start is a common belief. The procurator is of that opinion for twice he has put the merchant to torture."

Judah gripped the rope he was holding with crushing force.

"It is said," the narrator continued, "that there is not a

sound bone in the man's body. The last time I saw him he sat in a chair, a twisted, shapeless, helpless cripple."

"So tortured!" exclaimed several listeners.

"Still the suffering made no impression upon him. All he had was his lawfully, and he was making lawful use of it—that was the most they wrung from him. Now, however, he is past persecution. He has a license to trade signed by Tiberius himself."

"He paid roundly for it, I warrant."

"These ships are his," the Hebrew continued, passing the remark. "It is a custom among his sailors to salute each other by throwing out yellow flags, which means they have had a fortunate voyage."

When the transport was fairly in the channel of the river, Judah spoke to the Hebrew. "What was the name the merchant's master?"

"Ben-Hur, Prince of Jerusalem."

"What became of the prince's family?"

"The boy was sent to the galleys. I may say he is dead. One year is the ordinary limit of life under that sentence. The widow and daughter have not been heard of; those who know what became of them will not speak. They died doubtless in the cells of one of the wayside castles of Judea."

Judah walked to the pilot's quarter. The sunlight lay in hazy warmth upon the land and the water; nowhere except over his life was there a shadow.

Once only he awoke to a momentary interest, and that was when some one pointed out the Grove of Daphne, discernible from a bend in the river.

## CHAPTER II.

WHEN THE city came into view, the passengers were still on deck, eager that nothing of the scene might escape them. The venerable Jew was the principal spokesman. "The Grove of Daphne?" he said to an inquirer. "Nobody can describe it; only beware! Apollo, they say, prefers it to Olympus. People go there for one look—just one—and never come away. They have a saying which tells it all—'Better be a worm and feed on the mulberries of Daphne than be a king's guest.'"

"Then you advise me to stay away from it?"

"Not I! Go you will. Everybody goes—cynic philosopher, virile boys, women, and priests—all go. So sure am I of what you will do that I assume to advise you. Do not take quarters in the city—that will be loss of time; but go at once to the village in the edge of the grove. The way is through a garden, under the spray of fountains. The lovers of the god and his

Penæan maid built the town; and in its porticos and paths and thousand retreats you will find characters and habits and sweets and kinds elsewhere impossible. But the wall of the city! there it is. . . ."

The ship turned and made slowly for her wharf under the wall. Finally, the lines were thrown, the oars shipped, and the voyage was done.


CHAPTER III.

NEXT DAY early, after lodging for the night at a khan near the bridge on the Seleucian road, Ben-Hur sought the house of Simonides. Through an embattled gateway he passed to the wharves; thence up the river midst a busy throng, to the Seleucian Bridge, under which he paused to take in the scene.

There, directly under the bridge, was the merchant's house, a mass of unhewn gray stone, looking like a buttress of the wall against which it leaned. Two immense doors in front communicated with the wharf. Some holes near the top, heavily barred, served as windows. Weeds waved from the crevices, and in places black moss splotched the otherwise bald ston s.

The doors were open. Through one of them business t in; through the other it came out; and there was hurry, in all its movements.

On the wharf there were piles of goods in every kind o crate, bale, barrel and box, and groups of slaves, stripped to the waist, were working the landed cargoes.

Below the bridge lay a fleet of galleys, some loading, others unloading. A yellow flag blew out from each masthead. From fleet and wharf, and from ship to ship, the workmen and porters passed in clamorous counter-currents.

Above the bridge, across the river, a wall rose from the water's edge over which towered the fanciful cornices and turrets of an imperial palace, covering every foot of an island. But Ben-Hur scarcely noticed it. Now, at last, he thought to hear of his people—this, certainly, if Simonides had indeed been his father's slave. But would the man acknowledge the relation? That would be to give up his riches and the sovereignty of so royal a trade witnessed on the wharf and river. And what was of still greater consequence to the merchant, it would be to forego his career in the midst of amazing success, and yield himself voluntarily once more to the status of a slave. Simple thought of the demand seemed a monstrous audacity. Stripped of diplomatic address, it was to say, You are my slave; give me all you have—and yourself as well!

Yet Ben-Hur derived strength for the interview from faith in his rights and the hope uppermost in his heart. For the wealth, be it said in justice, he cared nothing; he was already counted a rich man in Rome, since the death of his foster-father. When he started to the door, it was with a promise to himself—"Let him tell me of mother and Tirzah, and I will give him his freedom without account."

He passed boldly into the house. The interior was that of a vast depot where, in ordered spaces, and under careful arrangement, goods of every kind were heaped and pent. Though the light was murky and the air stifling, men moved about briskly; and in places he saw workmen with saws and hammers making crates for shipments. Down a path between the piles he walked slowly, wondering if the man whose genius presented here such abounding proofs actually could have been his father's slave? If so, to what class had he belonged? If a Jew, was he the son of a servant? Or was he a debtor or a debtor's son? Or had he been sentenced and sold for theft? These thoughts in nowise disturbed the growing respect for the merchant.

At length a man approached.

"I would see Simonides, the merchant."

Among the stowage, the man led him to a flight of steps; ascending which, he found himself on the roof of the depot, and in front of a smaller stone house built upon another, invisible from the landing below, and under the open sky. The roof, hemmed in by a low wall, was a terrace and brilliant with flowers. A dustless path led to the door, through a bordering of Persian roses.

At the end of a darkened passage within, they stopped before a half parted curtain. The man called out, "A stranger to see the master."

A clear voice replied, "In God's name, let him enter."

A Roman might have called the apartment into which the visitor was ushered his atrium. The walls were panelled; each panel was comparted like a modern office-desk, and each compartment crowded with labelled folios discolored with age and use. Above a cornice of gilded balls, the ceiling rose in pavilion style until it broke into a shallow dome set with hundreds of panes of violet mica, permitting a flood of restful light. The floor was carpeted with gray rugs so thick that an invading foot fell half buried and soundless.

In the midlight of the room were two persons—a man resting in a chair high-backed, broad-armed, and lined with pliant cushions; and at his left, leaning against the back of the chair, a girl well forward into womanhood. At sight of them Ben-Hur felt the blood redden his forehead; bowing, as much to recover himself as in respect, he lost the lifting of the hands, and the almost imperceptible change of expression—could it have been a flash of fear?—with which the sitter caught

77

sight of him—an emotion as swift to go as it had been to come. When he raised his eyes the girl's hand was resting lightly upon the elder's shoulder; both of them were regarding him fixedly.

"If you are Simonides, the merchant, and a Jew"—Ben-Hur stopped an instant—"then the peace of the God of our father Abraham upon you and—yours."

The last word was addressed to the girl.

"I am the Simonides of whom you speak, by birthright a Jew," the man made answer, in a voice singularly clear. "I return you your salutation, with prayer to know who calls upon me."

Ben-Hur looked and where the figure of the man should have been, there was only a formless heap sunk in the depths of the cushions and covered by a quilted robe of sombre silk. Over the heap shone a head royally proportioned—the ideal head of a statesman and conqueror—such as Angelo would have modelled for Cæsar. White hair dropped in thin locks over the white brows, deepening the blackness of the eyes shining through them like sullen lights. The face was bloodless, and puffed with folds, especially under the chin. Here was a man who might be twice twelve times tortured into the shapeless cripple he was, without a groan, much less a confession; a man to yield his life, but never a purpose or point; a man born in armor, and assailable only through his loves. To him Ben-Hur stretched his hands, open and palm up, as he would offer peace at the same time he asked it.

"I am Judah, son of Ithamar, late head of the House of Hur, and a prince of Jerusalem."

The merchant's right hand lay outside the robe—a long, thin hand, articulate to deformity with suffering. It closed tightly; otherwise there was not the slightest expression of feeling of any kind on his part; nothing to warrant an inference of surprise or interest; nothing but this calm answer,

"The princes of Jerusalem, of the pure blood, are always welcome in my house; you are welcome. Give the young man a seat, Esther."

The girl took an ottoman near by, and carried it to Ben-Hur. As she arose from placing the seat, their eyes met.

"The peace of our Lord with you," she said modestly. "Be seated and at rest."

Ben-Hur did not take the offered seat, but said, deferentially, "I pray the good master Simonides that he will not hold me an intruder. Coming up the river yesterday, I heard he knew my father."

"I knew the Prince Hur. We were associated in some enterprises lawful to merchants who find profit in lands beyond the sea and the desert. But sit, I pray you—and, Esther, some

78

wine for the young man. Nehemiah speaks of a son of Hur who once ruled the half part of Jerusalem; an old house; very old, by the faith! In the days of Moses and Joshua even some of them found favor in the sight of the Lord, and divided honors with those princes among men."

Esther stood before Ben-Hur with a silver cup filled from a vase upon a nearby table. She offered the drink with downcast face. He touched her hand gently to put it away. Again their eyes met; whereat he noticed that she was small, not nearly to his shoulder in height; but very graceful, and fair and sweet of face, with eyes black and inexpressibly soft. She is kind and pretty, he thought, and looks as Tirzah would were she living. Then he said aloud,

"No, thy father—if he is thy father?"—he paused.

"I am Esther, the daughter of Simonides," she said, with dignity.

"Then, fair Esther, thy father, when he has heard my further speech, will not think worse of me if yet I am slow to take his wine; nor less I hope not to lose grace in thy sight. Stand thou here with me a moment!"

Both of them, as in common cause, turned to the merchant. "Simonides!" he said, firmly, "my father, at his death, had a trusted servant of thy name, and it has been told me that thou art the man!"

There was a sudden start of the wrenched limbs under the robe, and the thin hand clenched. "Esther, Esther!" the man called, sternly; "here, not there, as thou art thy mother's child and mine—here, not there, I say!"

The girl looked once from father to visitor; then she replaced the cup upon the table, and went dutifully to the chair, her countenance filled with wonder and alarm.

Simonides lifted his left hand and gave it into hers, lying lovingly upon his shoulder, and said dispassionately, "I have grown old in dealing with men—old before my time. If he who told thee of this was acquainted with my history, he must have persuaded thee that I could not be else than distrustful of other men. My loves are few, but they are. One of them"—he carried Esther's hand to his lips in manner unmistakable—"is a soul which is of such sweet comfort that, were it taken from me, I would die.

"The other love is but a memory; of which I will say further that, like a benison of the Lord, it hath encompassed a whole family, if only"—his voice trembled—"if only I knew where they were."

Ben-Hur's face suffused, and he cried, impulsively, "My mother and sister! Oh, it *is* of them you speak!"

Esther, as if spoken to, raised her head; but Simonides answered coldly, "Hear me to the end. Because of the loves

79

of which I have spoken, before I make return to thy demand touching my relations to the Prince Hur, and as something which of right should come first, do thou show me proofs of who thou art. Is thy witness in writing! Or cometh it in person?"

The demand was plain, and the right of it indisputable. Ben-Hur clasped his hands, stammered, and turned away at loss. Simonides pressed him.

"The proofs—the proofs, I say! Set them before me—lay them in my hands!"

Yet Ben-Hur made no answer. He had not anticipated the requirement; and, now that it was made, to him as never before came the awful fact that the three years in the galley had carried away all the proofs of his identity; mother and sister gone, he did not live in the knowledge of any human being. Many were acquainted with him, but that was all. Had Quintus Arrius been present, what could he have said more than where he found him, and that he believed the pretender to be the son of Hur? Judah had felt the loneliness before; to the core of life the sense struck him now. Simonides waited in silence.

"Master Simonides," he said, at length, "I can only tell my story; and I will not that unless you stay judgment, and with good-will deign to hear me."

"Speak," said Simonides, now master of the situation—"speak, and I will listen the more willingly that I have not denied you to be the very person you claim yourself."

Ben-Hur proceeded then, and told his life down to his landing at Misenum, in company with Arrius, returned victorious from the Ægean.

"My benefactor was loved and trusted by the emperor, who heaped him with honorable rewards. The merchants of the East contributed magnificent presents, and he became doubly rich among the rich of Rome. The good man adopted me his son by formal rites of law; and I strove to make him just return; no child was ever more dutiful to father than I to him. He would have had me a scholar; in art, philosophy, rhetoric, oratory, he would have furnished me the most famous teacher. I declined his insistence, because I was a Jew, and could not forget the Lord God, or the glory of the prophets, or our city of David and Solomon. Why did I accept any of the benefactions of the Roman? I loved him; and again, I thought I could, with his help, unseal the mystery locking the fate of my mother and sister; and to these there was yet another motive. I shall not speak of this except to say it controlled me so far that I devoted myself to arms, and the acquisition of everything deemed essential to thorough knowledge of the art of war. In the palæstræ and circuses of the city I toiled, and in the camps no less; and in all of them I have a name, but not that of my fathers. The crowns I won—and on the walls of the villa by Misenum there are many of them—all came to me as the son of Arrius, the duumvir. In that relation only am I known among Romans. . . . In pursuit of my secret aim, I left Rome for Antioch, intending to accompany the Consul Maxentius in the campaign he is organizing against the Parthians. Master of personal skill in all arms, I seek now the higher knowledge of the conduct of bodies of men in the field. The consul has admitted me one of his military family. But yesterday, as our ship entered the Orontes, two other ships sailed in with us flying yellow flags. A fellow-passenger and countryman from Cyprus explained that the vessels belonged to Simonides, the master-merchant of Antioch; he said Simonides was a Jew, once the servant of the Prince Hur, nor did he conceal the cruelties of Gratus, or the urpose of their infliction."

Simonides raised his eyes, and said in a clear voice, "I am tening."

"O good Simonides!" Ben-Hur said, "I see yet I stand in the shadow of thy distrust."

The merchant held his features fixed as marble, and waited.

"And not less clearly, I see the difficulties of my position," Ben-Hur continued. "All my Roman connection I can prove; I have only to call upon the counsel, now the guest of the ernor of the city; but I cannot prove I am my father's son. who could serve me in that are dead or lost."

covered his face with his hands; whereupon Esther arose, and, taking the rejected cup to him, said, "The wine is of the country we all so love. Drink, I pray thee!"

He saw the tears in her eyes, and he drank, saying, "Daughter of Simonides, thy heart is full of goodness. Be thou blessed of our God! I thank thee."

Then he addressed himself to the merchant again: "As I have no proof that I am my father's son, I will withdraw what I demanded of thee, O Simonides, and go hence to trouble you no more; only let me say I did not seek thy return to servitude nor an account of thy fortune. In any event, I would have said, as now I say, that all which is product of thy labor and genius is thine; keep it in welcome. I have no need of any part thereof. If, therefore, thou dost think of me again, be it with remembrance of this question, which, as I do swear by the prophets and Jehovah, was the chief purpose of my coming here: What dost thou know—what canst thou tell me—of my mother and Tirzah, my sister?"

"I have said that I knew the Prince Hur," Simonides replied, "and I remember hearing of the misfortune which overtook his family. I remember the Roman who wrought such misery to the widow of my friend is the same who hath since wrought upon me. I will go further, and say to you, I have made diligent quest concerning the family, but—I have nothing to tell you of them. They are lost."

"Then—then it is another hope broken!" Ben-Hur said. "I pray you pardon my intrusion; and if I have occasioned you annoyance, forgive it because of my sorrow." At the curtain he turned, and said, "I thank you both."

"Peace go with you," the merchant said.


## Chapter IV.

Scarcely was Ben-Hur gone, when Simonides seemed to wake as from sleep: his countenance flushed; the sullen light of his eyes changed to brightness; and he said, cheerily,

"Esther, ring—quick!"

She went to the table, and rang a service-bell

One of the panels in the wall swung back, exe    a do way which gave admittance to a man who passed    to th merchant's front, and saluted him with a half-salaa.

"Malluch, here—nearer—to the chair," the master    , imperiously. "Hearken! A young man is now descending to the store-room—tall, comely, and in the garb of Israel; follow him, his shadow not more faithful; and every night send me reports of where he is, what he does, and the company he keeps, and if, without discovery, you overhear his conversations, report them word for word, together with whatever will serve to expose him, his habits, motives, life. Understand you? If he leave the city, go after him—and, mark you, Malluch, be as a friend. If he bespeak you, tell him what you will to the occasion most suited, except that you are in my service; of that, not a word. Haste—make haste!"

The man saluted as before, and was gone.

Then Simonides rubbed his wan hands together, and laughed. "What is the day, daughter?" he said. "What is the day? I wish to remember it for happiness come. See, and look for it laughing, and tell me, Esther."

The merriment seemed unnatural to her; and, as if to entreat him from it, she answered sorrowfully, "Woe's me, father, that I should ever forget this day!"

His hands fell down the instant, and his chin dropped upon his breast. "True, most true, my daughter!" he said, without looking up. "This is the twentieth day of the fourth month. To-day, five years ago, my Rachel, thy mother, fell down and died. They brought me home broken as thou seest me, and we found her dead of grief. We laid her away in a lonely place— in a tomb cut in the mountain; no one near her. Yet in the

82

darkness she left me a little light, which thy years have increased to a brightness of morning." He raised his hand and rested it upon his daughter's head. "Dear Lord, I thank thee that now in my Esther my lost Rachel liveth again!"

Directly he lifted his head, and said, as with a sudden thought, "Is it not clear day outside?"

"It was, when the young man came in."

"Then let Abimelech come and take me to the garden, where I can see the river and the ships, and I will tell thee, dear Esther, why but now my mouth filled with laughter and my tongue with singing."

In answer to the bell a servant came and at her bidding pushed the chair, set on little wheels, out of the room to the roof of the lower house, called by him his garden. Out through the roses, he was rolled to a position from which he could view the palace-tops on the island. There the servant left him with Esther.

"When the young man was speaking, Esther, I observed thee, and thought thou wert won by him."

Her eyes fell as she replied, "I k you of faith, father, I believed him."

"In thy eyes, then, he is the lost son of the Prince Hur?"

"If he is not—" She hesitated.

"And if he is not, Esther?"

"Father, since my mother answered the call of the Lord God, by thy side I have heard and seen thee deal in wise ways with all manner of men seeking profit, holy and unholy; and now I say, if indeed the young man be not the prince he claims to be, then before me falsehood never played so well the part of righteous truth."

"By the glory of Solomon, daughter, thou speakest earnestly. Dost thou believe that I was his father's servant?"

"I understood him mention that as something he had but heard."

For a time Simonides' gaze swam among his swimming ships, though they had no place in his mind.

"Well, thou art a good child, Esther, of genuine Jewish shrewdness, and of years and strength to hear of myself and of thy mother, and of many things of the past not in thy knowledge or thy dreams—things withheld from the persecuting Romans for a hope's sake, and from thee so that thy nature should grow towards the Lord straight as the reed to the sun. . . . My father and mother were Hebrew bond-servants, tenders of the fig and olive trees growing, with many vines, in the King's Garden hard by Siloam; and in my boyhood I helped them. They were of the class bound to serve forever. They sold me to the Prince Hur, then, next to Herod the King, the richest man in Jerusalem. From the garden he transferred me to his storehouse in Alexandria of Egypt, where I came of age. I served him six years, and in the seventh, by the law of Moses, I went free."

"Oh, then, thou art not his father's servant!"

"Nay, daughter, hear. Now, in those days there were lawyers in the cloisters of the Temple who disputed vehemently, saying the children of servants bound forever took the condition of their parents; but the Prince Hur was a man righteous in all things, and an interpreter of the law after the strictest sect, though not of them. He said I was a Hebrew servant bought, in the true meaning of the great lawgiver, and, by sealed writings which I yet have, he set me free."

"And my mother?" Esther asked.

"Thou shalt hear all, Esther. . . . At the end of my service, I came up to Jerusalem to the Passover. My master entertained me. I loved him already, and I prayed to be continued in his service. He consented, and I served him yet another seven years but as a hired son of Israel. In his behalf I had charge of ventures on the sea by ships, and of ventures on land by caravans eastward to Susa and Persepolis, and the lands of silk beyond them. Perilous passages were they, my daughter; but the Lord blessed all I undertook. I brought home vast gains for the prince, and richer knowledge for myself, without which I could not have mastered the charges since fallen to me.

". . . One day I was a guest in his house in Jerusalem. A servant entered with some sliced bread on a platter. She came to me first. It was then I saw thy mother, and loved her, and took her away in my secret heart. After a while came a time when I sought the prince's permission to make her my wife. He told me she was bond-servant forever; but if she wished, he would set her free that I might be gratified. She gave me love for love, but was happy where she was, and refused her freedom. I prayed and besought, going again and again after long intervals. She would be my wife, she said, if I would become her fellow in servitude. Our father Jacob served yet other seven years for his Rachel. Could I not do as much for mine? But thy mother said I must become as she, to serve forever. I came away, but went back. Look, Esther, look here."

He pulled out the lobe of his left ear. "See you the scar of the awl?"

"I see it," she said; "and, oh, I see how thou didst love my mother!"

"Love her, Esther! She was to me a fountain of gardens, a well of living waters, and streams from Lebanon. The master, even as I required him, took me to the judges, and then back to his door, and thrust the awl through my ear into

84

door, and I was his servant forever. So I won my Rachel. And was ever love like mine?"

Esther stooped and kissed him, and they were silent.

"When the good prince was lost," the merchant continued, "I had risen to be his chief steward, with everything of property belonging to him in my management and control. The widow continued me in the stewardship. The business prospered, and grew year by year. Ten years passed; then came the blow which you heard the young man tell about. The Procurator gave it out an attempt to assassinate him. Under that pretext, by leave from Rome, he confiscated to his own use the immense fortune of the widow and children. That there might be no reversal of the judgment, he removed all the parties interested. From that dreadful day to this the family of Hur have been lost. The son, whom I had seen as a child, was sentenced to the galleys. The widow and daughter are supposed to have been buried in some of the many dungeons of Judea, which, once closed upon the doomed, are _____ ____ sealed and locked. They passed from the ____ ____ of men as utterly as if the sea had swallowed them unseen. We could not hear how they died—nay, not even that they were dead."

Esther's eyes were filled with tears.

"Thy heart is good, Esther, good as thy mother's was; and I pray it have not the fate of most good hearts—to be trampled upon by the unmerciful and blind. I went up to Jerusalem to give help to my benefactress, and was seized at the gate of the city and carried to the sunken cells of the Tower of Antonia; why, I knew not, until Gratus himself came and demanded of me the moneys of the House of Hur, which he knew, after our Jewish custom of exchange, were subject to my draft in the different marts of the world. He required me to sign to his order. I refused. He had the movable property of those I served; he had not their moneys. I saw how, if I kept favor in the sight of the Lord, I could rebuild their broken fortunes. I refused the tyrant's demands. He put me to torture; my will held good, and he set me free, nothing gained. I came home and began again, in the name of Simonides of Antioch, instead of the Prince Hur of Jerusalem. Thou knowest, Esther, how I have prospered; that the increase of the millions of the prince in my hands was miraculous; thou knowest how, at the end of three years, while going up to Cæsarea, I was taken and a second time tortured by Gratus to compel a confession that my goods and moneys were subject to his order of confiscation; thou knowest he failed as before. Broken in body, I came home and found my Rachel dead of fear and grief for me. The Lord our God reigned, and I lived. From the emperor himself I bought immunity

85

and license to trade throughout the world. To-day, Esther, the business which was in my hands for stewardship is multiplied into talents sufficient to enrich a Cæsar."

He lifted his head proudly; their eyes met; each read the other's thought. "What shall I do with the treasure, Esther?" he asked, without lowering his gaze.

"My father," she answered in a low voice, "did not the rightful owner call for it just now?"

Still his look did not fall. "And thou, my child; shall I leave thee a beggar?"

"Nay, father, am not I, because I am thy child, his bond-servant?"

A gleam of ineffable love lighted his face as he said, "The Lord hath been good to me in many ways; but thou, Esther, art the sovereign excellence of his favor."

He drew her to his breast and kissed her many times.

"Hear now," he said, with clearer voice—"hear now why I laughed this morning. The young man was the very apparition of his father as a comely youth. My spirit arose to salute him. I felt my trial-days were over and my labors ended. I longed to take him by the hand and show the balance I had earned, and say, 'Lo, 'tis all thine! and I am thy servant, ready now to be called away.'

"And so I would have done, Esther, but that moment three thoughts rushed to restrain me. I will be sure he is my master's son,—such was the first thought; if he is my master's son, I will learn somewhat of his nature. Of those born to riches, bethink you, Esther, how many there are in whose hands riches are but breeding curses." He paused, his hands clenched, his voice shrill. "Esther, consider the pains I endured at the Roman's hands; not Gratus's alone: the merciless wretches who did his bidding the first time and the last were Romans, and they all alike laughed to hear me scream. Consider my broken body, and the years I have gone shorn of my stature; consider thy mother yonder in her lonely tomb; and the sorrows of my master's family and the cruelty of their fate; consider all, and, with Heaven's love about thee, tell me, daughter, shall not a hair fall or a drop of blood run in expiation? Tell me not that vengeance is only the Lord's. Is not his the law, Eye for eye, hand for hand, foot for foot? Oh, in all these years I have dreamed of vengeance, thinking and promising, as the Lord liveth, it will one day buy me punishment of the wrong-doers. And when, speaking of his practice with arms, the young man said it was for a nameless purpose, I named the purpose even as he spoke—vengeance! and that, Esther, that it was—the third thought which held me still and hard while his pleading lasted, and made me laugh when he was gone."

86

Esther caressed the faded hands, and said, as if her spirit with his were running forward to results, "He is gone. Will he come again?"

"Ay, Malluch the faithful goes with him, and will bring him back when I am ready."

"And when will that be, father?"

"Not long, not long. He thinks all his witnesses dead. There is one living who will not fail to know him, if he be indeed my master's son."

"His mother?"

"Nay, daughter, I will set the witness before him; till then let us rest the business with the Lord."


## CHAPTER V.

WHEN BEN-HUR emerged from the great warehouse, it was with the thought that another failure was to be added to the many he had already met in the quest for his people. Then, in counteraction of the spell, the saying of the voyager flashed into memory—"Better a worm feeding upon the mulberries of Daphne, than be a king's guest." He turned, and walked rapidly down the landing and back to the khan.

"The road to Daphne!" the steward said, surprised at Ben-Hur's question. "You have not been here before? Well, count this the happiest day of your life. You cannot mistake the road, the next street to the left. . . ."

It was about the fourth hour of the day when he passed out the gate, and found himself one of a procession apparently interminable, moving to the famous Grove. The road was divided into separate ways for footmen, for men on horses, and men in chariots; and those again into separate ways for outgoers and incomers. The lines of division were guarded by low balustrading, broken by massive pedestals, many of which were surmounted with statuary. Right and left of the road extended margins of sward perfectly kept, relieved at intervals by groups of oak and sycamore trees, and vine-clad summer-houses for the accommodation of the weary, of whom, on the return side, there were always multitudes.

In his wretchedness, Ben-Hur barely noticed the crowd going with him. He treated the processional displays with like indifference. Besides his self-absorption, he had not a little of the complacency of a Roman visiting the provinces. It was not possible for the provinces to offer anything new or superior. He pushed forward through the companies in the way, and too slow-going for his impatience. Once a pair of goats led by a beautiful woman, woman and goats alike brilliant with ribbons and flowers, attracted his attention. Then he stopped to look at a bull of mighty girth, and snowy-white, covered with vines freshly cut, and bearing on its broad back a naked child in a basket, the image of a young Bacchus, squeezing the juice of ripened berries into a goblet, and drinking with libational formulas. Often after that he turned his head at hearing the rumble of wheels and the dull thud of hoofs; unconsciously he was becoming interested in the styles of chariots and charioteers, as they rustled past him. Nor was it long until he began to make notes of the people around him. He saw they were of all ages, sexes, and conditions, and all in holiday attire. At last, following the pointing of many fingers, he saw upon the brow of a hill the templed gate of the consecrated Grove. Borne along by the impulsive current, and sharing the common eagerness, he passed in, and, Romanized in taste as he was, fell to worshipping the place.

He stood upon a broad esplanade paved with polished stone; around him a restless exclamatory multitude, in gayest colors, relieved against the iridescent spray flying from fountains; before him, off to the southwest, dustless paths radiated out into a garden, and beyond that into a forest, over which rested a veil of pale-blue vapor. Ben-Hur gazed wistfully, uncertain where to go. A woman that moment exclaimed,

"Beautiful! But where to now?"

Her companion, wearing a chaplet of bays, laughed an answered, "The winds which blow here are respirations of the gods. Let us give ourselves to waftage of the winds."

"But if we should get lost?"

"O thou timid! No one was ever lost in Daphne, except those who have yielded to the charms of the place and chosen it for life and death. Stand here, and I will show you of whom I speak."

Upon the marble pavement there was a skurry of sandalled feet; the crowd opened, and a party of girls rushed about the speaker and his fair friend, and began singing and dancing to the tabrets they themselves touched. The woman, scared, clung to the man, who put an arm about her, and, with kindled face, kept time to the music with the other hand overhead. The hair of the dancers floated free, and their limbs blushed through the robes of gauze which scarcely draped them in the voluptuousness of the dance. One brief round, and they darted off through the yielding crowd lightly as they had come.

"Now what think you?" cried the man to the woman.

"Who are they?" she asked.

"Devadasi—priestesses devoted to the Temple of Apollo. There is an army of them. This is their home. Sometimes they wander off to other cities, but all they make is brought here to enrich the house of the divine musician. Shall we go now?"

Next minute the two were gone.

Ben-Hur took comfort in the assurance that no one was ever lost in Daphne, and he, too, set out—where, he knew not.

A sculpture of a centaur in the garden attracted him first. In his hand he held a scroll, on which, graven in Greek, were paragraphs of a notice:

O Traveller!
Art thou a stranger?

I. Hearken to the singing of the brooks, and fear not the rain of the fountains; so will the Naiades learn to love thee.

II. The shades of the Grove are thine in the day; at night they belong to Pan and his Dryads. Disturb them not.

III. Eat of the Lotus and the brooksides sparingly, unless thou wouldst have surcease of memory, which is to become a child of Daphne.

IV. Walk thou round the weaving spider—'tis Arachne at work for Minerva.

V. Wouldst thou behold the tears of Daphne, break but a bud from a laurel bough—and die.

Heed thou!
And stay and be happy.

Ben-Hur was angry; not as the irritable, from chafing of a trifle; nor was his anger like the fool's, pumped from the wells of nothing, to be dissipated by a reproach or a curse; it was the wrath peculiar to ardent natures rudely awakened by the sudden annihilation of a hope in which the choicest happinesses were thought to be certainty in reach.

In ordinary mood, Ben-Hur would have availed himself of his position in the consul's family, and made provision against wandering idly about, unknowing and unknown; or, wishing to squander days of leisure in the beautiful place, he would have had in hand a letter to the master of it all, whoever he might be. Now, however, he was a man in the blindness of bitter disappointment, adrift, not waiting for Fate, but seeking it as a desperate challenger.

CHAPTER VI.

BEN-HUR ENTERED the woods with the processions. He had a vague impression that they were in movement to the temples, which were the central objects of the Grove, supreme in attractions.

Presently, he began repeating to himself, "Better a worm, feeding on the mulberries of Daphne than be a king's guest." Then arose questions: Was life in the Grove so very sweet? Wherein was the charm? Did it lie in some philosophy? Or was it something discernible to every-day wakeful senses? Every year thousands, foreswearing the world, gave themselves to service here. If the Grove were so good for them, why should it not be good for him? He was a Jew; could it be that the excellences were for all the world but children of Abraham?

Farther on, out of the woods at his right hand, a breeze poured across the road, splashing him with a wave of sweet smells, of roses and consuming spices. He stopped, as did others, looking the way the breeze came.

"A garden over there?" he said, to a man at his elbow.

"Rather some priestly ceremony in performance—something to Diana, or Pan, or a deity of the woods."

The answer was in his mother tongue. Ben-Hur gave the speaker a surprised look. "A Hebrew?" he asked him.

The man replied with a deferential smile,

"I was born within a stone's-throw of the market-place in Jerusalem."

Ben-Hur was proceeding to further speech, when the crowd surged forward, thrusting him out of the side of the walk next the woods, and carrying the stranger away.

A path into the woods here offered a happy escape from the noisy processions. He walked first into a thicket which from the road, appeared in a state of nature, close, impenetrable, a nesting-place for wild birds. A few steps, however, gave him to see the master's hand even there. The shrubs were flowering or fruit-bearing; under the bending branches the ground was carpeted with brightest blooms. From lilac and rose, and lily and tulip, from oleander and strawberry-tree, the air loaded itself with exhalations; and that nothing might be wanting to the happiness of the nymphs and naiads, down through the flower-lighted shadows of the mass a brook went its course by many winding ways.

Out of the thicket, as he proceeded, a nightingale kept its place fearless, though he passed in arm's-length; a quail ran before him at his feet, whistling to the brood she was leading, and as he paused for them to get out of his way, a figure crawled from a bed of honeyed musk brilliant with golden blossoms. Ben-Hur was startled. Had he, indeed, been permitted to see a satyr at home? The creature looked up at him, and showed in its teeth a hooked pruning-knife; he smiled at his own scare, and, lo! the charm was evolved! Peace without fear—peace a universal condition—that was it!

The charm of the Grove seemed now plain to him; he was glad, and determined to render himself one of the lost in Daphne. Could not he, like the man with the pruning-knife in his mouth, forego the days of his troubled life—forego them, forgetting and forgotten?

But by-and-by his Jewish nature began to stir within him. The charm might be sufficient for some people. Of what kind were they?

Love is delightful—ah! how pleasant as a successor to wretchedness like this. But was it all there was of life! All?

There was an unlikeness between him and those who buried themselves contendedly here. They had no duties—they could not have had; but he—

"God of Israel?" he cried aloud, springing to his feet, with burning cheeks—"Mother! Tirzah! Cursed be the moment, cursed the place, in which I yield myself happy in your loss!"

He hurried away through the thicket, and came to a stream. A bridge carried the path he was traversing across the stream; and, standing upon it, he saw a landscape of wide valleys and irregular heights, with groves and lakes and fanciful houses linked together by white paths and shining streams. The valleys were spread below, that the river might be poured upon them for refreshment in days of drought, and they were as green carpets figured with beds and fields of flowers, and flecked with flocks of sheep white as balls of snow; and the voices of shepherds following the flocks were heard afar. The altars out under the open sky seemed countless, each with a white-gowned figure attending it, while processions in white went slowly hither and thither between them; and the smoke of the altars half-risen hung collected in pale clouds over the devoted places.

Suddenly a revelation dawned upon him—the Grove was, in fact, a temple—one far-reaching, wall-less temple where peace and love reigned supreme.

The architect had not concerned himself with columns and porticos, proportions or interiors, or any limitation upon the epic he sought to materialize; he had simply made a servant of Nature. So the cunning son of Jupiter and Callisto built the old Arcadia; and in this, as in that, the genius was Greek.

From the bridge Ben-Hur went forward into the nearest valley. He came to a flock of sheep. The shepherd was a girl, and she beckoned him, "Come!"

Farther on, the path was divided by an altar—a pedestal of black gneiss, capped with a slab of white marble. Close by it, a woman, seeing him, waved a wand of willow, and as he passed called him, "Stay!" And the temptation in her smile was that of passionate youth.

On yet farther, he met one of the processions; at its head a troop of little girls, nude except as they were covered with garlands, piped their shrill voices into a song; then a troop of boys, also nude, their bodies deeply sunbrowned, came dancing to the song of the girls; behind them the procession, all women, bearing baskets of spices and sweets to the altars

—women clad in simple robes, careless of exposure. As he went by they held their hands to him, and said, "Stay, and go with us."

But he pursued his way indifferent, and came next to a grove luxuriant, in the heart of the vale at the point where it would be most attractive to the observing eye. As it came close to the path he was travelling, there was a seduction in its shade, and through the foliage he caught the shining of what appeared a pretentious statue; so he turned aside, and entered the cool retreat.

The statue proved to be a Daphne of wondrous beauty. Hardly, however, had he time to more than glance at her face; at the base of the pedestal a girl and a youth were lying upon a tiger's skin asleep in each other's arms; close by them the implements of their service—his axe and sickle, her basket—flung carelessly upon a heap of fading roses.

The exposure startled him. Back in the hush of the perfumed thicket he discovered, as he thought, that the charm of the great Grove was peace without fear, and almost yielded to it; now, in this sleep in the day's broad glare—this sleep at the feet of Daphne—he read a further chapter. The law of the place was Love, but Love without Law.

And this was the sweet peace of Daphne!

The votaries of the great out-door temple were of the sybarites of the world, and of the herds in number vaster and in degree lower—devotees of the unmixed sensualism to which the East was almost wholly given. N ʼ to any of the exaltations—not to the singing-god, or his unhappy mistress; not to any philosophy requiring the calm of retirement, nor to any service for the comfort there is in religion, nor to love in its holier sense—were they abiding their vows.

Ben-Hur walked with a quicker step, holding his head higher; and, while not less sensitive to the delightfulness of all about him, he made his survey with calmer spirit; he could not so soon forget how nearly he himself had been blinded to his dedicated purpose.


CHAPTER VII.

IN FRONT of Ben-Hur there was a forest of cypress-trees, each a column tall and straight as a mast. Venturing into the shady precinct, he heard a trumpet gayly blown, and an instant after saw lying upon the grass close by the countryman whom he had met in the road going to the temples. The man arose, and came to him.

"I give you peace again," he said, pleasantly.

"Thank you," Ben-Hur replied, then asked, "Go you my way?"

"I am for the stadium, if that is your way. The trumpet you just heard was a call for the competitors."

"Good friend," said Ben-Hur frankly, "I admit my ignorance of the Grove; if you will let me be your follower, I will be glad."

"That will delight me. I hear the wheels of the chariots. They are taking the track."

Ben-Hur listened a moment, then put his hand upon the man's arm, saying, "I am the son of Arrius, the duumvir, and thou?"

"I am Malluch, a merchant of Antioch."

"Well, good Malluch, the trumpet and the gride of wheels excite me. I have some skill in the exercise. In the palæstræ of Rome I am not unknown. Let us to the course."

Malluch said quickly, "The duumvir was a Roman, yet I see his son in the garments of a Jew."

"The noble Arrius was my father by adoption," Ben-Hur answered.

Soon they came to a field with a track laid out upon it, exactly like those of the Roman stadia. The track proper was of soft earth rolled and sprinkled, and on both sides defined by ropes, stretched loosely upon upright javelins. In one of the stands the two new-comers found places.

Ben-Hur counted the chariots as they went by—nine in all.

"I commend the fellows," he said. "Here in the East, I thought they aspired to nothing better than the two; but they are ambitious, and play with royal fours. Let us study their performance."

Eight of the fours passed the stand, some walking, others on the trot, and all unexceptionally handled; then the ninth one came on the gallop. Ben-Hur burst into exclamation.

"I have been in the stables of the emperor, Malluch, but, by our father Abraham I never saw the like of these."

The last four was then sweeping past. All at once they fell into confusion. Some one on the stand uttered a sharp cry. Ben-Hur turned, and saw an old man half-risen from an upper seat, his hands clenched and raised, his eyes fiercely bright, his long white beard fairly quivering. Some of the spectators nearest him began to laugh.

"They should respect his beard at least. Who is he?" asked Ben-Hur.

"A mighty man from the Desert, somewhere beyond Moab, an owner of camels and horses descended, they say, from the racers of the first Pharaoh—Sheik Ilderim, by name.

The driver meanwhile exerted himself to quiet the four,

but without avail. Each ineffectual effort excited the sheik the more.

"Abaddon seize him!" yelled the patriarch, shrilly. "Run! fly! do you hear, my children?" The question was to his attendants, apparently of the tribe. "Do you hear? They are Desert-born, like yourselves. Catch them—quick!"

The plunging of the animals increased.

"Accursed Roman!" and the sheik shook his fist at the driver. "Did he not swear he could drive them—swear it by all his brood of bastard Latin gods? Cursed be he—cursed the mother of liars who calls him son! See them, the priceless! Let him touch one of them with a lash, and"—the rest of the sentence was lost in a furious grinding of his teeth. "To their heads, some of you, speak them—a word, one is enough, from the tentsong your mothers sang you. Oh, fool, fool that I was to put trust in a Roman!"

Some of the shrewder of the old man's friends planted themselves between him and the horses. An opportune failure of breath on his part helped the stratagem.

Ben-Hur, thinking he comprehended the sheik, sympathized with him. Far more than mere pride of property—more than anxiety for the result of the race, the patriarch loved those animals with a tenderness akin to the most sensitive passion.

They were all bright bays, unspotted, perfectly matched and so proportioned as to seem less than they really were. Delicate ears pointed ʘ    heads; the faces were broad and full between the eyes; the   ʼls in expansion disclosed membrane so deeply red as to suggest the flashing of flame; the necks were arches, overlaid with fine abundant manes. The sheik spoke of them as the priceless, and it was a good saying.

In this second and closer look at the horses, Ben-Hur read the story of their relation to their master. They had grown up under his eyes, objects of his special care in the day, his visions of pride in the night, with his family at home in the black tent out on the shadeless bosom of the desert, as his children beloved. That they might win him a triumph over the haughty and hated Roman, the old man had brought his loves to the city, never doubting they would win, if only he could find a trusty expert to take them in hand; not merely one with skill, but of a spirit which their spirits would acknowledge. Unlike the colder people of the West, he could not protest the driver's inability, and dismiss him civilly; an Arab and a sheik, he had to explode, and rive the air about him with clamor.

Before the patriarch was done with his expletives, a dozen hands were at the bits of the horses, and their quiet assured. About that time, another chariot appeared upon the track;

and, unlike the others, driver, vehicle, and racers were precisely as they would be presented in the Circus the day of final trial.

There should be no difficulty in understanding the carriage known to us all as the chariot of classical renown. One has but to picture to himself a dray with low wheels and broad axle, surmounted by a box open at the tail-end. Such was the primitive pattern. Artistic genius came along in time, and touching the rude machine, raised it into a thing of beauty— that, for instance, in which Aurora, riding in advance of the dawn, is given to our fancy.

The jockeys of the ancients, as shrewd and ambitious as their successors of the present, called their humblest turnout a *two,* and their best in grade a *four;* in the latter, they contested the Olympics and the other festal shows founded in imitation of them.

The same sharp gamesters preferred to put t⸍ ⸍horses to the chariot all abreast; and for distinction they t⸍ ⸍d the two next the pole *yoke-steeds,* and those on the rig⸍ ⸍nd left outside *trace-mates.* It was their judgment, also, t⸍ ⸍t, by a⸍ ⸍ng the fullest freedom of action, the greatest s⸍eed wa⸍ able; accordingly, the harness resorted to was nothing save a collar round the animal's neck, and a trace fixed to the collar.

The other contestants had been received in silence; the last comer was vigorously applauded. His yoke-steeds were black, while the trace-mates were snow-white. In conformity to the Roman taste, their tails had been clipped, and their shorn manes were divided into knots tied with flaring red and yellow ribbons.

As the chariot came into view from the stand, its appearance itself justified the shouting. Stout bands of burnished bronze reinforced the wheel hubs, the spokes were sections of ivory tusks, set in with the natural curve outward to perfect the dishing, bronze tires held the felloes which were of shining ebony. The axle was tipped with brass tiger heads and the bed was of woven willow gilded.

The coming of the beautiful horses and resplendent chariot drew Ben-Hur to look at the driver with increased interest.

Who was he?

Ben-Hur could not see the man's face, or even his full figure; yet the air and manner were familiar, and pricked at his memory.

From the shouting and the gorgeousness of the turnout, he might be some official favorite or famous prince, for kings often struggled for the crown of leaves which was the prize of victory. Ben-Hur arose and forced a passage down nearly to the railing in front of the lower seat of the stand.

And directly the whole person of the driver was in view. A companion rode with him, called Myrtilus, permitted men of high estate indulging their passion for the race-course. Ben-Hur saw only the driver, standing erect in the chariot, with the reins passed several times round his body—a handsome figure, scantily covered by a tunic of light-red cloth; in the right hand a whip; in the other, the arm raised and lightly extended, the four lines. The pose was exceedingly graceful and animated. The cheers and clapping of hands were received with statuesque indifference. Ben-Hur stood transfixed—his instinct and memory had served him faithfully—the driver was Messala. Messala unchanged, as haughty, confident, and audacious as ever, the same in ambition, and mocking cynicism.

## Chapter VIII.

As Ben-Hur descended the steps of the stand, an Arab arose and cried out, "Men of the East and West—hearken! The good Sheik Ilderim giveth greeting. With four horses, sons of the favorites of Solomon the Wise, he hath come against the best. Now needs he most a mighty man to drive them. Whoso will take them to the Sheik's satisfaction, is promised enrichment forever. Here—there—in the city and in the Circuses and wherever the strong congregate, tell ye of his offer. So saith my master, Sheik Ilderim the Generous."

The proclamation awakened a great buzz among the people under the awning. By night it would be repeated and discussed in all the sporting circles of Antioch. Ben-Hur, hearing it, stopped and looked hesitatingly from the herald to the sheik. Malluch thought he was about to accept the offer, but was relieved when he presently turned to him, and asked, "Good Malluch, where to now?"

"Would you liken yourself to others visiting the Grove for the first time, you will straightway to hear your fortune told at the Fountain of Castalia."

Ben-Hur shrugged. "I have heard of it. Very well, if you wish, let us thither."

Malluch kept watch on his companion as they went, and saw that for the moment at least his good spirits were out. Silently, sullenly, he kept a slow pace.

Sight of Messala had set Ben-Hur to thinking. It seemed scarce an hour ago that the strong hands had torn him from his mother, scarce an hour ago that the Roman had put seal upon the gates of his father's house. He recalled how, in the hopeless misery of the galleys, he had had little else to do, aside from labor, than dream dreams of vengeance, in all of which Messala was the object. There might be, he used to say to himself, escape for Gratus, but for Messala—never!

And now the meeting was at hand.

So what Malluch had accounted as a passing loss of spirit was an absorption in when the meeting should be, and in what manner he could make it most memorable.

They turned after a while into an avenue of oaks, among pedestrians and horsemen; women in litters borne by slaves; and now and then chariots rolling thunderously. Then they came in view of the famous Fountain of Castalia.

Edging through a company assembled at the point, Ben-Hur beheld a jet of sweet water pouring from the crest of a stone into a basin of black marble, where, after much boiling and foaming, it disappeared as through a funnel.

By the basin, under a small portico cut in the solid wall, sat a priest, old, bearded, wrinkled, and cowled. Occasionally a visitor extended a hand to him with a coin in it. With a cunning twinkle of the eyes, he took the money, and gave the party in exchange a leaf of papyrus. Before Ben-Hur could test the oracle, some other visitors were seen approaching across the meadow, and their appearance piqued the curiosity of the company, his not less than theirs.

He saw first a camel, very tall and very white, in leading of a driver on horseback. A houdah on the animal, besides being unusually large, was of crimson and gold. Two other horsemen followed the camel with tall spears in hand.

"A prince from afar," said one of the company.

"More likely a king."

"If he were on an elephant, I would say he was a king."

But who were the man and woman under the houdah?

Every eye saluted them with the inquiry. When they saw the thin, shrunken face buried under an immense turban, the skin of the hue of a mummy, making it impossible to form an idea of his nationality, they were pleased to think the limit of life was for the great as well as the small. They saw about his person nothing so enviable as the shawl which draped him.

The woman was seated in the manner of the East, amidst veils and laces of surpassing fineness. Above her elbows she wore armlets fashioned like coiled asps, and linked to bracelets at the wrists by strands of gold; otherwise the arms were bare and of singular natural grace. One of the hands rested upon the side of the carriage, showing tapered fingers glittering with rings. From her elevated seat she looked upon the people calmly, pleasantly, and apparently so intent upon studying them as to be unconscious of the interest she herself was exciting; and, what was in violent contravention of the custom among women of rank in public—she looked at them with an open face.

It was a fair face to see; youthful; complexion not white

like the Greek; nor brunet like the Roman; nor blond like the Gaul; but rather the tinting of the sun of the Upper Nile upon a skin of delicate transparency. The eyes, naturally large, were touched along the lids with the black paint immemorial throughout the East. The lips were slightly parted, disclosing, through their scarlet lake, teeth of glistening whiteness.

As if satisfied with the survey of people and locality, the girl spoke to the driver—an Ethiopian of vast brawn, naked to the waist—who led the camel nearer the fountain, and caused it to kneel; after which he received from her hand a cup, and proceeded to fill it at the basin. That instant the sound of wheels and the trampling of horses in rapid motion broke the silence her beauty had imposed, and, with a great outcry, the bystanders parted in every direction, hurrying to get away.

"The Roman has a mind to ride us down. Look out!" Malluch shouted to Ben-Hur, setting him at the same time an example of hasty flight.

The latter faced to the direction the sounds came from, and beheld Messala in his chariot pushing the four straight at the crowd. This time the view was near and distinct.

The parting of the company uncovered the camel; the hoofs were almost upon him, and he resting with closed eyes, chewing the endless cud. The Ethiopian wrung his hands afraid. In the houdah, the old man was hampered with age, and could not, even in the face of danger, forget the dignity which was plainly his habit. It was too late for the woman to save herself. Ben-Hur stood nearest them, and he called to Messala,

"Hold! Look where thou goest! Back, back!"

The patrician was laughing in hearty good umor; and, seeing there was but one chance of rescue, Ben-Hur stepped in, and caught the bits of the left yoke-steed and his mate. "Dog of a Roman! Carest thou so little for life?" he cried, putting forth all his strength. The two horses reared, and drew the others round; the tilting of the pole tilted the chariot; Messala barely escaped a fall, while his complacent Myrtilus rolled back like a clod to the ground. Seeing the peril past, all the bystanders burst into derisive laughter.

The matchless audacity of the Roman then manifested itself. Loosing the lines from his body, he tossed them to one side, dismounted, walked round the camel, looked at Ben-Hur, and spoke partly to the old man and partly to the woman.

"Pardon, I pray you—I pray you both. I am Messala," he said; "and, by the old Mother of the earth, I swear I did not see you or your camel! As to these good people—perhaps I trusted too much to my skill. I sought a laugh at them—the laugh is theirs. Good may it do them!"

when they dragged her away. Hardly may one say which graves deepest in memory, love or hate. To-day I knew him afar—and, Malluch—" He caught the listener's arm again. "And, Malluch, he knows and takes with him now the secret I would give my life for: he could tell if they live, and where they are, and their condition; if they are dead, he could tell where they died, and of what, and where lie their bones."

"And why will he not?"

"Because I am a Jew, and he is a Roman."

"But Romans have tongues, and Jews, though so despised, have methods to beguile them."

"For such as he? No; and, besides, the secret is one of state. All my father's property was confiscated and divided."

Malluch nodded his head slowly, much as to admit the argument; then he asked anew, "Did he not recognize you?"

"He could not. I was sent to death in life, and have been long since accounted of the dead."

"I wonder you did not strike him," said Malluch, yielding to a touch of passion.

"That would have been to put him past serving me forever. I would have had to kill him, and Death keeps secrets better even than a guilty Roman."

The man who, with so much to avenge, could so calmly put such an opportunity aside must be confident of his future or have ready some better design, and Malluch's interest changed with the thought; it ceased to be that of an emissary in duty bound to another. Malluch was preparing to serve him with good heart and from downright admiration.

"I would not take his life, good Malluch; his secret is for the present his safeguard; yet I may punish him, and if you give me help, I will try."

"He is a Roman," said Malluch, without hesitation; "and I am of the tribe of Judah. I will help you. If you choose, put me under oath—under the most solemn oath."

"Give me your hand, that will suffice."

As their hands fell apart, Ben-Hur said, with lightened feeling, "That I would charge you with is not difficult, good friend; neither is it dreadful to conscience. Let us move on."

They took the road which led across the meadow. Ben-Hur was the first to break the silence.

"Do you know Sheik Ilderim the Generous?"

"Yes."

"Where is his Orchard of Palms? How far is it beyond the village of Daphne?"

Malluch was touched by a doubt; he recalled the prettiness of the favor shown him by the woman at the fountain, and wondered if he who had the sorrows of a mother in mind was about to forget them for a lure of love; yet he replied, "The

Orchard of Palms lies beyond the village two hours by horse, and one by a swift camel."

"Thank you; and to your knowledge once more: Have the games of which you told me been widely published? And when will they take place?"

The questions were suggestive; and if they did not completely restore Malluch his confidence in Ben-Hur, they at least stimulated his curiosity.

"They will be of ample splendor. The prefect is rich, yet, to gain a friend at court, he must put himself out for the Consul Maxentius, who is coming to campaign against the Parthians. A month ago heralds proclaimed the opening of the Circus for the celebration. The name of the prefect would be of itself good guarantee of magnificence, particularly throughout the East; but when to his promises Antioch joins hers, all the islands and the cities by the sea stand assured of the extraordinary, and will be here in person or by their most famous professionals. The fees offered are royal."

"And the Circus—I have heard it is second only to the Maximus."

"At Rome, you mean. Well, ours seats two hundred thousand people, yours seats seventy-five thousand more; yours is of marble, so is ours; in arrangement they are exactly the same."

"Are the rules the same?"

"The laws of the Circus Maximus govern except in one particular: there but four chariots may start at once, here all start without reference to number."

"So then, Malluch, I may choose my own chariot?"

"Your own chariot and horses. There is no restriction upon either."

"One thing more now, O Malluch. When will the celebration be?"

"Ah! your pardon," the other answered. "To-morrow—and the next day," he said, counting aloud, "then the consul arrives. Yes, the sixth day from this we have the games."

"The time is short, Malluch, but it is enough. By the prophets of our old Israel, I will take to the reins again! But there is one condition: is there assurance that Messala will be a competitor?"

Malluch now saw the plan and all its opportunities for the humiliation of the Roman; and he had not been true descendant of Jacob if he had not considered the chances. His voice trembled as he said, "Have you the practice?"

"Fear not, my friend. The winners in the Circus Maximus have held their crowns these three years at my will. Ask the best of them and they will tell you so. In the last great games the emperor himself offered me his patronage if I would take his horses in hand and run them against the entries of the world."

Malluch spoke eagerly. "But you did not?"

"I—I am a Jew"—Ben-Hur seemed shrinking within himself as he spoke—"and, though I wear a Roman name, I dared not do professionally a thing to sully my father's name in the Temple. In the palæstræ I could indulge practice which, if followed into the Circus, would become an abomination; and if I take to the course here, Malluch, I swear it will not be for the prize or the winner's fee."

"Hold—swear not so!" cried Malluch. "The fee is ten thousand sestertii—a fortune for life!"

"Not for me, though the prefect trebled it fifty times. Better than that, better than all the imperial revenues from the first Cæsar—I will make this race to humble my enemy. Vengeance is permitted by the law."

Malluch smiled and nodded. "The Messala will drive," he said, directly. "He is committed to the race in many ways— by publication in the streets, and in the baths and theatres, the palace and barracks; and, to fix him past retreat, his name is on the wager tablets of every young spendthrift in Antioch."

"Ah! and that is the chariot, and those the horses, with which he will make the race? Thank you, thank you, Malluch! You have served me well already. I am satisfied. Now my guide to the Orchard of Palms, and give me introduction to Sheik Ilderim the Generous. I must go today, for his horses may be engaged to-morrow."

"You like them, then?"

"I never saw the kind before, except in the stables of Cæsar; but once seen, they are always to be known. If all that is said of them be true, and I can bring their spirit under control of mine, I can—"

"Win the sestertii!" said Malluch, laughing.

"No," answered Ben-Hur as quickly. "I will do what better becomes a man born to the heritage of Jacob—I will humble mine enemy in a most public place. But," he added, impatiently, "we are losing time. Let us most quickly reach the tents of the sheik."


CHAPTER X.

AT THE Orchard of the Palms, Ben-Hur was admitted into a tract of land apparently without limit and level as a floor. All under foot was fresh grass, in Syria the rarest and most beautiful production of the soil; if he looked up, it was to see the sky through the groinery of countless date-bearers,

103

very patriarchs of their kind, numerous and old, and of mighty girth.

The road wound parallel with the shore of the lake; and when it carried the travellers down to the water's edge, Malluch pointed to a giant palm tree. "Each ring upon its trunk marks a year of its life. Count them from root to branch, and if the sheik tells you the grove was planted before the Seleucidæ were heard of in Antioch, do not doubt him."

"As I saw him at the stand to-day, good Malluch, Sheik Ilderim appeared to be a very common man. The rabbis in Jerusalem would look down upon him, I fear, as a son of a dog of Edom. How come he in possession of the Orchard? And how has he been able to hold it against the greed of Roman governors?"

Malluch spoke warmly. "All his fathers before him were sheiks. One of them helped a king who was being hunted with swords. The story says he loaned him a thousand horsemen, who knew the paths of the wilderness and its hiding-places, and they carried him here and there until the opportunity came, and then with their spears they slew the enemy, and set him upon his throne again. And the king, it is said, remembered the service, and brought the son of the Desert to this place, and bade him set up his tent and bring his family and his herds, for the lake and trees, and all the land from the river to the nearest mountains, were his and his children's forever. And they have never been disturbed in the possession. The rulers succeeding have found it policy to keep good terms with the tribe, to whom the Lord has given increase of men and horses, and camels and riches, making them masters of many highways between cities; so that it is with them any time they please to say to commerce, 'Go in peace,' or 'Stop,' and what they say shall be done."

"How is it, then?" said Ben-Hur, who had been listening unmindful of the slow gait of the dromedaries. "I saw the sheik tear his beard while he cursed himself that he had put trust in a Roman. Cæsar, had he heard him, might have said, 'I like not such a friend as this; put him away.'"

"It would be but shrewd judgment," Malluch replied, smiling. "Ilderim is not a lover of Rome; he has a grievance. Three years ago the Parthians rode across the road from Bozra to Dasmascus, and fell upon a caravan laden, among other things, with the incoming tax-returns of a district over that way. They slew every creature taken, which the censors in Rome could have forgiven if the imperial treasure had been spared and forwarded. The taxed farmers being chargeable with the loss, complained to Cæsar, and Cæsar held Herod to payment, and Herod, on his part, seized property of Ilderim, whom he charged with treasonable neglect of duty. The sheik

104

appeared to Cæsar, and Cæsar has made him such answer as might be looked for from the unwinking sphinx. The old man's heart has been aching sore ever since, and he nurses his wrath, and takes pleasure in its daily growth."

"He can do nothing, Malluch?"

"Well," said Malluch, "that involves another explanation. You must know Simonides gives me his confidence, and sometimes flatters me by taking me into council; and as I attend him at his house, I have made acquaintance with many of his friends, who, knowing my footing with the host, talk to him freely in my presence. In that way I became intimate with Sheik Ilderim.

"A few week ago," said Malluch, continuing, "the old Arab called on Simonides, and found me present. I observed he seemed much moved about something, and, in deference, offered to withdraw, but he himself forbade me. 'As you are an Israelite,' he said, 'stay, for I have a strange story to tell.' This is in substance his story: A good many years ago, three men called at Ilderim's tent out in the wilderness. They were all foreigners, a Hindoo, a Greek, and an Egyptian; and they had come on camels, the largest he had ever seen, and all white. He welcomed them, and gave them rest. Next morning th~y arose and prayed a prayer new to the sheik—a prayer ~ ~ssed to God and his son—this with much mystery be-~s. After breaking fast with him, the Egyptian told who ..iey were, and whence they had come. Each had seen a star, out of which a voice had bidden them go to Jerusalem and ask, 'Where is he that is born King of the Jews?' They obeyed. From Jerusalem they were led by a star to Bethlehem, where, in a cave, they found a child newly born, which they worshipped; and after giving it costly presents, and bearing witness of what it was, they took to their camels, and fled without pause to the sheik, because if Herod—meaning him surnamed the Great—could lay hands upon them, he would certainly kill them. And, faithful to his habit, the sheik took care of them, and kept them concealed for a year, when they departed, leaving with him gifts of great value, and each going a separate way."

"It is, indeed, a most wonderful story," Ben-Hur exclaimed at its conclusion. "What did you say they were to ask at Jerusalem?"*

"They were to ask, 'Where is he that is born King of the Jews?' There was more to the question, but I cannot recall it."

"It is a miracle, Malluch."

"Ilderim is a grave man, though excitable as all Arabs are. A lie on his tongue is impossible."

"Has Ilderim heard nothing more of the three men?" asked Ben-Hur. "What became of them?"

"Ah, yes, that was the cause of his coming to Simonides the day of which I was speaking. Only the night before that day the Egyptian reappeared to him. Here at the door of the tent to which we are coming. He rode the same great white camel, and gave him the same name—Balthasar, the Egyptian."

Ben-Hur spoke with excitement. "It is a wonder of the Lord's! Balthasar, the Egyptian was the name the old man gave us at the fountain today."

Then Malluch became excited, "It is true," he said, "and the camel was the same—and you saved the man's life."

"And the girl," said Ben-Hur, like one speaking to himself, "she was his daughter."

"Tell me again," he said, presently. "Were the three to ask, 'Where is he that is to be King of the Jews?' "

"Not exactly. The words were *'born to be* King of the Jews.' Those were the words as the old sheik caught them first in the desert, and he has ever since been waiting the coming of the king; nor can any one shake his faith that he will come."

"How—as king?"

"Yes, and bringing the doom of Rome—so says the sheik."

Ben-Hur kept silent awhile, thinking. "The old man is one of many millions," he said, slowly, "one of many millions each with a wrong to avenge; and this strange faith, Malluch, is bread and wine to his hope; for who but a Herod may be King of the Jews while Rome endures? But did you hear what Simonides said to him?"

"I listened, and he said— But wait! Some one comes overtaking us."

The noise grew louder, until presently they heard the rumble of wheels mixed with the beating of horse-hoofs—a moment later Sheik Ilderim himself appeared on horse-back followed by a train, among which were the four wine-red Arabs drawing the chariot.

"Peace to you!—Ah, my friend Malluch! Welcome! I have bread and leben, or, if you prefer it, arrack, and the flesh of young kid. Come!"

They followed after him to the door of the tent, in which, when they were dismounted, he stood to receive them, holding a platter with three cups filled with creamy liquor just drawn from a great smoke-stained skin bottle.

And when they were gone in, Malluch took the sheik aside, and spoke to him privately; after which he went to Ben-Hur and excused himself.

"I have told the sheik about you, and he will give you the trial of his horses in the morning. He is your friend. Having done for you all I can, you must do the rest, and let me return to Antioch. I will come back to-morrow prepared, if all goes well in the meantime, to stay with you until the games are over."

## CHAPTER XI.

THE PEOPLE of Antioch were out on their house-tops comforting themselves with the night breeze when Simonides sat in his chair, and from the terrace looked down over the river, and his ships a-swing at their moorings. Above him the endless tramp upon the bridge went on. Esther was holding a plate for him containing his frugal supper—some wheaten cakes, light as wafers, some honey, and a bowl of milk, into which he now and then dipped the wafers after dipping them into the honey.

"Malluch is a laggard to-night," he said, showing where his thoughts were.

"Do you believe he will come?" Esther asked.

"Unless he has taken to the sea or the desert, and is yet following on, he will come."

"I hope so," she said, very softly.

Something in the utterance attracted his attention; it might have been the tone, it might have been the wish.

"You wish him to come, Esther?" he asked.

"Yes," she said, lifting her eyes to his.

"Why? Can you tell me?" he persisted.

"Because"—she hesitated, then began again—"because the young man is—" The stop was full.

"Our master. Is that the word?"

"Yes."

"And you still think I should not suffer him to go away without telling him to come, if he chooses, and take us—and all we have—all, Esther—the goods, the shekels, the ships, the slaves, and the mighty credit, which is a mantle of cloth of gold spun for me by the greatest of the angels of men—Success."

She made no answer.

"Does that not move you? No?" he said, with the slightest taint of bitterness. "Well, I have found, Esther, the worst reality is never unendurable when we meet it directly—not even the rack. I suppose it will be so with death. It pleases me even now to think what a favored man our master is. The fortune cost him nothing—not an anxiety, not a drop of sweat, not so much as a thought; it attaches to him undreamed of, and in his youth. And, Esther, let me waste a little vanity with the reflections; he gets what he could not go into the market and buy with all the pelf in a sum—thee, my child, my darling; thou blossom from the tomb of my lost Rachel!"

He drew her to him, and kissed her twice—once for herself, once for her mother.

"Say not that," she said, when his hand fell from her neck. "Let us think better of him; he knows what sorrow is, and will set us free."

"Ah, thy instincts are fine, Esther. But—but"—his voice rose and hardened—"these limbs upon which I cannot stand —this body drawn and beaten out of human shape—they are not all I bring him of myself. I bring him a soul which has triumphed over torture and Roman malice keener than any torture—I bring him a mind which has eyes to see gold at a distance farther than the ships of Solomon sailed, and power to bring it to hand—ay, Esther, into my palm here for the fingers to grip and keep lest it take wings at some other's word—a mind skilled at scheming"—he stopped and laughed —"Why, Esther, before the new moon passes into its next quartering I could ring the world so as to startle even Cæsar; for know you, child, I have that faculty which is better than any one sense, better than a perfect body, better than courage and will, better than experience—the faculty of drawing men to my purpose and holding them faithfully to its achievement. By that, as against things to be done, I multiply myself into hundreds and thousands. So the captains of my ships plough the seas, and bring me honest returns; so Malluch follows the youth, our master, and will"—Just then a footstep was heard upon the terrace—"Ha, Esther! said I not so? He is here— and we will have tidings. Now we will know if he will let thee go with all thy beauty, and me with all my faculties."

Malluch came to the chair and greeted them, and his attitude left it difficult to define his relation to them; whether that of a servant, or that of a friend. On the other side, Simonides, as was his habit in business, after answering the salutation went straight to the subject.

"What of the young man, Malluch?"

The events of the day were told quietly and in the simplest words, and until he was through there was no interruption, nor did the listener in the chair so much as move a hand.

"Thank you, thank you, Malluch," he said, heartily, at the conclusion; "you have done well—no one could have done better. He appears to have told you but little of his life."

"He has somewhere learned to be prudent. I might call him distrustful. He baffled all my attempts upon his confidence until we started from the Castalian fount going to the village of Daphne."

"A place of abomination! Why went he there?"

"I would say from curiosity, the first motive of the many who go; but, very strangely, he took no interest in the things he saw. Good master, the young man has a trouble of mind from which he would hide, and he went to the Grove, I think, as we go to sepulchres with our dead—he went to bury it."

"That were well, if so," Simonides said, in a low voice; then louder, "Malluch, the curse of the time is prodigality. Saw you signs of this weakness in the youth? Did he display money?"

"None, none, good master."

"In what he said or did, Malluch, could you in anywise detect his master-idea?—his main motive for his words and actions?

"As to that, Master Simonides, I can answer with much assurance. He is devoted to finding his mother and sister—that first. Then he has a grievance against Rome; and as the Messala of whom I told you had something to do with the wrong, the great present object is to humiliate him. The meeting at the fountain furnished an opportunity, but it was put aside as not sufficiently public."

"The Messala is influential," said Simonides thoughtfully.

"Yes; but the next meeting will be in the Circus. And the son of Arrius will win."

"How know you?"

Malluch smiled.

"I am judging by what he says."

"Is that all?"

"No; there is a much better sign—his spirit."

"Ay; but, Malluch, his idea of vengeance—what is its scope? Is his feeling but the vagary of a sensitive boy, or has it the seasoning of suffering manhood to give it endurance?"

"Good master," Malluch replied, "I saw his hate blaze—once when he wanted to know Ilderim's feeling towards Rome, and again when I told him the story of the sheik and the wise man, and spoke of the question, 'Where is he that is born King of the Jews?'"

Simonides leaned forward quickly. "Ah, Malluch, his words —give me his words."

"He wanted to know the exact words. Were they *to be* or *born to be?* It appeared he was struck by a seeming difference in the effect of the two phrases."

Simonides settled back into his pose of listening judge.

"Then," said Malluch, "I told him Ilderim's view of the mystery—that the king would come with the doom of Rome. The young man's blood rose over his cheeks and forehead."

Simonides gazed for a time at the ships and their shadows slowly swinging together in the river: when he looked up, it was to end the interview.

"Enough, Malluch," he said. "Get you to eat, and make ready to return to the Orchard of Palms; you must help the young man in his coming trial."

When Malluch was gone, Simonides took a deep draught of milk.

"Here now, Esther."

She resumed her place upon the arm of his chair.

"God is good to me, very good," he said, fervently. "I see now a reason for the gift of my great riches, and the end for which they were designed. "When the king comes he will need money and men, for as he was a child born of woman he will be but a man after all, bound to human ways as you and I are. And for the money he will have need of getters and keepers, and for the men leaders. There! See you not a broad road for my walking, and the running of the youth, our master?—and at the end of it glory and revenge for us both?"

She sat still, saying nothing.

"Of what are you thinking, Esther?" he said. "If the thought have the form of a wish, give it to me, while the power remains mine."

She answered with a simplicity almost childish, "Send for him, father. Send for him to-night, and do not let him go into the Circus."

"Ah!" he said, prolonging the exclamation; and a ⁀ his eyes fell upon the river. If she should really love the ⁀ ⁀ master! She was sixteen. It was not sufficient that she shoulᵈ enter upon her young womanhood a servant, but she must carry to her master her affections, the truth and tenderness which the father knew so well, because to this time they had all been his own. He controlled himself and asked calmly, "Not go into the Circus, Esther? Why, child?"

"It is not a place for a son of Israel, father."

"Rabbinical, rabbinical, Esther! Is that all?"

The tone of the inquiry was searching, and went to her heart, which began to beat loudly. A confusion, new and strangely pleasant, fell upon her.

"The young man is to have the fortune," he said, taking her hand, and speaking more tenderly; "he is to have the ships and the shekels—all, Esther, all. Yet I did not feel poor, for thou wert left me, and thy love so like the dead Rachel's. Tell me, is he to have that too?"

She bent over him, and laid her cheek against his head.

"Speak, Esther. I will be the stronger of the knowledge."

She sat up then, and spoke as if she were Truth's holy self. "Comfort thee, father. I will never leave thee; though he take my love, I will be thy handmaid ever as now."

And, stooping, she kissed him.

"The pleading of his voice drew me to him, and I shudder to think of him in danger. Yes, father, I would be more than glad to see him again. Still, the love that is unrequited

110

cannot be perfect love, wherefore I will wait a time, remembering I am thy daughter and my mother's."

"A very blessing of the Lord art thou, Esther! A blessing to keep me rich, though all else be lost. Thou shalt not suffer."

## CHAPTER XII.

THE PALACE across the river nearly opposite Simonides' place was surrounded by the wall enclosing the whole island to the water's edge. No longer in general use, the huge, sprawling pile was kept in perpetual readiness for state visitors; and when a consul, general of the army, king, or potentate arrived at Antioch, quarters were at once assigned him on the island.

In one of its many luxuriously appointed apartments was an elaborately decorated dining hall of vast proportions, and on this evening, about the tables, seated or moving restlessly from one to another, there were probably a hundred young Romans. They wore the in-door dress of the great capital; tunics short of sleeve and skirt, a style well adapted to the summer climate of Antioch. On the divan here and there togas and lacernæ lay where they had been carelessly tossed, some of them significantly bordered with purple. On the divan also lay sleepers stretched at ease; overcome by the heat and  ̄̇ ̇.   .  by Bacchus.

The num of voices was loud and incessant. Sometimes there was an explosion of laughter, sometimes a burst of rage or exultation; but over all prevailed the sharp, prolonged rattle of the tesseræ, or ivory dice, loudly shaken, and the moving of the *hostes* on the checkered boards.

"Good Flavius," said a player, holding his piece in suspended movement, "thou seest yon lacerna on the divan. It is fresh from the shop, and hath a shoulder-buckle of gold broad as a palm. Gladly I would give it to find a man who knows the minute that Maxentius will arrive to-morrow."

"Good play, good play! I have you! And why the minute?"

"Hast thou ever stood uncovered in the Syrian sun on the quay at which he will land? The fires of the Vesta are not so hot; and, by the Stator of our father Romulus, I would die, if die I must, in Rome rather than be cooked to death in Antioch. . . . Ha, by Venus, my Flavius, thou didst beguile me! I have lost. O fortune!"

And they played again and again; and when day, stealing through the skylights, began to dim the lamps, it found the two still at the game. Like most of the company, they were military attachés of the consul, awaiting his arrival.

111

A group of young men entered the room, and unnoticed at first, proceeded to the central table. Some of them kept their feet with difficulty. Around the leader's brow was a chaplet which marked him master of the feast, if not the giver. Apparently the wine had made no impression upon him; he carried his head high; the blood flushed his lips and cheeks; his eyes glittered; though the manner in which he walked was too nearly imperial for one sober and not a Cæsar. In going to the table, he made room for himself and his followers with little ceremony and no apologies; and when at length he stopped, and looked over it and at the players, they all turned to him, with a shout like a cheer.

"Messala! Messala!"

Instantly there were dissolutions of groups, and breaking-up of games, and a general rush towards the centre.

Messala took the demonstration indifferently, and proceeded to show the ground of his popularity. "A health to thee, Drusus, my friend," he said to the player next at his right; "a health—and thy tablets a moment."

He raised the waxen boards, glanced at the memoranda of wagers, and tossed them down.

"Denarii, only denarii—coin of cartmen and butchers!" he said, with a scornful laugh. "By the drunken Semele, to what is Rome coming, when a Cæsar sits o'nights waiting a turn of fortune to bring him but a beggarly denarius!"

The scion of the Drusi reddened to his brows, but the by-standers broke in upon his reply by surging closer around the table, and shouting, "The Messala! The Messala!"

"Men of the Tiber," Messala continued, wrestling a box with the dice in it from a hand near-by, "who is he most favored of the gods? A Roman. Who is he lawgiver of the nations? A Roman. Who is he, by sword right, the universal master?"

"A Roman, a Roman!" they shouted.

"Yet—yet"—he lingered to catch their ears—"yet there is a better than the best of Rome." He tossed his patrician head and paused, as if to sting them with his sneer.

"Ay—Hercules!" cried one.

"Bacchus!" yelled a satirist.

"No," Messala answered, "among men."

"Name him, name him!"

"I will," he said, the next lull. "He who to the perfection of Rome hath added the perfection of the East; who to the arm of conquest, which is Western, hath also the art needful to the enjoyment of dominion, which is Eastern. In the East we have no gods, only Wine, Women, and Fortune, and the greatest of them is Fortune; wherefore our motto, 'Who dareth what I dare?'—fit for the senate, fit for battle, fittest for him who, seeking the best, challenges the worst."

His voice dropped into an easy, familiar tone, but without relaxing the ascendency he had gained.

"In the great chest up in the citadel I have five talents coin current in the markets, and here are the receipts for them."

From his tunic he drew a roll of paper, and, flinging it on the table, continued, amidst breathless silence, every eye having him in view fixed on his, every ear listening:

"The sum lies there the measure of what I dare. Who of you dares so much? You are silent. Is it too great! I will strike off one talent. What! still silent? Come, then, throw me once for these three talents—only three; for two; for one—one at least—one for the honor of the river by which you were born —Rome East against Rome West!—Orontes the barbarous against Tiber the sacred!"

He rattled the dice overhead while waiting.

Not a man moved; then he flung the box upon the table, and, laughi... ...ok up the receipts.

He turned ... ...rusus, with a laugh heard throughout the apartment. "Ha, ha, m... friend! Be thou not offended because I levelled the Cæsar in thee down to the denarii. I did but use the name to try fine fledgings of our old Rome. Come, my Drusus, come!" He took up the box again and rattled the dice merrily. "Here, for what sum thou wilt, let us measure for-unes."

The manner was frank, cordial, winsome. Drusus melted in a moment.

"By the Nymphæ, yes!" he said laughing. "I will throw with thee, Messala—for a denarius.

"But hold, Messala, hold!" cried Drusus. "I know not if it be ominous to stay the poised dice with a question; but one occurs to me, and I must ask it though Venus slap me with her girdle."

"Nay, my Drusus, Venus with her girdle off is Venus in love. To thy question."

And Drusus asked, "Did you ever see one Quintus Arrius?"

"The duumvir?"

"No—his son."

"I knew not he had a son."

"It is nothing," Drusus said; "only, my Messala, Pollux was not more like Castor than Arrius is like thee."

The remark had the effect of a signal: twenty voices took it up. "True, true! His eyes—his face," they cried.

"What!" answered one, disgusted. "Messala is a Roman; Arrius is a Jew."

There was promise of a dispute; seeing which, Messala interposed. "The wine is not come, my Drusus; and, as thou seest, I have the dice as they were dogs in leash. As to Arrius, I will accept thy opinion of him, so thou tell me more about him."

"Well, be he Jew or Roman—and, by the great god Pan, I say it not in disrespect of thy feelings, my Messala!—this Arrius is handsome and brave and shrewd. The emperor offered him favor and patronage, which he refused. He came up through mystery, and keepeth distance as if he felt himself better or knew himself worse than the rest of us. In the palæstræ he was unmatched; he played with the blue-eyed giants from the Rhine as they were willow wisps. The duumvir left him vastly rich. He has a passion for arms, and thinks of nothing but war. Maxentius admitted him into his family, and he was to have taken ship with us, but we lost him at Ravenna. Nevertheless he arrived safely. We heard of him this morning. *Perpol!* Instead of coming to the palace or going to the citadel, he dropped his baggage at the khan, and hath disappeared again."

Messala took his hand from the dice-box, and called out, "Ho, my Caius! Dost thou hear?"

A youth at his elbow—his Myrtilus, or comrade, in the day's chariot practice—answered, pleased with the attention,

"Dost thou remember the man who gave thee the fall today?"

"By the love-locks of Bacchus, have I not a brui͞ ͟ ͟ ͟ ͞er to help me keep it in mind?"

"Well, be thou grateful to the Fates—I have found thy enemy. Listen."

Thereupon Messala turned to Drusus. "Tell us more of him —*perpol!*—of him who is both Jew and Roman—by Phœbus, a combination to make a Centaur lovely! What garments doth he affect, my Drusus?"

"Those of the Jews."

"Hearest thou, Caius?" said Messala. "The fellow is young —one; he hath the visage of a Roman—two; he loveth best the garb of a Jew—three; and in the palæstræ fame and fortune come of arms to throw a horse or tilt a chariot, as the necessity may order—four. And, Drusus, help thou my friend again. Doubtless this Arrius hath tricks of language; otherwise he could not so confound himself, to-day a Jew, to-morrow a Roman; but of the tongue of Athene—speaketh he in that as well?"

"With such purity, Messala, he might have been a contestant in the Isthmia."

"Art thou listening, Caius?" said Messala. "The fellow is qualified to salute a woman in the Greek; and as I keep the count, that is five. What sayest thou?"

"Thou hast found him, my Messala," Caius answered, "or I am not myself."

"Thy pardon, Drusus—and pardon of all—for speaking in riddles thus," Messala said, in his winsome way. "Thou didst speak, I think, of mystery in connection with the coming of the son of Arrius. Tell me of that."

" 'Tis nothing, Messala," Drusus replied. "When Arrius, the father, sailed in pursuit of the pirates, he was without wife or family; he returned with a boy—him of whom we speak—and next day adopted him."

"Adopted him?" Messala repeated. "By the gods, Drusus, thou dost, indeed, interest me! Where did the duumvir find the boy? And who was he?"

"Who shall answer thee that, Messala, but the young Arrius himself? *Perpol!* in the fight the duumvir—then but a tribune—lost his galley. A returning vessel found him and one other—all of the crew who survived—afloat upon the same plank. I give you now the story of the rescuers, which hath never been contradicted. They say, the duumvir's companion on the plank was a Jew—"

"A Jew!" echoed Messala.

"And a slave."

"How Drusus? A slave?"

"When the two were lifted to the deck, the duumvir was in his tribune's armor, and the other in the vesture of a rower."

Messala arose from leaning against the table. "A galley"—he checked the debasing word, and looked around frowning, for once in his life at loss. Just then a procession of slaves filed into the room; some were men who bore great jars of wine; others, comely, dark-haired young women, carried baskets of fruits and confections, others again with cups and flagons of gold and silver. There was inspiration in the sight. Instantly Messala climbed upon a stool.

"Men of the Tiber," he said in a clear voice, "let us turn this waiting for our chief into a feast of Bacchus. Whom choose ye for master?"

Drusus arose. "Who shall be master but the giver of the feast?" he said. "Answer, Romans."

They gave their reply in a shout.

Messala took the chaplet from his head, gave it to Drusus, who climbed upon the table, and, in the view of all, solemnly replaced it, making Messala master of the night.

## CHAPTER XIII.

SHEIK ILDERIM was a man of too much importance to go about with a small establishment. He had a reputation to keep with his tribe, such as became a prince and patriarch of the greatest following in all the Desert east of Syria; with the people of the cities he had another reputation, which was that of one of the richest personages not a king in all the East; and, being rich in fact—in money as well as in servants, camels, horses, and flocks of all kinds—he took pleasure in a certain state, which, besides magnifying his dignity with strangers, contributed to his personal pride and comfort.

Servants were already waiting the master's direction. One of them took off his sandals; another unlatched Ben-Hur's Roman shoes; then the two exchanged their dusty outer garments for fresh ones of white linen.

"Enter—in God's name, enter, and take thy rest," said the host, heartily, in the dialect of the Market-place of Jerusalem; forthwith he led the way to the divan.

"I will sit here," he said next, pointing; "and there the stranger."

A handmaid answered, and dexterously piled the pillows and bolsters as rests for the back; after which they sat upon the side of the divan, while water was brought fresh from the lake, and their feet bathed and dried with napkins.

Ilderim clapped his hands. "Seek the stranger in the guest-tent, and say I, Ilderim, send him a prayer that his peace may be as incessant as the flowing of waters."

The man in waiting bowed.

"Say, also," Ilderim continued, "that I have returned with another for breaking of bread; and, if Balthasar the wise careth to share the loaf 'hree may partake of it, and the portion of the birds b‾ e the less."

The second serv .. went away.

"Let us take our rest now."

Thereupon Ilderim settled himself upon the divan, and when fairly at rest, he stopped combing his beard, and said, gravely, "That thou art my guest, and hast drunk my leben, and art about to taste my salt, ought not to forbid a question: Who art thou?"

"So it please thee," said Ben-Hur, "first, I am not a Roman, as the name given thee as mine implieth."

Ilderim clasped the beard overflowing his breast, and gazed at the speaker with eyes faintly twinkling through the shade of the heavy, close-drawn brows.

"In the next place," Ben-Hur continued, "I am an Israelite of the tribe of Judah."

The sheik raised his brows a little.

"Nor that merely. Sheik, I am a Jew with a grievance against Rome compared with which thine is but a child's trouble."

The old man combed his beard with nervous haste, and let fall his brows until even the twinkle of the eyes went out.

"Still further: I swear to thee, Sheik Ilderim—I swear by the covenant the Lord made with my fathers—so thou but give me the revenge I seek, the money and the glory of the race shall be thine."

Ilderim's brows relaxed; his head arose; his face began to beam; and it was almost possible to see the satisfaction taking possession of him.

"Enough!" he said. "If at the roots of thy tongue there is a lie in coil, Solomon himself had not been safe against thee. But as to thy skill. What experience hast thou in racing with chariots? And the horses—canst thou make them creatures of thy will to come at call? To go, if thou sayest it, to the last extreme of breath and strength—and then, out of the depths of thy life thrill them to one exertion the mightiest of all? The gift, my son, is not to everyone. Ah, by the splendor of God! I knew a king who governed millions of men, their perfect master, but could not win the respect of a horse."

At his command, a servant came forward. "Let my Arabs come!"

The man drew aside part of the division curtain of the tent, exposing to view a group of horses, which lingered a moment where they were as if to make certain of the invitation.

"Come!" Ilderim said to them. "Why stand ye there? What have I that is not yours? Come, I say!"

They stalked slowly in.

A head of exquisite turn—with large eyes, soft as a deer's, and half hidden by the dense forelock, and small ears, sharp-pointed and sloped well forward—approached then quite to his breast, the nostrils open, and the upper lip in motion. "Who are you?" it asked, plainly as ever man spoke. Ben-Hur recognized one of the four racers he had seen on the course, and gave his open hand to the beautiful brute.

Ilderim clapped his hands. "Bring me the records," he said to a servant.

While waiting, the sheik played with the horses, patting their cheeks, combing their forelocks with his fingers, giving each one a token of remembrance. Presently the man appeared with a chest of cedar reinforced by bands, and hinged and bolted with brass.

The chest was opened, disclosing a mass of ivory tablets strung on rings of silver wire; each ring held several hundreds of them.

"Know thou, each tablet records the name of a foal of the pure blood born to my fathers through the hundreds of years passed; and also the names of sire and dam. Take them, and note their age, that thou mayst the more readily believe."

Some of the tablets were nearly worn away. All were yellow with age.

"Now, O son of Israel, thou mayest believe my declaration —if I am a lord of the Desert, behold my ministers! Take them from me, and I become as a sick man left by the caravan to die. Thanks to them, age hath not diminished the terror of me on the highways between cities; and it will not while I have strength to go with them. They were never overtaken in retreat; nor, by the sword of Solomon, did they ever fail in pursuit! That, mark you, on the sands and under saddle; but now—I do not know—I am afraid, for they are under yoke the first time, and the conditions of success are so many. They have the pride and the speed and the endurance. If I find them a master, they will win. Son of Israel, if thou art the man, I swear it shall be a happy day that brought thee thither. Of thyself now speak."

"I know now," said Ben-Hur, "why it is that in the love of an Arab his horse is next to his children; and I know, also, why the Arab horses are the best in the world; but, good sheik, I would not have you judge me by words alone; for, as you know, all promises of men sometimes fail. Give me the trial first on some plain hereabout, and put the four in my hand to-morrow."

Ilderim's face beamed again.

"From the masters in Rome," said Ben-Hur, "I ...... ed many lessons, little thinking they would serve me in a time like this. I tell thee thy sons of the Desert, though they have separately the speed of eagles and the endurance of lions, will fail if they are nc trained to run together under the yoke. For bethink th-e,      in every four there is one the slowest and one the    'test; it vas so to-day; the driver could not reduce the      to harmonious action with the poorest. Can I get them t  .n together, moved by my will, the four as one, thou shal' nave the sestertii and the crown, and I my revenge. What sayest thou?"

Ilderim listened, combing his beard. At the end he said, with a laugh, "We have a saying in the Desert, 'If you will cook the meal with words, I will promise an ocean of butter.' Thou shalt have the horses in the morning."

At that moment there was a stir at the rear entrance to the tent.

"The supper—it is here! and yonder my friend Balthasar, whom thou shalt know. He hath a story to tell which an Israelite should never tire of hearing."

## Chapter XIV.

Balthasar was conducted to the divan, where Ilderim and Ben-Hur received him standing. A loose black gown covered his person; his step was feeble, and his whole movement slow

118

and cautious, apparently dependent upon a long staff and the arm of a servant.

"This is he, O Balthasar," said the sheik, his hand on Ben-Hur's arm, "who will break bread with us this evening."

The Egyptian glanced at the young man, and looked again surprised and doubting; seeing which the sheik continued, "I have promised him my horses for trial to-morrow; and if all goes well, he will drive them in the Circus."

Balthasar continued his gaze.

"He came well recommended," Ilderim pursued, puzzled. "You may know him as the son of Arrius, who was a noble Roman sailor, though"—the sheik hesitated, then resumed, with a laugh—"though he declares himself an Israelite of the tribe of Judah; and, by the splendor of God, I believe what he tells me!"

Balthasar could no longer withhold explanation. "To-day, O most generous sheik, my life was in peril, and would have been lost had not a youth, the counterpart of this one—if, indeed, he be not the very same—intervened when all others fled, and saved me." Then he addressed Ben-Hur direct.y, "Art thou not he?"

"I cannot answer so far," Ben-Hur replied, with modest deference. "I am he who stopped the horses of the insolent Roman when they were rushing upon thy camel at the Fountain of Castalia. Thy daughter left a cup with me." From the bosom of his tunic he produced the cup, and gave it to Balthasar.

A glow lighted the faded countenance of the Egy in. "The Lord sent thee to me at the Fountain to-day," he said, in a tremulous voice, stretching his hand towards Ben-Hur; "and he sends thee to me now. I give him thanks; and praise him thou, for of his favor I have wherewith to give thee great reward, and I will. The cup is thine; keep it."

Ben-Hur took back the gift, and Balthasar, seeing the inquiry upon Ilderim's face, related the occurrence at the Fountain.

"What!" said the sheik to Ben-Hur. "Thou saidst nothing of this to me, when better recommendation thou couldst not have brought. Am I not an Arab, and sheik of my tribe of tens of thousands? And is not he my guest? And is it not in my guest-bond that the good or evil thou dost him is good or evil done to me? Whither shouldst thou go for reward but here? And whose the hand to give it but mine?" His voice at the end of the speech rose to cutting shrillness.

"Good sheik, spare me, I pray. I came not for reward, great or small; the help I gave this excellent man would have been given as well to thy humblest servant."

"But he is my friend, my guest—not my servant; and seest

119

thou not in the difference the favor of Fortune?" Then to Balthasar the sheik subjoined, "Ah, by the splendor of God! I tell thee again he is not a Roman."

With that he turned away, and gave attention to the servants.

Ben-Hur gave his arm to Balthasar, and conducted him to the table, where shortly they were all seated on their rugs. The lavers were brought them, and they washed and dried their hands; then the sheik made a sign, the servants stopped, and the voice of the Egyptian arose tremulous with holy feeling.

"Father of All—God! What we have is of thee; take our thanks, and bless us, that we may continue to do thy will."

It was the grace the good man had said simultaneously with his brethren Gaspar the Greek and Melchior the Hindoo, the utterance in diverse tongues at the meal in the desert, years before.


Chapter XV.

THE EGYPTIAN told his story of the meeting of the three in the desert, and agreed with the sheik that it was in December, twenty-seven years before when he and his companions, fleeing from Herod, arrived at the tent praying shelter. Balthasar was heard with intense interest; even the servants lingering when they could to catch its details. Ben-Hur received it as became a man listening to a revelation of deep concern to all humanity, and to none of more concern than the people of Israel. In his mind, as we shall presently see, there was crystallizing an idea which was to change his course of life, if not absorb it absolutely.

As the recital proceeded, the impression made by Balthasar upon the young Jew increased; at its conclusion, his feeling was too profound to permit a doubt of its truth; indeed, there was nothing left him desirable in the connection but assurances, if such were to be had, pertaining exclusively to the consequences of the amazing event.

To Sheik Ilderim the story was not new. He had heard it from the three wise men together under circumstances which left no room for doubt; he had acted upon it seriously, for helping a fugitive escape from the anger of the first Herod was dangerous. Now one of the three sat at his table again, a welcome guest and revered friend. Sheik Ilderim was an Arab, whose interest in the consequences was but general; on the other hand, Ben-Hur was an Israelite, with more than a special interest in the true interpretation of the fact. He laid hold of the circumstance with a purely Jewish mind.

From his cradle, he had heard of the Messiah; at the colleges he had been made familiar with all that was known of that Being at once the hope, the fear, and the peculiar glory of the chosen people; the prophets from the first to the last of the heroic line foretold him; and the coming had been, and yet was, the theme of endless exposition with the rabbis until all the children of Abraham, wherever their lots were cast, bore the Messiah in expectation, and by it ruled and moulded their lives.

There were two circumstances in Ben-Hur's life the result of which had been to keep him in a state comparatively free from the narrowing influence and hard effects of the audacious faith of his Separatist countrymen.

In the first place, his father followed the faith of the Sadducees, who may, in a general way, be termed the Liberals of their time. They were unquestionably a sect, yet their religion was more a philosophy than a creed; they did not deny themselves the enjoyments of life, and saw many admirable methods and productions among the Gentile divisions of the race. In politics they were the active opposition of the Separatists. Ben-Hur was in course of acquiring these opinions when the second saving event overtook him.

Upon a youth of Ben-Hur's mind and temperament the influence of five years of affluent life in Rome can be appreciated best by recalling that the great city was then, in fact, the meeting-place of the nations—politically and commercially, as well as for the indulgence of pleasure without restraint. Round and round the golden milestone in front of the Forum flowed all the active currents of humanity. How could he, as the son of Arrius, pass day after day, from the beautiful Misenum villa into the receptions of Cæsar, and be wholly uninfluenced by what he saw there of kings, princes, ambassadors, hostages, and delegates, suitors from every known land, waiting humbly the yes or no which was to make or unmake them? And when he sat under the purple velaria of the Circus Maximus, one of three hundred and fifty thousand spectators, he must have been visited by the thought that possibly there might be some branches of the human family worthy of divine mercy, though they were of the uncircumcised—some, by their sorrows, and, yet worse, by their hopelessness fitted for brotherhood in the promises to his countrymen.

That he should have had such a thought under such circumstances was but natural. The wretchedness of the masses, and their hopeless condition, had no relation whatever to religion; their groans were not against their gods or for want of gods. No, the unhappy condition was from misgovernment and usurpations and countless tyrannies. The Avernus men had been tumbled into, and were praying to be relieved from, was terribly but essentially political. And the supplication— everywhere alike, in Lodinum, Alexandria, Athens, Jerusalem —was for a king to conquer with—not a god to worship.

The people, even the discerning and philosophical, discovered no hope except in crushing Rome; that done, the relief would follow in restorations and reorganizations; therefore they prayed, conspired, rebelled, fought, and died, drenching the soil to-day with blood, to-morrow with tears— and always with the same result.

Ben-Hur was in agreement with the mass of non-Romans. The five years' residence in the capital served him with opportunity to see and study the miseries of the subjugated world. And in full belief that the evils which afflicted it were political, and to be cured only by the sword, he was going forth to fit himself for a part in the day of the heroic remedy. By practice of arms he was a perfect soldier; but war has its higher fields; the consummate captain is a fighting-man armed with an army. He was further swayed by the reflection that the vengeance he dreamed of would be more surely found in some of the ways of war than in any pursuit of peace.

All this colored his feelings as he listened to Balthasar. The story touched two of the most sensitive points of his being. His heart beat fast when he found not a doubt either that the recital was true in every particular, or that the Child so miraculously found was the Messiah. Marvelling much that Israel rested so dead to the revelation, and that he had never heard of it before that day, two questions resented themselves to him:

Where was the Child then?

And what was his mission?

## Chapter XVI.

"If I could answer you," Balthasar said, in his simple, earnest, devout way—"oh, if I knew where he is, how quickly I would go to him! The seas should not stay me, nor the mountains."

"You have tried to find him, then?" asked Ben-Hur.

A smile flitted across the face of the Egyptian.

"The first task I charged myself with after leaving the shelter given me in the desert was to learn what became of the Child. But a year had passed, and I dared not go up to Judea in person, for Herod still held the throne, as bloody-minded as ever. In Egypt, upon my return, there were a few friends to believe the wonderful things I told them. Some of them came up for me looking after the Child. They went first to Bethlehem, and found there the khan and the cave;

but the steward—he who sat at the gate the night of the birth, and the night we came following the star—was gone. The king had taken him away, and he was no more seen."

"But they found some proofs, surely," said Ben-Hur, eagerly.

"Yes, proofs written in blood. You must know, when Herod heard of our flight, he sent down and slew the youngest-born of the children of Bethlehem. Not one escaped. The faith of my messengers was confirmed; but they came to me saying the child was dead, slain with the other innocents."

"Dead!" exclaimed Ben-Hur, aghast. "Dead, sayest thou?"

"Nay, my son, I did not say so. I said *they*—my messengers —told me the Child was dead. I did not believe the report then; I do not believe it now."

"I see—thou hast some special knowledge."

"Not so, not so," said Balthasar, dropping his gaze. "The Spirit was to go with us no farther than to the Child. The last inspiration of the Holy One was that which sent us to Ilderim for safety."

"Yes," said the sheik, fingering his beard nervously. "You told me you were sent to me by a Spirit—I remember it."

"I have no special knowledge," Balthasar continued, observing the dejection which had fallen upon Ben-Hur; "but, my son, I will tell you why I believe the Child is living.

"The voice, which was his, speaking to me by the lake, said, 'Blessed art thou, O son of Mizraim! The Redemption cometh. With two others from the remotenesses of the earth, thou shalt see the Saviour.' I have seen the Saviour—blessed be his name!—but the Redemption, which was the second part of the promise, is yet to come. Seest thou now? If the Child be dead, there is no agent to bring the Redemption about, and the word is naught, and God—nay, I dare not say it!

"The Redemption was the work for which the Child was born; and so long as the promise abides, not even death can separate him from his work until it is fulfilled, or at least in the way of fulfilment. Take that now as one reason for my belief; then give me further attention."

Balthasar drank, and, seeming refreshed, continued: "The Saviour I saw was born of woman, in nature like us, and subject to all our ills—even death. Let that stand as the first proposition. Consider next the work set apart to him. Was it not a performance for which only a man is fitted—a man wise, firm, discreet—a man, not a child? To become such he had to grow as we grow. Consider now the dangers his life was subject to in the interval between childhood and maturity. The existing powers were his enemies; Herod was his enemy; and what would Rome have been? And as for Israel—that he should not be accepted by Israel was the motive for cutting

123

him off. See you now? What better way was there to take care of his life than by passing him into obscurity? Wherefore I say to myself he is not dead, but lost; and, his work remaining undone, he will come again. There you have the reasons for my belief. Are they not good?"

Ilderim's eyes were bright with understanding, and Ben-Hur, lifted from his dejection, said heartily, "I, at least, may not gainsay them. What further, pray?"

"Hast thou not enough, my son? Well," he began, in calmer tone, "seeing that it was God's will that the Child should not be found—I settled my faith into the keeping of patience, and took to waiting. What though I cannot go to him, or name the hill or vale of his abiding-place? By the certainty there is in the promise and reason of God, I know he lives."

"Where thinkest thou he is?" asked Ben-Hur in a low voice.

Balthasar looked at him kindly. "In my house on the Nile, I sat thinking. A man thirty years old, I said to myself, should have his fields of life all ploughed, and his planting well done; for after that it is summer-time, with space scarce enough to ripen his sowing. The Child, I said further, is now twenty-seven—his time to plant must be at hand. I asked myself, as you here asked me, my son, and answered by coming hither, as to a good resting-place close by the land thy fathers had from God. Where else should he appear, if not in Judea? In what city should he begin his work if not in Jerusalem? Who should be first to receive the blessings he is to bring, if not the children of Abraham, Isaac, and Jacob; in love, at least, the children of the Lord? If I were bidden go seek him, I would search well the hamlets and villages on the slopes of the mountains of Judea and Galilee falling into the valley of the Jordan. He is there now."

"I see, good Balthasar," Ben-Hur said, "that thou hast been much and strangely favored. I see, also that thou art a wise man indeed. I pray thee, tell further of the mission of him whom thou art waiting, and for whom I too shall wait as becomes a believing son of Judea. He is to be a Saviour, thou saidst; is he not to be King of the Jews also?"

"My son," said Balthasar, in his benign way, "the mission is yet a purpose in the bosom of God. All I think about it is wrung from the words of the Voice.

"The cause of my disquiet," Balthasar went on calmly—"that which made me a preacher in Alexandria and in the villages of the Nile—was the fallen condition of men, occasioned, as I believed, by loss of knowledge of God. I sorrowed for the sorrows of my kind—not of one class, but all of them. So utterly were they fallen it seemed to me there could be no Redemption unless God himself would make it his work; and I prayed him to come, and that I might see him. 'Thy good works have conquered. The Redemption cometh; thou shalt see the Saviour'—thus the Voice spake; and with the answer I went up to Jerusalem rejoicing. Now, to whom is the Redemption? To all the world. And how shall it be? Men say, I know, that there will be no happiness until Rome is razed from her hills. That is to say, the ills of the time are not, as I thought them, from ignorance of God, but from the misgovernment of rulers. Oh no, no! The Redemption cannot be for a political purpose—to pull down rulers and powers, and vacate their places merely that others may take and enjoy them. If that were all of it, the wisdom of God would cease to be surpassing. I tell you, though it be but the saying of blind to blind, he that comes is to be a Saviour of souls; and the Redemption means God once more on earth."

Disappointment showed plainly on Ben-Hur's face—his head drooped; and if he was not convinced, he yet felt himself incapable of disputing the Egyptian. Not so Ilderim.

"By the splendor of God!" he cried impulsively, "the judgment does away with all custom. The ways of the world cannot be changed. There must be a leader in every community clothed with power, else there is no reform."

Balthasar received the burst gravely. "Thy wisdom, good sheik, is of the world; and thou dost forget that it is from the ways of the world we are to be redeemed. Man as a subject is the ambition of a king; the soul of a man for its salvation is the desire of a God."

Ilderim, though silenced, shook his head, unwilling to believe. Ben-Hur took up the argument for him.

"Father—I call thee such by permission," he said, "for whom wert thou required to ask at the gates of Jerusalem?"

"I was to ask of the people," said Balthasar, quietly, "'Where is he that is born King of the Jews?'"

"And you saw him in the cave by Bethlehem?"

"We saw and worshipped him, and gave him presents—Melchior, gold; Gaspar, frankincense; and I, myrrh."

"When thou dost speak of fact, O father, to hear thee is to believe," said Ben-Hur; "but in the matter of opinion, I cannot understand the kind of king thou wouldst make of the Child—I cannot separate the ruler from his powers and duties."

"Son," said Balthasar, "we have the habit of studying closely the things which chance to lie at our feet, giving but a look at the greater objects in the distance. Thou seest now but the title—*King of the Jews;* wilt thou lift thine eyes to the mystery beyond it, the stumbling-block will disappear. Of the title, a word. Thy Israel hath seen better days—days in which God called thy people endearingly his people, and dealt with them through prophets. Now, if in those days he promised

125

them the Saviour I saw—promised him as *King of the Jews*—the appearance must be according to the promise. Bethink thee—what is it to be a successor of Herod? Could not God benefit better his beloved? If thou canst think of the Almighty Father stooping to borrow the inventions of men, why was I not bidden to ask for a Cæsar at once? Oh, for the substance of that whereof we speak, look higher, I pray thee! Ask rather of what he shall be king; for I do tell, my son, that is the key to the mystery, which no man shall understand without the key."

Balthasar raised his eyes devoutly. "There is a kingdom on the earth, though it is not of it—a kingdom of wider bounds than the sea and the earth. Its existence is a fact as our hearts are facts, and we journey through it from birth to death without seeing it; nor shall any man see it until he hath first known his own soul; for the kingdom is not for him, but for his soul."

"What thou sayest, father, is a riddle to me," said Ben-Hur. "I never heard of such a kingdom."

"Nor did I," said Ilderim.

"And I may not tell more of it," Balthasar added humbly. "What it is, what it is for, how it may be reached, none can know until the Child comes to take possession of it as his own."

After that there was silence, which Balthasar accepted as the end of the conversation. "Good sheik," he said, in his placid way, "to-morrow or the next day I will go up to the city for a time. My daughter wishes to see the preparations for the games. And, my son, I will see you again. To you both, peace and good-night."

They all arose. The sheik and Ben-Hur remained looking after the Egyptian until he was conducted out of the tent.

"Sheik Ilderim," said Ben-Hur then, "I have heard strange things to-night. Give me leave, I pray, to walk by the lake that I may think of them."

"Go; and I will come after you."


CHAPTER XVII.

THE NIGHT was quiet. Not a ripple broke upon the shore. The old stars of the old East were all out, and there was summer everywhere—on land, on lake, in the sky.

Ben-Hur's imagination was heated, his feelings aroused, his will unsettled.

So the palms, the sky, the air, seemed to him of the far south zone into which Balthasar had been driven by despair for men; the lake, with its motionless surface, was a suggestion of the Nilotic mother by which the good man stood praying when the Spirit made its radiant appearance. He feared, yet wished, and even waited for the vision.

In all reflection about his life there had been one hiatus which he had not been able to bridge or fill up. When, finally, he was graduated a captain as well as a soldier, to what object should he address his efforts? Revolution he contemplated, of course; but the processes of revolution have always been the same, and to lead men into them there must be first, a cause to enlist adherents; second, an end, as a practical achievement.

To determine the sufficiency of either the cause or the end, it was needful that Ben-Hur would have to study the adherents to whom he looked when all was ready for action. Very naturally, they were his countrymen. The wrongs of Israel were to every son of Abraham, and each was a holy cause.

Ay, the cause was there! But the end—what should it be?

The days he had given this branch of his scheme were past calculation—all with the same conclusion: a dim, uncertain, general idea of national liberty. Was it suffiicient? He could not say no, for that would have been the death of his hope; he shrank from saying yes, because he could not assure himself that Israel was able single-handed to successfully combat Rome. He knew the resources of that great enemy; he knew her art was superior to her resources. A universal alliance might suffice, but, that was impossible, except a hero would come from one of the suffering nations, and by martial successes accomplish a renown to fill the whole earth. Wnat glory to Judea could she prove the Macedonia of the new Alexander! Under the rabbis valor was possible, but not discipline. And then the taunt of Messala in the garden of Herod: "All you conquer in the six days, you lose on the seventh."

So it happened he never approached the chasm thinking to surmount it but he was beaten back; and so incessantly had he failed in the object that he had about given it over, except as a thing of chance. The hero might be discovered in his day, or he might not. God only knew. The story of Balthasar offered him, clearly, the solution of the trouble. Here was the requisite hero found at last; and he a son of the Lion tribe, and King of the Jews! Behind the hero—the world in arms.

The king implied a kingdom; he was to be a warrior glorious as David, a ruler wise and magnificent as Solomon; the kingdom was to be a power against which Rome was to dash itself to pieces. There would be colossal war, and the agonies of death and birth—then peace, meaning Judean dominion forever.

"What of this kingdom? And what is it to be?" Ben-Hur asked himself.

But there were only the words of Balthasar, "On the earth, yet not of it—not for men, but for their souls—a dominion, nevertheless, of unimaginable glory."

"The hand of man is not in it," he said, despairingly. "Nor has the king of such a kingdom use for men; neither toilers, nor councillors, nor soldiers. The earth must die, or be made anew, and for government new principles must be discovered —something besides armed hands—something in place of Force. But what?"

In the midst of his reverie a hand was laid upon his shoulder.

"I have a word to say, O son of Arrius," said Ilderim, stopping by his side—"A word, and then I must return, for the night is going."

"I give you welcome, sheik."

"As to the things you have heard but now," said Ilderim, almost without pause, "take in belief all save that relating to the kind of kingdom the Child will set up when he comes; keep an open mind until you hear Simonides the merchant, to whom  will make you known. The Egyptian gives you coinage of his dreams which are too good for the earth; Simonides is wiser; he will give you the sayings of your prophets by book and pages, so you cannot deny that the Child will be King of the Jews in fact—ay, by the splendor of God! a king as Herod was, only better and far more magnificent. And then we will taste the sweetness of vengeance. I have said. Peace to you!"

Ilderim did not stay.

"Simonides again!" said Ben-Hur bitterly. "Simonides here, Simonides there; from this one now, then from that! I am like to be well ridden by my father's servant, who knows at least to hold fast that which is mine; wherefore he is richer, if indeed he be not wiser than the Egyptian. By the covenant! it is not to the faithless a man should go to find a faith—" He broke off suddenly, listening.

Down the lake towards the dowar came a woman singing. Her voice floated along the hushed water melodious as a flute, growing louder each instant. Directly the dipping of oars was heard in slow measure; a little later the words were distinguishable in purest Greek.

Then the singer was past the palms. The passing of the boat was as the passing of a deeper shadow into the deeper night.

"I know her voice—the daughter of Balthasar." He recalled her large eyes curtained slightly by the drooping lashes, the lips full and deep with dimpling in the corners, and all the grace of the tall, lithe figure.

Then, almost the same instant, another face, younger and quite as beautiful—more childlike and tender, if not so passionate—appeared as if held up to him out of the lake.

"Esther!" he said, smiling. "As I wished, a star has been sent to me."

He turned, and passed slowly back to the tent.

# BOOK FIFTH

## Chapter I.

THE MORNING after the bacchanalia in the dining hall of the palace, the divan was covered with young patricians. Maxentius might come, and the city throng to receive him; the legion might descend in glory of arms; yet would the many continue to sleep on the divan where they had fallen or been carelessly tumbled by the indifferent slaves.

Not all, however, who participated in the celebration were in the shameful condition. When full daylight began to peer through the skylights, Messala arose, and took the chaplet from his head, in sign that the revel was at end; then he gathered his robes about him, gave a last look at the scene, and, without a word, departed for his quarters. Cicero could not have retired with more gravity from a night-long senatorial debate.

Three hours afterwards two couriers entered his room and from his own hand received each a despatch, sealed and in duplicate, and consisting chiefly of a letter to Valerius Gratus, the procurator, still resident in Cæsarea. One courier was to proceed overland, the other by sea; both were to make the utmost haste.

ANTIOCH, *XII. Kal. Jul.*
*Messala to Gratus.*

O my Midas!

I have to relate to thee an astonishing event, which, though as yet somewhat in the field of conjecture, will, I doubt not, justify thy instant consideration.

Allow me first to revive thy recollection. Remember, a good many years ago, by name Ben-Hur. If thy memory have a limp there is, if I mistake not, a wound on thy head which may help thee to a revival of the circumstance.

Next to arouse thy interest. In punishment of the attempt upon thy life the family were seized and summarily disposed of, and their property confiscated. And inasmuch, O my Midas! as the action had the approval of our Cæsar, there should be no shame in referring to the sums which were realized to us respectively from that source, for which I can never cease to be grateful to thee, certainly not while I continue the enjoyment of the part which fell to me.

In vindication of thy wisdom I recall further that thou madest disposition of the family of Hur, both of us at the time supposing the plan to be most effective for the purposes in view, which were silence and delivery over to inevitable but natural death. Thou wilt remember what thou didst with the mother and sister of the malefactor; yet now I yield to a desire to learn whether they be living or dead.

Remember that the actual criminal was sent to the galleys for life. I myself saw and read the receipt for his body delivered to the tribune commanding a galley.

Referring to the limit of life at the oar, the outlaw thus justly disposed of should be dead, or drowned. Of opinion that he was certainly dead, I have lived five years in calm and innocent enjoyment of the fortune for which I am in a degree indebted to him.

Last night, while acting as master of the feast for a party just from Rome I heard a singular story. Maxentius, the consul, as you know, comes to-day to conduct a campaign against the Parthians. Of the ambitious who are to accompany him there is one, a son of the late duumvir Quintus Arrius. The son and heir of whom I speak is he whom thou didst send to the galleys—the very Ben-Hur who should have died at his oar five years ago—returned now with fortune and rank, and possibly as a Roman citizen, to— Well, thou art too firmly seated to be alarmed, but I am in danger—no need to tell thee of what.

When Arrius, the father by adoption of this outlaw, joined battle with the pirates, his vessel was sunk and but two of all her crew escaped drowning—Arrius himself, and this one, his heir.

When the officers took them from the sea the associate of the tribune was a young men who, when lifted to the deck, was in the dress of a galley slave.

Yesterday, by good chance, I met the mysterious son of Arrius face to face; and I declare now that, though I did not then recognize him, he is the very Ben-Hur who was for years my playmate; the very Ben-Hur who, if he be a man, though of the commonest grade, must this very moment be thinking of vengeance not to be satisfied short of life; vengeance for country, mother, sister, self, and for fortune lost.

Ben-Hur's going and coming will of course be regulated by his master, the consul, who, though he exert himself without rest day and night, cannot get away under a month.

I saw the Jew yesterday in the Grove of Daphne; and if he be not there now, he is certainly in the neighborhood. Indeed, he is to be found at the old Orchard of Palms, under the tent of the traitor Sheik Ilderim, who cannot long escape our strong hand. Be not surprised if Maxentius, as his first measure, places the Arab on the ship for Rome.

I am so particular about the whereabouts of the Jew because it will be important to thee, when thou consider what is to be done; for already I know that in every scheme involving human action there are three elements always to be taken in account—time, place, and agency.

If thou sayest this is the place, have thou no hesitancy in trusting the business to thy most loving friend,

MESSALA.

## CHAPTER II.

ABOUT THE time the couriers departed with the despatches Ben-Hur entered Ilderim's tent.

The sheik saluted him from the divan.

"I give thee peace, son of Arrius," he said. "The horses are ready, I am ready."

"Are they yoked?"

"No."

"Then I will serve myself," said Ben-Hur. "I must make the acquaintance of thy Arabs. I must know their temper, for they are like men; if bold, the better of scolding; if timid the better of praise and flattery. Let the servants bring me the harness."

"And the chariot?" asked the sheik.

"I will let the chariot alone to-day. In its place, let them bring me a fifth horse, if thou hast it; he should be bare-backed, and fleet as the others."

Ilderim's wonder was aroused, and he summoned a servant. "Bid them bring the harness for the four," he said, "and the bridle for Sirius."

Ilderim then arose. "Sirius is my love, and I am his, O son of Arrius. We have been comrades for twenty years—in tent, in battle, in all stages of the desert we have been comrades. I will show him to you."

Going to the division curtain, he held it, while Ben-Hur passed under. The horses came to him in a body. One with a small head, luminous eyes, neck like the segment of a bended bow, and mighty chest, nickered gladly at sight of him.

"Good horse," said the sheik, patting the dark-brown cheek.

132

"Good horse, good-morning." Turning to Ben-Hur, he added, "This is Sirius, father of the four here. Mira, the mother, awaits our return, being too precious to be hazarded in a region where there is a stronger hand than mine. And much I doubt," he laughed as he spoke—"O son of Arrius, if the tribe could endure her absence. She is their glory; did she gallop over them, they would laugh. Ten thousand horsemen, sons of the desert, will ask to-day, 'Have you heard of Mira?' And to the answer, 'She is well,' they will say, 'God is good! blessed be God!' "

The harness was brought. With his own hands Ben-Hur equipped the horses; with his own hands he led them out of the tent, and there attached the reins.

"Bring me Sirius," he said.

An Arab could not have better sprung to seat on the courser's back.

"And now the reins."

They were given him, and carefully separated.

"Good sheik," he said, "I am ready. Let a guide go ⌐fore me to the field, and send some of thy men with water."

There was no trouble at starting. Already there seemed a tacit understanding between the horses and the new driver. The order of going was precisely that of driving, except that Ben-Hur sat upon Sirius instead of standing in the chariot. Ilderim's spirit arose. He combed his beard, and smiled with satisfaction. He followed on foot, the entire tenantry of the dowar—men, women, and children—pouring after him.

The field proved well fitted for the training, which Ben-Hur began immediately by driving the four at first slowly, and in perpendicular lines, and then in wide circles. He put them next into a trot; again progressing, he pushed into a gallop; at length he contracted the circles, and yet later drove eccentrically right, left, forward, and without a break. An hour was thus occupied. Slowing the gait to a walk, he drove up to Ilderim.

"The work is done, nothing now but practice," he said, dismounting and going to the horses. "See, the gloss of their coats is without spot; they breathe lightly as when I began. I give thee great joy, and it will go hard if we have not the victory and our—"

He stopped, colored, bowed. At the sheik's side he observed, for the first time, Balthasar, leaning upon his staff, and two women closely veiled.

"The victory, and our revenge!" Ilderim finished for him. Then he said, "Son of Arrius, thou art the man. Be the end like the beginning, and thou shalt see what lines the hand of an Arab who is able to give."

Remounting Sirius, Ben-Hur renewed the training, going as

before from walk to trot, from trot to gallop; finally, he pushed the steady racers into the run, gradually quickening it to full speed. The four were the same, whether they flew forward or wheeled in varying curvature. In their action there were unity, power, grace, pleasure, all as effortless as swallows in their evening flight.

In the midst of the exercises, and the attention they received from all the bystanders, Malluch came upon the ground, seeking the sheik.

"I have a message for you, O sheik," he said, "from Simonides, the merchant."

"Simonides!" ejaculated the Arab. "Ah! 'tis well. May Abaddon take all his enemies!"

Ilderim broke the seal of the package and read the two letters.

## No. 1.
### Simonides to Sheik Ilderim.

O friend!

There is in thy dowar a youth of fair presence, calling himself the son of Arrius; and such he is by adoption.

He is very dear to me.

Come thou to-day or to-morrow, that I may tell thee his history, and have thy counsel. Meantime, favor all his requests, be they not against honor. Should there be need of reparation, I am bound to thee for it.

That I have interest in this youth, keep thou private.

Remember me to thy other guest. He, his daughter, thyself, and I whom thou mayst choose to be of thy company, must depend upon me at the Circus the day of the games. I have seats engaged.

To thee and all thine, peace.

SIMONIDES.

## No. 2.
### Simonides to Sheik Ilderim.

O friend!

There is a sign which all persons not Romans, and who have moneys or goods subject to despoilment, accept as warning—that is, the arrival at a seat of power of some high Roman official charged with authority.

To-day comes the Consul Maxentius.

Be thou warned!

Another word of advice.

A conspiracy, to be against thee, O friend, must include the Herods as parties; thou hast great properties in their dominions. Wherefore keep thou watch.

Send this morning to thy trusty guardians of the roads leading south from Antioch, and bid them search every courier going and coming, if they find private despatches relating to thee or thine affairs, *thou shouldst see them.*

If couriers left Antioch this morning, your messengers know the byways, and can intercept them.

Do not hesitate.

Burn this after reading.

SIMONIDES.

Ilderim read and refolded the letters in the linen wrap, and put the package under his girdle.

Ben-Hur brought the four to a walk, and drove to Ilderim. "With leave, O sheik," he said, "I will return thy Arabs to the tent, and bring them out again this afternoon."

Ilderim walked to him as he sat on Sirius, and said, "I give them to you, son of Arrius, to do with as you will until after the games. You have done with them in two hours what the Roman—may jackals gnaw his bones fleshless!—could not in as many weeks. By the splendor of God, we will win!"

At the tent Ben-Hur remained with the horses while they were being cared for; then, after a plunge in the lake and a cup of arrack with the sheik, whose flow of spirits was royally exuberant, he dressed himself in his Jewish garb again and walked with Malluch on into the Orchard.

"I will give you," Ben-Hur said, "an order for my property stored in the khan by the Seleucian Bridge. Bring it to me to-day, if you can. And, good Malluch—as you are a man of business, which I much fear Sheik Ilderim is not—"

"Arabs seldom are," said Malluch, gravely.

"I do not impeach their shrewdness, Malluch. It is well, however, to look after them. To save all forfeit or hindrance in connection with the race, you would put me perfectly at rest by going to the office of the Circus, and seeing that he has complied with every preliminary rule; and if you can get a copy of the rules, it may be of great help to me. I would like to know the colors I am to wear, and particularly what crypt I am to occupy at the starting; if it be next Messala's on the right or left, it is well; if not, and you can have it changed so as to bring me next the Roman, do so.

"I saw yesterday that Messala was proud of his chariot, as he might be, for the best of Cæsar's scarcely surpass it. Can you not make its display an excuse which will enable you to find if it be light or heavy? I would like to have its exact weight and measurements—and, Malluch, though you fail in all else, bring me exactly the height his axle stands above the ground. You understand, Malluch? I do not wish him to have any actual advantage of me. I do not care for his splendor; if I beat him, it will make his fall the harder, and my triumph the more complete. If there are advantages I want them."

At the door of the tent they found a servant replenishing the smoke-stained bottles and stopped to refresh themselves.

135

Shortly afterwards Malluch returned to the city.

During their absence, a messenger well mounted had been despatched with orders as suggested by Simonides. He was an Arab, and carried nothing written.

## CHAPTER III.

"IRAS, THE daughter of Balthasar, sends me with salutation and a message," said a servant to Ben-Hur, who was taking his ease in the tent. "Would it please you to accompany her upon the lake?"

"I will carry the answer myself. Tell her so."

His shoes were brought him, and in a few minutes Ben-Hur sallied out to find the fair Egyptian. The shadow of the mountains was creeping over the Orchard of Palms. Afar through the trees came the tinkling of sheep-bells, the lowing of cattle, and the voices of the herdsmen bringing their charges home.

Sheik Ilderim had gone to the city in answer to the invitation of Simonides. Ben-Hur, thus left alone, had seen his horses cared for; cooled himself in the lake; and exchanged the field garb for his customary white vestments.

The Egyptian was to Ben-Hur a wonderfully beautiful woman—beautiful of face, beautiful of form, and as she returned to his fancy, the whole passionate Song of Solomon came with her, inspired by her presence. It was not love that was taking him, but admiration and curiosity, which might be the heralds of love.

The landing was a simple affair, consisting of a short stairway, and a platform garnished by lamp-posts; yet at the top of the steps he paused, arrested by what he beheld.

There was a shallop resting lightly as an egg-shell upon the clear water. An Ethiop—the camel-driver at the Castalian fount—occupied the rower's place, his blackness intensified by a livery of shining white. All the boat aft was cushioned and carpeted with stuffs brilliant with Tyrian red. On the rudder seat sat the Egyptian herself, sunk in Indian shawls and a vapor of delicate veils and scarfs. Her arms were bare to the shoulders: and their expression, the hands, the fingers even, seemed endowed with graces and meaning; each was an object of beauty.

In the glance he gave her, Ben-Hur paid no attention to these details. There was simply an impression made upon him; and, like strong light, it was a sensation, not a thing of sight or enumeration. Thy lips are like a thread of scarlet; thy temples are like a piece of pomegranate within thy locks. Rise up, my love, my fair one, and come away; for, lo! the winter is past, the rain is over and gone; the flowers appear on the earth; the time of the singing of birds is come, and the voice of the turtle is heard in the land. . . .

"Come," she said, observing him stop, "come, or I shall think you a poor sailor."

Did she know anything of his life upon the sea? He descended to the platform at once. "I was afraid," he said, as he took the vacant seat before her.

"Of what?"

"Of sinking the boat," he replied, smiling.

"Wait until we are in deeper water," she said, giving a signal to the black, who dipped the oars, and they were off.

If love and Ben-Hur were enemies, the latter was never more at mercy. The Egyptian sat where he could not but see her; with her eyes giving light to his, the stars might come out, and he not see them. The night might fall with unrelieved darkness everywhere else; her look would make illumination for him.

"Give me the rudder," he said.

"No," she replied, "that were to reverse the relation. Did I not ask you to ride with me? I am indebted to you, and would begin payment. You may talk and I will listen, or I will talk and you will listen: that choice is yours; but it shall be mine to choose where we go, and the course."

"And where may that be?"

"You are alarmed again."

"O fair Egyptian, I but asked you the first question of every captive."

"Call me Egypt."

"I would rather call you Iras. Egypt is a country, and means many people."

"Yes, yes! And such a country!"

"I see; it is to Egypt we are going."

"Would we were! I would be so glad."

"You have no care for me, then," he said.

"Ah, by that I know you were never there."

"I never was."

"There, O son of Arrius, the happy find increase of happiness, and the wretched drink once of the sweet water of the sacred river, and laugh and sing, rejoicing like children."

"Are not the very poor with you there as elsewhere?"

"The very poor in Egypt are the very simple in wants and ways," she replied. "They have no wish beyond enough, and how little that is, a Greek or a Roman cannot know."

"But I am neither Greek nor Roman."

She laughed. "I have a garden of roses, and in the midst of it is a tree, and its bloom is the richest of all. Whence came it, think you?"

"From Persia, the home of the rose?"

"No. I will tell you," she said: "a traveller found it perishing by the roadside on the plain of Rephaim."

"Oh, in Judea!"

"I put it in the earth by the Nile, and the soft south wind nursed it, and the sun kissed it in pity; after which it could not help but grow and flourish. I stand in its shade now, and it thanks me with perfume. As with the roses, so with the men of Israel. Where shall they reach perfection but in Egypt?"

"Moses was but one of millions."

"Nay, there was a reader of dreams. Will you forget him?"

"The friendly Pharaohs are dead."

"Ah, yes! The river by which they dwelt sings to them in their tombs; yet the same sun tempers the same air to the same people."

"Alexandria is a Roman town."

"She has but exchanged sceptres. Cæsar took from her that of the sword, and in its place left that of learning. Go with me to the Brucheium, and I will show you the college of nations; to the Serapeion, and see the perfection of architecture; to the Library, and read the immortals; to the theatre, and hear the heroics of the Greeks and Hindoos; to the quay, and count the triumphs of commerce; descend with me into the streets, O son of Arrius, when nothing remains of the day but its pleasures, you shall hear the stories that have amused men from the beginning, and the songs which will never die."

Abruptly the keel of the boat grated upon the underlying sand, and, next moment, the bow ran upon the shore.

"A quick voyage, O Egypt!" he cried.

"And a briefer stay!" she replied, as, with a strong push, the black sent them shooting into the open water again.

"You will give me the rudder now."

"Oh, no," said she, laughing. "To you, the chariot; to me, the boat. We are merely at the lake's end, and having been to Egypt, let us go now—to the Grove of Daphne. And on the way, tell me something of the Roman from whom you saved us to-day."

The request struck Ben-Hur unpleasantly. "I wish this were the Nile," he said evasively. "The kings and queens, having slept so long, might come down from their tombs, and ride with us."

"They were of the colossi, and would sink our boat. But tell me of the Roman. He is very wicked, is he not?"

"I cannot say."

"Is he of noble family, and rich?"

"I cannot speak of his riches."

"How beautiful his horses were! and the bed of his chariot was gold, and the wheels ivory. And his audacity! The bystanders laughed as he rode away; they, who were so nearly under his wheels!" She laughed at the recollection.

"They were rabble," said Ben-Hur bitterly.

"He must be one of the monsters who are said to be growing up in Rome—Apollos ravenous as Cerberus. Does he reside in Antioch?"

"He is of the East somewhere."

"Egypt would suit him better than Syria."

"Hardly," Ben-Hur replied. "Cleopatra is dead."

That instant the lamps burning before the door of the tent came into view. "The dowar!" she cried.

"Ah, then, we have not been to Egypt. I have not seen Karnak or Philæ. This is not the Nile. I have but been boating in a dream."

"Philæ—Karnak. Mourn rather that you have not seen the Rameses at Aboo Simbel, looking at which makes it so easy to think of God, the maker of the heavens and earth. Or why should you mourn at all? Let us go on to the river."

"Go on! Ay, till morning comes, and the evening, and the next morning!" he said vehemently.

After a while, Ben-Hur was sitting at the Egyptian's feet, and her hand upon the tiller was covered by his hand. And with conversation and stories, they whiled the hours away. As they stepped ashore, she said, "To-morrow we go to the city."

"But you will be at the games?" he asked.

"Oh yes."

"I will send you my colors."


CHAPTER IV.

ILDERIM RETURNED to the dowar next day and as he dismounted, a man whom he recognized as of his own tribe came to him and said, "O sheik, I was bidden give thee this package, with request that thou read it at once. If there be answer, I was to wait thy pleasure."

Ilderim gave the package immediate attention. The seal was already broken. The address ran, *To Valerius Gratus at Cæsarea.*

"Abaddon take him!" growled the sheik, at discovering a letter in Latin.

Had the missive been in Greek or Arabic, he could have read it; as it was, the utmost he could make out was the signature in bold Roman letters—Messala—whereat his eyes twinkled.

"Where is the young Jew?" he asked.

"In the field with the horses," a servant replied.

139

The sheik replaced the papyrus in its envelopes, and, tucking the package under his girdle, remounted the horse. That moment a stranger appeared, coming, apparently, from the city. "I am looking for Sheik Ilderim, surnamed the Generous," he said. His language and attire bespoke him a Roman.

What he could not read, he yet could speak; so the old Arab answered, with dignity, "I am Sheik Ilderim."

The man's eyes fell; he raised them again, and said, with forced composure, "I heard you had need of a driver for the games."

Ilderim's lip under the white mustache curled contemptuously. "Go thy way," he said. "I have a driver."

He turned to ride away, but the man, lingering, spoke again. "Sheik, I am a lover of horses, and they say you have the most beautiful in the world."

The old man drew rein, as if on the point of yielding to the flattery, but finally replied, "Not to-day, not today; some other time I will show them to you. I am too busy just now."

He rode to the field, while the stranger betook himself to town again with a smiling countenance. He had accomplished his mission.

And every day thereafter, down to the great day of the games, a man—sometimes two or three men—came to the sheik, pretending to seek an engagement as driver.

In such manner Messala kept watch over Ben-Hur.


CHAPTER V.

THE SHEIK waited, well satisfied, until Ben-Hur drew his horses off the field for the forenoon—well satisfied, for he had seen them, after being put through all the other paces, run full speed as if the four were one.

"This afternoon, O sheik, I will give Sirius back to you." Ben-Hur patted the neck of the horse as he spoke. "I will take the chariot."

"So soon?" Ilderim asked.

"With such as these, good sheik, one day suffices. They are not afraid; they have a man's intelligence, and they love the exercise. This one," he shook a rein over the back of the youngest of the four—"you called him Aldebaran, I believe—is the swiftest; in once round a stadium he would lead the others thrice his length."

Ilderim pulled his beard, and said, with twinkling eyes, "Aldebaran is the swiftest; but what of the slowest?"

"This is he." Ben-Hur shook the rein over the one named Antares. "This is he: but he will win, for he will run his utmost all day—and, as the sun goes down, then he will reach his swiftest."

"Right again," said Ilderim.

"I have but one fear, O sheik. In his greed of triumph, a Roman cannot keep honor pure. In the games—all of them, mark you—their tricks are infinite; in chariot-racing their knavery extends to everything—from horse to driver, from driver to master. Wherefore, good sheik, look well to all thou hast; from this till the trial is over, let no stranger so much as see the horses. Would you be perfectly safe, do more—keep over them armed guard day and night; then I will have no fear of the end." At the door of the tent they dismounted.

"What you say shall be attended to. But, son of Arrius"—Ilderim drew forth the package, and opened it slowly, while they walked to the divan and seated themselves—"help me with thy Latin."

He passed the despatch to Ben-Hur. "There; read—and read aloud, in the tongue of thy fathers."

Ben-Hur was in good spirits, and began the reading carelessly. *"Messala to Gratus!"* A premonition drove the blood to his heart. Ilderim observed his agitation.

"Well; I am waiting."

Ben-Hur started again to read one of the duplicates of the letter despatched to Gratus by Messala the morning after the palace revel.

When he came to the parts intended to refresh the memory of Gratus, his voice trembled. " 'I recall further,' " he read, " 'that thou made disposition of the fam, y of Hur' "—there he drew a long breath—" 'both of us at the time supposing the plan to be the most effective for the purposes in view, which were silence and delivery over to inevitable but natural death.' "

Here the paper fell from Ben-Hur's hands, and he covered his face. "They are dead—dead. I alone am left."

The sheik had been a silent witness of the young man's suffering; now he arose and said, "Son of Arrius, it is for me to beg thy pardon. Read the paper by thyself. When thou art strong enough to give the rest of it to me, send word, and I will return."

He went out of the tent.

Ben-Hur, when somewhat recovered, resumed reading. "Thou wilt remember," the missive ran, "what thou didst with the mother and sister of the malefactor; yet now I yield to a desire to learn if they be living or dead"—Ben-Hur started, and read again, and then again, and at last broke into exclamation. "He does not *know* they are dead! There is yet hope." He went on to the end of the letter.

"They are not dead," he said, after reflection; "they cannot

141

be dead, or he would have heard of it." Then he sent for the sheik.

"In coming to your hospitable tent, O sheik," he said, "it was in my mind to speak of myself to assure you I only could be intrusted with your horses. I declined to tell you my history. But the chance which sent this paper to my hand is so strange that I feel bidden to trust you with everything. And I am more inclined to do so by the knowledge that we are both threatened by the same enemy, against whom we must make common cause. I will read the letter and perhaps then you may see why I was so moved."

The sheik listened closely, until Ben-Hur came to the paragraph in which he was particularly mentioned: " 'I saw the Jew yesterday in the Grove of Daphne; and if he be not there now, he is certainly in the neighborhood. Indeed, he is to be found at the old Orchard of Palms.' "

"A—h!" exclaimed Ilderim, in surprise and anger.

" 'At the old Orchard of Palms,' " Ben-Hur repeated, " 'under the tent of the traitor, Sheik Ilderim.' "

"Traitor!—I?" the old man cried, in his shrillest tone, while in his forehead and neck the veins swelled as they would burst.

"A moment, sheik," said Ben-Hur. "Such is Messala's opinion of you. Now hear his threat." And he read on: " '. . . . under the tent of the traitor Sheik Ilderim, who cannot long escape our strong hand. Be not surprised if Maxentius, as his first measure, places the Arab on ship for Rome.' "

"To Rome! Me—Ilderim—sheik of ten thousand horsemen with spears—*me* to Rome!"

He leaped to his feet, his arms outstretched, his fingers curved like claws, his eyes glittering. "O God! When shall this insolence end? A freeman am I; free are my people. Must we die slaves? Or, worse, must I live a dog, crawling to a master's feet? Must I lick his hand lest he lash me? What is mine is not mine; I am not my own; for breath of body I must be beholden to a Roman. Oh, could I shake off twenty years— or ten—or five!"

He ground his teeth and shook his hands overhead; then, under the impulse of another idea, he caught Ben-Hur's shoulder with a strong grasp.

"If I were as thou, son of Arrius—as young, as strong, as practised in arms; if I had a motive, a motive like thine, great enough to make hate holy— Son of Hur, son of Hur, I say—"

At that name Ben-Hur's blood stopped; surprised, bewildered, he gazed into the Arab's eyes, now close to his, and fiercely bright.

"Son of Hur, I say, had I half thy wrongs, I could not rest." Never pausing, the old man swept on. "To all my grievances, I would add those of the world, and devote myself to venge-

142

ance. From land to land I would go, firing all mankind. No war for freedom but should find me engaged; no battle against Rome in which I would not bear a part. I would turn Parthian, if I could not do better. If men failed me, still I would never give up! By the splendor of God! I would herd with wolves, and make friends of lions, in hope of marshalling them against the enemy. I would use every weapon. So my victims were Romans, I would rejoice in slaughter. To the flames everything Roman; to the sword every Roman born. Of nights I would pray the gods, the good and the bad alike, to lend me their special terrors—tempests, drought, heat, cold, and all the nameless poisons they let loose in air, all the thousand things of which men die on sea and on land. Oh, I could not sleep. I—I—"

The sheik stopped, panting, wringing his hands. And of all the passionate outburst Ben-Hur retained but a vague impression wrought by fiery eyes, a piercing voice, and a rage too intense for coherent expression.

For the first time in years, he heard himself addressed by his proper name. One man at least knew him, and acknowledged it without demand of identity; and that man an Arab, fresh from the desert!

How came the man by his knowledge? The letter? No. It told the story of his misfortunes, but it did not identify him as the same victim whose escape from doom was its theme.

"Good sheik, tell me how you came by this letter."

"My people watch the roads between cities," Ilderim answered, bluntly. "They took it from a courier."

"Are they known to be thy people?"

"No. To the world they are robbers, whom it is my duty to catch and slay."

"Again, sheik. You call me son of Hur—my father's name. I did not think myself known to a person on earth. How came you by the knowledge?"

Ilderim hesitated. "I know you, yet I am not free to tell you more." The sheik walked away; but, observing Ben-Hur's disappointment, he came back, and said, "Let us say no more about the matter now. I will go to town; when I return, I may talk to you fully. Give me the letter."

Ilderim rolled the papyrus carefully, restored it to its envelopes, and became once more all energy.

"What sayest thou?" he asked, while waiting for his horse and retinue. "I told what I would do, were I thou, and thou hast made no answer."

Ben-Hur's countenance and voice changed with feeling. "All thou hast said, I will do—all, at least, in the power of a man. I devoted myself to vengeance long ago. Every hour of the five years passed I have lived with no other thought. I have taken no respite. I have had no pleasures of youth. The blandishments of Rome were not for me. I wanted her to educate me for revenge. I went to her most famous masters and professors of the arts essential to a fighting-man. I associated with gladiators, and with winners of prizes in the Circus; and they were my teachers. The drill-masters in the great camp were proud of my attainments in their line. O sheik, I am a soldier; but the things of which I dream require me to be a captain. With that thought, I have taken part in the campaign against the Parthians; when it is over, if the Lord spare my life—then"—he raised his clenched hands—"then Rome shall account to me in Roman lives! You have my answer, sheik."

Ilderim put an arm over his shoulder. "If thy God favor thee not, son of Hur, it is because he is dead. Take thou this from me—sworn to, if so thy preference run: thou shalt have my hands, and their fulness—men, horses, camels, and the desert for preparation. I swear it! For the present, enough. Thou shalt see or hear from me before night."

Turning abruptly, the sheik was soon on the road to the city.

## CHAPTER VI.

WHEN ILDERIM left the tent, Ben-Hur h   much to think about, requiring immediate action. His enemies were as adroit and powerful as any in the East. If they were afraid of him, he had greater reason to be afraid of them. There was a certain qualified pleasure in the assurance that his mother and sister were alive, even if the assurance was based on mere inference. That there was one person who could tell him where they were seemed as if discovery were now close at hand.

Occasionally he wondered whence the Arab derived his information about him; not from Malluch certainly; nor from Simonides, whose interests all adverse, would hold him dumb. Could Messala have been the informant? No, no; disclosure might be dangerous in that quarter. Conjecture was vain; at the same time he was consoled with the thought that whoever the person with the knowledge might be, he was a friend, and, being such, would reveal himself in good time. A little more waiting—a little more patience. Possibly the letter might precipitate a full disclosure.

Occupied with his thoughts, he wandered far through the Orchard, pausing by the lake. He might not look upon the water and its sparkling ripples, without thinking of the Egyptian and her beauty, and of floating with her through the night; he might not forget her sensuous charms, the lightness of her laugh, the flattery of her attention, the warmth of her little hand under his. From thoughts of her it was but a short way to Balthasar, and the strange things of which he had been witness, unaccountable by any law of nature; and from him, again, to the King of the Jews, whom the good man was holding in holy promise. And there his mind stayed. Because nothing is so easy as denial of an idea not agreeable to our wishes, he rejected the definition given by Balthasar of the abstract kingdom of souls the king was coming to establish. A kingdom of Judea, on the other hand, was more than comprehensible: such had been, and might be again. And he envisioned a new kingdom broader of domain, richer in power, and of far more splendor than the old; of a new king wiser and mightier than Solomon under whom he could find both service and revenge. In that mood he returned to the dowar.

The mid-day meal disposed of, Ben-Hur had the chariot rolled out for inspection. No point or part of it escaped him. With pleasure, he saw the pattern was Greek, in his judgment preferable to the Roman in many respects; it was wider between the wheels, and lower and stronger, and the disadvantage of greater weight would be more than compensated by the greater endurance of his Arabs. Speaking generally, the carriage-makers of Rome built for the games almost solely, sacrificing safety to beauty, and durability to grace; while the chariots of Achilles and "the king of men," designed for war and all its extreme tests, still ruled the tastes of those who struggled for the crowns at the great games.

When he came away in the evening, it was with restored spirit, and a decision to defer the matter of Messala until after the race. He could not forego the pleasure of meeting his adversary under the eyes of the East; other competitors seemed not to enter his thought. His confidence in the result was absolute; no doubt of his own skill; and as to the four Arabians, they were his full partners in the game.

After nightfall, Ben-Hur waited for Ilderim, not yet returned from the city. Then, at last, there was a sound of horse's feet coming rapidly. But it was Malluch who rode up.

"Son of Arrius," he said cheerily, after salutation, "I salute you for Sheik Ilderim, who requests you to mount and go to the city. He is waiting for you."

Ben-Hur asked no questions. Very shortly the two were on the road, riding swiftly and in silence.

Down to Simonides' landing they rode, and in front of the great warehouse, under the bridge, Malluch drew rein.

"We are come," he said. "Dismount."

"Where is the sheik?" Ben-Hur asked.

"Come with me. I will show you."

A watchman took the horses, and almost before he realized it Ben-Hur stood once more at the door of the house up on the greater one, listening to the response from within: "In God's name, enter."

## CHAPTER VII.

MALLUCH STOPPED at the door; Ben-Hur entered alone.

The room was the same in which he had formerly interviewed Simonides. Close by the arm-chair, a polished brazen rod, set on a broad wooden pedestal, arose higher than a tall man, holding lamps of silver on sliding arms.

Three persons were present, looking at him—Simonides, Ilderim, and Esther.

He glanced hurriedly from one to another, as if to find answer to the question half formed in his mind, What business can these have with me? He became calm, with every sense on the alert, for the question was succeeded by another, Are they friends or enemies?

At length his eyes rested upon Esther.

The men returned his look kindly; in her face there was something more than kindness—something which went to his inner consciousness without definition.

"Son of Hur—"

The guest turned to the speaker.

"Son of Hur," said Simonides, repeating the address slowly, and with distinct emphasis, "take thou the peace of the Lord God of our fathers—take it from me and mine."

The speaker sat in his chair; there were the royal head, the bloodless face, the masterful air, which caused visitors to forget the broken, distorted body of the man. Then he crossed his hands upon his breast.

The action, taken with the salutation, could not be misunderstood, and was not.

"Simonides," Ben-Hur answered, much moved, "the holy peace you tender is accepted. As son to father, I return it to you. Only let there be perfect understanding between us."

Thus delicately he sought to put aside the submission of the merchant, and, in place of the relation of master and servant, substitute one higher and holier.

Simonides let fall his hands, and, turning to Esther, said, "A seat for the master, daughter."

She brought a stool, and stood looking from one to the other—from Ben-Hur to Simonides, from Simonides to Ben-Hur; and they waited, each declining the superiority direction would imply. At length, Ben-Hur advanced, and gently took the stool from her, and going to the chair, placed it at the merchant's feet.

"I will sit here," he said.

146

His eyes met hers—an instant only. He recognized her gratitude, she his generosity and forbearance.

Simonides bowed his acknowledgment. "Esther, child, bring me the paper," he said, with a breath of relief.

"Thou saidst well, son of Hur," Simonides began, while unrolling the sheets. "Let us understand each other. In anticipation of the demand—which I would have made hadst thou waived it—I have here a statement covering everything necessary to the understanding required. I could see but two points involved—the property first, and then our relation. The statement is explicit as to both."

Ben-Hur glanced at Ilderim.

"Nay," said Simonides, "the sheik shall not deter thee from reading. The account is of a nature requiring a witness. In the attesting place at the end thou wilt find, when thou comest to it, the name—Ilderim, Sheik. He knows all. He is thy friend. All he has been to me, that will he be to thee also."

Ben-Hur replied, "I know already the excellence of his friendship, and have yet to prove myself worthy of it." Immediately he continued, "Later, O Simonides, I will read the papers carefully; for the present give me their substance."

Esther took a place by her father's chair, letting her right arm fall lightly across his shoulder, so, when he spoke, the account seemed to have rendition from them jointly.

"This," said Simonides, drawing out the first leaf, "shows the money I had of thy father's, being the amount saved from the Romans; there was no property saved, only money, and that the robbers would have taken but for our Jewish custom of bills of exchange. The amount saved, being sums I drew from Rome, Alexandria, Damascus, Carthage, Valentia, and elsewhere within the circle of trade, was one hundred and twenty talents, Jewish money."

He gave the sheet to Esther, and took the next one.

"With that amount—one hundred and twenty talents—I charged myself. Hear now my credits. I use the word, as thou wilt see, with reference to the proceeds gained from the use of the money."

From separate sheets he then read footings, which totalled five hundred and fifty-three talents.

"To the five hundred and fifty-three talents gained, add the original capital I had from thy father, and thou hast six hundred and seventy-three talents—and all thine—making thee, O son of Hur, the richest subject in the world."

He took the papyri from Esther, and reserving one, rolled them and offered them to Ben-Hur. "And now," he added, dropping his voice, "there is nothing thou mayst not do."

Simonides crossed his hands upon his breast again; Esther was anxious; Ilderim nervous. Taking the roll, Ben-Hur arose.

"All this is to me as a light from heaven, sent to drive away a night which has been so long I feared it would never end," he said in a husky voice. "I give first thanks to the Lord, who has not abandoned me, and my next to thee, O Simonides. Thy faithfulness outweighs the cruelty of others, and redeems our human nature. Shall any man in this hour of such mighty privilege be more generous than I? Serve me as a witness now, Sheik Ilderim. Hear thou my words as I shall speak them— hear and remember. And thou, Esther, good angel of this good man, hear thou also."

He stretched his hand with the roll to Simonides. "The things these papers take into account—all of them: ships, houses, goods, camels, horses, money; the least as well as the greatest—give I back to thee, O Simonides, making them all thine, and sealing them to thee and thine forever."

Esther smiled through her tears, Ilderim pulled his beard, his eyes glistening like beads of jet. Simonides alone was calm.

"Sealing them to thee and thine forever," Ben-Hur continued, with better control of himself, "with one exception, and upon one condition."

The listeners waited upon his words.

"The hundred and twenty talents which were my father's thou shalt return to me."

Ilderim's countenance brightened.

"And thou shalt join me in search of my mother and sister, holding all thine subject to the expense of discovery, even as I will hold mine."

Simonides, stretching out his hand, said, "I see thy spirit, son of Hur, and I am grateful to the Lord that he hath sent thee to me. If I served well thy father in life, and his memory afterwards, be not afraid of default to thee; yet must I say the exception cannot stand."

Exhibiting, then, the reserved sheet, he continued. "Thou hast not all the account. Take this and read aloud."

Ben-Hur took the supplement, and read it.

Statement of the servants of Hur, rendered by Simonides, steward of the estate.

1. Amrah, Egyptian, keeping the palace in Jerusalem.
2. Simonides, the steward, in Antioch.
3. Esther, daughter of Simonides.

Now, in all his thoughts of Simonides, not once had it entered Ben-Hur's mind that, by the law, a daughter followed the parent's condition. In all his visions of her, the sweet-faced Esther had figured as the rival of the Egyptian, and an object of possible love. He shrank from the revelation so suddenly brought him, and looked at her blushing; and, blushing, she dropped her eyes before him. Then he said, while the papyrus rolled itself together,

"A man with six hundred talents is indeed rich, and may do what he pleases; but, rarer than the money, more priceless than the property, is the mind which amassed the wealth, and the heart it could not corrupt when amassed. O Simonides— and thou, fair Esther—have no fear. Sheik Ilderim here shall be witness that in the same moment ye were declared my servants, that moment I declared ye free; and what I declare, that will I put in writing. Can I do more?"

"Son of Hur," said Simonides, "verily thou dost make servitude lightsome. But I was wrong; there are some things thou canst not do: thou canst not make us free in law. I am thy servant forever, because I went to the door with thy father one day, and in my ear the awl-marks yet abide."

"Did my father do that?"

"Judge him not," cried Simonides quickly. "He accepted me a servant because I prayed him to do so. I never repented the step. It was the price I paid for Rachel, the mother of my child here; for Rachel, who would not be my wife unless I became what she was—a servant forever."

Ben-Hur walked the floor. "I was rich before," he said, stopping suddenly. "I was rich with the gifts of the generous Arrius; now comes this greater fortune, and the mind which achieved it. Is there not a purpose of God in it all? Counsel me, O Simonides! Help me to see the right and do it. Help me to be worthy of my name, and what thou art in law to me, that will I be to thee in fact and deed. I will be thy servant forever."

Simonides' face glowed. "O son of my dead master! I will do better than help; I will serve thee with all my might of mind and heart. Body, I have not; it perished in thy cause; but with mind and heart I will serve thee. Only make me legally what I have assumed to be."

"Name it," said Ben-Hur eagerly.

"As steward in the care of your property."

"Count thyself steward now; or wilt thou have it in writing?"

"Thy word simply is enough; it was so with the father, and I will not more from the son. And now, if the understanding be perfect"—Simonides paused.

"It is with me," said Ben-Hur.

"And thou, daughter of Rachel, speak!" said Simonides, lifting her arm from his shoulder.

Esther stood a moment abashed, her color coming and

149

going; then she went to Ben-Hur, and said, "I am not better than my mother was; and, as she is gone, I pray you, O my master, let me care for my father."

Ben-Hur took her hand, and led her back to the chair, saying, "Thou art a good child. Have thy will."

## Chapter VIII.

"Esther," Simonides said quietly, "the night is going fast; let the refreshments be brought."

She rang a bell. A servant answered with wine and bread, which she bore round.

"The understanding, good master," continued Simonides, when all were served, "is not perfect in my sight. Henceforth our lives will run on together like rivers which have met and joined their waters. I think their flowing will be better if every cloud is blown from the sky above them. You left my door the other day with what seemed a denial of the claims which I have just allowed in the broadest terms; but it was not so, indeed it was not. Esther is witness that I recognized you; and that I did not abandon you, let Malluch say."

"Malluch!" exclaimed Ben-Hur.

"One bound to a chair, like me, must have many hands if he would move the world from which he is barred. I have many such, and Malluch is one of the best. And, sometimes" —he cast a grateful glance at the sheik—"sometimes I borrow from others good of heart, like Ilderim the Generous—good and brave. Let him say if I either denied or forgot you."

Ben-Hur looked at the Arab.

"This is he, good Ilderim, this is he who told you of me?"

Ilderim's eyes twinkled as he nodded.

"How, O my master," said Simonides, "may we without trial tell what a man is? I knew you; I saw your father in you; but the kind of man you were I did not know. There are people to whom fortune is but a curse. Were you of them? I sent Malluch to find out for me. Do not blame him. He brought me report of you which was all good."

"I do not," said Ben-Hur, heartily. "There was wisdom in your goodness."

"I am compelled now by truth," the merchant continued. "As in my hands the fortune grew, I wondered at the increase. I could see a hand not my own guarded the enterprises I set going. The simooms which smote others on the desert jumped over the things which were mine. The storms which heaped the seashore with wrecks did but blow my ships the sooner into port. Strangest of all, I, fixed to one place like a dead thing, had never a loss by an agent—never. The elements stooped to serve me, and all my servants were faithful."

"It is very strange," said Ben-Hur.

"So I said, and kept saying. Finally, O my master, finally I came to be of your opinion—God was in it—and, like you, I asked, What can his purpose be? Intelligence like God's never stirs except with design. I felt sure, if God were in it, some day, in his own way he would show me his purpose. And I believe now he has done so."

Ben-Hur listened closely.

"Many years ago—thy mother was with me, Esther—I sat by the wayside out north of Jerusalem, when three men passed by riding great white camels, such as had never been seen in the Holy City. The men were from far countries. The first one stopped and asked me a question. 'Where is he that is born king of the Jews?' As if to allay my wonder, he went on to say, 'We have seen his star in the east, and have come to worship him.' I could not understand, but followed them to the Damascus Gate; and of every person they met on the way —of the guard at the Gate, even—they asked that question. All who heard it were amazed like me. In time I forgot the circumstance, though there was much talk of it as a presage of the Messiah. When God walks the earth, his steps are often centuries apart. You have seen Balthasar?"

"And heard him tell his story," said Ben-Hur.

"A miracle!" cried Simonides. "As he told it to me, I seemed to hear the answer I had so long waited; God's purpose burst upon me. Poor will the King be when he comes— poor and friendless; without following, without armies, without cities or castles; a kingdom to be set up, and Rome reduced and blotted out. See, O my master! thou flushed with strength, trained to arms, burdened with riches; behold the opportunity the Lord hath sent thee! Shall not his purpose be thine? Could a man be born to a more perfect glory?"

"But the kingdom, the kingdom!" Ben-Hur answered eagerly. "Balthasar says it is to be of souls."

Pride of race was strong in Simonides, and therefore the slightly contemptuous tone with which he replied: "Balthasar has been a witness of wonderful things—of miracles, O my master; and when he speaks of them, I bow with belief, for they are of sight and sound personal to him. But he is a son of Mizraim, and not even a proselyte. Hardly may he be supposed to have special knowledge in a matter of God's dealing with our Israel. The prophets had their light from Heaven directly. I must believe the prophets.

"May the testimony of a whole people be slighted, my master? Though you travel from Tyre to the capital of Idumea, you will not find any one who has ever eaten of the lamb of

151

the Passover, to tell you that the kingdom the King will build for us is other than of this world, like our father David's. The way to the fountain's head is open. Let us go to it at once. Some wine, Esther, and then the Torah and the words of Isaiah."

He took one of the rolls and read, " 'The people that walked in darkness have seen a great light: they that dwell in the land of the shadow of death, upon them hath the light shined. . . . For unto us a child is born, unto us a son is given: and the government shall be upon his shoulder. . . . Of the increase of his government and peace there shall be no end, upon the throne of David, and upon his kingdom, to order it, and to establish it with judgment and with justice from henceforth even forever.'—Believest thou the prophets, O my master?—Now, Esther, the word of the Lord that came to Micah."

And the merchant read on, through the visions of Jeremiah and of Daniel. Then he looked up at Ben-Hur. "Believest thou the prophets, O my master?"

"It is enough. I believe," cried Ben-Hur.

"If the King come poor, will not my master, of his abundance, give him help?"

"Help him? To the last shekel and the last breath. But why speak of his coming poor?"

"Give me, Esther, the word of the Lord as it came to Zechariah," said Simonides. Then he read, "Rejoice greatly, O daughter of Zion. . . . Behold, thy King cometh unto thee with justice and salvation; lowly, and riding upon an ass, and upon a colt, the foal of an ass."

Ben-Hur looked away.

"What see you, O my master?"

"Rome!" he answered gloomily—"Rome, and her legions. I have dwelt with them in their camps. I know them."

"Ah!" said Simonides. "Thou shalt be a master of legions for the King, with millions to choose from."

"Millions?" cried Ben-Hur.

Simonides sat a moment thinking. "The question of power should not trouble you," he said. "You were seeing the lowly King in the act of coming to his own. And balanced against him you saw the brassy legions of Cæsar, and you were asking, 'What can he do against such might?' "

"It was my very thought."

"O my master!" Simonides continued. "You do not know how strong is our Israel. Go up to Jerusalem next Passover, and see us as we are. The promise of the Lord to father Jacob was a law under which our people have not ceased multiplying—they grew under foot of the Egyptian; the clench

152

of the Roman has been but wholesome nurture to them; now they are indeed 'a nation, and a company of nations.' Nor that only, my master; in fact, to measure the strength of Israel you shall not bide solely by the rule of natural increase, but add thereto the spread of the faith, which will carry you over the whole known earth. Further, the habit is to think and speak of Jerusalem as Israel, but Jerusalem is only a stone of the Temple. Turn from beholding the legions, and count the hosts of the faithful. Count the many in Persia, children of those who chose not to return with the returning; count the brethren who swarm the marts of Egypt and Farther Africa; count the Hebrew colonists eking profit in the West—in Lodinum, and the trade-courts of Spain; count the pure of blood and the proselytes in Greece and in the isles of the sea, and here in Antioch, and, for that matter, those of that city accursed—Rome herself; count the worshippers of the Lord dwelling in tents along the deserts next us. . . . And when you have done counting the census of the sword hands that await you, you see a kingdom ready fashioned for him who is to do 'judgment and justice in the whole earth'—in Rome not less than in Zion. Have then the answer, 'hat Israel can do, that also can the King."

Upon Ilderim, the merchant's words were as the blowing of a trumpet. "Oh that I had back my youth!" he cried, starting to his feet.

Ben-Hur sat still. The speech, he saw, was an invitation to devote his life and fortune to the mysterious Being who was palpably as much the center of a great hope with Simonides as with the devout Egyptian. The idea had come to him repeatedly; but it had come and gone only a idea. Not so now; already Simonides had exalted it into a cause brilliant with possibilities and infinitely holy. The effect was as if a door had suddenly opened, admitting Ben-Hur to a service rich with the rewards of duty done, and prizes to soothe his ambition. One touch more was needed.

"Let us concede all you say, O Simonides," said Ben-Hur, "that the King will come, and his kingdom be as Solomon's; say also I am ready to give myself and all I have to him and his cause; then what? Shall we proceed like blind men building? Shall we wait till the King comes? Or until he sends for me? You have age and experience on your side. Answer."

Simonides answered at once. "We have no choice; none. This letter"—he produced Messala's despatch as he spoke—"is the signal for action. The alliance proposed between Messala and Gratus we have not the influence at Rome nor the force here to resist. They will kill you if we wait. How merciful they are, look at me and judge.

"O my master," he continued, "how strong are you in purpose? For well I remember how pleasant the world was to me in my youth."

"Yet," said Ben-Hur, "you were capable of a great sacrifice."

"Yes; for love."

"Has not life other motives as strong?"

Simonides shook his head.

"What, then, of revenge?"

The man's eyes gleamed; his hands shook; he answered, quickly, "Revenge is a Jew's of right; it is the law."

"A camel, even a dog, remembers a wrong," cried Ilderim.

Simonides picked up the thread of his thought.

"There is work for the King which should be done in advance of his coming. We may not doubt that Israel is to be his right hand; but, it is a hand without cunning in war. Of the millions, there is not one trained band, not a captain. The condition is as the Roman would have it; but the time of change is at hand, when the shepherd shall put on armor, and take the spear and sword, and the feeding flocks be turned to fighting lions. Some one, my son, must station himself at the King's right hand. Who shall it be if not he who is skilled in the arts of war?"

Ben-Hur flushed. "A deed to be done is one thing; but how to do it is another."

Simonides sipped the wine Esther brought him, and replied, "The sheik, and thou, my master, shall be principals, each with a part. I will remain here, carrying on as now. Thou shalt betake thee to Jerusalem, and thence to the wilderness, and begin numbering the fighting-men of Israel, telling them into tens and hundreds, choosing captains and training them, and in secret places hoarding arms, for which I shall keep thee supplied. Commencing over in Perea, thou shalt go then to Galilee, whence it is but a step to Jerusalem. In Perea, the desert will be at thy back, and Ilderim in reach of thy hand. He will guard the roads, so that nothing shall pass without thy knowledge. He will help thee in many ways. Until the ripening time no one shall know what is here contracted. Mine is but a servant's part. I have spoken to Ilderim. What sayest thou?"

Ben-Hur looked at the sheik.

"It is as he says, son of Hur," the Arab responded. "I have given my word, and he is content with it; but thou shalt have my oath, binding me, and the ready hands of my tribe, and whatever serviceable thing I have."

The three—Simonides, Ilderim, Esther—gazed at Ben-Hur fixedly.

"Every man," he answered, "has a cup of pleasure poured for him, and soon or late it comes to his hand, every man

154

but me. I see, Simonides, and thou, O generous sheik!—I see whither the proposal tends. If I enter upon the course, farewell peace, and the hopes which cluster around it. Rome's outlawry will follow me, and her hunters; and in the tombs near cities and the caverns of remotest hills I must eat and take my rest."

The speech was broken by a sob. All turned to Esther, who hid her face upon her father's shoulder.

"I did not think of you, Esther," said Simonides gently.

"It is well enough, Simonides," said Ben-Hur. "I have no choice, but to take the part you assign me, at once."

"Shall we have writings?" asked Simonides, moved by his habit of business.

"I rest upon your word," said Ben-Hur.

Thus simply was effected the treaty which was to alter Ben-Hur's life.

"One word now, my friends," Ben-Hur said, more cheerfully. "By your leave, I will be my own man until after the games. It is not probable Messala will attack me until he has given the procurator time to answer his letter, say seven days. Meeting him in the Circus is a pleasure I would buy at any risk."

Ilderim, well pleased, assented readily, and Simonides, intent on business, added, "It is well; for the delay will give me time to do you a good part. I understood you to speak of an inheritance derived from Arrius. Is it in property?"

"A villa near Misenum, and houses in Rome."

"I suggest, then, the sale of the property, and a safe deposit of the proceeds. Give me an account of it, and I will have despatched an agent on the mission. We will forestall the imperial robbers at least this once. Then, if there be nothing more, the work of the night is done."

"Let the horses be brought," said Ben-Hur. "I will return to the orchard. The enemy will not discover me if I go now, and"—he glanced at Ilderim—"the four will be glad to see me."

As the day dawned, he and Malluch dismounted at the door of the tent.

## CHAPTER IX.

NEXT NIGHT Ben-Hur stood on the terrace of the great warehouse with Esther. Below them on the landing there was running about and shifting of packages and boxes, and shouting of men, whose figures, stooping, heaving, hauling in the light of the crackling torches looked like laboring genii. A galley was being laden for instant departure. Simonides had not yet come from his office, where he would deliver to the captain of the vessel instructions to proceed to Ostia, the seaport of Rome, landing a passenger there.

The passenger was the agent going to dispose of Ben-Hur's Roman estate. When the lines of the vessel were cast off, and she put about, Ben-Hur was committed irrevocably to the work undertaken the night before.

Young, handsome, rich, only recently returned from the patrician circles of Roman society, for a moment the world seemed to offer a far more attractive life than that he had pledged himself to with such zeal under the fiery enthusiasm of Simonides. Too, there was the hopelessness of contention with Cæsar; the uncertainty veiling everything connected with the King and his coming; the ease and honors which could so easily be his, and, strongest of all, the sense newly acquired of home, with friends to make it delightful.

Such temptations were now helped by Ben-Hur's companion.

"Were you ever at Rome?" he asked Esther, standing closely at his side.

"No," Esther replied. "Nor have I desire to go there."

"Why?"

"I am afraid of Rome," she answered.

He looked down at her then, noting that she appeared little more than a child. In the dim light he could not see her face distinctly; but again he was reminded of Tirzah, and a sudden tenderness fell upon him—just so the lost sister had stood with him on the house-top the calamitous morning of the accident to Gratus. That she was his servant by law would make him always the more considerate and gentle towards her.

"I cannot think of Rome," she continued, "as a city of palaces and temples; she is to me a monster which has possession of one of the beautiful lands, and lies there luring men to ruin and death—a ravenous beast gorging with blood. Why—" She faltered, looked down, stopped.

"Go on," said Ben-Hur reassuringly.

She drew closer to him, looked up again, and said, "Why must you make her your enemy? Why not rather make peace with her, and be at rest? You have had many ills and borne them; you have survived the snares laid for you by foes. Sorrow has consumed your youth; must you give it the remainder of your days?"

The delicate face seemed to come nearer as the pleading went on; he inclined his head to her. "What would you have me do, Esther?"

She hesitated a moment, then asked, in return, "Is the property near Rome a residence?"

"Yes."

"And pleasant?"

"It is beautiful—a palace in the midst of gardens and shell-strewn walks; fountains without and within; hills around covered with vines and so high that Neapolis and Vesuvius are in sight, and the sea a purpling blue expanse dotted with sails. Cæsar has a county-seat near by, but in Rome they say the old Arrian villa is the prettiest."

"And the life there, is it quiet?"

"There was never a summer day, never a moonlit night, more quiet, save when visitors come. The life, Esther, was all too quiet for me. It made me restless by keeping always present a feeling that I was tying myself with silken chains, and after a while—and not a long while either—would end with nothing done."

She looked off over the river.

"Why did you ask?"

"I cannot understand," she said, "the nature which prefers the life you are going to—a life—"

"Of violence, and it may be of blood," he finished for her.

"Yes," she added, "the nature which could prefer tha⁴ life to such as might be in the beautiful villa."

"Esther, there is no preference, no choice. I am going of necessity. To stay here is to die; and if I go there, the end will be the same—a poisoned cup, a bravo's blow, or a judge's sentence obtained by perjury. Messala and the procurator Gratus are rich with plunder of my father's estate, and it is important to them to keep their gains. Ah, Esther, if I cou'¹ buy them, I do. not know that I would. Peace is not possible to me while my people are lost, for I must be watchful to find them. If I find them, and they have suffered wrong, shall not the guilty suffer for it? If they are dead by violence, shall the murderers escape? Not the holiest love, by any strata-gem, could lull me to rest."

"Is it so bad then?" she asked, her voice tremulous with feeling. "Can nothing be done?"

Ben-Hur took her hand. "Do you care so much for me?"

"Yes," she answered simply.

The hand was warm, and in his palm it was lost. He felt it tremble. Then he thought the Egyptian came, so much the opposite of this little one; so tall, so audacious, with a flattery so cunning, a wit so ready, a beauty so wonderful, a manner so bewitching. He carried the hand to his lips, and gave it back.

"You shall be another Tirzah to me, Esther. The little sister the Roman stole from me, and whom I must find before I can rest or be happy."

Just then a gleam of light flashed across the terrace and

fell upon the two; and, looking round, they saw a servant roll Simonides in his chair out of the door. They went to the merchant, and in the after-talk he was principal.

## CHAPTER X.

THE DAY before the games, all Ilderim's racing property was taken to the city, and put in quarters adjoining the Circus. Along with it the good man carried a great deal of other property; so with servants, retainers mounted and armed, horses in leading, cattle driven, camels laden with baggage, his outgoing from the Orchard was like a tribal migration. The people along the road laughed at his motley procession; yet with all his irascibility, he was not in the least offended by their rudeness. If he was under surveillance, as he had reason to believe, the informer would describe the semi-barbarous show with which he came up to the races. The Romans would laugh; the city would be amused; but what difference? Next morning the procession would be far on the road to the desert, and going with it would be everything of value belonging to the Orchard, save such as were essential to the success of his four. He was, in fact, started home; his tents were all folded; the dowar was no more; in twelve hours all would be out of reach of pursuit. A man is never safer than when he is ridiculed; and the shrewd old Arab knew it.

Neither he nor Ben-Hur overestimated the influence of Messala; it was their opinion, however, that he would not begin active measures against them until after the race; if defeated there by Ben-Hur, they might instantly look for the worst he could do; he might not even wait for Gratus's advices. With this view, they were prepared to take themselves out of harm's way. They rode together now in good spirits, calmly confident of success on the morrow.

On the way, they came upon Malluch in waiting for them. He gave no sign of the relationship so recently admitted between Ben-Hur and Simonides, or of the treaty between them and Ilderim. He exchanged salutations as usual, and produced a paper, saying to the sheik, "I have here the notice of the editor of the games, just issued, in which you will find your horses published for the race. You will find in it also the order of exercises. Without waiting, good sheik, I congratulate you upon your victory."

He gave the paper over, and turned to Ben-Hur. "To you, also, son of Arrius, my congratulations. There is nothing now to prevent your meeting Messala. Every condition preliminary to the race is complied with. Your color is white, and Messala's mixed scarlet and gold. The good effects of the choice are visible already. Boys are now hawking white ribbons along the streets; to-morrow every Arab and Jew in the city will wear them. In the Circus you will see the white fairly divide the galleries with the red."

"The galleries—but not the tribunal over the Porta Pompæ."

"No; the scarlet and gold will rule there. But if we win how the dignitaries will tremble! They will bet, of course, according to their scorn of everything not Roman—two, three, five to one on Messala, because he is Roman." Dropping his voice yet lower, he added, "In confidence, I will have a friend next behind the consul's seat to accept offers of three to one, or five, or ten—the madness may go to such height. I have put to his order six thousand shekels for the purpose."

"Nay, Malluch," said Ben-Hur. "A Roman will wager only in his Roman coin. Suppose you find your friend to-night, and place to his order sestertii in such amount as you choose. And look you, Malluch—let him be instructed to seek wagers with Messala and his supporters; Ilderim's four against Messala's."

Malluch reflected a moment. "The effect will be to center interest upon your contest."

"The very thing I seek, Malluch. Help me to fix the public eye upon our race—Messala's and mine."

Malluch spoke quickly. "Enormous wagers offered will answer; if the offers are accepted, all the better." Malluch turned his eyes watchfully upon Ben-Hur.

"Shall I not have back the equivalent of his robbery?" said Ben-Hur, partly to himself. "Another opportunity may not come. And if I could break him in fortune as well as in pride! Hark, Malluch! Stop not in thy offer of sestertii. Advance them to talents, if there be any who dare so high. Five, ten, twenty talents; ay, fifty, so the wager be with Messala himself. Go to Simonides, and tell him I wish the matter arranged. Tell him my heart is set on the ruin of my enemy, and that the opportunity holds such excellent promise that I choose the risk. Go, good Malluch. Let this not slip."

"Your pardon," Malluch said to Ben-Hur. "There was another matter. I found that the hub of Messala's chariot stands quite a palm higher from the ground than yours."

"A palm! So much?" cried Ben-Hur, joyfully.

Then he leaned over to Malluch. "As thou art a son of Judah, Malluch, get thee a seat in the gallery over the Gate of Triumph, down close to the balcony in front of the pillars, and watch well when we make the turns there; watch well, for if I have any fortune at all, I will— Nay, Malluch, let it go unsaid! Only get thee there, and watch well."

At that moment a cry burst from Ilderim. "Ha! By the splendor of God! what is this?"

He drew near Ben-Hur with a finger pointing on the face of the notice.

Ben-Hur took the paper, which, signed by the prefect of the province as editor, gave the details of the various contests. First would be a procession of extraordinary splendor; the procession would be succeeded by the customary honors to the god Consus, whereupon the games would begin; running, leaping, wrestling, and boxing. The names of the competitors were given, with their several nationalities and schools of training, the trials in which they had been engaged, the prizes won, and the money prizes offered.

Over these Ben-Hur sped with rapid eyes. At last he came to the announcement of the race. He read it slowly. The city offered the spectacle in honor of the visiting consul. One hundred thousand sestertii and a crown of laurel were the prizes. Then followed the particulars. The entries were six in all— fours only permitted; and, to further interest in the performance, the competitors would be turned into the course together. Each four then received description.

I. A four of Lysippus the Corinthian—two grays, a bay, and a black; entered at Alexandria last year, and again at Corinth, where they were winners. Lysippus, driver. Color, yellow.

II. A four of Messala of Rome—two white, two black; victors of the Circensian as exhibited in the Circus Maximus last year. Messala, driver. Colors, scarlet and gold.

III. A four of Cleanthes the Athenian—three gray, one bay; winners at the Isthmian last year. Cleanthes, driver. Color, green.

IV. A four of Dicæus the Byzantine—two black, one gray, one bay; winners this year at Byzantium. Dicæus, driver. Color, black.

V. A four of Admetus the Sidonian—all grays. Thrice entered at Cæsarea, and thrice victors. Admetus, driver. Color, blue.

VI. A four of Ilderim, sheik of the Desert. All bays; first race. Ben-Hur, a Jew, driver. Color, white.

*Ben-Hur, a Jew driver!*
Why that name instead of Arrius?
Ben-Hur raised his eyes to Ilderim. He had found the cause of the Arab's outcry. Both rushed to the same conclusion.
The hand was the hand of Messala!


## Chapter XI.

EVENING WAS hardly upon Antioch, when the Omphalus, in the center of the city, became a troubled fountain from which in every direction flowed currents of people, for the time given up to Bacchus and Apollo.

They thronged the great roofed streets, which were miles

on miles of porticos wrought of marble, polished to the last degree of finish, and all gifts to the voluptuous city by princes. Darkness was not permitted anywhere; and the singing, the laughter, the shouting, were incessant, and in compound like the roar of waters dashing through hollow grottos, confused by a multiude of echoes.

Nearly everyone wore the colors of the morrow's race; a scarf, a badge, a ribbon or a feather. And three colors predominated—the green of Cleanthes the Athenian, the white of Ben-Hur, and Messala's scarlet and gold.

Meanwhile, in the vast dining hall of the palace apartment, the divan still held its burden of corpselike sleepers and carelessly flung garments, and the tables still resounded with the rattle of dice. Yet the greater part of the company walked idly about, yawning, pausing to exchange a few desultory words, waiting with ill-concealed boredom. Would the weather be fair for the games to-morrow? Did the laws of the Circus in Antioch differ from those of Rome? The young men's heavy work was done; the wagers on every event had been duly noted on the ivory memorandum tablets; wagers all made, that is, excepting on the main contest—the chariot race.

Not one of that company of bored, wearied young patricians could find anyone to hazard so much as a denarius against the high favorite, Messala.

There were no colors in the great hall but his scarlet and gold.

No one thought of anything but his victory. For them there was not the slightest possibility of any other outcome.

Was he not perfect in training? Had he not graduated from the imperial *lanista?* Had not his horses been winners at the Circensian, as well as in the Circus Maximus? And then—above all—was he not a Roman?

In a corner, at ease on the divan, Messala himself was the center of attention to his admirers who plied him with questions.

At that point, Drusus and Cecilius entered the chamber.

"Ah!" cried the young prince, throwing himself on the divan at Messala's feet, "Ah, by Bacchus, I am tired! What a day for a walk up to the Omphalus, and beyond—who shall say how far? Rivers of people; never so many in the city before. They say we will see the whole world at the Circus."

Messala laughed scornfully. "The idiots! *Perpol!* They never beheld a Circensian with Cæsar himself for editor. But, my Drusus, what found you?"

"Nothing."

"O—ah! You forget," said Cecilius. "The procession of whites."

*"Mirabile!"* cried Drusus, half rising. "We met a faction of

whites, and they had a banner. But—ha, ha, ha!—scum of the desert were they, my Messala, and garbage-eaters from the Jacob's Temple in Jerusalem. What had I to do with them?"

"Nay," said Cecilius, "Drusus is afraid of a laugh, but I am not, my Messala. We stopped the crowd, and—"

"—offered them a wager," said Drusus, taking the word from the shadow's mouth. "And—ha, ha, ha!—one fellow with not enough skin on his face to make a worm for a carp stepped forth, and—ha, ha, ha!—said Yes. I drew my tablets. 'Who is your man?' I asked. 'Ben-Hur, the Jew,' said he. Then I: 'What shall it be? How much?' He answered, 'A—a—' Excuse me, Messala. By Jove's thunder, I cannot go on for laughter!"

The listeners leaned forward. Messala looked to Cecilius.

"A—shekel!" gasped the latter shaking with his mirth.

A burst of laughter ran fast on his words.

"And what then?" asked Messala.

An outcry over about the door just then occasioned a rush to that quarter and, as the noise there grew louder, even Cecilius took himself off, pausing only to say, "The noble Drusus, my Messala, put away his tablets and—lost the shekel."

"A white! A white!"

"Let him come!"

The dice-players quit their games; the sleepers awoke, rubbed their eyes, drew their tablets and hurried to the common center.

"I offer you—"

"And I—"

"I—"

The person so warmly received was the venerable Jew, Ben-Hur's fellow-voyager from Cyprus. He entered, grave, quiet and observant. His robe was spotlessly white; so was the cloth of his turban. Bowing and smiling at the welcome, he moved slowly towards the central table. Arrived there, he drew his robe about him in a stately manner, took seat, and waved his hand. The gleam of a jewel on a finger helped him not a little to the silence which ensued.

"Romans—most noble Romans—I salute you!" he said.

"Easy, by Jupiter! Who is he?" asked Drusus.

"A dog of Israel—Sanballat by name—purveyor for the army; residence, Rome; vastly rich. He spins mischiefs, nevertheless, finer than spiders spin their webs. Come—by the girdle of Venus! let us hear him!"

Messala arose and with Drusus joined the crowd.

"It came to me on the street," said that person, producing his tablets, and opening them on the table with an air of business, "that there was great discomfort in the palace because offers on Messala were going without takers. The gods, you know, must have sacrifices; here am I. You see my color; let us to the matter. Odds first, amounts next. What will you give me?"

The audacity seemed to stun his hearers.

"Haste!" he said. "I have an engagement with the consul."

The spur was effective. "Two to one," cried half a dozen.

"What!" exclaimed the purveyor, astonished. "Only two to one, and yours a Roman? Give me four."

"Four it is," said a boy, stung by the taunt.

"Five—give me five," cried the purveyor instantly.

A stillness fell on the assemblage.

"The consul—your master and mine—is waiting for me. Give me five—for the honor of Rome, five."

"Five let it be," said one.

There was a sharp cheer—a commotion—and Messala edged forward.

Sanballat smiled, and made ready to write. "If Cæsar die to-morrow," he said, "Rome will not be all bereft. There is at least one other with spirit to take his place. Give me six."

"Six be it," answered Messala. "Six to one—the difference between a Roman and a Jew. And, having found it, now, let us get on. The amount—and quickly. The consul may send for thee, and I will then be bereft."

Sanballat took the laugh against him coolly, wrote, and offered the writing to Messala.

And Messala read:

*Mem.—Chariot-race.* Messala of Rome, in wager with Sanballat, also of Rome, says he will beat Ben-Hur, the Jew. Amount of wager, twenty talents. Odds to Sanballat, six to one.

Witnesses:

SANBALLAT.

There was no noise, no motion. Messala stared at the memorandum and thought rapidly. So lately he stood in the same place, and in the same way hectored the countrymen around him. They would remember it. If he refused to sign, his leadership was lost. And sign he could not; he was not worth one hundred talents, nor the fifth part of the sum. Suddenly his mind became a blank; he stood speechless; the color fled his face. An idea at last came to his relief.

"Thou Jew!" he said. "Where hast thou twenty talents? Show me."

Sanballat's provoking smile deepened. "There," he replied, offering Messala a paper.

163

Again Messala read:

AT ANTIOCH, *Tammuz 16th day*.
The bearer, Sanballat of Rome, hath now to his order with me fifty talents, coin of Cæsar.

SIMONIDES.

"Fifty talents!" echoed the throng in amazement.

Then Drusus came to the rescue. "By Hercules!" he shouted. "The Jew is a liar. Who but Cæsar hath fifty talents at order? Down with the insolent white!"

The cry was angry, and it was angrily repeated; yet Sanballat kept his seat, and his smile grew more exasperating as he waited. At length Messala spoke.

"Hush! One to one, my countrymen—one to one, for love of our ancient Roman name."

The action recovered him his ascendency. "O thou circumcised dog!" he continued, to Sanballat. "I gave thee six to one, did I not?"

"Yes," said the Jew quietly.

"Well, give me now the fixing of the amount."

"With reserve, if the amount be trifling, have thy will."

"Write, then, five in place of twenty."

"Hast thou so much?"

"By the mother of the gods, I will show you receipts."

"Nay, the word of so brave a Roman must pass. Only make the sum even in accordance with the odds—six make it, and I will write."

"Write it so."

And they exchanged writings. Sanballat immediately arose and looked around him, a sneer in place of his smile. No man better than he knew those with whom he was dealing.

"Romans," he said, "another wager, if you dare! Five talents against five talents—an even wager—that the white will win. I challenge you collectively."

They were again surprised.

"What!" he cried louder. "Shall it be said in the Circus to-morrow that a dog of Israel went into the palace full of Roman nobles—among them even the scion of a great Cæsar —and laid five talents before them in challenge, and they lacked the courage to take it up?"

The sting was unendurable. "Have done, O insolent!" said Drusus, "write the challenge, and leave it on the table; and to-morrow, if we find thou hast indeed so much money to put at such hopeless hazard, I Drusus, promise it shall be taken."

Sanballat wrote again, and, rising, said unmoved as ever, "See, Drusus, I leave the offer with you. When it is signed, send it to me any time before the race begins. I will be found with the consul in a seat over the Porta Pompæ. Peace to you; peace to all."

That night the story of the prodigious wager flew along the streets; and Ben-Hur, lying with his four, was told of it, and also that Messala's whole fortune was on the hazard.

And he slept never so soundly.

## Chapter XII.

The Circus at Antioch stood on the south bank of the river nearly opposite the island. At midnight the entrances had been thrown wide, and the rabble, surging in, occupied the quarters assigned to them, from which nothing less than an army with spears could have dislodged them. They dozed the night away on the benches, and breakfasted there; and there the close of the exercises found them, patient and sight-hungry as in the beginning.

The wealthier people, their seats secured, began moving towards the Circus about the first hour of the morning, the noble and very rich among them distinguished by litters and retinues of liveried servants.

By the second hour, the efflux from the city was a stream unbroken and innumerable.

Exactly as the official dial up in the citadel pointed the second hour half gone, the legion, in full panoply, descended from Mount Sulpius; and when the rear of the last cohort disappeared in the bridge, Antioch was abandoned.

A great crowd on the river shore witnessed the consul come over from the island in a barge of state. As the great man landed, and was received by the legion, the martial show for one brief moment transcended the attraction of the Circus.

At last, a flourish of trumpets called for silence, and instantly the gaze of over a hundred thousand persons was directed towards a pile forming the eastern section of the building.

There was a basement first, broken in the middle by a broad arched passage, called the Porta Pompæ, over which, on an elevated tribunal magnificently decorated with insignia and legionary standards, the consul sat in the place of honor.

Across this sanded arena stood a pedestal of marble supporting three low conical pillars of carved gray stone. Many an eye would hunt for those pillars before the day was done, for they were the first goal, and marked the beginning and end of the race-course. Behind the pedestal, leaving a passage-way and space for an altar, commenced a wall ten or twelve feet in breadth and five or six in height, extending exactly two hundred yards, or one Olympic stadium. At the farther extremity of the wall there stood another pedestal, surmounted with pillars which marked the second goal.

The racers would enter the course on the right of the first goal, and keep the wall all the time to their left. The beginning and ending points of the contest lay, consequently, directly in front of the consul across the arena; and for that reason his seat was admittedly the most desirable in the Circus.

Out of the Porta Pompæ over in the east now rose a sound mixed of voices and instruments harmonized. Presently, forth issued the chorus of the procession which marked the start of the celebration. The editor and civic authorities of the city, givers of the games, followed in robes and garlands; then the gods, some on platforms borne by men, others in great four-wheel carriages gorgeously decorated; and then the contestants of the day, each in costume exactly as he would run, wrestle, leap, box, or drive.

If there had been a question as to the popularity of the several games, it was now put to rest. To the splendor of the chariots and the excellent beauty of the horses, the charioteers added the personality necessary to perfect the display. A horseman accompanied each one of them except Ben-Hur, who, for some reason—possibly distrust—chose to go alone; so, too, they were all helmeted but him. As they approached the spectators stood upon the benches, and the gay bouquets flying from the balcony thickened into a storm, dropping into the chariot-beds, which threatened to fill to the tops. Even the horses had a share in the ovation; nor were they less conscious than their masters of the honors.

Nearly every individual on the benches, women and children as well as men, were a color, now green, now yellow, now blue; but there was a preponderance of white, and scarlet and gold.

As the charioteers moved on in the circuit, the excitement increased; at the second goal, where, especially in the galleries, white was the ruling color, the people exhausted their flowers and filled the air with screams.

When at length the march was ended and the Porta Pompæ received back the procession, Ben-Hur knew he had his greatest wish.

The eyes of the East were upon his contest with Messala.

CHAPTER XIII.

ABOUT THREE o'clock the programme was concluded except the chariot-race. The editor wisely chose that time for a recess. At once the *vomitoria* were thrown open, and all who could hastened to the portico outside where the restaurants had their quarters. Those who remained yawned, talked, gossiped, consulted their tablets, and, all distinctions else forgotten, merged into but two classes—the winners, who were happy, and the losers, who were grum and captious.

Now, however, a third class of spectators, composed of citizens who desired only to witness the chariot-race, availed themselves of the recess to come in and take their reserved seats; by so doing they thought to attract the least attention and give the least offence. Among these were Simonides and his party, whose places were in the vicinity of the main entrance on the north side, opposite the consul.

As the four stout servants carried the merchant in his chair up the aisle, curiosity was excited. Presently some one called out his name and there was hurried climbing on seats to see the fabled rich man about whom report had circulated a romance mixed of good fortune and bad.

Ilderim was also recognized and warmly greeted; but no body knew Balthasar or the two women who followed him closely veiled.

The people made way for the party respectfully, and the ushers seated them in easy speaking distance of each other down by the balustrade overlooking the arena.

The women were Iras and Esther.

Upon being seated, the latter cast a frightened look over the Circus, and drew the veil closer about her face; while the Egyptian, letting her veil fall upon her shoulders, gave herself to view, and gazed at the scene with the seeming unconsciousness of being stared at.

The new-comers were yet making their first examination of the spectacle, beginning with the consul and his attendants, when some workmen ran in and commenced to stretch a chalk rope across the arena from balcony to balcony in front of the pillars of the first goal.

These gate-keepers were dressed in tunics colored like those of the competing charioteers; so, when they took their stations, everybody knew the particular stall in which his favorite was that moment waiting.

"Did you ever see Messala?" the Egyptian asked Esther.

The Jewess shuddered as she answered no. If not her father's enemy, the Roman was Ben-Hur's.

"He is beautiful as Apollo."

Presently Sanballat came to the party. "I am just from the stalls, O sheik," he said, bowing gravely to Ilderim, who began combing his beard, while his eyes glittered with eager inquiry. "The horses are in perfect condition."

Ilderim replied, "If they are beaten, I pray it be by some other than Messala."

Turning then to Simonides, Sanballat drew out a tablet, saying, "I bring you also something of interest. I reported, you will remember, the wager concluded with Messala last night, and stated that I left another which, if taken, was to be delivered to me before the race began. Here it is."

Simonides took the tablet and read the memorandum. "Yes," he said, "their emissary came to ask me if you had so much money with me. Keep the tablet close. If you lose, you know where to come; if you win"—his face knit hard— "see the signers escape not; hold them to the last shekel. That is what they would do with us."

"Trust me," replied the purveyor.

The trumpeters blew a call at which the absentees rushed back to their places. At the same time, some attendants appeared in the arena, and, climbing upon the division wall, went to an entablature near the second goal at the west end, and placed upon it seven wooden balls; then returning to the first goal, upon an entablature there they set up seven other pieces of wood hewn to represent dolphins.

"What shall they do with the balls and fishes, O sheik?" asked Balthasar.

"They are to keep the count. At the end of each round run thou shalt see one ball and one fish taken down."

The preparations were now complete, and presently a trumpeter in gaudy uniform arose by the editor, ready to blow the signal of commencement promptly at his order. Straightway the stir of the people and the hum of their conversation died away. Every face turned to the east, as all eyes settled upon the gates of the six stalls which shut in the competitors.

"Look now for the Roman," said Iras to Esther, who did not hear her, for, with close-drawn veil and beating heart, she sat watching for Ben-Hur.

The trumpet sounded short and sharp; whereupon the starters, one for each chariot, leaped down from behind the pillars of the goal, ready to give assistance if any of the fours proved unmanageable.

Again the trumpet blew, and simultaneously the gate-keepers threw the stalls open.

The gate-keepers called their men; instantly the ushers on the balcony waved their hands, and shouted with all their strength, "Down! down!"

As well have whistled to stay a storm.

Forth from each stall, like missiles in a volley from so many great guns, rushed the six fours; and up the vast assemblage arose, electrified and irrepressible, and, leaping upon the benches, filled the Circus and the air above it with yells and screams. This was the time for which they had so patiently waited!—this moment of supreme interest treasured up in talk and dreams since the proclamation of the games!

"He is come—there—look!" cried Iras, pointing to Messala.

"I see him," answered Esther, looking at Ben-Hur.

The veil was withdrawn. For an instant she was brave. An idea of the joy there is in doing an heroic deed under the eyes of a multitude came to her, and she understood how, at such times, men laugh at death or forget it utterly.

The competitors were now under view from nearly every part of the Circus, yet the race was not begun; they had first to make the chalked line successfully.

The line was stretched for the purpose of equalizing the start. If it were dashed upon, discomfiture of man and horses resulted; on the other hand, to approach it timidly was to incur the hazard of being thrown behind in the beginning of the race; and that was certain forfeit of the position next the wall on the inner line of the course.

The arena swam in a dazzle of light; yet each driver looked first for the rope, then for the coveted inner line. So all six aiming at the same point and speeding furiously, a collision seemed inevitable.

The crossing was about two hundred and fifty feet in width. If now a driver look away, or his mind wander, or a rein slip! Calculating upon the natural impulse to give one glance —just one—in curiosity or vanity, malice might be there with an artifice; while friendship and love might prove as deadly as malice.

The competitors, having started each on the shortest line for the position next the wall, yielding would be like giving up the race; and who dared yield? The cries of encouragement from the balcony were indistinguishable and indescribable: a roar which had the same effect upon all the drivers.

The fours neared the rope together. Then the trumpeter by the editor's side blew a signal vigorously. Seeing the action, however, the judges dropped the rope, and not an instant too soon, for the hoof of one of Messala's horses struck it as it fell. Nothing daunted, the Roman shook out his long lash, loosed the reins, leaned forward, and, with a triumphant shout, took the inside track next to the wall.

"Jove with us! Jove with us!" yelled all the Roman faction, in a frenzy of delight.

As Messala turned in, the bronze lion's head at the end of

his axle caught the fore-leg of the Athenian's right-hand trace-mate, flinging the brute over against its yoke-fellow. Both staggered, struggled, and lost their headway. The ushers had their will at least in part. The thousands held their breath with horror; only up where the consul sat was there shouting.

"Jove with us!" screamed Drusus frantically.

"He wins! Jove with us!" answered his friends, seeing Messala speed on.

Tablet in hand, Sanballat turned to them; but a crash from the course below turned his attention that way.

Messala having passed, the Corinthian was the only contestant on the Athenian's right, and to that side the latter tried to turn his broken four; and then, as ill-fortune would have it, the wheel of the Byzantine, who was next on the left, struck the tail-piece of his chariot, knocking his feet from under him. There was a crash, a scream of rage and fear, and the unfortunate Cleanthes fell under the sharp pounding hoofs.

On swept the Corinthian, on the Byzantine, on the Sidonian.

Sanballat looked for Ben-Hur, and turned again to Drusus and his coterie.

"A hundred sestertii on the Jew!" he cried.

"Taken!" answered Drusus.

"Another hundred on the Jew!" shouted Sanballat.

Nobody appeared to hear him. He called again; the  ...tion below was too absorbing, and they were too busy shouting, "Messala! Messala! Jove with us!"

When Esther ventured to look again, a party of workmen were removing the horses and broken chariot; another party were taking off the man himself; and every Greek was vocal with execrations and prayers for vengeance. Suddenly she dropped her hands; Ben-Hur, unhurt, was to the front, coursing freely forward along with the Roman! Behind them, in a group, followed the Sidonian, the Corinthian and the Byzantine.

The race was on; the souls of the racers were in it; over them bent the multitude.


CHAPTER XIV.

WHEN THE dash for position began, Ben-Hur was on the extreme left of the six. For a moment, like the others, he was half blinded by the light in the arena; yet he managed to catch sight of his antagonists and divine their purpose. At Messala, who was more than an antagonist, he gave one searching look. The air of passionless hauteur was there as

170

of old, and so were the Italian god-like features; but more—it may have been a jealous fancy, still the Israelite thought he saw the soul of the man, darkly cruel, cunning, desperate; a soul in a tension of watchfulness and fierce resolve.

Ben-Hur felt his own resolution harden to a like temper. At whatever cost, at all hazards, he would humble this enemy! Prize, friends, wages, honor—everything was lost in the one deliberate purpose. Regard for life even should not hold him back. Yet there was no passion; no blinding rush of heated blood from heart to brain and back again. He had his plan, and confiding in himself, he settled to the task never more observant, never more capable. The air about him seemed aglow with a renewed and perfect transparency.

When not half-way across the arena, he saw that Messala's rush would, if there was no collision and the rope fell, give him the wall; that the rope would fall, he ceased to doubt; and further it came to him that Messala knew it was to be let drop at the last moment—prearrangement with the editor, could safely reach that point in the contest—and it suggested, what more Roman-like than for the official to lend himself to a countryman who, besides being so popular, had so much at stake? There could be no other accounting for the confidence with which Messala pushed his four forward the instant his competitors were prudentially checking their fours in front of the obstruction—no other except madness. Ben-Hur yielded the wall for the time.

The rope fell, and all the fours but his sprang into the course under urgency of voice and lash. He drew head to the right, and, with all the speed of his Arabs, darted across the trails of his opponents. So while the spectators were shivering at the Athenian's mishap, and the Sidonian, Byzantine, and Corinthian were striving to avoid involvement in the wreck, Ben-Hur swept around and took the course neck and neck with Messala, though on the outside. The marvelous skill shown in making the change thus from the extreme left across to the right without appreciable loss did not fail the sharp eyes upon the benches: the Circus seemed to rock and rock again with applause. Then Esther clasped her hands in glad surprise; then Sanballat, smiling, offered his hundred sestertii a second time without a taker; and then the Romans began to consider, thinking Messala might have found an equal, if not a master, and that in an Israelite!

And now, racing together side by side, a narrow interval between them, the two neared the second goal.

The pedestal of the three pillars there, viewed from the west, was a stone wall in the form of a half-circle. Making this turn was considered in all respects the most telling test of a charioteer. A hush fell over all the Circus, so that for

171

the first time in the race the rattle and clang of the cars plunging after the tugging steeds were distinctly heard. Then, it would seem, Messala observed Ben-Hur, and recognized him; and at once the audacity of the man flamed out in an astonishing manner.

"Down Eros, up Mars!" he shouted, whirling his lash with practised hand—"Down Eros, up Mars!" he repeated, and caught the well-doing Arabs of Ben-Hur a vicious cut, the like of which they had never known.

The blow was seen in every quarter, and amazement swept the stands. The awed hush deepened; up on the benches behind the consul the boldest held his breath, then, involuntarily, down from the balcony burst the indignant roar of the people.

Forward sprang the four as with one impulse, and forward leaped the chariot. Where got Ben-Hur the large hand and mighty grip which helped him now so well? Where but from the oar with which so long he fought the sea? And what was this spring of the floor under his feet to the dizzy eccentric lurch of the deck of the storm-tossed ship? So he kept his pace, and gave the four free rein, and called to them in soothing voice, trying merely to guide them round the dangerous turn; and before the fever of the people began to abate, he had back the mastery. Nor that only: on approaching the first goal, he was again even with Messala, bearing with him the sympathy and admiration of every one not a Roman. So clearly was the feeling shown, so vigorous its manifestation, that Messala, with all his boldness, felt it unsafe to trifle further.

As the car whirled round the goal, Esther caught sight of Ben-Hur's face—a little pale, a little higher raised, otherwise calm, even placid.

Immediately a man climbed on the entablature at the west end of the division wall, and took down one of the conical wooden balls. A dolphin on the east entablature was taken down at the same time.

Again, the second ball and second dolphin disappeared.

And then the third ball and third dolphin.

Three rounds concluded: still Messala held the inside position; still Ben-Hur moved with him side by side; still the other competitors followed as before. In the fifth round the Sidonian succeeded in getting a place outside Ben-Hur, but lost it directly.

The sixth round was entered upon without change of relative position.

Gradually the speed had been quickened—gradually the blood of the competitors warmed with the work. Men and beasts seemed to know alike that the final crisis was near, bringing the time for the winner to assert himself.

The interest which from the beginning had centered chiefly in the struggle between the Roman and the Jew, with an intense and general sympathy for the latter, was fast changing to anxiety on his account. On all the benches the spectators bent forward motionless, except as their faces turned following the contestants. Ilderim quit combing his beard, and Esther forgot her fears.

"A hundred sestertii on the Jew!" cried Sanballat to the Romans under the consul's awning.

"I will take thy sestertii," answered a Roman youth, preparing to write.

"Do not so," interposed a friend. "Messala hath reached his utmost speed. Look then at the Jew."

"By Hercules!" the first one replied, his countenance falling. "The dog throws all his weight on the bits. If the gods help not our friend, the Israelite will run away. No, not yet. Look! Jove with us, Jove with us!"

The cry, swelled by every Latin tongue, shook the *velaria* over the consul's head.

If it were true that Messala had attained his utmost speed, the effort was with effect; slowly but certainly he was beginning to forge ahead. His horses were running with their heads down; from the balcony their bodies appeared actually to skim the earth; their expanded nostrils showed blood-red; their eyes strained in their sockets. How long could they keep the pace? On they dashed. As they neared the second goal, Ben-Hur turned in behind the Roman's car.

The joy of the Messala faction reached its bound: they screamed and howled, and tossed their colors; and Sanballat filled his tablets with wagers of their tendering.

Malluch, in the lower gallery over the Gate of Triumph, found it hard to keep his cheer. He had cherished the vague hint dropped to him by Ben-Hur of something to happen in the turning of the western pillars. It was the fifth round, yet the something had not come; and he had said to himself, the sixth will bring it; but Ben-Hur was hardly holding a place at the tail of his enemy's car.

Over in the east end, Simonides' party held their peace. The merchant's head was bent low. Ilderim tugged at his beard, and dropped his brows till there was nothing of his eyes but an occasional sparkle of light. Esther scarcely breathed. Iras alone appeared glad.

Along the home-stretch—sixth round—Messala leading, next him Ben-Hur, and so close it was the old story:

Thus to the first goal, and round it. Messala, fearful of

losing his place, hugged the stony wall perilously close; a foot to left, and he would have been dashed to pieces; yet when the turn was finished, no man, looking at the wheel-tracks of the two cars, could have said, Here went Messala, there the Jew. They left but one trace behind them.

As they whirled by, Esther saw Ben-Hur's face again, and it was whiter than before.

Simonides, shrewder than Esther, said to Ilderim, the moment the rivals turned into the course, "I am no judge, good sheik, if Ben-Hur be not about to execute some plan. His face hath that look."

To which Ilderim answered, "Saw you how clean they were and fresh? By the splendor of God, friend, they have not been running! But now watch!"

One ball and one dolphin remained on the entablatures; and all the people drew a long b eath, for the beginning of the end was at hand.

First, the Sidonian gave the scourge to his four, and, smarting with fear and pain, they dashed desperately forward, promising for a brief time to go to the front. The effort ended in promise. Next, the Byzantine and Corinthian each made the trial with like result, after which they were practically out of the race. Thereupon, with a readiness perfectly explicable, all the factions except the Romans joined hope in Ben-Hur, and openly indulged their feeling.

"Ben-Hur! Ben-Hur!" they shouted, and the voicees rolled overwhelmingly against the consul stand.

From the benches above him as he passed, the favor descended in fierce injunctions.

"Take the wall now!"

"On! loose the Arabs! Given them rein and scourge!"

Over the balustrade they stooped low, stretching their hands imploringly to him.

Either he did not hear, or could not do better, for halfway round the course he was still following; at the second goal still no change!

And now, to make the turn, Messala began to draw in his left-hand steeds, an act which necessarily slackened their speed. His spirit was high; more than one altar was richer of his vows; the Roman genius was still president. On the three pillars only six hundred feet away were fame, increase of fortune, promotions, and a triumph sweetened by hate, all in store for him! That moment Malluch, in the gallery, saw Ben-Hur lean forward over his Arabs, and give them the reins. Out flew the many-folded lash in his hand; over the backs of the startled steeds it writhed and hissed, and hissed and writhed again and again; and though it fell not, there were both sting and menace in its quick report; and as the man passed thus to resistless action, his face suffused, his eyes gleaming, along the reins he seemed to flash his will; and instantly not one, but the four as one, answered with a leap that landed them alongside the Roman's car. Messala, on the perilous edge of the goal, heard, but dared not look to see what the awakening portended. From the people he received no sign. Above the noises of the race there was but one voice, and that was Ben-Hur's. In the old Aramaic, as the sheik himself, he called to the Arabs,

"On, Atair! On, Rigel! What, Antares! dost thou linger now? Good horse—oho, Aldebaran! I hear them singing in the tents. I hear the children singing and the women—singing of the stars, of Atair, Antares, Rigel, Aldebaran, victory!— and the song will never end. Well done! Home to-morrow, under the black tent—home! On, Antares! The tribe is waiting for us, and the master is waiting!"

There had never been anything of the kind more simple; seldom anything so instantaneous.

At the moment chosen for the dash, Messala was moving in a circle round the goal. To pass him, Ben-Hur had to cross the track on a like circle limited to the least possible increase. The thousands on the benches understood it all: they saw the signal given—the magnificent response; the four close outside Messala's outer wheel, Ben-Hur's inner wheel behind the other's car—all this they saw. Then they heard a crash loud enough to send a thrill through the Circus, and, quicker than thought, out over the course a spray of shining white and yellow flinders flew. Down on its right side toppled the bed of the Roman's chariot. There was a rebound as of the axle hitting the hard earth; another and another: then the car went to pieces; and Messala, entangled in the reins, pitched forward headlong.

The Sidonian, who had the wall next behind, could not stop or turn out. Into the wreck full speed he drove; then over the Roman, and into the latter's four, all mad with fear. Presently, out of the turmoil, the fighting of horses, the sound of blows, the murky cloud of dust and sand, he crawled, in time to see the Corinthian and Byzantine go on down the course after Ben-Hur, who had not been an instant delayed.

The people arose, leaped upon benches, and shouted and screamed. Those who looked that way caught glimpses of Messala, now under the trampling of the fours, now under the abandoned cars. He was still; they thought him dead; but far the greater number followed Ben-Hur in his career. They had not seen the cunning touch of the reins by which, turning a little to the left, he caught Messala's wheel with the iron-shod point of his axle, and crushed it; but they had seen the transformation of the man, and themselves felt the heat and glow

of his spirit, the heroic resolution; the maddening energy of
action with which, by look, word, and gesture, he had so
suddenly inspired his Arabs. And such running! It was rather
the long leaping of lions in harness; but for the lumbering
chariot, it seemed the four were flying. When the Byzantine
and Corinthian were half-way down the course, Ben-Hur
turned the first goal.

And the race was won!

The consul arose; the people shouted themselves hoarse;
the editor came down from his seat, and crowned the victors.

The fortunate man among the boxers was a low-browed,
yellow-haired Saxon, of such brutalized face as to attract
a second look from Ben-Hur, who recognized a teacher with
whom he himself had been a favorite at Rome. From him
the young Jew looked up and beheld Simonides and his party
on the balcony. They waved their hands to him. Esther kept
her seat; but Iras arose, and gave him a smile and a wave
of her fan.

The procession was then formed, and passed out of the
Gate of Triumph.

The day was over.

## CHAPTER XV.

BEN-HUR TARRIED across the river with Ilderim; for at midnight, as previously determined, they would take the road
which the caravan, then thirty hours out, had pursued.

The sheik was happy; his offers of gifts had been royal;
but Ben-Hur had refused everything, insisting that he was
satisfied with the humiliation of his enemy. The generous
dispute was continued.

"Think," the sheik would say, "what thou hast done for
me. In every black tent down to the Akaba and to the ocean,
and across to the Euphrates, and beyond to the sea of the
Scythians, the renown of my Mira and her children will go;
and they who sing of them will magnify me, and forget that
I am in the wane of life; and all the spears now masterless
will come to me, and my sword-hands multiply past counting.
Thou dost not know what it is to have sway of the Desert
such as will now be mine. I tell thee it will bring tribute incalculable from commerce, and immunity from kings. Ay,
by the sword of Solomon, doth my messenger seek favor
for me of Cæsar, that will he get. Yet nothing—nothing?"

And Ben-Hur answered, "Nay, sheik, have I not thy hand
and heart? Let thy increase of power and influence inure to
the King who comes. In the work I am going to, I may have
great need. Saying no now will leave me to ask of thee with
better grace hereafter."

In the midst of this controversy, two messengers arrived—Malluch and one unknown. The former was admitted first. The good fellow did not attempt to hide his joy over the event of the day.

"The master Simonides sends me to say that, upon the adjournment of the games, some of the Roman faction made haste to protest against payment of the money prize."

Ilderim started up, crying, in his shrillest tones, "By the splendor of God! the East shall decide whether the race was fairly won."

"Nay, good sheik," said Malluch, "the editor has paid the money. When they said Ben-Hur struck Messala's wheel, the editor laughed, and reminded them of the blow the Arabs had at the turn of the goal. The Athenian is dead."

"Dead!" echoed Ilderim. "What fortune these Roman monsters have! Messala escaped?"

"Escaped—yes, O sheik, with life; but it shall be a burden to him. The physicians say he will live, but never walk again."

Ben-Hur had a vision of Messala, chair-bound like Simonides, and, like him, going abroad on the shoulders of servants. The good man had carried his burden well; but could Messala survive, with his pride and ambition so badly wounded?

"Simonides bade me say further," Malluch continued, "Sanballat is having trouble. Drusus, and those who signed with him, referred to the Consul Maxentius the question of paying the five talents they lost, and he has referred it to Cæsar. Messala also refused his losses, and Sanballat, in imitation of Drusus, went to the consul, where the matter is still in advisement. The better Romans say the protestants shall not be excused; and all the adverse factions join with them. The city rings with the scandal."

"What says Simonides?" asked Ben-Hur.

"The master laughs, and is well pleased. If the Roman pays, he is ruined; if he refuses to pay, he is dishonored. Imperial policy will decide the matter. To offend the East would be a bad beginning with the Parthians; to offend Sheik Ilderim would be to antagonize the Desert, over which lie all Maxentius's lines of operation. Wherefore Simonides bade me tell you to have no disquiet; Messala will pay."

Malluch retired, and was succeeded by the other messenger, a lad of gentle manners and delicate appearance, who knelt upon one knee, and said, winningly, "Iras, the daughter of Balthasar, well known to good Sheik Ilderim, hath intrusted me with a message to the sheik, who, she saith, will do her great favor to receive her congratulations on account of the victory."

"The daughter of my friend is kind," said Ilderim, with sparkling eyes. "Give her this jewel, in sign of the pleasure

I have from her message." He took a ring from his finger as he spoke.

"I will, as thou sayest, O sheik," the lad replied, and continued, "The daughter of the Egyptian charged me further. She prays the good Sheik Ilderim to send word to Ben-Hur that her father hath taken residence for a time in the palace of Idernee, where she will receive him after the fourth hour to-morrow. And if, with her congratulations, Sheik Ilderim will accept her gratitude for this other favor done, she will be ever so pleased."

The sheik looked at Ben-Hur, whose face was suffused with pleasure. "By your leave, O sheik, I will see the fair Egyptian."

Ilderim laughed, and said, "Shall not a man enjoy his youth?"

At midnight Ilderim took the road, having arranged to leave a horse and a guide for Ben-Hur, who was to follow him.

## Chapter XVI.

Going next day to fill his appointment with Iras, Ben-Hur turned from the Omphalus into the Colonnade of Herod, and so came shortly to the palace of Idernee.

From the street he passed first into a vestibule, on the sides of which stairways led up to a portico. Winged lions sat by the stairs; in the middle there was a gigantic ibis spouting water over the floor; the lions, ibis wall, and floor, all of massive gray stone, were reminders of the Egyptians.

Ben-Hur moved on slowly. Iras was waiting for him; waiting with song and badinage, sparkling, fanciful, capricious —with smiles which glorified her glance, and glances which lent voluptuous suggestion to her whisper.

The passage brought him to a closed double door, in front of which he paused; and, as he did so, the broad leaves began to open of themselves, without creak or sound of lock or latch, or touch of foot or finger.

Looking through the doorway, he beheld the atrium of a Roman house, roomy and rich to a fabulous degree of magnificence.

When he looked down upon the floor, he was standing upon the breast of a Leda, represented as caressing a swan; and, looking farther, he saw the whole floor was similarly laid in mosaic pictures. And there were stools and chairs, and couches which were invitations of themselves. The reflections of the furniture were on the polished floor as distinctly as if they floated upon unrippled water; even the panelling of the walls and the fresco of the ceiling were reflected. Here was an interior that would have fitted well the house on the Palatine Hill which Cicero bought of Crassus.

Still in his dreamful mood, Ben-Hur sauntered about. When Iras was ready, she would come or send a servant. Twice, thrice, he made the round, yet nobody came. Time began at length to impress itself upon him, and he wondered why Iras stayed so long. He paused often to listen: and impatience blew a little fevered breath upon his spirit; and at last he woke to the silence which held the house in thrall, and the thought of it made him uneasy and distrustful. "Oh, she is giving the last touch to her eyelids, or she is arranging a chaplet for me; she will come presently, more beautiful of the delay!" He sat down then to admire a bronze candelabrum, the post at one end, and on the end opposite it an altar and a female celebrant. But the silence would obtrude itself: he listened but there was not a sound; the palace was still as a tomb.

There might be a mistake. No, the messenger had come from the Egyptian, and this was the palace of Idernee. Then he remembered how mysteriously the door had opened, so soundlessly, so of itself. He would see!

He went to the same door. Though he walked ever so lightly, the sound of his stepping was loud and harsh, and he shrank from it. He was getting nervous. The cumbrous Roman lock resisted his first effort to raise it; and the second —the blood chilled in his cheeks—he wrenched with all his might: in vain—the door was not even shaken. A sense of danger seized him, and for a moment he stood irresolute.

Who in Antioch had the motive to do him harm?

Messala!

And this palace of Idernee? He had seen Egypt in the vestibule, but here, in the atrium, was Rome; everything about him betrayed Roman ownership. The atrium underwent a sudden change, with all its elegance and beauty, it was no more than a trap.

The idea irritated Ben-Hur. There were many doors on the right and left of the atrium, leading, doubtless, to sleeping-chambers; he tried them, but they were all firmly fastened. Knocking might bring response. Ashamed to make outcry, he lay down on a couch, and tried to reflect.

All too plainly, he was a prisoner; but for what purpose? And by whom?

If the work were Messala's. . . . He sat up, looked about, and smiled defiantly. There were weapons in every table; the couches would serve him as battering-rams; and he was strong, and there was always increase of might in rage and despair!

Messala himself could not come for he was a cripple like Simonides; still he could move others. Ben-Hur arose, and tried the doors again. Once he called out; the room echoed so that he was startled. He made up his mind to wait before attempting to break out. At length he came to the conclusion that the affair was an accident or mistake. The palace certainly belonged to somebody; it must have care and keeping: and the keeper would come; the evening or the night would bring him.

Half an hour passed. He was sitting at the farther end of the room when a footstep startled him.

"At last she has come!" he thought, with a throb of relief and pleasure, and arose. But the step was heavy, and accompanied with the gride of coarse sandals. The gilded pillars were between him and the door; he advanced quietly and leaned against one of them. Presently he heard the voices of men, one of them rough and guttural. What was said he could not understand, as the language was strange.

After a general survey of the room the strangers were brought into Ben-Hur's view—two men, one very stout, both tall, and both in short tunics. Everything they saw appeared wonderful to them; everything they stopped to examine they touched. The atrium seemed profaned by their presence. At the same time, their assurance pointed to some business; if business, with whom?

With much loud, rough talk they sauntered this way and that, while gradually approaching the pillar by which Ben-Hur was standing. Where a slanted gleam of the sun fell with a glare upon the mosaic floor, a statue attracted their notice. In examining it they stopped in the light.

The mystery surrounding his own presence in the palace had tended to make Ben-Hur nervous. So now, when in the tall, stout stranger he recognized a Northman whom he had known in Rome, and seen crowned only the day before in the Circus as the winning pugilist; when he saw the man's scarred face, and his shoulders of Herculean breadth, a thought of personal danger started a chill along every vein. Here, the opportunity for murder was too perfect to have come by chance. He turned an anxious eye upon the Northman's comrade—young, black-eyed, black-haired, altogether Jewish in appearance; he observed, also, that both the men were dressed exactly as professionals of the arena. Ben-Hur could not be longer in doubt: he had been lured into the palace with design. Out of reach of aid, in this remote privacy, he was to die.

He gazed at them, while the quick flash of instinct, the alarm of self-preservation, told him that the boldest step was now the best one; he must be the aggressor and strike first and with force. Yesterday, by permission of the Lord, he had triumphed; and now he drew faith and strength from the circumstance.

He undid the sash around his waist, and, baring his head and casting off his white Jewish gown, stood forth in an under-tunic not unlike those of the enemy, and was ready, body and mind. Folding his arms, he placed his back against the pillar, and calmly waited.

The examination of the statue was brief. Directly the Northman turned, and said something in the unknown tongue; then both looked at Ben-Hur. A few more words and they advanced towards him.

"Who are you?" he asked in Latin.

The Northman fetched a pugnacious grin. "Barbarians."

"This is the palace of Idernee. Whom seek you? Stand and answer."

The words were spoken in the tone of command. The strangers stopped; and in his turn the Northman asked, "Who are you?"

"A Roman."

The giant broke into a guffaw. "Ha, ha, ha! I have heard how a god once came from a cow licking a salted stone; but not even a god can make a Roman of a Jew."

They moved nearer. "Hold!" said Ben-Hur, quitting the pillar. "One word."

The Saxon folded his immense arms across his breast. "A word! Speak."

"You are Thord the Northman and were *lanista* in Rome."

Thord nodded, his blue eyes wide.

"I was your scholar."

"No," said Thord, shaking his head. "By the beard of Irmin, I had never a Jew to make into a fighting-man."

"But I will prove it. You came here to kill me."

"That is true."

"Then let this man fight me singly, and I will make the proof on his body."

A gleam of humor shone in the Northman's face. He spoke to his companion who made answer; then he replied with the pleasure of a diverted child, "Wait till I say begin."

By repeated touches of his foot, he pushed a couch out on the floor, and proceeded leisurely to stretch his burly form upon it; when perfectly at ease, he said, "Now begin."

Without ado, Ben-Hur walked to his antagonist.

"Defend thyself," he said.

The man put up his hands.

As the two confronted each other in the classic position, they seemed as like as brother. To the stranger's confident smile, Ben-Hur opposed an earnestness which, had his skill been known, would have been accepted fair warning of danger. Both knew the combat was to be mortal.

Ben-Hur feinted with his right hand. The stranger parried,

181

slightly advancing his left arm. Before he could return to guard, Ben-Hur caught him by the wrist in a grip which years at the oar had made terrible as a vise. The surprise was complete, and no time given. To throw himself forward; to push the arm across the man's throat and over his right shoulder, and turn him left side front; to strike surely with the ready left fist at the bare neck under the ear—were but minor divisions of the same act. The man fell without a cry, and lay still.

"Ha! What! By the beard of Irmin!" cried Thord in astonishment, rising to a sitting posture. Then he laughed. "I could not have done it better myself." He viewed Ben-Hur coolly from head to foot, and, rising, faced him with undisguised admiration. "It was *my* trick—the trick I have practised for ten years in the schools of Rome. You are not a Jew. Who are you?"

"You knew Arrius the duumvir?"

"Quintus Arrius? Yes, he was my patron. And I knew his son; he would have made a king gladiator. I taught him the very trick you played on this one here—a trick impossible except to a hand and arm like mine. It has won me many a crown."

"I am that son of Arrius."

Thord drew nearer, and viewed him carefully; then his eyes brightened with genuine pleasure, and, laughing, he held out his hand.

"Ha, ha, ha! He told me I would find a Jew here—killing whom was serving the gods."

"Who told you so?" asked Ben-Hur, taking the hand.

"He—Messala—ha, ha, ha! Last night on his bed he told me between groans."

Ben-Hur saw that the Roman, if he lived, would still be capable and dangerous, and follow him unrelentingly. Revenge remained to sweeten the ruined life; to buy it he must cling to the fortune lost in the wager with Sanballat. Ben-Hur ran the ground over. Why not he resort to the Roman's methods? The man hired to kill him could be hired to strike back! Half yielding, he looked down at his late antagonist lying still, with white upturned face, so like himself. He asked, "Thord, what was Messala to give you for killing me?"

"A thousand sestertii."

"You shall have them; and if you do now what I tell you, I will add three thousand more." The giant reflected aloud. "I won five thousand yesterday; from the Roman—six. Give me four, good Arrius—four more—and I will stand firm for you, though old Thor, my namesake, strike me with his hammer. Make it four, and I will kill the lying patrician, if you

182

say so. I have only to cover his mouth and nose with my hands—thus." He illustrated the process.

"I see," said Ben-Hur. "With ten thousand sestertii you can return to Rome, open a wine-shop near the Great Circus, and live as becomes the first of the *lanistæ*."

The giant's scarred face glowed afresh.

"I will make it four thousand," Ben-Hur continued, "and to earn the money there will be no blood on your hands, Thord. Hear me now. Did not your friend here look like me?"

"I would have said he was an apple from the same tree."

"Well, if I put on his tunic, and dress him in my clothes, and you and I go away together, leaving him here, can you not get your sestertii from Messala all the same? You have only to make him believe that I am dead."

Thord laughed till the tears ran into his mouth.

"Ha, ha, ha! Ten thousand sestertii were never won so easily. And a wine-shop by the Great Circus!—all for a lie without blood in it. Give me thy hand, O son of Arrius. Get on now, and—ha, ha, ha!—if ever you come to Rome, fail not to ask for the wine-shop of Thord the Northman. By the beard of Irmin, you will have the best, if I steal it from Cæsar!"

They shook hands again; after which the exchange of clothes was made. It was arranged that a messenger would go at night to Thord's lodging-place with the four thousand sestertii. When they were done, the giant knocked at the front door; it opened to him; and, passing out of the atrium, he led Ben-Hur into a room adjoining, where the latter completed his attire from the coarse garments of the dead pugilist. They separated in the Omphalus.

"Fail not, O son of Arrius, fail not the wine-shop near the Great Circus! By the beard of Irmin, there was never fortune gained so cheap. The gods keep you!"

Upon leaving the atrium, Ben-Hur gave a last look at the assassin as he lay in the Jewish vestments, and was satisfied. The likeness was striking. If Thord kept faith, the secret would endure forever.

At night, in the house of Simonides, Ben-Hur told the good man all that had taken place in the palace of Idernee; and it was agreed that, after a few days, public inquiry should be set afloat for the discovery of the whereabouts of the son of Arrius. Eventually the matter was to be carried boldly to Maxentius; then, if the secret was sustained both Messala and Gratus would be happy, and Ben-Hur free to go to Jerusalem to search for his lost people.

At the leave-taking, Simonides sat in his chair on the terrace and gave his farewell with the warmth of a father. Esther went with the young man to the head of the steps.

"If I find my mother, Esther, thou shalt go to her at Jerusalem, and be a sister to Tirzah."

And with the words he kissed her.

He crossed the river where he found Ilderim's guide. The horses were brought out.

"This one is thine," said the Arab.

It was Aldebaran, the swiftest and brightest of the sons of Mira, and, next to Sirius, the beloved of the sheik; and Ben-Hur knew the old man's heart came to him along with the gift.

The corpse in the atrium was taken up and buried by night; and, as part of Messala's plan, a courier was sent off to Gratus to make him at rest by the announcement of Ben-Hur's death—this time past question.

And soon, in Rome, a wine-shop was opened near the Circus Maximus, with inscription over the door:

THORD THE NORTHMAN.

# BOOK SIXTH

WITHIN A month from the night Ben-Hur left Antioch to go out with Sheik Ilderim into the desert, Valerius Gratus had been succeeded by Pontius Pilate.

The removal cost Simonides exactly five talents Roman money paid to Sejanus, then in height of power as imperial favorite, the object being to help Ben-Hur, by lessening his exposure while on his mission in Jerusalem. To such pious use the faithful steward put the winnings from Drusus and his associates; all of whom, having paid their wagers, became at once and naturally the enemies of Messala, whose repudiation was still an unsettled question in Rome.

Brief as the time was, already the Jews knew the change of rulers was not for the better.

The cohorts sent to relieve the garrison of Antonia made their entry into the city by night; next morning the first sight that greeted the residents was the walls of the old Tower decorated with military ensigns, which unfortunately consisted of busts of the emperor mixed with eagles and globes. A multitude marched to Cæsarea, where Pilate was lingering, and implored him to remove the detested images. Five days and nights they beset his palace gates; at last he appointed a meeting with them in the Circus. When they were assembled, he encircled them with soldiers; instead of resisting, they offered him their lives. At that, he recalled the images and ensigns to Cæsarea, where Gratus, with more consideration, had kept such abominations housed during the eleven years of his reign.

The worst of men once in a while vary their wickedness

by good acts; so with Pilate. He ordered an inspection of all the prisoners in Judea, and a list of the persons in custody, with a statement of the crimes for which they had been committed. The revelations were astonishing. Hundreds of persons were released against whom there were no accusations; many others came to light who had long been accounted dead; yet more amazing, there was opening of dungeons not merely unknown by the people, but actually forgotten by the authorities.

The Tower of Antonia, occupying the sacred area on Mount Moriah, was originally a castle built by the Macedonians. When Herod came he strengthened its walls and extended them to include offices, barracks, armories, magazines, cisterns, and last, though not least, prisons of all grades. He levelled the solid rock, and tapped it with deep excavations, and built over them; connecting the whole great mass with the Temple by a beautiful colonnade. In such condition the Tower fell at last out of his hands into those of the Romans. All through the administration of Gratus it had been a garrisoned citadel and underground prison terrible to revolutionists. Woe when the cohorts poured from its gates to suppress disorder. Woe not less when a Jew passed the same gates going in under arrest.

The order of the new procurator requiring a report of the persons in custody was promptly executed; and two days had gone since the last unfortunate was brought up for examination. The tabulated statement, ready for forwarding, lay on the table of the tribune in command; ready to go to Pilate, in the palace on Mount Zion.

The tribune was weary and anxious to relax from his duties by watching the Jews over in the courts of the Temple. His clerks shared his impatience.

In the spell of waiting a man appeared in a doorway leading to an adjoining apartment. He rattled a bunch of keys, each heavy as a hammer, and at once attracted the chief's attention.

"Ah, Gesius! come in," the tribune said.

As the new-comer approached the chief's table everybody present observed the expression of alarm and mortification on his face.

"O tribune!" he began, bending now, "I fear to tell what now I bring you."

"A breach of duty, ha, Gesius? Thou mayst laugh at Cæsar, or curse the gods, and live; but if the offence be to the eagles —ah, thou knowest, Gesius—go on!"

"It is now about eight years since Valerius Gratus selected me to be keeper of prisoners here in the Tower," said the

186

man deliberately. "I remember the morning I entered upon the duties of my office. He gave me these keys, numbered to correspond with the number of the cells; they were the badges of my office, he said, and not to be parted with. 'Here are maps of the cells,' said he. There were three of them. 'This one,' he went on, 'shows the arrangement of the upper floor; this second one gives you the second floor; and this last is of the lower floor. I give them to you in trust. Go immediately and visit each cell, and see to its condition. When anything is needed for the security of a prisoner, order it according to your judgment, for you are the master under me, and no other.'

"I turned to go away; he called me back. 'Ah, I forgot,' he said. 'Give me the map of the lower floor.' I gave it to him, and he spread it upon the table. He laid his finger on the one numbered Five. 'There are three men confined in that cell, desperate characters, who by some means got hold of a state secret, and suffer for their curiosity. Accordingly, they are blind and tongueless, and are placed there for life. They shall have nothing but food and drink, to be given them through a hole, which you will find in the wall covered by a slide. One thing more which you shall not forget: The door of their cell—cell number Five—shall never be opened for any purpose, neither to let one in nor out, not even yourself. If they die,' he said, 'the cell shall be their tomb. They were put there to die, and be lost. The cell is leprous. Do you understand?' With that he let me go."

Gesius stopped, and from the breast of his tunic drew three parchments, all much yellowed by time and use; selecting one of them, he spread it upon the table before the tribune, saying, "This is the lower floor."

| Passage | | | | |
|---|---|---|---|---|
| V | IV | III | II | I |

"I see," the tribune replied. "Go on now. The cell marked Five was leprous, Gratus said."

"I would like to ask you a question," remarked the keeper. "Had I not a right, under the circumstances, to believe the map a true one?"

"What else couldst thou?"

"It is not a true one," the keeper said. "It shows but five cells upon the floor, while in all truth there are six!"

187

"Six, sayest thou?"

"I will show you the floor as I believe it to be."

Upon a page Gesius drew the following diagram:

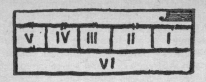

"Thou hast done well," said the tribune, examining the drawing. "I will have the map corrected, and given thee. Come for it in the morning."

"But hear me further, O tribune."

"To-morrow, Gesius, to-morrow."

"That which I have yet to tell will not wait."

The tribune shrugged and resumed his chair.

"I will hurry," said the keeper, humbly, "only let me ask another question. Had I not a right to believe Gratus in what he further told me as to the prisoners in cell number Five—three prisoners of state—blind and without tongues? But, O tribune, that was not true either."

"No!" said the tribune, with returning interest.

"Hear, and judge for yourself. I visited all the cells, beginning with those on the first floor, and ending with those on the lower. The order that the door of number Five should not be opened had been respected; through all the eight years food and drink for three men had been passed through a hole in the wall. I went to the door yesterday, curious to see the wretches, who, against all expectations, had lived so long. The door fell down, rusted from its hinges. Going in, I found but one man, old, blind, tongueless, and naked. His hair dropped in stiffened mats below his waist. His skin was like the parchment there. He held his hands out and the finger-nails curled and twisted like the claws of a bird. I asked him where his companions were. He shook his head in denial. We searched the cell. The floor was dry; so were the walls. If three men had been shut in there, and two of them had died, at least their bones would have endured.

"I think, O tribune, there has been but one prisoner there in the eight years."

The chief regarded the keeper sharply. "Have a care; thou art more than saying Gratus lied."

Gesius bowed, but said, "He might have been mistaken."

"No," said the tribune warmly. "By thine own statement he was right. Didst thou not say but now that for eight years food and drink had been furnished three men?"

The bystanders approved the shrewdness of their chief; yet Gesius did not seem discomfited.

"You have but half the story, O tribune. You know what I did with the man: I sent him to the bath, had him shorn and clothed, then took him to the gate of the Tower, and bade him go free. To-day he came back, and by signs and tears made me understand he wished to return to his cell, and I so ordered. As they were leading him off, by piteous dumb imploration, he insisted I go with with him; and I went. The mystery of the three men stayed in my mind. I was not satisfied about it.

"When we were in the cell again, the prisoner led me to a hole in the inner wall like that through which we passed him his food, and which escaped me yesterday. Still holding my hand, he put his face to the hole and gave a beast-like cry. A sound came faintly back. I was astonished, and drew him away, and called out, 'Ho, here!' At first there was no answer. I called again, and heard these words, 'Be thou praised, O Lord!' And I asked, 'Who are you?' and had reply, 'A woman of Israel, entombed here with her daughter. Help us quickly, or we die.' I told them to be of cheer, and hurried here to know your will."

The tribune arose hastily. "Thou wert right, Gesius," he said, "and I see now. The map was a lie, and so was the tale of the three men. There have been better Romans than Valerius Gratus."

"Yes," said the keeper. "I gleaned from the prisoner that he had given the women of the food he had received.

"It is accounted for," replied the tribune, and observing the countenances of his friends, and reflecting it that would be well to have witnesses, he added, "Let us rescue the women. Come all."

Gesius was pleased. "We will have to pierce the wall," he said. "I found where a door had been, but it was filled solidly with stones and mortar."

The tribune turned to a clerk, "Send workmen after me with tools. Make haste; but hold the report, for it will have to be corrected."

## Chapter II.

The morning of their seizure, eight years before, Ben-Hur's mother and sister had been carried to the Tower, where Gratus proposed to put them out of the way. He had chosen the tower as more immediately in his own keeping, and cell VI because, first, it could be better lost than any other, and, secondly, it was infected with leprosy; for these prisoners were to be put in a place to die. They were, accordingly, taken down by slaves in the night-time, when there was no witness; then the same slaves walled up the door, after which they were sent away never to be heard of more. That they might linger, Gratus selected a convict who had been made blind and tongueless, and sank him in the only connecting cell, there to serve them with food and drink. So, with a cunning partly due to Messala, under color of punishing a brood of assassins, the two smoothed a path to confiscation of the estate of the Hurs, of which no portion ever reached the imperial coffers.

As the last step in the scheme, Gratus summarily removed the old keeper of the prison; because, knowing the underground floors as he did, it would be next to impossible to keep the transaction from him. Then, with masterly ingenuity, the procurator had new maps drawn for delivery to a new keeper, with the omission, as we have seen, of cell VI. Thus he accomplished the design—the cell and its unhappy tenants were alike lost.

Before the sound of the keeper's voice came to them, the two women were grouped close by a narrow ventilating aperture; one was seated, the other half-reclining against her; there was nothing between them and the bare rock. The light, slanting upward, struck them with ghastly effect; they were without vesture or covering.

Where the two were thus grouped the stony floor was polished shining-smooth. How much of the eight years had they spent in front of the aperture, nursing their hope of rescue by that timid yet friendly ray of light? When brightness came creeping in, they knew it was dawn; when it began to fade, they knew the world was hushing for the night, which could not be anywhere in the world so utterly dark as with them. Through that crevice they went to the world in thought, and passed the weary time going up and down as spirits go, looking and asking, the one for her son, the other for her brother. On the seas they sought him, and on the islands of the seas; to-day he was in this city, to-morrow in that other; and everywhere, and at all times, he was a flitting sojourner; for, as they lived waiting for him, they knew that he lived looking for them. And always they told each other, "While he lives, we shall not be forgotten; so long as he remembers us, there is hope!"

The mother had been beautiful as a woman, the daughter beautiful as a child; but now their hair was long, unkempt, and strangely white; they were enduring the tortures of hunger and thirst, not having had food or drink since the convict had been taken away yesterday.

Tirzah, reclining against her mother in half embrace, moaned piteously.

"Be quiet, Tirzah. They will come. God is good. We have forgotten not to pray at every sounding of the trumpets in the Temple. Somebody will come to us. Let us have faith. God is good."

"I will try to be strong, mother," she said, "to live for you and my brother! But my tongue burns, my lips scorch."

There was in the voices an unexpected tone, sharp, dry, metallic, unnatural.

The mother drew the daughter closer to her breast, and said, "I dreamed about him last night, and saw him as plainly, Tirzah, as I see you. I thought we were in the Woman's Court just before the Gate Beautiful; and he came and stood in the shade of the Gate. I knew he was looking for us, and stretched my arms to him, and ran, calling him. He heard me and saw me, but he did not know me. In a moment he was gone."

"Would it not be so, mother, if we were to meet him? We are so changed."

"It might be so; but—" The mother's head drooped, and her face knit with pain—"but we could make ourselves known to him."

Tirzah tossed her arms and moaned again. "Water, mother, water."

Hardly knowing what she was doing, speaking aimlessly, because speak she must, she said again, "Patience, Tirzah; they are coming—they are almost here."

She thought she heard a sound over by the little door in the partition-wall and she was not mistaken. A moment, and the cry of the convict rang through the cell. Tirzah heard it also; and they both arose, still keeping hold of each other.

"Ho there!" they heard; and then, "Who are you?"

The voice was strange. Except from Tirzah, they were the first and only words the mother had heard in eight years. The change was mighty—from death to life—and instantly!

"A woman of Israel, entombed with her daughter. Help us quickly, or we die."

"Be of cheer. I will return."

Soon she heard another sound in another place, as of blows on the wall—blows quick, ringing, and delivered with iron tools. She did not speak, nor did Tirzah, but they listened, knowing that a way to liberty was being made for them. Their eyes were fixed upon the spot whence the sounds proceeded and they dared not look away, lest the work should cease and they be returned to despair.

Each instant the blows sounded more plainly; now and then a piece fell with a crash; and liberty came nearer. Presently the workmen could be heard speaking. Then through a crevice flashed the red ray of torches. Into the darkness it cut beautiful as if from a spear of the morning.

A block fell inside, and another—then a great mass, and the door was open. A man grimed with mortar and stonedust stepped in, and stopped, holding a torch above his head. Others followed with torches, and stood aside for the tribune to enter.

The tribune stopped, because they fled from him partly in shame; nor yet from shame alone. From the obscurity of their partial hiding he heard these words, the saddest, most dreadful, most utterly despairing of the human tongue:

"Come not near us—unclean, unclean!"

The men flared their torches while they stared at each other.

"Unclean, unclean!" came from the corner again, a slow tremulous wail of sorrow.

So the mother performed her duty, and in the moment realized that the freedom she had prayed for and dreamed of, fruit of scarlet and gold seen afar, was an empty futile hope. She and Tirzah were lepers.

To be a leper was to be treated as dead—to be excluded from the city as a corpse; to be spoken to by the best beloved only at a distance; to dwell with none but lepers; to be denied the rites of the Temple and the synagogue; to go about in rent garments and with covered mouth, except when crying, "Unclean, unclean!" to find refuge in the wilderness or in abandoned tombs; to become a materialized spectre of Hinnom and Gehenna; to be at all times less a living offence to others than a breathing torment to self; afraid to die, yet without hope except in death.

Once—she could not have told the day or the year, for down in the haunted hell even time was lost—once the mother felt a dry scurf in the palm of her right hand, a trifle which she tried to wash away. It clung; yet she thought but little of the sign till Tirzah complained that she, too, was attacked in the same way. The supply of water was scant, and they denied themselves drink that they might use it as a curative. At length the whole hand was attacked; the skin cracked open, the finger-nails loosened from the flesh. There was not much pain, chiefly a steadily increasing discomfort. Later their lips began to parch and seam. One day the mother, who struggled against the impurities of the dungeon with all ingenuity, thinking the malady was taking hold on Tirzah's face, led her to the light, and saw with anguish and terror that the young girl's eyebrows were white as snow.

Speechless, motionless, the mother was capable of but one thought—leprosy!

When she began to think, it was not of herself, but of her child, and, mother-like, her natural tenderness turned to courage. So she made ready for the last sacrifice of perfect heroism. She buried her knowledge in her heart; hopeless

192

herself, she redoubled her devotion to Tirzah, and with wonderful ingenuity continued to keep the daughter ignorant of what they were beset with, and even hopeful that it was nothing. She repeated her little games, and retold her stories, and invented new ones, and listened with pleasure to the songs she would have from Tirzah, while from her own wasting lips the sacred psalms served to keep alive in them both the recollection of the God who would seem to have abandoned them.

Slowly, steadily, with horrible certainty, the disease spread, after a while bleaching their heads white, eating holes in their lips and eyelids, and covering their bodies with scales; then it fell to their throats, shrilling their voices, and to their joints, hardening the tissues and cartileges. Slowly, and as the mother well knew, past a remedy, it was affecting their lungs and arteries and bones, at each advance making the sufferers more loathsome; and so it would continue till death, which might yet be years before them.

The day came at last when the mother, under impulsion of duty, told Tirzah the name of their ailment; and the two, in agony of despair, prayed that the end might come quickly.

But one tie to earth remained to them; unmindful of their own loneliness, they kept up a certain spirit by talking and dreaming of Ben-Hur. The mother promised reunion with him to the sister, and she to the mother, not doubting, either of them, that he was equally faithful to them, and would be equally happy of the meeting. And with the spinning and re-spinning of this slender thread they found pleasure, and excused their not dying. . . .

Not all the joy over the prospect of release could keep the mother blind to its consequences now that it was at hand. If she went near the house called home, she must stop at the gate and cry, "Unclean, unclean!" She must go about with the love alive in her breast strong as ever, yet knowing that the son of whom she had so constantly thought must stand afar. If he held out his hands to her and called "Mother, mother," for very love of him she must fend him off. And this other child, before whom, in want of other covering, she was spreading her long, tangled locks, she must continue as sole partner of her blasted life.

"Who are you?" the tribune asked.

"Two women dying of hunger and thirst. Yet come not near us, nor touch the floor or the wall. Unclean, unclean!"

"Give my thy story, woman—thy name, when thou wert put here, by whom, and for what."

"There was once in this city of Jerusalem a Prince Ben-Hur, the friend of all generous Romans, and who had Cæsar for his friend. I am his widow, and this one with me is his child. How may I tell you for what we were sunk here, when

I do not know, unless it was because we were rich? Valerius Gratus can tell you who our enemy was, and when our imprisonment began. I cannot. See to what we have been reduced—oh, see, and have pity!"

The air was heavy with the pest and the smoke of the torches, yet the Roman called one of the torch-bearers to his side, and wrote the answer nearly word for word. It was terse and comprehensive, containing at once a history, an accusation, and a prayer.

"Thou shalt have relief, woman," he said, closing the tablets. "I will send thee food and drink. Make preparation, and to-night I will have thee taken to the gate of the Tower, and set free. Thou knowest the law. Farewell."

He spoke to the men, and went out the door.

About the middle of the first watch, the two were conducted to the gate, and turned into the street. So the Roman quit himself of them, and in the city of their fathers they were once more free.

Up to the stars, twinkling as of old, they looked; then they asked themselves,

"What next? And where to?"

## CHAPTER III.

ABOUT THE hour Gesius, the keeper, made his appearance before the tribune in the Tower of Antonia, Ben-Hur was climbing the eastern face of Mount Olivet. The road was rough and dusty, and vegetation on that side burned brown, for it was the dry season in Judea.

He proceeded slowly, looking often to his right and left, with the expression, half of pleasure, half of inquiry; as if he were saying, "I am glad to be with you again; let me see how you are changed." When at length he drew near the summit, he quickened his step, unmindful of fatigue, and hurried on without pause or turning of the face. There he came to a dead stop, arrested as if by a strong hand. His cheeks flushed, his breath quickened at the city of Jerusalem that lay before him.

Though he had seen Rome to familiarity, here he was gratified. The sight filled a measure of pride which would have made him drunk with vainglory but for the thought, princely as the city was, it no longer belonged to his countrymen; the worship in the Temple was by permission of strangers; the hill where David dwelt was an office from which the chosen of the Lord were wrung and wrung for taxes, and scourged for very deathlessness of faith. These however were pleasures and griefs of patriotism common enough; in addition Ben-Hur brought with him a personal history which the spectacle below freshened and vivified.

The sun stooped low, rimming the walls and towers with the brightness of gold. Then it disappeared as with a plunge. The quiet turned Ben-Hur's thought homeward. There was a point in the sky a little north of the Holy of Holies; under it, straight as a lead-line would have dropped, lay his father's house, if yet the house endured.

He thought of the duty that was bringing him to Jerusalem.

Out in the desert while with Ilderim, looking for strong places and acquainting himself with it generally, as a soldier studies a country in which he has projected a campaign, a messenger came one evening with the news that Gratus was removed, and Pontius Pilate sent to take his place.

Messala was disabled and believed him dead; Gratus was powerless and gone; why should Ben-Hur longer defer the search for his mother and sister? There was nothing to fear now. If he could not himself see into the prisons of Judea, he could examine them through the eyes of others. If the lost were found, Pilate could have no motive in holding them in custody—none, at least, which could not be overcome by purchase. If found, he would carry them to a place of safety, and then he could give himself more entirely to the King Who Was Coming. That night he counselled with Ilderim, and obtained his assent. Three Arabs came with him to Jericho, where he left them and the horses, and proceeded alone and on foot. Malluch was to meet him in Jerusalem.

In view of the future, it was advisable to keep himself in hiding from the authorities, particularly the Romans. Malluch was shrewd and trusty; the very man to charge with the conduct of the investigation.

Where to begin, was the first point. He had no clear idea about it. His wish was to commence with the Tower of Antonia. Tradition planted the gloomy pile over a labyrinth of prison-cells, which kept it a terror to the Jewish fancy. A burial, such as his people had been subjected to, might be possible there. If his mother and Tirzah were not there now, but had been, some record must remain, a clew which had only to be followed faithfully to the end.

Under this inclination, moreover, there was a hope which he could not forego. From Simonides he knew Amrah, the Egyptian nurse, was living. During the years Simonides had kept her supplied; so she was there now, sole occupant of the great house, which Gratus had not been able to sell. The story of its rightful owners sufficed to secure the property from strangers, whether purchasers or mere occupants. People going to and fro passed it with whispers. Its reputation was that of a haunted house; derived probably from the infrequent glimpses of poor old Amrah, sometimes on the roof, sometimes in a latticed window. Now, if he could get to her, Ben-Hur fancied she could help him to knowledge which, though faint, might yet be serviceable. Anyhow, sight of her in that place, so endeared by recollections, would be to him a pleasure next to finding his mother and sister.

So, first he would go to the old house, and look for Amrah.

Thus resolved, he began descent of the Mount. In due time, he passed by Gethsemane on into the city through the Fish Gate.

## CHAPTER IV.

IT WAS dark when Ben-Hur turned into a narrow lane leading to the south. A few of the people whom he met saluted him. The houses on both sides were low, dark, and cheerless; the doors all closed: from the roofs, occasionally, he heard women crooning to children. With feelings sinking lower, he came presently to the deep reservoir now known as the Pool of Bethesda, in which the water reflected the over-pending sky. Looking up, he beheld the northern wall of the Tower of Antonia, a black frowning heap reared into the dim steel-gray sky. He halted as if challenged by a threatening sentinel.

The Tower stood up so high, and seemed so vast, resting apparently upon foundations so sure! If his mother were there in living burial, what could he do for her? An army might beat the stony face with ballista and ram, and be laughed at. Against him alone the gigantic southeast turret looked down in the self-containment of a hill.

In doubt and misgiving, he turned into the street in front of the Tower and followed it slowly on to the west.

The old formal salutation which he received from the few people who passed him had never sounded so pleasantly. Presently all the eastern sky began to silver and shine, and the tall towers on Mount Zion emerged floating, as it were, above the yawning blackness of the valley below.

He came, at length, to his father's house.

At the gate on the north side of the old house Ben-Hur stopped. In the corners the wax used in the sealing-up was still plainly seen, and nailed across the gate doors was the board with the inscription—

THIS IS THE PROPERTY OF
THE EMPEROR.

Nobody had gone in or out the gate since the dreadful day of the separation. Should he knock as of old? It was useless, he knew it; yet he could not resist the temptation. Amrah might hear, and look out of one of the windows on that side. Taking a stone, he mounted the broad stone step, and tapped three times. A dull echo replied. He tried again, louder than before; and again, pausing each time to listen. The silence was mocking. Retiring into the street, he watched the windows; but they, too, were lifeless. The parapet on the roof was defined sharply against the brightening sky; nothing could have stirred upon it unseen by him, and nothing did stir.

Silently, then, he stole round to the south. There, too, the gate was sealed and inscribed. The mellow August moon, pouring over the crest of Olivet, since termed the Mount of Offence, brought the lettering boldly out; and he was filled with rage. All he could do was to wrench the board from its nailing, and hurl it into the ditch. Then he sat upon the step, and prayed for the New King, and that his coming might be hastened. As his blood cooled, insensibly he yielded to the fatigue of long travel in the summer heat, and sank down lower, and, at last, slept.

About that time two women came down the street from the direction of the Tower of Antonia, approaching the palace of the Hurs. They advanced stealthily, with timid steps, pausing often to listen. At the corner of the rugged pile one said to the other, in a low voice:

"This is it, Tirzah!"

And Tirzah, after a look, caught her mother's hand, and leaned upon her heavily, sobbing, but silent.

"Let us go on, my child, because when morning comes they will put us out of the gate of the city, to return no more."

Tirzah sank almost to the stones. "Ah, yes!" she said, between sobs; "I forgot. I had the feeling of going home. But we have no home; we belong to the dead!"

The mother stooped and raised her tenderly, saying, "We have nothing to fear. Let us go on."

And, creeping in close to the rough wall, they glided on, like two ghosts, till they came to the gate, before which they also paused. Seeing the board, they stopped upon the stone and read the inscription: "This is the Property of the Emperor."

Then the mother clasped her hands, and, with upraised eyes, moaned. "Oh, Tirzah, the poor are dead! Your brother is dead! They took everything from him—everything—even this house!"

"Poor!" said Tirzah vacantly.

"He will never be able to help us. To-morrow—to-morrow, my child, we must find a seat by the wayside, and beg alms, beg, or—"

She caught Tirzah's hand as she spoke, and hastened to the west corner of the house, keeping close to the wall. They shrank from the moonlight, which lay exceedingly bright over the whole south front, and along a part of the street. Casting one look back and up to the windows on the west side, she stepped out into the light, drawing Tirzah after her: and the extent of their affliction was then to be seen—on their lips and cheeks, in their bleared eyes, in their cracked hands; especially in the long, snaky locks, stiff with loathsome ichor, and, like their eyebrows, ghastly white. Nor was it possible to have told which was mother, which daughter; both alike seemed witch-old.

"Wait!" the mother whispered. "Some one is lying upon the step—a man. Let us go round him."

They crossed to the opposite side of the street quickly, and in the shade there, moved on till they stopped before the gate.

"He is asleep, Tirzah! Stay here, and I will try the gate."

The mother stole noiselessly across, and touched the wicket; she never knew if it yielded, for that moment the man sighed, and, turned restlessly, so that the face was left up-turned in the moonlight. She looked down at it and started; then looked again, stooping a little, and arose and clasped her hands and raised her eyes to heaven. Then she ran back to Tirzah.

"As the Lord liveth, the man is my son—thy brother!" she whispered. The mother caught · her hand eagerly. "Come!" she said, "let us look at him together—once more—only once."

They crossed the street hand in hand ghostly-quick, ghostly-still. When their shadows fell upon him, they stopped. One of his hands was lying out upon the step palm up. Tirzah fell upon her knees, and would have kissed it; but the mother drew her back.

"Not for thy life; not for thy life! Unclean, unclean!" she whispered.

Tirzah shrank from him, as if he were the leprous one. She knelt down, and, crawling to his feet, touched the sole of one of his sandals with her lips, yellow with the dust of the street—and touched it again and again; and her soul was in the kisses.

He stirred, and tossed his hand. They moved back, but heard him mutter in his dream, "Mother! Amrah! Where is—"

He fell off into the deep sleep.

Tirzah stared wistfully. Almost the mother wished he might waken.

He had asked for her; she was not forgotten; in his sleep he was thinking of her. Was it not enough?

Presently the mother beckoned to Tirzah, and they arose, and taking one more look, as if to print his image past fading, hand in hand they crossed the street. Back in the shade of the wall, they retired and knelt, looking at him, waiting for him to wake.

By-and-by, another woman appeared at the corner of the palace. The two in the shade saw her plainly in the light; a small figure, bent, dark-skinned, gray-haired, dressed neatly in servant's garb, and carrying a basket of vegetables.

At sight of the man upon the step the new-comer stopped; then, as if decided, she walked on—very lightly as she drew near the sleeper. Passing round him, she went to the gate, slid the wicket latch easily to one side, and put her hand in the opening. One of the broad boards in the left valve swung ajar without noise. She put the basket through, and was about to follow, when, yielding to curiosity, she lingered to have one look at the stranger.

The spectators across the street heard a low exclamation, and saw the woman bend closer down, clasp her hands, gaze wildly around, stoop and raise the hand and kiss it fondly—that which they wished so mightily to do, but dared not.

Awakened, Ben-Hur instinctively withdrew the hand; as he did so, his eyes met the woman's. "Amrah! O Amrah, is it thou?" he said.

The good nurse made no answer in words, but fell upon his neck crying for joy.

Gently he put her arms away, and, lifting the dark face wet with tears, kissed it, his joy only a little less than hers. Then those across the way heard him say, "Mother—Tirzah—O Amrah, tell me of them!"

Amrah cried afresh.

So entreated, Amrah only wept the more.

"Wert thou going in?" he asked, presently, seeing the board swung back. "Come, then. I will go with thee." He arose as he spoke. "The Romans—the curse of the Lord upon them!—the Romans lied. The house is mine. Rise, Amrah, and let us go in."

A moment and they were gone, leaving the two in the shade to behold the gate staring blankly at them—the gate which they might not ever more enter. They nestled together in the dust.

Next morning they were found, and driven out the city with stones.

"Begone! Ye are of the dead; go to the dead!"

So they went forth.

CHAPTER V.

THE BLUFF FACE of the hill of Evil Counsel opposite the city on the southeast is seamed and pitted with tombs which have been immemorially the dwelling-places of lepers. There they set up their government and established their society; there they founded a city and dwelt by themselves, avoided as the accursed of God.

The second morning after Ben-Hur's mother and sister had been driven from the city, Amrah drew near the well En-rogel, and seated herself upon a stone. She brought with her a water-jar and a basket, the contents of the latter covered with a snow-white napkin. Placing them on the ground at her side, she loosened the shawl which fell from her head, knit her fingers together in her lap, and gazed demurely up to where the hill drops steeply down into the Potter's Field.

It was very early, and she was the first to arrive at the well. Soon, however, a man came bringing a rope and a leathern bucket. Saluting the little dark-faced woman, he undid the rope, fixed it to the bucket, and waited customers. Others who chose to do so might draw water for themselves; he was a professional in the business, and for a *gerah* would fill the largest jar the stoutest woman could carry.

Seeing the jar, the man asked after a while if Amrah wished it filled; she answered him civilly, "Not now"; whereupon he gave her no more attention. When the dawn was fairly defined over Olivet, his patrons began to arrive, and he had all he could do to attend to them. All the time she kept her seat, looking intently up at the hill.

Her custom had been to go to market after nightfall. Stealing out unobserved, she would seek the shops over by the Fish Gate, make her purchases of meat and vegetables, and return and shut herself up again.

She had nothing to tell Ben-Hur of her mistress or Tirzah —nothing. He would have had her move to a place not so lonesome; she refused. She would have had him take his own room again, which was just as he had left it; but the danger of discovery was too great, and he wished above all things to avoid inquiry. He would come and see her often as possible. Coming in the night, he would also go away in the night. She was compelled to be satisfied, and at once occupied herself contriving ways to make him happy. That he was a man now did not occur to her; nor did it enter her mind that he might have put by his boyish tastes; to please him, she thought to go on her old round of services. He used to be fond of confections; she remembered the things in that line which

200

delighted him most, and resolved to make them, and have a supply always ready when he came. Could anything be happier? So next night, earlier than usual, she stole out with her basket, and went over to the Fish Gate Market. Wandering about, seeking the best honey, she chanced to hear a man telling a story.

The narrator was one of the men who had held torches for the commandant of the Tower of Antonia when, down in cell VI, the Hurs were found. The particulars of the finding were all told, and she heard them, with the names of the prisoners, and the widow's account of herself.

As in a dream, Amrah listened to the recital, made her purchases, and returned home. What a happiness she had in store for her boy!

She put the basket away, now laughing, now crying. Suddenly she stopped and thought. It would kill him to be told that his mother and Tirzah were lepers. He would go through the awful city over on the Hill of Evil Counsel—into each infected tomb he would go without rest, asking for them, and the disease would catch him, and their fate would be his. She wrung her hands. What should she do? Then she came to a singular conclusion.

The lepers, she knew, were accustomed of mornings to come down from their hill, and take a supply of water for the day from the well En-rogel. Bringing their jars, they would set them on the ground and wait, standing afar until they were filled. To that the mistress and Tirzah must come; for the law was inexorable, and admitted no distinction. A rich leper was no better than a poor one.

So Amrah decided not to speak to Ben-Hur of the story she had heard, but go alone to the well and wait. Hunger and thirst would drive the unfortunates there, and she believed she could recognize them at sight. If not, they might recognize her.

Meantime Ben-Hur came, and they talked much. To-morrow Malluch would arrive; then the search should be immediately begun. He was impatient to be about it. To amuse himself until then he would visit the sacred places in the vicinity.

When he was gone she busied herself in the preparation of things good to eat, applying her utmost skill to the work. At the approach of day, she filled the basket, selected a jar, and took the road to En-rogel.

Shortly after sunrise, when business at the well was most pressing, and the drawer of water most hurried; when half a dozen buckets were in use at the same time, everybody making haste to get away before the cool of the morning melted into the heat of the day, the tenantry of the hill began to appear and move about the doors of their tombs. Somewhat later they were discernible in groups, of which not a few were children. They came momentarily around the turn of the bluff—women with jars upon their shoulders, old and very feeble men hobbling along on staffs and crutches. Some leaned upon the shoulders of others; a few—the utterly helpless—lay, like heaps of rags, upon litters.

From her seat by the well Amrah kept watch upon the spectral groups. That they were there upon the hill she had no doubt; that they must come down and near she knew; when the people at the well were all served they would come.

Now, at the base of the bluff there was a tomb which had attracted Amrah by its wide gaping. A stone of large dimensions stood near its mouth. The sun looked into it through the hottest hours of the day, and altogether it seemed uninhabitable by anything living, unless, perchance, by some wild dogs returning from scavenger duty down in Gehenna. Thence, however, two women came, one half supporting, half leading, the other. They were both white-haired; both looked old; but their garments were not rent, and they gazed about them as if the locality were new. Amrah thought she even saw them shrink terrified at the spectacle offered by the hideous assemblage of which they found themselves part.

The two moved slowly, painfully, and with much fear towards the well, whereat several voices were raised to stop them; yet they kept on. The drawer of water picked up some pebbles, and made ready to drive them back. The company cursed them. The greater company on the hill shouted shrilly, "Unclean, unclean!"

"Surely," thought Amrah of the two, as they kept coming, "they are strangers to the usage of lepers."

She arose, and went to meet them, taking the basket and jar. The alarm at the well immediately subsided.

"What a fool," said one, laughing, "what a fool to give good bread to the dead!"

Could that be the mistress she loved—whose image of matronly loveliness she had treasured in memory so faithfully? And that the Tirzah she had nursed through babyhood! The soul of the woman sickened at the sight.

"These are old women," she said to herself. "I never saw them before. I will go back." She turned away.

"Amrah," said one of the lepers.

The Egyptian hastily set down the jar, and looked back, trembling. "Who called me?" she asked. The servant's wondering eyes settled upon the speaker's face. "Who are you?" she cried.

"We are they you are seeking."

Amrah fell upon her knees. "O my mistress, my mistress!

202

As I have made your God my God, be he praised that he has led me to you!"

And upon her knees the overwhelmed woman began moving forward.

"Stay, Amrah! Come not nearer. Unclean, unclean!"

The words sufficed. Amrah fell upon her face, sobbing. Suddenly she arose upon her knees again.

"O my mistress, where is Tirzah?"

"Here I am, Amrah, here! Will you not bring me a little water?"

Putting back the hair fallen over her face, Amrah arose and went to the basket and uncovered it. "See," she said, "here are bread and meat."

She would have spread the napkin upon the ground, but the mistress spoke again.

"No, Amrah. Those yonder may stone you, and refuse us drink. Leave the basket with me. Take up the jar and fill it, and bring it here. We will carry them to the tomb with us. For this day you will then have rendered all the service that is lawful. Haste, Amrah."

The people who had watched all this made way for the servant, and even helped her fill the jar, so piteous was her grief.

"Who are they?" a woman asked.

Amrah answered, "They used to be good to me."

Raising the jar upon her shoulder, she hurried back. Placing the water by the basket, she stepped back, and stood off a little way.

"Thank you, Amrah," said the mistress, taking the articles. "This is good of you."

"Is there nothing more I can do?" asked Amrah.

The mother's hand was upon the jar, and she was fevered with thirst; yet she paused, and, rising, said firmly, "Yes, I know that Judah has come home. I saw him at the gate night before last asleep on the step. I saw you wake him."

"O my mistress! You saw it, and did not come!"

"That would have been to kill him. I can never take him in my arms again. I can never kiss him more. O Amrah, Amrah, you love him, I know!"

"Yes," said the nurse. "I would die for him."

"Prove to me what you say, Amrah."

"I am ready."

"Then you shall not tell him where we are or that you have seen us—only that, Amrah."

"But he is looking for you. He has come from afar to find you."

"He must not find us. He shall not become what we are. Hear, Amrah? You shall bring us the little we need—not long

203

now. You shall come every morning and evening thus, and—and you shall tell us of him, Amrah; but to him you shall say nothing of us."

"The burden will be heavy, O my mistress, and hard to bear," said Amrah.

"How much harder would it be to see him as we are," the mother answered as she gave the basket to Tirzah. "Come again this evening," she said taking up the water and starting for the tomb.

Amrah waiting until they had disappeared; then she took the road home.

## CHAPTER VI.

LITTLE TIME had been lost in consultation upon the arrival of Malluch. The latter began the search at the Tower of Antonia, and began it boldly, by a direct inquiry of the tribune commanding. He gave the officer a history of the Hurs, and all the particulars of the accident to Gratus, describing the affair as wholly without criminality. The object of the quest now, he said, was if any of the unhappy family were discovered alive to carry a petition to the feet of Cæsar, praying restitution of the estate and return to their civil rights. Such a petition, he had no doubt, would result in an investigation by the imperial order, a proceeding of which the friends of the family had no fear.

In reply the tribune told of the discovery of the women in the Tower, and permitted a reading of the memorandum he had taken of their account of themselves.

Malluch thereupon hurried to Ben-Hur.

The pain was too deep for expression. He sat still a long time, with pallid face and laboring heart. One moment he was torn by a virtuous rage of sorrow, next by a longing for vengeance.

"I must look for them. There is but one place for them to go."

Together they went to the gate opposite the Hill of Evil Counsel, immemorially the lepers' begging-ground. There they stayed all day, giving alms, asking for the two women, and offering rich rewards for their discovery. So they did in repetition day after day through the remainder of the fifth month, and all the sixth. There was diligent scouring of the dread city on the hill by lepers to whom the rewards offered were mighty incentives, for they were only dead in law. Over and over again the gaping tomb down by the well was invaded, and its tenants subjected to inquiry; but they kept their secret fast. The result was failure. And now, the morning of the first day of the seventh month, the extent of the additional information gained was that not long before two leprous women had been stoned from the Fish Gate by the authorities. A little pressing of the clew, together with some shrewd comparison of dates, led to the sad assurance that the sufferers were the Hurs, and left the old question darker than ever. Where were they? And what had become of them?

"It was not enough that my people should be made lepers," said the son, with increasing bitterness, "that was not enough. They must be stoned from their native city! My mother is dead; she has wandered to the wilderness! Tirzah is dead; I alone am left. And for what? How long, O God, thou Lord God of my fathers, how long shall this Rome endure?"

Angry, hopeless, vengeful, he entered the court of the khan where he lodged and found it crowded with people come in during the night. While he ate his breakfast, he listened. To one party he was specially attracted. They were mostly young, active, hardy men, in manner and speech provincial. In their look, the certain indefinable air, the pose of the head, glance of the eye, there was a spirit which did not, as a rule, belong to the outward seeming of the 'ower orders of Jerusalem; the spirit thought to be engendered by the freedom of life in mountainous districts. They were Galileans, in the city for various purposes, but chiefly to take part in the Feast of Trumpets, set for that day. They interested him at once, as hailing from the region in which he hoped to find readiest support for his projected work.

While observing them, visualizing the achievements possible to a legion of such spirits disciplined in the severe Roman style, a man came into the court, his eyes bright with excitement.

"Why are you here?" he said to the Galileans. "The rabbis and elders are going from the Temple to see Pilate. Come, make haste, and let us go with them."

"To see Pilate! For what?"

"They have discovered a conspiracy. Pilate's new aqueduct is to be paid for with money of the Temple."

"What, with the sacred treasure? It is Corban—money of God. Let him touch a shekel of it if he dare!"

"Come," cried the messenger. "We may be needed. Make haste!"

As if the thought and the act were one, there was quick putting-away of useless garments, and the party stood forth bareheaded, and in the short sleeveless under-tunics they were used to wearing as reapers in the field and boatmen on the lake—the garb in which they climbed the hills following the herds, and plucked the ripened vintage, careless of the sun.

Then Ben-Hur spoke. "Men of Galilee," he said, "I am a son of Judah. Will you take me in your company?"

"You seem stout enough. Come along."

Ben-Hur put off his outer garments. "You think there may be fighting?" he asked quietly, as he tightened his girdle.

"Yes, with the guard."

"Legionaries?"

"Whom else can a Roman trust?"

"What weapons have you to fight with?"

They looked at him silently.

"Well," he continued, "we will have to do the best we can; but had we not better choose a leader? The legionaries always have one, and so are able to act with one mind."

The Galileans stared more curiously, as if the idea were new to them. "Let us at least agree to stay together," he said. "Now, let us go."

They passed rapidly round the Akra district to the Tower of Mariamne, which was a short way to the grand gate of the Praetorium on Mount Zion. In going, they were joined by people like themselves stirred to wrath by news of the proposed desecration. When, at length, they reached the gate of the Prætorium, the procession of elders and rabbis had passed in with a large following, leaving a greater crowd clamoring outside.

A centurion kept the entrance with a guard drawn up full armed under the marble battlements. The sun struck the soldiers fervidly on helmet and shield; but they remained indifferent alike to its heat and to the imprecations of the rabble. Through the open bronze gates a current of citizens poured in, while a much lesser one poured out.

"What is going on?" one of the Galileans asked an outcomer.

"Nothing," was the reply. "The rabbis are before the door of the palace asking to see Pilate. He has refused to come out. They have sent one to tell him they will not go away till he has heard them. They are waiting."

"Let us go in," said Ben-Hur, in his quiet way, seeing what his companions probably did not, that there was not only a disagreement between the suitors and the governor, but an issue already joined.

Turning to the right, the party proceeded a short distance to a spacious square, on which stood the residence of the governor. An excited multitude filled the square. Every face was directed towards a portico built over a broad closed doorway. Under the portico there was another array of legionaries.

The throng was so close that the friends could not advance;

they remained in the rear, observers of what was going on. About the portico they could see the high turbans of the rabbis, whose impatience communicated at times to the mass behind them; a cry was frequent: "Pilate, if thou be a governor, come forth, come forth!"

An hour passed, and though Pilate deigned them no answer, the rabbis and crowd remained. Noon came, bringing a shower from the west; by now the multitude was larger and much noiser, and the feeling more decidedly angry. The shouting for Pilate to appear grew louder; often it was with disrespectful variations. Meanwhile Ben-Hur held his Galilean friends together. He judged the pride of the Roman would eventually get the better of his discretion. Pilate was but waiting for the people to furnish him an excuse for resort to violence.

And at last the end came. In the midst of the assemblage they heard the sound of blows, succeeded instantly by yells of pain and rage, and a most furious commotion. The venerable men in front of the portico faced about aghast. The people in the rear at first pushed forward; in the centre, the effort was to get out; and for a short time the pressure of opposing forces was like that of a giant vise. A thousand voices made inquiry, raised all at once; as no one had time to answer, the surprise speedily became a panic.

Ben-Hur kept his senses. "You cannot see?" he said to one of the Galileans.

"No."

He caught the man about the middle, and lifted him bodily.

"I see now," said the man. "There are some armed with clubs, and they are beating the people. They are dressed like Jews. But they are Romans in disguise. Their clubs fly like flails! There, I saw a rabbi struck down—an old man! They spare nobody!"

Ben-Hur let the man down. "Men of Galilee," he said, "it is a trick of Pilate's. Now, if you will do what I say, we will get even with the club-men."

"Yes, yes!" they answered.

"Let us go back to the trees by the gate."

They ran back; and, by throwing their united weight upon the limbs, tore them from the trunks. In a brief time they, too, were armed. Returning, at the corner of the square they met the crowd rushing madly for the gate. Behind, the clamor continued—a medley of shrieks, groans, and execrations.

"To the wall!" Ben-Hur shouted. "To the wall—and let the herd go by!"

So, clinging to the masonry at the right hand, they escaped the might of the rush, and little by little made headway until, at last, the square was reached.

"Keep together now, and follow me!"

By this time Ben-Hur's leadership was perfect; and as he pushed into the seething mob his party closed after him in a body. And when the Romans, clubbing the people and making merry as they struck them down, came hand to hand with the Galileans, eager for the fray, and equally armed, they were in turn surprised. Then the shouting was close and fierce; the crash of sticks rapid and deadly; the advance as furious as hate could make it. No one performed his part as well as Ben-Hur whose training served him admirably; for not merely he knew to strike and guard; his long arm, perfect co-ordination, and incomparable strength helped him to success in every encounter. He was at once fighting-man and leader. He had need to strike a man but once. He seemed, moreover, to have eyes for each of his friends, and the faculty of being at the right moment exactly where he was most needed. Thus surprised and equally matched, the Romans at first retired, but finally turned their backs and fled to the portico. The impetuous Galileans would have pursued them to the steps, but Ben-Hur restrained them.

"Stay, my men!" he said. "The centurion yonder is coming with the guard. They have swords and shields; let us get back and out of the gate while we may."

They obeyed him, though slowly; for they had frequently to step over their countrymen lying where they had been felled; some writhing and groaning, some praying help, other mute as the dead. But the fallen were not all Jews. In that there was consolation.

The centurion shouted to them as they went off; Ben-Hur laughed at him, and replied in his own tongue, "If we are dogs of Israel, you are jackals of Rome. Remain here, and we will come again."

The Galileans cheered, and laughing, went on.

Outside the gate there was a multitude the like of which Ben-Hur had never seen, not even in the Circus at Rome. The house-tops, the streets, the slope of the hill, were all densely covered with people wailing and praying.

The party were permitted to pass without challenge by the outer guard. But hardly were they out before the centurion in charge at the portico appeared, and in the gateway called to Ben-Hur.

"Ho, insolent! Art thou a Roman or a Jew?"

Ben-Hur answered, "I am a son of Judah, born here. What wouldst thou with me?"

"Stay and fight."

"Singly?"

"As thou wilt!"

Ben-Hur laughed derisively. "O brave Roman! Worthy son of the bastard Roman love! I have no arms."

"Thou shalt have mine," the centurion answered. "I will borrow of the guard here."

The people hearing this, became silent; and the hush spread. But lately Ben-Hur had beaten a Roman under the eyes of Antioch and the Farther East; now, could he beat another under the eyes of Jerusalem, the honor might be vastly profitable to the cause of the New King. He did not hesitate. Going to the centurion, he said, "I am willing. Lend my thy sword and shield."

The arms were as delivered, and at once the centurion was ready. Only when the combatants advanced to begin the fight the question sped from mouth to mouth, "Who is he?" And no one knew.

The Roman supremacy in arms lay in three things—submission to discipline, the legionary formation of battle, and a peculiar use of the short sword. In combat, they never struck or cut; from first to last they thrust—they advanced thrusting, they retired thrusting; and generally their aim was at the foeman's face. All this was well known to Ben-Hur.

As they were about to engage he said, "I told thee I was a son of Judah; but I did not tell that I am *lanista*-taught. Defend thyself!"

At the last word Ben-Hur closed with his antagonist. A moment, standing foot to foot, they glared at each other over the rims of their embossed shields; then the Roman pushed forward and feinted an under-thrust. The Jew laughed at him. A thrust at the face followed. The Jew stepped lightly to the left; quick as the thrust was, the step was quicker. Under the lifted arm of the foe he slid his shield, advancing it until the sword and sword-arm were both caught on its upper surface; another step, this time forward and left, and the man's whole right side was offered to the point. The centurion fell heavily on his breast, clanging the pavement, and Ben-Hur had won. With his foot upon his enemy's back, he raised his shield overhead after the gladiatorial custom, and saluted the soldiers by the gate.

On the houses far as the Xystus, the people waved shawls and handkerchiefs and shouted; and if he had consented, the Galileans would have carried Ben-Hur off upon their shoulders.

To a petty officer who then advanced from the gate he said, "Thy comrade died like a soldier. I leave him undespoiled. Only his sword and shield are mine."

With that, he walked away. Off a little he spoke to the Galileans. "Brethren, you have behaved well. Let us now separate, lest we be pursued. Meet me to-night at the khan.

I have something to propose to you of great interest to Israel."

"Who are you?" they asked him.

"A son of Judah," he answered. "Bring with you this sword and shield that I may know you."

Pushing brusquely through the increasing crowd, he speedily disappeared.

At the instance of Pilate, the people went up from the city and carried off their dead and wounded, and there was much mourning for them; but the grief was greatly lightened by the victory of the unknown champion. The fainting spirit of the nation was revived; insomuch that in the streets and up in the Temple even, amidst the solemnities of the feast, old tales of the Maccabees were told again, and thousands shook their heads whispering wisely, "A little longer, only a little longer, brethren, and Israel will come to her own. Let there be faith in the Lord, and patience."

# BOOK SEVENTH

## CHAPTER I.

THE MEETING took place in the khan of Bezetha as appointed. Thence Ben-Hur went with the Galileans into their country, where his exploits up in the old Market place gave him fame and influence. Before the winter was gone he raised three legions, and organized them after the Roman pattern. He could have had as many more, for the martial spirit of that gallant people never slept. The proceeding, however, required careful guarding against both Rome and Herod Antipas. Contenting himself for the present with the three, he strove to train and educate them for systematic action. For that purpose he carried the officers over into the lava-beds of Trachonitis, and taught them the use of arms, particularly the javelin and sword, and the manœuvring peculiar to the legionary formation; after which he sent them home as teachers. And soon the training became the pastime of the people.

The task called for patience, skill, zeal, faith, and devotion on his part. Yet he would have failed but for the support he had from Simonides, who furnished him arms and money, and from Ilderim, who kept watch and brought him supplies. And still he would have failed but for the genius of the Galileans.

Under that name were comprehended the four tribes— Asher, Zebulon, Issachar, and Naphthali—and the districts originally set apart to them. The Jew born in sight of the Temple despised these brethren of the north; but the Talmud itself has said, "The Galilean loves honor, and the Jew money."

Hating Rome as fervidly as they loved their own country,

in every revolt they were first in the field and last to leave it. For the great festal days they went up to Jerusalem marching and camping like armies; yet they were liberal in sentiment, and even tolerant to heathenism. In Herod's beautiful cities, which were Roman in all things, in Sepphoris and Tiberias especially, they took pride, and in the building them gave loyal support. They had for fellow-citizens men from the outside world everywhere, and lived in peace with them. To the glory of the Hebrew name they contributed poets like the singer of the Song of Songs, and prophets like Hosea.

Upon such a people, so quick, so proud, so brave, so devoted, so imaginative, a tale like that of the coming of the King was all-powerful. That he was coming to put Rome down would have been sufficient to enlist them in the scheme proposed by Ben-Hur; but when, besides, they were assured he was to rule the world, more mighty than Cæsar, more magnificent than Solomon, and that the rule was to last forever, the appeal was irresistible, and they vowed themselves to the cause body and soul. They asked Ben-Hur his authority for the sayings, and he quoted the prophets, and told them of Balthasar in waiting over in Antioch; and they were satisfied, for it was the old much-loved legend of the Messiah, familiar to them almost as the name of the Lord: the long-cherished dream with a time fixed for its realization. The King was not merely coming now; he was at hand.

So with Ben-Hur the winter months rolled by, and spring came, with gladdening showers blown over from the summering sea in the west; and by that time so earnestly and successfully had he toiled that he could say to himself and his followers, "Let the good King come. He has only to tell us where he will have his throne set up. We have the sword-hands to keep it for him."

And in all his dealings with the many men they knew him only as a son of Judah, and by that name.

One evening, over in Trachonitis, Ben-Hur was sitting with some of his Galileans at the mouth of the cave in which he quartered, when an Arab courier rode to him, and delivered a letter. Breaking the package, he read,

JERUSALEM, *Nisan IV.*

A prophet has appeared who men say is Elias. He has been in the wilderness for years, and to our eyes he is a prophet; and such also is his speech, the burden of which is of one much greater than himself, who, he says, is to come presently, and for whom he is now waiting on the eastern shore of the River Jordan. I have been to see and hear him, and the one he is waiting for is certainly the King you are awaiting. Come and judge for yourself.

MALLUCH.

Ben-Hur's face flushed with joy. "By this word, O my friends," he said, "our waiting is at end. The herald of the King has appeared and announced him."

Upon hearing the letter read, they also rejoiced at the promise it held out.

"Get ready now," he added, "and in the morning set your faces homeward; when arrived there, send word to those under you, and bid them be ready to assemble as I may direct. For myself and you, I will go see if the King be indeed at hand, and send your report. Let us, in the meantime, live in the pleasure of the promise."

Going into the cave, he addressed a letter to Ilderim, and another to Simonides, giving notice of the news received, and of his purpose to go up immediately to Jerusalem. When night fell, he mounted, and with an Arab guide set out for the Jordan, intending to strike the track of the caravans between Rabbath-Ammon and Damascus.

## CHAPTER II.

IT WAS Ben-Hur's purpose to turn aside at the break of day, and find a safe place in which to rest; but the dawn overtook him while out in the Desert, and he kept on, the guide promising to bring him to a vale shut in by great rocks, where there were a spring, some mulberry-trees, and graze for the horses.

As he rode thinking of the wonderous events so soon to happen, the guide, ever on the alert, called attention to an appearance of strangers behind them. "It is a camel with riders," the guide said.

A little later Ben-Hur could see the camel was white and unusually large, reminding him of the wonderful animal he had seen bring Balthasar and Iras to the fountain in the Grove of Daphne. There could be no other like it. Thinking then of the fair Egyptian, his gait became slower, and at length fell into the merest loiter, until finally he could discern a curtained houdah, and two persons seated within it. He heard the ringing of the tiny bells, and beheld the rich housings which had been so attractive to the crowd at the Castalian fount. He beheld also the Ethiopian, always attendant upon the Egyptians. The tall camel stopped close by his horse, and Ben-Hur, looking up, saw Iras herself under the raised curtain looking down at him, her great swimming eyes bright with astonishment and inquiry.

After greetings had been exchanged, Balthasar said, "There is a caravan a short way behind us going to Alexandria; and as it is to pass through Jerusalem, I thought best to avail myself

213

of its company as far as the Holy City, whither I am journeying. This morning, however, in discontent with its slow movement—slower because of a Roman cohort in attendance upon it—we rose early, and ventured thus far in advance. As to robbers along the way, we are not afraid, for I have here a signet of Sheik Ilderim; against beasts of prey, God is our sufficient trust."

Ben-Hur bowed and said, "The good sheik's signet is a safeguard wherever the wilderness extends, and the lion shall be swift that overtakes this king of his kind." He patted the neck of the camel as he spoke.

"Yet," said Iras, with a smile which was not lost upon Ben-Hur, whose eyes had turned to her during the conversation with the elder, "yet even he would be better if his fast were broken. Kings have hunger and headaches. You will be happy, I am sure, to show us some near path to living water, that we may grace a morning's meal in the Desert."

Ben-Hur hastened to answer. "We will find the spring you ask for. With leave, we will make haste."

Afterwhile the party came to a shallow wady, down which, turning to the right hand, the guide led them. Finally, from a narrow passage, the travellers entered a spreading vale which, come upon suddenly from the yellow verdureless plain, had the effect of a freshly discovered Paradise. The water-channels winding here and there, appeared like threads tangled among islands green with grasses and fringed with reeds. One palm-tree arose in royal assertion. The bases of the boundary-walls were cloaked with clambering vines, and under a leaning cliff the mulberry grove had planted itself, proclaiming the spring which the party were seeking. And there the guide conducted them.

The water started from a crack in the cliff which some hand had enlarged into an arched cavity. Graven over it in bold Hebraic letters was the word God. From the arch the stream ran merrily over a flag spotted with bright moss, and leaped into a pool glassy clear; thence it stole away between grassy banks, nursing the trees before it vanished in the thirsty sand. The horses were presently turned loose, and from the kneeling camel the Ethiopian assisted Balthasar and Iras; whereupon the old man, turning his face to the east, crossed his hands reverently upon his breast and prayed.

"Bring me a cup," Iras said with some impatience.

From the houdah the slave brought her a crystal goblet; then she said to Ben-Hur, "I will be your servant at the fountain."

They walked to the pool together. He would have dipped the water for her, but she refused his offer, and, kneeling,

214

held the cup to be filled by the stream itself; when it was cooled and overrunning, she tendered him the first draught.

"No," he said, putting the graceful hand aside, and seeing only the large eyes half hidden beneath the arches of the upraised brows, "be the service mine, I pray."

She persisted in having her way. "In my country, O son of Hur, we have a saying, 'Better a cup-bearer to the fortunate than minister to a king.'"

"Fortunate?" he said.

"The gods give us success as a sign by which we may know them on our side. Were you not winner in the Circus? That was one sign. There is another. In a combat with swords you slew a Roman."

His cheeks flushed, not so much for the triumphs themselves as the thought that she had followed his career with interest. A moment, and the pleasure was succeeded by a reflection. The combat, he knew, was matter of report throughout the East; but the name of the victor had been committed to a very few—Malluch, Ilderim, and Simonides. Could they have made a confidante of the girl? So with wonder and gratification he was confused.

Seeing it, she arose and said, holding the cup over the pool, "O gods of Egypt! I give thanks for a hero discovered—thanks that the victim in the Palace of Idernee was not my king of men. And so, O holy gods, I pour and drink."

Part of the contents of the cup she returned to the stream, the rest she drank. When she took the crystal from her lips, she laughed at him.

"O son of Hur, is it a fashion of the very brave to be so easily overcome by a woman? Take the cup now, and see if you cannot find a happy word in it for me."

He took the cup, and stooped to refill it. "A son of Israel has no gods whom he can libate," he said, playing with the water to hide his amazement, now greater than before. What more did the Egyptian know about him? Had she been told of his relations with Simonides? And there was the treaty with Ilderim—had she knowledge of that also? He was struck with mistrust. Somebody had betrayed his secrets, and they were serious. And, besides, he was going to Jerusalem, just then of all the world the place where such intelligence possessed by an enemy, might be most dangerous to him, his associates, and the cause. But was she an enemy?

When the cup was fairly cooled, he filled it and arose, saying, with indifference well affected, "Most fair, were I an Egyptian or a Greek or a Roman, I would say"—he raised the goblet overhead as he spoke—"O ye better gods! I give thanks that there are yet left to the world, despite its wrongs

215

and sufferings, the charm of beauty and the solace of love, and I drink to her who best represents them—to Iras, loveliest of the daughters of the Nile!"

She laid her hand softly upon his shoulder. "You have offended against the law. The gods you have drunk to are false. Why shall I not tell the rabbis on you?"

"Oh!" he replied laughing, "that is very little to tell for one who knows so much else that is really important."

"I will go further—I will go to the little Jewess who makes the roses grow and the shadows flame in the house of the great merchant over in Antioch. To the rabbis I will accuse you of impenitence; to her—"

"Well, to her?"

"I will repeat what you have said to me under the lifted cup, with the gods for witnesses."

He was still a moment. With quickened fancy he saw Esther at her father's side listening to the despatches he had forwarded—sometimes reading them. In her presence he had told Simonides the story of the affair in the Palace of Idernee. She and Iras were acquainted; this one was shrewd and worldly; the other was simple and affectionate, and therefore easily won. Simonides could not have broken faith—nor Ilderim—for if not held by honor, there was no one, unless it might be himself, to whom the consequences of exposure were more serious and certain. Could Esther have been the Egyptian's informant—even though perhaps an unwitting one? He did not accuse her; yet a suspicion was sown with the thought, and suspicions are weeds of the mind which grow most rapidly when least wanted. Before he could answer the allusion to the little Jewess, Balthasar came to the pool.

"We are greatly indebted to you, son of Hur," he said, in his grave manner. "This vale is very beautiful; the grass, the trees, the shade, invite us to stay and rest. Come sit with us, and taste our bread."

"Suffer me first to serve you."

With that Ben-Hur filled the goblet, and gave it to Balthasar,

Immediately the slave brought napkins; and the three seated themselves in Eastern style under the tent which years before had served the Wise Men at the meeting in the Desert.

## CHAPTER III.

THE RESTFULNESS of the vale, the freshness of the air, the garden beauty, the Sabbath stillness, seemed to have affected the spirits of the elder Egyptian; his voice, gestures, and whole manner were unusually gentle; and often as he bent his eyes upon Ben-Hur conversing with Iras, they softened with pity.

"When we overtook you, son of Hur," he said, at the conclusion of the repast, "it seemed your face was also turned towards Jerusalem. May I ask if you are going so far?"

"I am going to the Holy City."

"Is there a shorter road than that by Rabbath-Ammon?"

"A rougher route, but shorter, lies by Gerasa and Rabbath-Gilead. It is the one I am taking."

"I am impatient," said Balthasar. "Latterly my sleep has been visited by the same dream in repetition. A voice—it is nothing more—comes and tells me, 'Haste—arise! He whom thou hast so long awaited is at hand.' "

"You mean he that is to be King of the Jews?" Ben-Hur asked, gazing at the Egyptian in wonder.

"Even so."

"Then you have heard nothing of him?"

"Nothing, except the words of the voice in the dream."

"Here, then, are tidings to make you glad as they made me."

From his gown Ben-Hur drew the letter received from Malluch. The Egyptian read aloud, and as he read the veins in his neck swelled and throbbed. At the conclusion he raised his eyes in thanksgiving.

"Thou hast been very good to me, O God," he said. "Give me, I pray thee, to see the Saviour again, and worship him, and thy servant will be ready to go in peace."

The words, the manner, the simplicity of the prayer, touched Ben-Hur with a sensation new and abiding. God never seemed so actual and so near by; it was as if he were there bending over them or sitting at their side—a Father to whom all his children were alike in love—Father, not more of the Jew than of the Gentile, who needed no intermediates, no rabbis, no priests, no teachers. The idea that such a God might send mankind a Saviour instead of a king appeared to Ben-Hur in a light not merely new, but so plain that he could almost discern both the greater want of such a gift and its greater consistency with the nature of such a Diety.

"Now that he has come, O Balthasar, you still think he is to be a Saviour, and not a king as Cæsar is; you thought his sovereignty would be spiritual, not of the world."

"Oh, yes," the Egyptian answered; "and I am of the same opinion now. I see the divergence in our faith. You are going to meet a king of men, I a Saviour of souls."

"Let me try, O son of Hur," he said, "and help you to a clear understanding of my belief; then it may be, seeing that the spiritual kingdom I expect him to set up can be more excellent in every sense than anything of mere Cæsarean splendor, you will better understand the reason of the interest I take in the mysterious person we are going to welcome. . . ."

The good man then spoke at length of his conviction of the nature of the coming Kingdom, and of the glory of the soul's immortality, as opposed to the ephemeral quality of earthly joys and splendor. When he stopped and drank, the hand carrying the cup to his lips trembled; and both Iras and Ben-Hur shared his emotion and remained silent. Upon the latter a light was breaking. He was beginning to see, as never before, that there might be a spiritual kingdom of more import to men than any earthly empire; and that after all a Saviour would indeed be a more godly gift than the greatest king.

"A practical question presents itself," Balthasar continued. "How shall we know him at sight? If you continue in your belief—that he is to be a king as Herod was—of course you will keep on until you meet a man clothed in purple and with a sceptre. On the other hand, I look for one poor, humble, undistinguished—a man in appearance as other men; and the sign by which I will know him will be never so simple. He will offer to show me and all mankind the way to the eternal life; the Life of the Soul."

The company sat a moment in silence which was broken by Balthasar. "Let us arise now," he said, "and set forward again. What I have said has caused a return of impatience to see him who is ever in my thought; and if I seem to hurry you, O son of Hur—and you, my daughter—be that my excuse."

In a little while they were retracing their steps back through the wady, intending to overtake the caravan if it had passed them by.


## CHAPTER IV.

THE CARAVAN, stretched out upon the Desert, was like a lazy serpent. By-and-by its stubborn dragging became intolerably irksome to Balthasar, patient as he was; so, at his suggestion, the party determined to go on by themselves.

Ben-Hur found a certain charm in Iras's presence. If she looked down upon him from her high place, he made haste to get near her; if she spoke to him, his heart beat out of its usual time. The desire to be agreeable to her was a constant impulse. Objects on the way, though ever so common, became interesting the moment she called attention to them; a black swallow in the air pursued by her pointing finger went off in a halo; if a flake of mica sparkled in the drab sand, at a word he turned aside and brought it to her; and if she threw it away in disappointment, far from thinking of the trouble he had been put to, he was sorry it proved so worthless, and kept

218

a lookout for something better—a ruby, perchance a diamond. And when, now and then, the curtain of the houdah fell down, it seemed a sudden dullness had dropped from the sky, bedraggling all the landscape.

There were signs, too, that she well knew the influence she was exercising over him. From some place she had drawn a caul of golden coins, and adjusted it so the gleaming strings fell over her forehead and upon her cheeks, blending lustrously with the flowing of her blue-black hair. She had also produced rings for fingers and ear, bracelets, a necklace of pearls, also a shawl embroidered with threads of fine gold—the effect of all which she softened with a scarf of Indian lace skillfully folded about her throat and shoulders. And so arrayed, she plied Ben-Hur with countless coquetries; showering him with smiles; and all the while following him with glances, now melting-tender, now sparkling-bright.

The sun at its going down behind a spur of the old Bashan left the party halted by a pool of clear water in the Abilene Desert. There the tent was pitched, the supper eaten, and preparations made for the night.

The second watch was Ben-Hur's; and he was standing, spear in hand, within arm-reach of the dozing camel, looking awhile at the stars, then over the veiled land. Yet in thought he entertained the Egyptian, recounting her charms, and sometimes debating how she came by his secrets, the uses she might make of them, and the course he should pursue with her. And through all his reflections the girl was a strong temptation, the stronger of a gleam of policy behind. At the very moment he was most inclined to yield to the allurement, a soft hand was laid upon his shoulder. The touch thrilled him; he started, turned—and she was there.

"I thought you asleep," he said presently.

"Sleep is for old people and little children, and I came out to look at my friends, the stars over the Nile. But confess yourself surprised!"

He took the hand which had fallen from his shoulder, and said, "Well, was it by an enemy?"

"Oh, no! To be an enemy is to hate, and hating is a sickness which Isis will not suffer to come near me. She kissed me, you should know, on the heart when I was a child."

"Your speech does not sound in the least like your father's. Are you not of his faith?"

She laughed low. "I might have been, had I seen what he has. I may be when I get old like him. There should be no religion for youth, only poetry and philosophy; and no poetry except that of wine and mirth and love, and no philosophy that does not excuse follies which cannot outlive a season. My father's God is too awful for me. I failed to find him in the

Grove of Daphne. He was never heard of as present in the atria of Rome. But, son of Hur, I have a wish."

"A wish! Where is he who could deny you?"

"It is very simple. I wish to help you." She drew closer as she spoke.

He laughed, and replied lightly, "O Egypt!—I came near saying *dear* Egypt!—does not the sphinx abide in your country?"

"Well?"

"You are one of its riddles. In what do I need help? And how can you help me?"

She took her hand from him, and, turning to the camel, spoke to it endearingly, and patted its monstrous head as it were a thing of beauty.

"Sometimes thou, too, goest stumbling because the way is rough and stony and the burden grievous. How is it thou knowest the kind intent by a word, and always makest answer gratefully, though the help offered is from a woman? I will kiss thee, thou royal brute!"—she stooped and touched its broad forehead with her lips, saying immediately, "because in thy intelligence there is no suspicion!"

And Ben-Hur, restraining himself, said calmly, "The reproach has not failed its mark, O Egypt! If I seem to say thee no, may it not be because I am under seal of honor, and by my silence cover the lives and fortunes of others?"

"May be!" she said quickly. "It is so."

He asked, his voice sharp with amazement, "What all knowest thou?"

She answered, after a laugh, "Why do men deny that the senses of women are sharper than theirs? Your face has been under my eyes all day. I had but to look at it to see you bore some weight in mind; and to find the weight, what had I to do more than recall your debates with my father? Son of Hur!"—she lowered her voice and, going nearer, spoke so her breath was warm upon his cheek—"son of Hur! he thou art going to find is to be King of the Jews, is he not?"

His heart beat fast and hard.

"A King of the Jews like Herod, only greater," she continued.

He looked away—into the night, up to the stars; then his eyes met hers, and lingered there; and her breath was on his lips.

"Since morning," she said further, "we have been having visions. Now if I tell you mine, will you serve me as well? What? Silent still?"

She pushed his hand away, and turned as if to go; but he caught her and said eagerly, "Stay—stay and speak!"

She went back, and with her hand upon his shoulder, leaned

against him; and he put his arm around her, and drew her close, very close; and in the caress was the promise she asked.

"Speak, and tell me thy visions, O Egypt, dear Egypt! I am at thy will."

The entreaty passed apparently unheard, for looking up and nestling in his embrace, she said, slowly, "The vision which followed me was of magnificent war—war on land and sea—with clashing of arms and rush of armies, as if Cæsar and Pompey were come again, and Octavius and Antony. A cloud of dust and ashes arose and covered the world, and Rome was not any more; all dominion returned to the East; out of the cloud issued another race of heroes; and there were vaster satrapies and brighter crowns for giving away than were ever known. And, son of Hur, while the vision was passing, and after it was gone, I kept asking myself, 'What shall he not have who served the King earliest and best?'"

Again Ben-Hur recoiled. The question was the very question which had been with him all day. Presently he fancied he had the clew he wanted.

"So," he said, "I have you now. The satrapies and crowns are the things to which you would help me. I see, I see! And there never was such a queen as you would be, so shrewd, so beautiful, so royal—never! But, alas, dear Egypt! by the vision as you show it the prizes are all of war, and you are but a woman, though Isis did kiss you on the heart. And crowns are starry gifts beyond your power to help, unless, indeed, you have a way to them more certain than that of the sword. If so, O Egypt, Egypt, show it, and I will walk in it, if only for your sake."

She removed his arm, and said, "Spread your cloak upon the sand—here, so I can rest against the camel. I will sit, and tell you a story which came down the Nile to Alexandria, where I had it."

He did as she said, first planting the spear in the ground.

"And what shall I do?" he said, ruefully, when she was seated. "In Alexandria is it customary for the listeners to sit or stand?"

From the comfortable place against the camel she answered, laughing, "The audiences of story-tellers are wilful, and sometimes they do as they please."

Without more ado he stretched himself upon the sand, and put her arm about his neck.

And she told of how beauty came to the earth; of the lovely Moon-Goddess, Isis, and her husband, the Sun-King Osiris; of how, after a jealous quarrel, Osiris in his pride boasted that he alone could create a perfectly happy creature without help from his wife. Isis, smiling wisely, retired to her silver moon palace, to watch, and as she watched she knit.

221

First, Osiris created the earth, a gray planet that shadowed the moon, and thereupon, in the midst of nature, he created the First Man. Soon, however, the man became listless and despondent. So Isiris caused the earth to flame with color, which for a brief span brought back happiness to the creature, but again he withered. Osiris then gave life and movement to the things of the earth, and once more, for a little time, the man was happy until he no longer took pleasure in the tumbling brooks, the movement of the foliage, the life of the beasts. And it was the same when Osiris gave sound and music to all the things of nature.

"Then," continued Iras, "Isis mused, thinking how wonderous well, her lord was doing; but presently she shook her head. For now, indeed, Osiris was done; and if the creature should again fall off into wretchedness, her help must be asked; and her fingers flew—two, three, five, even ten stitches she took at once.

"And the man was happy a long time; it seemed, indeed, he would never tire again. But Isis knew better; and she waited, nor minded the many laughs flung at her from the sun; and at last saw signs of the end. And he pined and sickened, and sought his place of moping by the river, and at last fell down motionless.

"Then Isis in pity spoke. " 'My lord,' she said, 'the creature is dying.'

"But Osiris held his peace; he could do no more.

" 'Shall I help him?' she asked.

"Osiris was too proud to speak.

"Then Isis took the last stitch in her knitting, and gathering her work in a roll of brilliance flung it off so it fell close to the man. And he, hearing the sound of the fall so near by, looked up, and lo! a Woman—the First Woman—was stooping to help him! She reached a hand to him; he caught it and arose; and nevermore was miserable, but evermore happy.

"Such, O son of Hur! is the genesis of the beautiful, as they tell it on the Nile."

"A pretty invention, and cunning," he said, "but it is imperfect. What did Osiris afterwards?"

"Oh yes," she replied. "He called the Divine Wife back to the sun, and they went on all pleasantly together, each helping the other."

"And shall I not do as the first man?" He carried the hand resting upon his neck to his lips and his head dropped softly into her lap.

"You will find the King," she said, placing her other hand caressingly upon his head. "You will go on and find the King and serve him. With your sword you will earn his richest gifts; and his best soldier will be my hero."

222

He turned his face, and saw hers close above. In all the sky there was that moment nothing so bright to him as her eyes. Presently he sat up, and put his arms about her, and kissed her passionately, saying, "O Egypt, Egypt! If the King has crowns in gift, one shall be mine; and I will bring it and put it here over the place my lips have marked. You shall be a queen—my queen—no one more beautiful! And we will be ever, ever so happy!"

"And you will tell me everything, and let me help you in all?" she said, kissing him in return.

"Is it not enough that I love you?" he asked.

"Perfect love means perfect faith," she replied. "But never mind—you will know me better." She took her hand from him and arose.

"You are cruel," he said.

Moving away, she stopped by the camel, and touched its front face with her lips.

"Oh thou noblest of thy kind!—that, because there is no suspicion in thy love."

An instant, and she was gone.


## CHAPTER V.

THE THIRD day of the journey the party nooned by the river Jabbok, where there were a hundred or more men, mostly of Peræa, resting themselves and their beasts. Hardly had they dismounted, before a man came to them with a pitcher of water and a bowl, and offered them drink. As they received the attention with courtesy, he said, looking at the camel, "I am returning from the Jordan, at Bethabara, where just now there are many people from distant parts, travelling as you are, illustrious friend; but they had none of them the equal of your servant here."

"Bethabara used to be a lonesome ford," said Ben-Hur. "I cannot understand how it can have become of such interest."

"I see," the stranger replied; "you, too, are from abroad, and have not heard the good tidings. A man has appeared out of the wilderness—a very holy man—with his mouth full of strange words, which take hold of all who hear them. He calls himself John the Nazarite, son of Zacharias, and says he is the messenger sent before the Messiah.

"They say of this John that he has spent his life from childhood in a cave down by En-Gedi, praying and living more strictly than the Essenes. Crowds go to hear him preach. I went to hear him with the rest."

"What does he preach?"

"A new doctrine—one never before taught in Israel, as all say. He calls it repentance and baptism. The rabbis do not know what to make of him; nor do we. Some have asked him if he is the Christ, others if he is Elias; but to them all he has the answer, 'I am the voice of one crying in the wilderness, Make straight the way of the Lord!' "

At this point the man was called away by his friends; as he was going, Balthasar spoke.

"Good stranger!" he said, tremulously, "tell us if we shall find the preacher at the place you left him."

"Yes, at Bethabara."

"Who should this Nazarite be?" said Ben-Hur to Iras, "if not the herald of our King?"

In so short a time he had come to regard the daughter as more interested in the mysterious personage he was looking for than the aged father! Nevertheless, the latter with a positive glow in his sunken eyes half arose, and said,

"Let us make haste. I am not tired."

They turned away to help the slave.

Next day out of the pass through which they had journeyed the party came upon the barren steppe east of the sacred river. Opposite them they saw the upper limit of the old palm lands of Jericho, stretching off to the hill-country of Judea. Ben-Hur's blood ran quickly, for he knew the ford was close at hand.

The driver quickened the camel's pace. Soon they caught sight of booths and tents and tethered animals; and then of the river, and a multitude collected down close by the bank, and yet another multitude on the western shore. Knowing that the preacher was preaching, they made greater haste; yet, as they were drawing near, suddenly there was a commotion in the mass, and it began to break up and disperse.

They were too late!

"Let us stay here," said Ben-Hur to Balthasar, who was wringing his hands. "The Nazarite may come this way."

The people were too intent upon what they had heard, and too busy in discussion, to notice the new-comers. When some hundreds were gone by, they beheld a person coming towards them of such singular appearance they forgot all else.

Outwardly the man was rude and uncouth, even savage. Over a thin, gaunt visage of the hue of brown parchment, over his shoulders and down his back below the middle, in witch-like locks, fell a covering of sun-scorched hair. His eyes were burning-bright. All his right side was naked, and of the color of his face, and quite as meagre; a shirt of the coarsest camel's hair clothed the rest of his person to the knees, being gathered at the waist by a broad girdle of untanned leather. His feet were bare. A scrip, also of untanned leather, was fastened to the girdle. He used a knotted staff to help him forward. His movement was quick, decided, and strangely watchful. Every little while he tossed the unruly hair from his eyes, and peered round as if searching for somebody.

The fair Egyptian surveyed the son of the Desert with surprise and disgust. Presently, raising the curtain of the houdah, she spoke to Ben-Hur, who sat his horse near by.

"Is *that* the herald of thy King?"

"It is the Nazarite," he replied, without looking up.

In truth, he was himself more than disappointed. Despite his familiarity with the ascetic colonists in En-Gedi—their dress, their indifference to all worldly opinion, their constancy to vows which gave them over to every imaginable suffering of body, still Ben-Hur's dream of the King had colored all his thought of him, so that he never doubted to find in the forerunner some sign or token of the goodliness and royalty he was announcing. Gazing at the savage figure before him, the long trains of courtiers whom he had been used to see in the imperial corridors at Rome arose before him, forcing a comparison. Shocked, shamed, bewildered, he could only answer,

"It is the Nazarite."

With Balthasar it was different. The ways of God, he knew, were not as men would have them. He had seen the Saviour a child in a manger, so he kept his seat, his hands crossed upon his breast, his lips moving in prayer. He was not expecting a king.

Another man, sitting by himself on a stone at the edge of the river, arose, and walked slowly up from the shore, in a course to take him across the line the Nazarite was pursuing and bring him near the camel.

And the two—the preacher and the stranger—kept on until they came, the former within twenty yards of the animal, the latter within ten feet. Then the preacher stopped, and flung the hair from his eyes, looked at the stranger, threw his hands up as a signal to all the people in sight; and they also stopped, each in the pose of a listener; and when the hush was perfect, slowly the staff in the Nazarite's right hand came down and pointed to the stranger.

At the same instant, under the same impulse, Balthasar and Ben-Hur fixed their gaze upon the man pointed out, and both took the same impression. He was moving slowly towards them in a clear space a little to their front, a form slightly above the average in stature, and slender, even delicate. His action was calm and deliberate, like that habitual to men much given to serious thought upon grave subjects; and it well became his costume, which was an undergarment full-sleeved and reaching to the ankles, and an outer robe called the talith; on his left arm he carried the usual handkerchief for the head. His

225

sandals were of the simplest kind. He was without scrip or girdle or staff.

But it was the face of the man which was the real source of the spell they caught in common with all who stood looking at him.

The head was open to the cloudless light, except as it was draped with hair long and slightly waved, and parted in the middle, and auburn in tint. Under a broad, low forehead, under black well-arched brows, beamed eyes dark-blue and large, and soft. The delicacy of the nostrils and mouth was unusual and when it was taken with the gentleness of the eyes, the pallor of the complexion, and the softness of the beard, never a soldier but would have laughed at him in encounter, never a woman who would not have confided in him at sight, never a child that would not, with quick instinct, have given him its hand and whole artless trust.

The features were ruled by intelligence, love, pity, or sorrow; though it was a blending of them all, yet withal no one could have observed the face with a thought of weakness in the man.

Slowly he drew nearer the three.

Now Ben-Hur, mounted and spear in hand, was an object to claim the glance of a king; yet the eyes of the man approaching were all the time raised above him—and not to Iras but to Balthasar, the old and unserviceable.

Presently the Nazarite, still pointing with his staff, cried, in a loud voice, "Behold the Lamb of God, which taketh away the sin of the world!"

The crowd, arrested by the action of the speaker, and listening for what might follow, were struck by words so strange; upon Balthasar they were overpowering. He was there to see once more the Redeemer of men. The faith which had brought him the singular privileges of the time long gone yet lived in his heart; and now it gave him a power of vision above that of his fellows. The ideal of his faith was before him, perfect in face, form, dress, action, age. Ah, now if something could only happen to identify the stranger beyond all doubt.

And that was what did happen.

Exactly at the fitting moment, as if to assure the trembling Egyptian, the Nazarite repeated the outcry,

"Behold the Lamb of God, which taketh away the sin of the world!"

Balthasar fell upon his knees. For him there was no need of explanation; and as if the Nazarite knew it, he turned to those more immediately about him staring in wonder, and continued:

"This is he of whom I said, 'After me cometh a man which

is preferred before me; for he was before me.' And I knew him not: but that he should be manifest to Israel, therefore am I come baptizing with water. I saw the Spirit descending from heaven like a dove, and it abode upon him. And I knew him not; but he that sent me to baptize with water, the same said unto me, 'Upon whom thou shalt see the Spirit descending and remaining on him, the same is he which baptizeth with the Holy Ghost.' And I saw and bare record, that this" —he paused, his staff still pointing at the stranger in the white garments. "I bare record, *that this is the Son of God!*"

"It is he, it is he!" Balthasar cried, with upraised tearful eyes.

Ben-Hur was studying the face of the stranger, though with an interest entirely different.. There was room in his mind for but one thought—who is this man? Messiah or king? Never was apparition more unroyal. Looking at that calm countenance, the very idea of war and conquest smote him like a profanation. He thought, as if speaking to his own heart, Balthasar must be right, and Simonides wrong. This man has not come to rebuild the throne of Solomon; he has neither the nature nor the genius of Herod; king he may be, but not of another and greater Rome.

It should be understood now that this was not a conclusion with Ben-Hur, but an impression; and while it was forming while yet he gazed at the countenance, his memory began to struggle. "Surely," he said to himself, "I have seen the man; but where and when?" That the eyes, so calm, so pitiful, had somewhere in the past time looked upon him, that moment they were looking upon Balthasar, became an assurance. Faintly at first, the scene by the well at Nazareth when the Roman guard was dragging him to the galleys returned. Those hands had helped him when he was perishing. The face was one of the pictures he had carried in mind ever since. In his effusion of feeling, the explanation of the preacher was lost by him, all but the last words: "—*this is the Son of God!*"

Ben-Hur leaped from his horse to render homage to his benefactor; but Iras cried to him, "Help, son of Hur, help, or my father will die!"

He stopped, looked back, then hurried to her assistance. She gave him a cup; and leaving the slave to bring the camel to its knees, he ran to the river for water. The stranger was gone when he came back.

At last Balthasar was restored to consciousness. Stretching forth his hands, he asked feebly, "Where is he?"

"Who?" asked Iras.

An intense instant interest shone upon the good man's face, as if a last wish had been gratified, and he answered,

"He—the Redeemer—the Son of God, whom I have seen again."

"Believest thou so?" Iras asked in a low voice of Ben-Hur.

"The time is full of wonders; let us wait," was all he said.

And next day while the three were listening to him, the Nazarite broke off in mid-speech, saying reverently, "Behold the Lamb of God!"

Looking to where he pointed, they beheld the stranger again. As Ben-Hur surveyed the slender figure, and countenance compassionate to sadness, a new idea broke upon him: "Balthasar was right—so was Simonides. Might not the Redeemer be a king also?"

And he asked one at his side, "Who is the man walking yonder?"

The other laughed and replied, "He is the son of a carpenter over in Nazareth."

# BOOK EIGHTH

## CHAPTER I.

IT WAS nearly three years after the annunciation of the Christ at Bethabara, and on this twenty-first day of March, on the summer-house terrace of the Hur palace in Jerusalem, Simonides turned to his daughter.

"Esther—Esther! Speak to the servant below that he may bring me a cup of wine.

From the parapet overlooking the court-yard Esther called to a man in waiting there; at the same moment another man-servant came up and saluted respectfully.

"A package for the master," he said, giving her a letter enclosed in linen cloth, tied and sealed.

In the meanwhile, Malluch, acting for Ben-Hur, who could not longer endure the emptiness and decay of his father's house, had bought it from Pontius Pilate; and, in process of repair, gates, courts, lewens, stairways, terraces, rooms, and roof had been cleansed and thoroughly restored. At every point, indeed, a visitor was met by evidences of the higher tastes acquired by the young proprietor during his years of residence in the villa by Misenum and in the Roman capital.

Ben-Hur had not yet publicly assumed ownership of the property. In his opinion, the hour for that was not yet come. Neither had he yet taken his proper name. Passing the time in the labors of preparation in Galilee, he waited patiently the action of the Nazarene, who became daily more and more a mystery to him, and by prodigies done, often before his eyes, kept him in a state of anxious doubt both as to his character and mission. Occasionally he came up to the Holy

City, stopping at the paternal house; always, however, as a stranger and a guest.

These visits of Ben-Hur, it should also be observed, were far more than mere rest from labor. Balthasar and Iras made their home in the palace; and the charm of the daughter was still upon him with all its original freshness, while the father, though feebler in body, held him an unflagging listener to speeches of astonishing power, urging the divinity of the wandering miracle-worker of whom they were all so expectant.

As to Simonides and Esther, they had arrived from Antioch only a few days before—a wearisome journey to the merchant, borne in a palaquin swung between two camels. But now that he had arrived the good man spent most of his day hours there seated in an arm-chair. In the shade of the summer-house he could drink fully of the inspiring air lying lightly upon the familiar hills; with Esther by him, it was so much easier to bring ba`  the other Esther, his wife. And yet every day a messenger b ought him a despatch from Sanballat, in charge of his commerce; with such detailed directions as to exclude all judgment save his own, and all chances.

As Esther started in return to the summer-house, the sunlight showed her a woman now—small, graceful in form, of regular features, rosy with youth and health, bright with intelligence, beautiful with the outshining of a devoted nature— a woman to be loved because loving was a habit of life irrepressible ..ith her.

She looked at the package as she turned, paused, looked at it a second time more closely than at first; and the blood rose reddening her cheeks—the seal was Ben-Hur's. With quickened steps she hastened on.

Simonides held the package a moment while he also inspected the seal. Breaking it open, he gave her the roll it contained.

"Read," he said.

His eyes were upon her as he spoke, and instantly a troubled expression fell upon his own face.

"You know who it is from, I see, Esther."

"Yes—from—our master."

Slowly his chin sank into the roll of flesh. "You love him, Esther?" he asked quietly.

"Yes," she answered.

"Have you thought well of what you do?"

"I have tried not to think of him, father, except as the master to whom I am dutifully bound. The effort has not helped me to strength."

"A good girl, a good girl, even as thy mother was," he said, dropping into reverie, from which she roused him by unrolling the paper.

"The Lord forgive me, but—but thy love might not have been vainly given had I kept fast hold of all I had, as I might have done—such power is there in money!" "Let me, for your sake, my child, show you the worst. His love, Esther, is all bestowed."

"I know it," she said calmly.

"The Egyptian has him in her net," he continued. "She has the cunning of her race, with beauty to help her—much beauty, great cunning; but, like her race again, no heart. The daughter who despises her father will bring her husband to grief."

"Does she that?"

Simonides went on: "Balthasar is a wise man who has been wonderfully favored for a Gentile, and his faith becomes him; yet she makes a jest of it. I heard her say, speaking of him yesterday, 'The follies of youth are excusable; nothing is admirable in the aged except wisdom, and when that goes from them, they should die.' A cruel speech, fit for a Roman. I applied it to myself, knowing a feebleness like her father's will soon come to me also. But you, Esther, will never say of me—no, never—'It were better he were dead.' No, your mother was a daughter of Judah."

With half-formed tears, she kissed him, and said, "I am my mother's child."

He laid his hand upon her shoulder and resumed: "When he has taken the Egyptian to wife, Esther, he will think of you with repentance and much calling of the spirit; for at last he will awake to find himself but the minister of her bad ambition. Rome is the center of all her dreams. To her he is the son of Arrius the duumvir, not the son of Hur, Prince of Jerusalem."

Esther made no attempt to conceal her feelings. "Save him, father! It is not too late!" she entreated.

He answered with a smile, "A man drowning may be saved; not so a man in love."

"But you have influence with him. He is alone in the world. Show him his danger. Tell him what she is."

"That might save him from her. But would it give him to you, Esther? I am a servant, as my fathers were for generations; yet I could not say to him, 'Lo, master, my daughter—she is fairer than the Egyptian, and loves thee better!' No, by the patriarchs, Esther, I would rather lay us both with your mother to sleep as she sleeps!"

A blush burned Esther's face. "I did not mean you to tell him so, father. I was concerned for him alone—for his happiness, not mine. Because I have dared love him, I shall keep myself worthy his respect; so only can I excuse my folly. Let me read his letter now."

On the road from Galilee to Jerusalem.

The Nazarene is on the way also. With him, though without his knowledge, I am bringing a full legion of mine. A second legion follows. The Passover will excuse the multitude. He said upon setting out, "We will go up to Jerusalem, and all things that are written by the prophets concerning me shall be accomplished."

Our waiting draws to an end.

Peace to thee, Simonides.

BEN-HUR.

Esther returned the letter to her father. There was not a word in the missive for her—not even in the salutation had she a share—and it would have been so easy to have written: "And to thine, peace." For the first time in her life she felt the smart of a jealous sting.

"The eighth day," said Simonides, "and this, Esther, this is the—"

"The ninth," she replied. Possibly we may see him to-night," she added, pleased into momentary forgetfulness.

"It may be, it may be! To-morrow is the Feast of Unleavened Bread, and he may wish to celebrate it; so may the Nazarene; and we may see him—we may see both of them, Esther."

At this point the servant appeared with the wine and water. Esther helped her father, and in the midst of the service Iras came upon the roof.

To the Jewess, the Egyptian never appeared so beautiful as at that moment. Her gauzy garments fluttered about her like a little cloud of mist; her countenance was suffused with pleasure. She moved with bouyant steps, and self-conscious, though without affectation. Esther at the sight shrank within herself, and nestled closer to her father.

"Peace to you, Simonides, and to the pretty Esther peace," said Iras, inclining her head. "You remind me, good master—if I may say it without offence—of the priests in Persia who climb their temples to send prayers after the departing sun. Is there anything in the worship you do not know, let me call my father. He is Magian-bred."

"Fair Egyptian," the merchant replied, nodding with grave politeness, "your father is a good man who would not be offended if he knew I told you his Persian lore is the least part of his wisdom."

Iras's lips curled slightly. "To speak like a philosopher, as you invite me," she said, "the least part always implies a greater. Let me ask what you esteem the greater part of his knowledge?"

Simonides turned upon her sternly. "Pure wisdom always

232

directs itself towards God; the purest wisdom is knowledge of God; and no man of my acquaintance has it in higher degree, than good Balthasar."

To end the parley, he raised the cup and drank.

The Egyptian turned to Esther a little testily. "A man who has millions in store, and fleets of ships at sea, cannot discern in what simple women find amusement. Let us leave him. By the wall yonder we can talk."

They went to the parapet then, stopping at the place where, years before, Ben-Hur loosed the broken tile upon the head of Gratus.

"You have not been to Rome?" Iras began, toying the while with one of her unclasped bracelets.

"No," said Esther demurely.

"Have you not wished to go?"

"No."

"Ah, how little there has been of your life!"

The sigh that succeeded the exclamation could not have been more piteously expressive had the loss been the Egyptian's own. Next moment her laugh might have been heard in the street below; and she said, "Oh, oh, my pretty simpleton! The half-fledged birds nested in the great bust out on the Memphian sands know nearly as much as you."

Then, seeing Esther's confusion, she changed her manner, and said in a confiding tone, "You must not take offence, my dear. I was playing. Here, let me kiss the hurt, and tell you what I would not to any other—not if Simbel himself asked me, offering a lotus-cup of the spray of the Nile!"

Another laugh, masking the look she turned sharply upon the girl, and she said, "The King is coming."

Esther gazed at her in innocent surprise.

"The Nazarene," Iras continued, "he whom our fathers have been talking about so much, whom Ben-Hur has been toiling for so long"—her voice dropped—"the Nazarene will be here to-morrow, and Ben-Hur to-night."

Esther struggled to maintain her composure, but failed: her eyes fell, blood surged to her cheek and forehead, and she was saved sight of the triumphant smile that passed like a gleam over the face of the Egyptian.

"See, here is his promise." And from her girdle she took a roll. "Rejoice with me, O my friend! He will be here to-night! On the Tiber there is a house, a royal property, which he has pledged to me; and to be its mistress is to be—"

A sound of some one walking swiftly along the street below interrupted the speech, and she leaned over the parapet to see. Then she drew back, and cried, with hands clasped above her head, "Now blessed be Isis! 'Tis he—Ben-Hur himself! That he should appear while I had such thought of him! There are no gods if it be not a good omen. Put your arms about me, Esther—and a kiss!"

The Jewess looked up. Upon each cheek was a glow; her eyes sparkled with a light more nearly of anger than ever her nature emitted before. It was not enough for her to be forbidden more than fugitive dreams of the man she loved; a boastful rival must tell her in confidence of her better success, and of the brilliant promises which were its rewards. Of her, the servant of a servant, there had been no hint of remembrance; this other could show her letter, leaving her to imagine all it breathed. So she said,

"Dost thou love him so much, then, or Rome so much better?"

The Egyptian drew back a step; then she bent her haughty head quite near her questioner.

"What is it to thee, daughter of Simonides?"

Esther, all thrilling, began, "He is my—" A warning thought stayed the words: she recovered and answered, "He is my father's friend."

She could not bring herself to admit her servile condition.

Iras laughed more lightly than before. "No more than that?" she said. "Ah, by the lover-gods of Egypt, thou mayst keep thy kisses—keep them. Thou hast taught me but now that there are others vastly more estimable waiting me here in Judea; and"—she turned away, looking back over her shoulder—"I will go get them. Peace to thee."

Esther saw her disappear down the steps, when, putting her hands over her face, she burst into tears so they ran scalding through her fingers—tears of shame and choking passion. And, with a new withering force echoed her father's words: "Thy love might not have been vainly given had I kept fast hold of all I had, as I might have done."

## CHAPTER II.

AN HOUR later, Balthasar and Simonides, the latter attended by Esther, met in the great chamber of the palace; and while they were talking, Ben-Hur and Iras came in together.

The young Jew, advancing in front of his companion, walked first to Balthasar, and saluted him, and received his reply; then he turned to Simonides, but paused at sight of Esther.

With Ben-Hur, much study of possibilities, indulgence of hopes and dreams, influences, born of the condition of his country, influences more direct—that of Iras, for example—had made him, in the worldly sense, ambitious; and as he had given the passion place, allowing it to become an imperious governor, the resolves and impulses of former days faded imperceptibly almost out of recollection. His own sufferings and the mystery darkening the fate of his family moved him less and less, as in hope at least, he approached nearer the goals which occupied his visions.

He paused in surprise at seeing Esther a woman now, and so beautiful; and as he stood looking at her a still voice reminded him of broken vows and duties undone: almost his old self returned.

For an instant he was startled; but recovering; he went to Esther, and said, "Peace to thee, sweet Esther—peace; and thou, Simonides, the blessing of the Lord be thine, if only because thou hast been a good father to the fatherless."

Esther heard him with downcast face; Simonides answered, "I repeat the welcome of the good Balthasar, son of Hur—welcome to thy father's house; and sit, and tell us of thy travels, and of thy work, and of the wonderful Nazarene—who he is, and what."

Esther stepped out quickly and brought a covered stool, and set it for him.

"Thanks," he said to her.

When seated, he addressed himself to the men. "I have come to tell you of the Nazarene. For many days now I have followed him with such watchfulness as one may give another upon whom he is waiting so anxiously. I have seen him under all circumstances said to be trials and tests of men; and while I am certain he is a man as I am, not less certain am I that he is something more."

Some one coming into the room interrupted him; he turned, and arose with extended hands. "Amrah! Dear old Amrah!"

She came forward; and they, seeing the joy in her face, thought not once how wrinkled and tawny it was. She knelt at his feet, clasped his knees, and kissed his hands over and over; and when he could he put the lank gray hair from her cheeks, and kissed them, saying, "Good Amrah, have you nothing, nothing of them—not a word—not one little sign?"

Then she broke into sobbing which made answer plainer than the spoken word.

"God's will has been done," he said, in a tone that plainly told he had no more hope of finding his people.

When he could again, he took seat, and said, "Come, sit by me, Amrah—here, for I have much to say to these good friends of a wonderful man come into the world."

But she went off, and stooping with her back to the wall, joined her hands before her knees, content, they all thought, with seeing him. Then Ben-Hur, bowing to the old men, began again. "I fear to answer the question asked me about the Nazarene without first telling you some of the things I have seen him do; and to that I am more inclined, my friends, because to-morrow he will come to the city, and go up into the Temple, which he calls his father's house, where, it is further said, he will proclaim himself. So, whether you are right, O Balthasar, or you, Simonides, we and all Israel shall know to-morrow."

Balthasar rubbed his hands and asked, "Where shall I go to see him?"

"The pressure of the crowd will be very great. Better, I think, that you all go upon the roof above the cloisters—say upon the porch of Solomon."

"Can you be with us?"

"No," said Ben-Hur, "my friends will require me, perhaps, in the procession."

"Procession!" exclaimed Simonides. "Does he travel in state?"

"He brings twelve men with him, fishermen, tillers of the soil, one a publican, all of the humbler class; and he and they make their journeys on foot, careless of wind, cold, rain, or sun. Seeing them stop by the wayside at nightfall to break bread or lie down to sleep, I have been reminded of a party of shepherds going back to their flocks from market, not of nobles and kings. Only occasionally am I made to know he is their teacher as well as their companion—their superior not less than their friend.

"You are shrewd men; you know what creatures of certain master motives we are, and that it has become little less than a law of our nature to spend life in eager pursuit of certain objects; now, appealing to that law, what would you say of a man who could be rich by making gold of the stones under his feet, yet is poor of choice?"

"The Greeks would call him a philosophei," said Iras.

"Nay, daughter," said Balthasar, "the philosophers had never the power to do such thing."

"How know you this man has?"

Ben-Hur answered quickly, "I saw him turn water into wine."

"Very strange, very strange," said Simonides; "but it is not so strange to me as that he should prefer to live poor when he could be so rich. Is he so poor?"

"He owns nothing, and envies nobody his owning. He pities the rich. But passing that, what would you say to see a man multiply seven loaves and two fishes, all his store, into enough to feed five thousand people, and have full baskets over? That I saw the Nazarene do."

"You saw it?" exclaimed Simonides.

"Ay, and ate of the bread and fish."

"More marvellous still," Ben-Hur continued, "what would

236

you say of a man in whom there is such healing virtue that the sick have but to touch the hem of his garment to be cured, or cry to him afar? As we came out of Jericho two blind men by the wayside called to the Nazarene, and he touched their eyes, and they saw. So they brought a palsied man to him, and he said merely, 'Go unto thy house,' and the man went away well. What say you to these things?"

The merchant had no answer.

"Think you now, as I have heard others argue, that what I have told you are tricks of jugglery? Let me answer by recalling greater things which I have seen him do. Look first to that curse of God—comfortless, as you all know, except by death—leprosy."

At these words Amrah dropped her hands to the floor, and in her eagerness to hear him half arose.

"What would you say," said Ben-Hur, with increased earnestness—"what would you say to have seen that I now tell you? A leper came to the Nazarene while I was with him down in Galilee, and said, 'Lord, if thou wilt, thou canst make me clean.' He heard the cry, and touched the outcast with his hand, saying, 'Be thou clean'; and forthwith the man was himself again, healthful as any of us who beheld the cure, and we were a multitude."

Here Amrah arose, and with her gaunt fingers held the wiry locks from her eyes. The brain of the poor creature had long since gone to heart, and she was troubled to follow the speech.

"Then, again," said Ben-Hur, without stopping, "ten lepers came to him one day in a body, and, falling at his feet, called out—I saw and heard it all—called out, 'Master, Master, have mercy upon us!' He told them, 'Go, show yourselves to the priest, as the law requires; and before you are come there ye shall be healed.' "

"And were they?"

"Yes. On the road their infirmity left them, so that there was nothing to remind us of it except their polluted clothes."

"Such thing was never heard before—never in all Israel!" said Simonides, in undertone.

And then, while he was speaking, Amrah turned away, and walked noiselessly to the door, and went out; and none of the company saw her go.

"But my misgivings, my amazement, were not yet at the full. The people of Galilee are, as you know, impetuous and rash; after years of waiting their swords burned their hands; nothing would do them but action. 'He is slow to declare himself; let us force him,' they cried to me. And I, too, became impatient. If he is to be king, why not now? The legions are ready. So as he was once teaching by the seaside we would have crowned him whether or not; but he disappeared, and was next seen on a ship departing from the shore. Good Simonides, the desires that make other men mad—riches, power, even kingships offered out of great love by a great people—move this one not at all. What say you?"

The merchant's chin was low upon his breast; raising his head, he replied, resolutely, "The Lord liveth, and so do the words of the prophets. Let to-morrow answer."

"Be it so," said Balthasar, smiling.

And Ben-Hur said, "Be it so. From these things, not above suspicion by those who did not see them in performance as I did, let me tell you now of others infinitely greater, acknowledged since the world began to be past the power of of man. Tell me, has any one to your knowledge ever reached out and taken from Death what Death has made his own? Who ever gave again the breath of a life lost?

"Mark you," Ben-Hur proceeded, "I do but tell you things of which I was a witness, together with a cloud of other men. On the way hither I saw another act still more mighty. In Bethany there was a man named Lazarus, who died and was buried; and after he had lain four days in a tomb, shut in by a great stone, the Nazarene was shown to the place. Upon rolling the stone away, we beheld the man lying inside bound and rotting. There were many people standing by, and we all heard what the Nazarene said, for he spoke in a loud voice: 'Lazarus, come forth!' I cannot tell you my feelings when in answer, as it were, the man arose and came out to us with all his cerements about him. 'Loose him,' said the Nazarene next, 'loose him, and let him go.' And when the napkin was taken from the face of the resurrected, lo, my friends! the blood ran anew through the wasted body, and he was exactly as he had been in life before the sickness took him off. He lives yet, and is hourly seen and spoken to. You may go see him to-morrow. And now I ask you that which I came to ask, it being but a repetition of what you asked me, O Simonides: What more than a man is this Nazarene?"

The question was put solemnly, and long after midnight the company sat and debated it; Simonides being yet unwilling to give up his understanding of the sayings of the prophets, and Ben-Hur contending that the elder disputants were both right—that the Nazarene was the Redeemer, as claimed by Balthasar, and also the destined king that the merchant would have.

"To-morrow we will see. Peace to you all."

So saying, Ben-Hur took his leave.

CHAPTER III.

THE FIRST person to go out of the city upon the opening of the Sheep's Gate next morning was Amrah, basket on arm.

Down the eastern valley she took her way. The side of Olivet, darkly green, was spotted with white tents recently put up by people attending the feasts; past Gethsemane; past the tombs at the meeting of the Bethany roads; past the sepulchral village of Siloam she went. Occasionally the decrepit little body staggered; once she sat down to get her breath; rising shortly, she struggled on with renewed haste.

When at last she reached the King's Garden she slackened her gait; for then the grim city of the lepers was in view, extending far around the pitted south hill of Hinnom.

Early as it was, Amrah's unhappy mistress was up and sitting outside, leaving Tirzah asleep within. The course of the malady had been terribly swift in the three years. Conscious of her appearance, with the refined instincts of her nature, she kept her whole person habitually covered. Seldom as possible she permitted even Tirzah to see her.

This morning she was taking the air with bared head, knowing there was no one to be shocked by the exposure. The light was not full, but enough to show the ravages to which she had been subject. Her hair was snow-white and unmanageably coarse, falling over her back and shoulders like so much silver wire. The eyelids, the lips, the nostrils, the flesh of the cheeks, were either gone or reduced to fetid rawness. The neck was a mass of ash-colored scales. One hand lay outside the folds of her habit rigid as that of a skeleton; the nails had been eaten away; the joints of the fingers, if not bare to the bone, were swollen knots crusted with red secretion. Head, face, neck, and hand indicated all too plainly the condition of the whole body.

When the sun would gild the crest of Olivet she knew Amrah would come, first to the well, then to a stone between the well and the foot of the hill, and that the good servant would there deposit the food and fill the water-jar afresh for the day. Of happiness, that brief visit was all that remained to her. She could then ask about her son, and be told of his welfare, with such bits of news concerning him as the messenger could glean. At times she heard he was at home; then she would issue from her dreary cell at break of day, and sit till sun set, a motionless figure draped in white, statue-like, with gaze fixed invariably over the Temple to the spot under the sky where the old house stood. Nothing else was left her. Tirzah she counted as dead; and as for herself, she simply waited the end, knowing every hour of life was an hour of dying.

About the hill every green thing perished in its first season; the winds warred upon the shrubs and venturous grasses, leaving to drought such as they could not uproot. Look where she would, the view was made depressingly suggestive by tombs—tombs above her, tombs below, tombs opposite her own tomb—all now freshly whitened in warning to visiting pilgrims.

While she sat there a woman came up the hill, staggering and spent with exertion.

The widow arose hastily, and, covering her head, cried, in a voice unnaturally harsh, "Unclean, unclean!"

In a moment, heedless of the notice, Amrah was at her feet. All the long-pent love of the simple creature burst forth: with tears and passionate exclamations she kissed her mistress's garments, and for a while the latter strove to escape from her; then, seeing she could not, she waited till the violence of the paroxysm was over.

"What have you done, Amrah?" she said. "Is it by such disobedience you prove your love for us? Wicked woman! You are lost; and he—your master—you can never go back to him.

"The ban of the Law is upon you, too: you cannot return to Jerusalem. What will become of us? Who will bring us bread? O wicked, wicked Amrah! We are all, all undone alike!"

"Mercy, mercy!" Amrah sobbed from the ground.

"You should have been merciful to yourself, and so doing been most merciful to us. Now where can we go? There is no one to help us. O false servant! The wrath of the Lord was already too heavy upon us."

Tirzah, awakened by the noise, appeared at the door of the tomb. In the half-clad apparition, patched with scales, lividly seamed, nearly blind, its limbs and extremities swollen to grotesque largeness, eyes however sharpened by love could not have recognized the creature of childish grace who had been the daughter of the great house of Hur.

"Is it Amrah, mother?"

The servant tried to crawl to her also.

"Stay, Amrah!" the widow cried imperiously. "I forbid you touching her. Rise, and go before any at the well see you here. Nay, I forgot—it is too late! You must remain now and share our misery. Rise, I say!"

Amrah rose to her knees. "O good mistress! I am not false —I am not wicked. I bring you good tidings."

"Of Judah?"

"There is a wonderful man," Amrah continued, "who has

240

power to cure you. He speaks a word, and the sick are made well, and even the dead come to life. I have come to take you to him."

"Poor Amrah!" said Tirzah compassionately.

"No," cried Amrah, detecting the doubt—"no, as the Lord lives, even the Lord of Israel, my God as well as yours, I speak the truth. Go with me, I pray, and lose no time. This morning he will pass by on his way to the city. See! the day is at hand. Take the food here—eat, and let us go."

The mother listened eagerly. "Who told you about this Nazarene?"

"Judah."

"Judah told you? Is he at home?"

"He came last night."

The widow was silent awhile. "Did Judah send you to tell us this?" she next asked.

"No. He believes you dead."

"There was a prophet once who cured a leper," the mother said thoughtfully to Tirzah, "but he had his power from God." Then addressing Amrah, she asked, "How does my son know this man so possessed?"

"He was travelling with him, and heard the lepers call, and saw them go away well. First there was one man; then there were ten; and they were all made whole."

The elder listener was silent again. The skeleton l and shook. She did not question the performance, for her own son was the witness testifying through the servant; but she strove to comprehend the power by which work so astonishing could be done by a man. With her, however, the hesitation was brief. To Tirzah she said, "This must be the Messiah! There was a time when Jerusalem and all Judea were filled with a story that he was born. I remember it. By this time he should be a man. It must be—it is he." She turned to Amrah. "We will go with you. Bring the water which you will find in the tomb in a jar, and set the food for us. We will eat and be gone."

Soon the three women set out. As Tirzah had caught the confident spirit of the others, there was but one fear that troubled the party. Bethany, Amrah said, was the town the man was coming from; now from that to Jerusalem there were three roads, or rather paths—one over the first summit of Olivet, a second at its base, a third between the second summit and the Mount of Offence. The three were not far apart; far enough, however, to make it possible for the unfortunates to miss the Nazarene if they failed the one he chose to come by.

A little questioning satisfied the mother that Amrah knew nothing of the country beyond the Cedron, and even less of the intentions of the man they were going to see, if they could. She discerned, also, that both Amrah and Tirzah looked to her for guidance; and she accepted the charge.

"We will go first to Bethphage," she said to them. "There, if the Lord favor us, we may learn what else to do."

They descended the hill to Tophet and the King's Garden, and paused in the deep trail furrowed through them by centuries of wayfaring.

"I am afraid of the road," the matron said. "Better that we keep to the country among the rocks and trees. This is feast-day, and on the hill-sides yonder I see signs of a great multitude in attendance. By going across the Mount of Offence here we may avoid them."

Tirzah had been walking with great difficulty; upon hearing this her courage began to fail her. "The mount is steep, mother; I cannot climb it."

"Remember, we are going to find health and life. See, my child, how the day brightens around us! And yonder are women coming this way to the well. They will stone us if we stay here. Come, be strong this once."

Thus the mother, not less tortured herself, sought to inspire the daughter; and Amrah came to her aid. To this time the latter had not touched them nor they her; now, in disregard of consequences as well as of command, the faithful nurse went to Tirzah and put her arm over her shoulder, and whispered, "Lean on me. I am strong, though I am old; and it is but a little way. There—now we can go."

The face of the hill they were crossing was broken with pits, and ruins of old structures; but when at last they stood upon the top to rest, and looked at the spectacle before them—at the Temple and its courtly terraces, at Zion, at the enduring towers white thrusting into the sky—the mother was strengthened with a love of life for life's sake.

"Look, Tirzah," she said—"look at the plates of gold on the Gate Beautiful. Do you remember we used to go up there? Will it not be pleasant to do so again? And think—home is but a little way off. And Judah will be there to receive us!"

From the side of the middle summit garnished green with myrtle and olive trees, thin columns of smoke arose straight into the pulseless morning, each a warning of restless pilgrims astir, and of the need of haste.

Though the good servant toiled faithfully to lighten the labor in descending the hill-side, the girl moaned at every step; sometimes in extremity of anguish she cried out. Upon reaching the road, she fell down exhausted.

"Go on with Amrah, mother, and leave me here," she said faintly.

"No, no, Tirzah. What would the gain be if I were healed

and you not? When Judah asks for you, what could I say to him were I to leave you?"

"Tell him I loved him."

The elder leper arose from bending over the fainting sufferer, and gazed about her, hope perishing. The joy of the thought of cure was inseparable from her thought of Tirzah. Even as the brave woman was committing their venture to the judgment of God, she saw a man walking rapidly up the road from the east.

"Courage, Tirzah!" she said. "Yonder comes one to tell us of the Nazarene."

Amrah helped the girl to a sitting posture, and supported her while the man advanced.

"In your goodness, mother, you forget what we are. The stranger will go around us; his best gift to us will be a curse, or a stone."

"We will see."

The road at the edge of which the trio was posted was little more than a worn path, winding crookedly through tumbled limestone. If the stranger kept it, he must meet them face to face; and he did so, until near enough to hear the cry she was bound to give. Then, uncovering her head, a further demand of the law, she shouted shrilly, "Unclean, unclean!"

To her surprise, the man came steadily on.

"What would you have?" he asked, stopping opposite them not four yards off.

"Thou seest us. Have a care," the mother said with dignity.

"Woman, I am the courier of him who but speaketh to such as thou and they are healed. I am not afraid."

"The Nazarene?"

"The Messiah," he said.

"Is it true that he cometh to the city to-day?"

"He is now at Bethphage and on this road."

She clasped her hands, and looked up thankfully.

"For whom takest thou him?" the man asked with pity.

"The Son of God," she replied.

"Stay thou here then; or, as there is a multitude with him, take thy stand by the white rock under the tree, then as he goeth by fail not to call to him; call, and fear not. If thy faith is strong, he will hear thee though all the heavens thunder. I go to tell the city that he is at hand, and to make ready to receive him. Peace to thee and thine, woman." The stranger moved on.

"Did you hear, Tirzah? Did you hear? Once more, my child—oh, only once—let us to the rock."

Thus encouraged, Tirzah took Amrah's hand and arose; but as they were going, Amrah said, "Stay; the man is returning." And they waited for him.

"I pray your grace, woman," he said. "Remembering that the sun will be hot before the Nazarene arrives, I thought this water would do thee better than it will me. Take it and be of good cheer. Call to him as he passes."

He offered a gourd full of water; and instead of placing the gift on the ground for her to take up when he was at a safe distance, he gave it into her hand.

"Art thou a Jew?" she asked, surprised.

"I am that, and better; I am a disciple of the Christ who teacheth daily by word and example this which I have done unto you. The world hath long known the word charity without understanding it. Peace and good cheer to thee and thine."

He went on, and they went slowly to the rock he had pointed out to them, high as their heads, and scarcely thirty yards from the road. There they cast themselves under the tree and drank of the gourd, and rested refreshed. Soon Tirzah slept, and fearing to disturb her, the others held silent.

## CHAPTER IV.

DURING THE third hour the road in front of the resting-place of the lepers became gradually frequented by people going toward Bethphage and Bethany; now, however, a great crowd appeared over the crest of Olivet, and as it defiled down the road, thousands in number, the two watchers noticed with wonder that every one in it carried a palm-branch freshly cut. As they sat watching, the noise of another multitude approaching from the east drew their eyes that way. Then the mother awoke Tirzah.

"What is the meaning of it all?" the girl asked.

"He is coming," answered the mother. "These we see are from the city going to meet him; those we hear in the east are his friends bearing him company; I think the processions will meet here before us."

"I fear, if they do, we cannot be heard."

The same thought was in the elder's mind.

"Amrah," she asked, "when Judah spoke of the healing of the ten, in what words did he say they called to the Nazarene?"

"Either they said, 'Lord, have mercy upon us,' or 'Master, have mercy.'"

"Only that?"

"No more I heard."

"Yet Judah said he saw them go away well."

Meantime the people in the east came up slowly. When the foremost of them were in sight, the gaze of the lepers fixed upon a man riding an ass in the midst of what seemed a selected company that sang and danced about him in extravagance of joy. The rider was bareheaded and clad in white. When he came closer, they saw an olive-hued face shaded by long chestnut hair and parted in the middle. He looked neither to the right nor left. In the noisy abandon of his followers he appeared to have no part; nor did their favor disturb him in the least, or raise him out of his profound melancholy. The sun beat upon the back of his head, and lighting up the floating hair gave it a likeness to a golden nimbus. Behind him the irregular procession, pouring forward with continuous singing and shouting, extended out of view. There was no need of any one to tell the lepers that this was he—the Nazarene!

"He is here, Tirzah," the mother said. "Come, my child."

As she spoke she glided in front of the white rock and fell upon her knees, the daughter and servant by her side. Then at sight of the procession in the west, the thousands from the city halted, and began to wave their green branches, chanting: "Blessed is the King of Israel that cometh in the name of the Lord!"

And all the thousands who were of the rider's company replied so the air shook with the sound. Amidst the din, the cries of the poor lepers were not more than the twittering of dazed sparrows.

The moment of the meeting of the hosts was come, and with it the opportunity the sufferers were seeking; if not taken, it would be lost forever, and they would be lost as well.

"Nearer, my child—let us get nearer. He cannot hear us," said the mother.

She arose and staggered forward. Her ghastly hands were up, and she screamed with horrible shrillness. The people saw her—saw her hideous face, and stopped awe-struck. Tirzah, behind her a little way, fell down, too faint and frightened to follow.

"The lepers! the lepers!"

"Stone them!"

"The accursed of God! Kill them!"

These, with other yells, broke in upon the hosannas of the multitude too far removed to see the cause of the interruption. Then in fair view, the Nazarene rode up and stopped in front of the woman. She beheld his face—calm, pitiful, and of exceeding peace.

"O Master, Master! Thou seest our need; thou canst make us clean. Have mercy upon us—mercy!"

"Believest thou I am able to do this?" he asked.

"Thou art he of whom the prophets spake—thou art the Messiah!" she replied.

His eyes grew radiant, his manner confident. "Woman," he said, "great is thy faith; be it unto thee even as thou wilt."

He lingered an instant after, apparently unconscious of the presence of the throng—an instant—then he rode away.

Immediately both the hosts, from the city and from Bethphage, closed around him with hosannas and waving of palms, and so he passed from the lepers forever. Covering her head, the elder hastened to Tirzah, and folded her in her arms, crying, "Daughter, look up! I have his promise; he is indeed the Messiah. We are saved—saved!" And the two remained kneeling while the procession, slowly going, disappeared over the mount. When the noise of its singing afar was scarcely heard the miracle began.

There was first in the hearts of the lepers a freshening of the blood; then it flowed faster and stronger, thrilling their wasted bodies with an infinitely sweet sense of painless healing. Each felt the scourge going from her; their strength revived; they were returning to be themselves. At once, as if to make the purification complete, from body to spirit the quickening ran, exalting them to a fervor of ecstasy.

To this transformation there was a witness other than Amrah. Ben-Hur had followed the Nazarene throughout his wanderings; and now, the young Jew was present when the leprous woman appeared in the path of the pilgrims. He heard her prayer and saw her disfigured face; he heard the answer also, and was not so accustomed to incidents of the kind, frequent as they had been, as to have lost interest in them. Besides, his hope to satisfy himself upon the mission of the mysterious man was still upon him, even stronger, because of a belief that now, before the sun went down, the man himself would mak  ll known by public proclamation. Consequently, Ben-H  had withdrawn from the procession, and seated himself upon a stone to wait its passage.

From his place he nodded recognition to many of the people—Galileans in his league, carrying short swords under their long *abbas*. After a little a swarthy Arab came up leading two horses; at a sign from Ben-Hur he also drew out.

"Stay here," the young master said when all were gone by, even the laggards. "I wish to be at the city early, and Aldebaran must do me service."

He stroked the forehead of the horse, then crossed the road towards the two women.

They were to him strangers in whom he felt interest only as they were subjects of a superhuman experiment, the result of which might possibly help him to solution of the mystery that had so long engaged him. As he proceeded, he glanced at the figure of the little woman standing by the white rock, her face hidden in her hands.

He hurried on, and passing by the other two, stopped before the servant. "Amrah," he said to her, "Amrah, what do you here?"

She rushed forward, and fell upon her knees before him, blinded by her tears, nigh speechless with contending joy and fear. "O master, master! Thy God and mine, how good he is!"

Amrah, aloof and hiding her face, knew the transformation the lepers were undergoing without a word spoken to her—knew it, and shared all their feeling to the full. Her countenance, her words, her whole manner, betrayed her condition; and with swift presentiment he connected it with the women he had just passed: he felt her presence there at that time was in some way associated with them, and turned hastily as they arose to their feet. His heart stood still; he became rooted in his tracks.

The woman he had seen before the Nazarene was standing with her hands clasped and eyes streaming, looking towards heaven. The mere transformation would have been a sufficient surprise; but it was the least of the causes of his emotion. Could he be mistaken? Never was there in life a stranger so like his mother; and like her, except for her white hair, as she was the day the Roman snatched her from him. And who was it by her side, if not Tirzah?—fair, beautiful, perfect, more mature, but in all other respects exactly the same as when she looked with him over the parapet the morning of the accident to Gratus. He had given them over as dead, and time had accustomed him to the bereavement; he had not ceased mourning for them, yet they had simply dropped out of his plans and dreams. Scarcely believing his senses, he laid his hand upon the servant's head, and asked, tremulously,

"Amrah, Amrah—my mother! Tirzah! Tell me if—"

"Speak to them, O master, speak to them!" she said.

He waited no longer, but ran, with outstretched arms, crying, "Mother! mother! Tirzah! Here I am!"

They heard his call, and with a cry as loving started to meet him. Suddenly the mother stopped, drew back, and uttered the old alarm,

"Stay, Judah, my son; come not nearer. Unclean, unclean!"

The utterance was from fear; and the fear was but another form of maternal love. Though they were healed in person, the taint of the scourge might be in their garments ready for communication. He had no such thought. They were before him; he had called them, they had answered. Who or what should keep them from him now? Next moment the three, so long separated, were mingling their tears in each other's arms.

The first ecstasy over, the mother said, "In this happiness, O my children, let us begin life anew by acknowledgment of him to whom we are all so indebted."

They fell upon their knees, Amrah with the rest; and the prayer of the elder outpoken was as a psalm.

Tirzah repeated it word for word; so did Ben-Hur, but not with the same questionless faith; for when they were risen, he asked, "In Nazareth, where the man was born, mother, they call him the son of a carpenter. What is he?"

She looked at him with all her old tenderness, and answered as she had answered the Nazarene himself: "He is the Messiah."

"And whence has he his power?"

"We may know by the use he makes of it. Can you tell me any ill he has done?"

"No."

"By that sign then I answer: He has his power from God."

It is not an easy thing to shake off in a moment the expectations nurtured through years, and Ben-Hur's ambition would not down. He persisted, as men do yet every day, in measuring the Christ by himself.

The mother was the first to think of the cares of life. "What shall we do now, my son? Where shall we go?" Then Ben-Hur, recalled to duty observed how completely every trace of the scourge had disappeared from his restored people; their flesh had come again like the flesh of a little child; and he took off his cloak, and threw it over Tirzah.

"Take it," he said, smiling, "the eye of the stranger would have shunned you before; now it shall not offend you." The act exposed a sword belted to his side.

"Is it a time of war?" asked the mother anxiously.

"No."

"Why, then, are you armed?"

"It may be necessary to defend the Nazarene." Thus Ben-Hur evaded the whole truth.

"Has he enemies? Who are they?"

"Alas, mother, they are not all Romans!"

"Is he not of Israel, and a man of peace?"

"There was never one more so; but in the opinion of the rabbis and teachers he is guilty of a great crime. In his eyes the uncircumcised Gentile is as worthy of favor as a Jew of the strictest habit. He preaches a new dispensation."

The mother was silent, and they moved to the shade of the tree by the rock. Calming his impatience to have them home again and hear their story, he showed them the necessity of obedience to the law governing in cases like theirs, and in conclusion called the Arab, bidding him take the horses to the gate by Bethesda and await him there; whereupon they set out, and with ease and in good time reached a tomb newly made near that of Absalom, overlooking the depths of Cedron. Finding it unoccupied, the women took possession, while he went on hastily to make the preparations necessary for their new condition.

## CHAPTER V.

BEN-HUR pitched two tents out on the Upper Cedron east a short space of the Tombs of the Kings, and furnished them with every comfort at his command; and there he conducted his mother and sister, to remain until the examining priest could certify their perfect healing.

In course of the duty, the young man had subjected himself to such serious defilement as to bar him from participation in the ceremonies of the great feast, then near at hand. He could not enter the least sacred of the courts of the Temple. Of necessity, not less than choice, therefore, he stayed at the tents with his beloved people. There was a great deal to hear from them, and a great deal to tell them of himself.

He listened to all they told him with outward patience masking inward feeling. In fact, his hatred of Rome and Romans had reached a higher mark than ever; his desire for vengeance became a thirst which attempts at reflection only intensified. In the almost savage bitterness of his humor many mad impulses took hold of him; he thought seriously of insurrection in Galilee; even the sea stretched itself map-like before his fancy, laced with lines of passage crowded with imperial plunder and imperial travellers; but each mental venture brought him back to the old conclusion—that there could be no sound success except in a war involving all Israel in solid union; and all musing upon the subject, all inquiry, all hope, ended where they began—in the Nazarene and his purposes.

At odd moments the excited schemer found a pleasure in fashioning a speech for that person: "Hear, O Israel! I am he, the promised of God, born King of the Jews—come to you with the dominion spoken of by the prophets. Rise now, and lay hold on the world!"

Would the Nazarene but speak these few words, what a tumult would follow! How many mouths performing the office of trumpets would take them up and blow them abroad for the massing of armies!

Would he speak then?

And eager to begin the work, and answering in the worldly way, Ben-Hur lost sight of the double nature of the man, and of the other possibility, that the divine in him might transcend the human. In the miracle of which Tirzah and his mother were the objects, he saw a power ample enough to raise and support a Jewish crown over the wrecks of the Italian, and more than ample to remodel society, and convert mankind into one purified happy family; and when that work was done, could any one say the peace then ordered was not a mission worthy a son of God? Could any one then deny the Redeemership of the Christ? And discarding all consideration of political consequences, what personal glory there would then be to him, as a man! It was not in the nature of any mere mortal to refuse such a career.

Meantime down the Cedron, and in towards Bezetha, especially on the roadsides up to the Damascus Gate, the country filled rapidly with all kinds of temporary shelters for pilgrims to the Passover. Ben-Hur visited the strangers, and talked with them; and returning to his tents, he was each time more and more astonished at the vastness of their numbers. And when he further discovered that every part of the world was represented among them—cities upon both shores of the Mediterranean far off as the Pillars of the West, river-towns in distant India, provinces in northernmost Europe; and that these representatives had all the same object—celebration of the notable feast—an idea tinged mistily with superstitious fancy forced itself upon him. Might he not after all have misunderstood the Nazarene? Might not that person, by patient waiting, be covering silent preparation, and proving his fitness for the glorious task before him? How much better this time for the movement than that other when the Galileans would have forced on him assumption of the crown! Then the support would have been limited to only a few thousands; now his proclamation would be responded to by—who could say how many? Pursuing this theory, Ben-Hur moved amidst brilliant promises, and glowed with the thought that the melancholy man, under gentle seeming and wonderous self-denial, was in fact carrying in disguise the subtlety of a politician and the genius of a soldier.

In the meanwhile, brawny men, bare-headed and black-bearded, came and asked for Ben-Hur at the tent; his interviews with them were always apart; and to his mother's question who they were he answered, "Some good friends of mine from Galilee."

Through them he kept informed of the movements of the Nazarene, and of the schemes of the Nazarene's enemies, rabbinical and Roman. That the good man's life was in danger, he knew; but that there were any bold enough to attempt to take it at that time, he could not believe. It seemed too securely intrenched in a great fame and an assured popularity. The very vastness of the attendance in and about the city brought with it a seeming guaranty of safety. And yet, Ben-Hur's confidence rested most certainly upon the miraculous power of the Christ. Pondering the subject in the purely human view, that the master over life and death would not exert his power in care of himself was simply past belief and understanding.

All these incidents occurred between the twenty-first day of March—by the modern calendar—and the twenty-fifth. The evening of the latter day Ben-Hur yielded to his impatience, and rode to the city, leaving behind him a promise to return that night.

The horse was fresh, and, choosing his own gait, sped swiftly. In the houses passed there were no tenants; the fires by the tent-doors were out; the road was deserted; for this was the first Passover eve, and the hour "between the evenings" when the visiting millions crowded the city, and the slaughter of lambs in offering reeked the forecourts of the Temple, and the priests in ordered lines caught the flowing blood and carried it swiftly to the dripping altars—when all was haste and hurry, racing with the stars fast coming with the signal after which the roasting and the eating and the singing might go on, but not the preparation.

## CHAPTER VI.

BEN-HUR left the horse at the khan and shortly after was at his father's house, in the great chamber. He called for Malluch first; that worthy being out, he sent a salutation to his friends the merchant and the Egyptian. But they were being carried abroad to see the celebration.

When Ben-Hur inquired for the good Balthasar, and with grave courtesy desired to know if he would be pleased to see him, he really addressed the daughter a notice of his arrival. While the servant was answering for the elder, the curtain of the doorway was drawn aside, and the younger Egyptian came in, and walked—or floated, upborne in a white cloud of the gauzy raiment she so loved and lived in—to the centre of the chamber, where the light cast by lamps from the seven-armed brazen stick planted upon the floor was the strongest. With her there was no fear of light.

The servant left the two alone.

In the excitement occasioned by the events of the few days past, Ben-Hur had scarcely given a thought to the fair Egyptian. If she came to his mind at all, it was merely as a briefest pleasure, a suggestion of a delight which could wait for him, and was waiting.

But now the influence of the woman revived with all its force the instant Ben-Hur beheld her. He advanced to her eagerly, but stopped and gazed. Such a change he had never seen!

251

Theretofore she had been a lover studious to win him—in manner all warmth, each glance an admission, each action an avowal. She had showered him with incense of flattery. While he was present, she had impressed him with her admiration; going away, he carried the impression with him to remain a delicious expectancy hastening his return. It was for him the painted eyelids drooped lowest over the lustrous almond eyes; for him the love-stories caught from the professionals abounding in the streets of Alexandria were repeated with emphasis and lavishment of poetry; for him endless exclamations of sympathy, and smiles, and little privileges with hand and hair and cheek and lips, and songs of the Nile, and displays of jewelry, and subtleties of lace in veils and scarfs. The idea, old as the oldest of peoples, that beauty is the reward of the hero had never such realism as she contrived for his pleasure; insomuch that he could not doubt he was her hero; she avouched it in a thousand artful ways as natural with her as her beauty—winsome ways reserved, it would seem, by the passionate genius of old Egypt for its daughters.

Such the Egyptian had been to Ben-Hur from the night of the boat-ride on the lake in the Orchard of Palms. But now her real nature made itself manifest.

It was not possible for her to have received a stranger with repulsion more incisive; yet she was apparently as passionless as a statue, only the small head was a little tilted, the nostrils a little drawn, and the sensuous lower lip pushed the upper the least bit out of its natural curvature.

She was the first to speak. "Your coming is timely, O son of Hur," she said in a voice sharply distinct. "I wish to thank you for hospitality; after to-morrow I may not have the opportunity to do so."

Ben-Hur bowed slightly without taking his eyes from her.

"I have heard of a custom which the dice-players observe with good result among themselves," she continued. "When the game is over, they refer to their tablets and cast up their accounts; then they libate the gods and put a crown upon the happy winner. We have had a game—it has lasted through many days and nights. Why, now that it is at an end, shall not we see to which the chaplet belongs?"

Yet very watchful, Ben-Hur answered, lightly, "A man may not balk a woman bent on having her way."

"Tell me," she continued, inclining her head, and permitting the sneer to become positive, "tell me, O prince of Jerusalem, where is he, that son of the carpenter of Nazareth, and son not less of God, from whom so lately such mighty things were expected?"

He waved his hand impatiently. "I am not his keeper."

The beautiful head sank yet lower. "Has he broken Rome to pieces?"

Again, but with anger, Ben-Hur raised his hand.

"Where has he seated his capital?" she proceeded. "Cannot I go see his throne and its lions of bronze? And his palace—he raised the dead; and to such a one, what is it to raise a golden house? He has but to stamp his foot and say the word, and the house is, pillared like Karnak, and wanting nothing."

There was by this time slight ground left to believe her playing; the questions were offensive, and her manner pointed with unfriendliness; seeing which, he became more wary and said with good-humor, "O Egypt, let us wait another day, even another week, for him, the lions and the palace."

She went on without noticing the suggestion. "And how is it I see you in that garb? Such is not the habit of governors in India or vice-kings elsewhère. I saw the satrap of Teheran once, and he wore a turban of silk and a cloak of cloth of gold, and the hilt and scabbard of his sword made me dizzy with their splendor of precious stones. I fear you have not entered upon your kingdom—the kingdom I was to share with you."

"The daughter of my wise guest is kinder than she imagines herself; she is teaching me that Isis may kiss a heart without making it better."

Ben-Hur spoke with cold courtesy, and Iras, after playing with the pendant solitaire of her necklace of coins, rejoined, "For a Jew, the son of Hur is clever. I saw your dreaming Cæsar make his entry into Jerusalem. You told us he would that day proclaim himself King of the Jews from the steps of the Temple. I beheld the procession descend the mountain bringing him. I heard their singing. They were beautiful with palms in motion. I looked everywhere among them for a figure with a promise of royalty—a horseman in purple, a chariot with a driver in shining brass, a stately warrior behind an orbed shield, rivalling his spear in stature. I looked for his guard. It would have been pleasant to have seen a prince of Jerusalem and a cohort of the legions of Galilee."

She flung her listener a glance of provoking disdain, then laughed heartily, as if the ludicrousness of the picture in her mind were too strong for contempt. "Instead of a Sesostris returning in triumph or a Cæsar helmed and sworded—I saw a man with a woman's face and hair, riding an ass's colt, and in tears. The King! the Son of God! the Redeemer of the world! ha, ha, ha!"

In spite of himself, Ben-Hur winced.

"I did not quit my place, O prince of Jerusalem," she said

253

before he could recover. "I did not laugh. I said to myself, 'Wait. In the Temple he will glorify himself as becomes a hero about to take possession of the world.' I saw him enter the Gate of Shushan and the Court of the Women. I saw him stop and stand before the Gate Beautiful. There were people with me on the porch and in the courts, and on the cloisters and on the steps of the three sides of the Temple there other people—all waiting breathlessly to hear his proclamation. The pillars were not more still than we. I fancied I heard the axles of the mighty Roman machine begin to crack. O prince, by the soul of Solomon, your King of the World drew his gown about him and walked away, and out by the farthest gate, nor opened his mouth to say a word; and—the Roman machine is running yet!"

In simple homage to a hope that instant lost—a hope which, while it was falling, he unconsciously followed with a parting look down to its disappearance, Ben-Hur lowered his eyes.

At no previous time, whether when Balthasar was plying him with arguments, or when miracles were being done before his face, had the disputed nature of the Nazarene been so plainly set before him. The best way, after all, to reach an understanding of the divine is by study of the human. So with the picture given by the Egyptian of the scene when the Nazarene turned from the Gate Beautiful; its central theme was an act utterly beyond a man of merely human inspirations. A parable to a parable-loving people, it taught what the Christ had so often asserted—that his mission was not political. There was not much more time for thought of all this than that allowed for a breath; yet the idea took fast hold of Ben-Hur, and in the same instant he followed his hope of vengeance out of sight. And the man with the woman's face and hair, and in tears, came near to him—near enough to leave something of his spirit.

"Daughter of Balthasar," he said, with dignity, "if this be the game of which you spoke to me, take the chaplet—I accord it yours. Only let us make an end of words. That you have a purpose I am sure. Get to it, I pray, and I will answer you; then let us go our several ways, and forget we ever met. Say on; I will listen, but not to more of what you have given me."

She regarded him intently, as if determining what to do, then she said coldly, "You have my leave—Go."

"Peace to you," he responded and walked away.

As he was about passing out of the door, she called to him. He stopped where he was, and looked back.

"Consider all I know about you."

"O most fair Egyptian," he said, returning, "what do you know about me?"

She looked at him absently. "You are more of a Roman, son of Hur, than any of your Hebrew brethren."

"Am I so unlike my countrymen?" he asked indifferently.

"The demi-gods are all Roman now," she rejoined.

"And therefore you will tell me what more you know about me?"

"The likeness is not lost upon me. It might induce me to save you."

"Save me!"

The pink-stained fingers toyed daintily with the lustrous pendant at the throat, and her voice was exceeding low and soft; only a tapping on the floor with her silken sandal admonished him to have a care.

"There was a Jew, an escaped galley-slave, who killed a man in the Palace of Idernee," she began slowly.

Ben-Hur was startled.

"The same Jew slew a Roman soldier before the Market-place here in Jerusalem; the same Jew has three trained legions from Galilee to seize the Roman governor to-night; the same Jew has alliances perfected for war upon Rome, and Ilderim the Sheik is one of his partners."

Drawing nearer him, she whispered, "You have lived in Rome. Suppose these things repeated in ears we know of. Ah! you change color."

He drew back from her with the look of a man who, thinking to play with a kitten, has run upon a tiger; and she proceeded:

"You are acquainted in the antechamber, and know the Lord Sejanus. Suppose he were given the proofs in hand— that the same Jew is the richest man in the East—nay, in all the empire. The fishes of the Tiber would have fattening other than they dig out of its ooze, would they not? And while they were feeding—ha! son of Hur!—what splendor there would be on exhibition in the Circus! Amusing the Roman people is a fine art; getting the money to keep them amused is another art even finer; and was there ever an artist the equal of the Lord Sejanus?"

Ben-Hur was not too much stirred by the evident baseness of the woman for recollection. Not infrequently when all the other faculties are numb and failing, memory does its office with the greatest fidelity. The scene at the spring on the way to the Jordan reproduced itself; and he remembered thinking then that Esther had betrayed him, and thinking so now, he said calmly as he could,

"To give you pleasure, daughter of Egypt, I acknowledge
255

your cunning, and that I am at your mercy. It may also please you to hear me acknowledge I have no hope of your favor. I could kill you, but you are a woman. The Desert is open to receive me; and though Rome is a good hunter of men, there she would follow long and far before she caught me, for in its heart there are wildernesses of spears as well as wildernesses of sand, and it is not beloved by the unconquered Parthian. In the toils as I am—dupe that I have been—yet there is one thing my due: who told you all you know about me? In flight or captivity, dying even, there will be consolation in leaving the traitor the curse of a man who has lived knowing nothing but wretchedness. Who told you all you know about me?"

It might have been a touch of art, or might have been sincere, the expression of the Egyptian's face became sympathetic.

"There are in my country, O son of Hur," she said presently, "workmen who make pictures by gathering vari-colored shells here and there on the sea-shore after storms, and cutting them up, and patching the pieces as inlaying on marble slabs. Can you not see the hint there is in the practice to such as go searching for secrets? Enough that from this person I gathered a handful of little circumstances, and from that other yet another handful, and that afterwhile I put them together, and was happy as a woman can be who has at disposal the fortune and life of a man whom"—she stopped, and beat the floor with her foot; and looked away as if to hide a sudden emotion; with an air of even painful resolution she presently finished the sentence—"whom she is at loss what to do with."

"No, it is not enough," Ben-Hur said, unmoved by the play. "To-morrow you will determine what to do with me. I may die."

"True," she rejoined quickly. "I had something from Sheik Ilderim as he lay with my father in a grove out in the Desert. The night was still, very still, and the walls of the tent were poor ward against ears outside listening to—birds and beetles flying through the air."

She smiled and proceeded: "Some other things—bits of shell for the picture—I had from the son of Hur himself."

"Was there no other who contributed?"

"No, not one."

Hur drew a breath of relief and said lightly, "Thanks. It were not well to keep the Lord Sejanus waiting for you. The Desert is not so sensitive. Again, O Egypt, peace!"

To this time he had been standing uncovered; now he took the handkerchief from his arm where it had been hanging, and adjusting it upon his head, turned to depart. But she arrested him; in her eagerness, she even reached a hand to him.

"Stay," she said.

He looked back at her, but without taking the hand, and he knew by her manner that the climax of the scene was now to come.

"Stay and do not distrust me, O son of Hur, if I declare I know why the noble Arrius took you for his heir. And, by Isis! by all the gods of Egypt! I swear I tremble to think of you, so brave and generous, under the hand of the remorseless minister. Consider, as I do, what the Desert will be to you in contrast of life. Oh, I give you pity—pity! And if you but do what I say, I will save you. That, also, I swear, by our holy Isis!"

"Almost—almost I believe you," Ben-Hur said, yet hesitatingly, for a doubt remained with him grumbling against yielding a good sturdy doubt, such as has saved many a life and fortune.

"The perfect life for a woman is to live in love; the greatest happiness for a man is the conquest of himself; and that, O prince, is what I have to ask of you."

She spoke rapidly, and with animation; indeed, she had never appeared to him so fascinating.

"You had once a friend," she continued. "It was in your boyhood. There was a quarrel, and you and he became enemies. He did you wrong. After many years you met him again in the Circus at Antioch."

"Messala."

"Yes, Messala. You are his creditor. Forgive the past; admit to friendship again; restore the fortune he lost in the great wager; rescue him. The six talents are as nothing to you; not so much as a bud lost upon a tree already in full leaf; but to him— Ah, he must go about with a broken body; wherever you meet him he must look up to you from the ground. O Ben-Hur, noble prince! to a Roman descended as he is beggary is the other most odious name for death. Save him from beggary!"

If the rapidity with which she spoke was a cunning invention to keep him from thinking, either she never knew or else had forgotten that there are convictions which derive nothing from thought, but drop into place without leave or notice. It seemed to him, when at last she paused to have his answer, that he could see Messala himself peering at him over her shoulder; and in its expression the countenance of the Roman was not that of a mendicant or a friend; the sneer was as patrician as ever, and the fine edge of the hauteur as flawless and irritating.

"The appeal has been decided then, and for once a Messala takes nothing. I must go and write it in my book of great occurrences—a judgment by a Roman against a Roman! But

257

did he—did Messala send you to me with this request, O Egypt?"

"He has a noble nature, and judged you by it."

Ben-Hur took the hand upon his arm. "As you know him in such friendly way, fair Egyptian, tell me, would he do for me, there being a reversal of the conditions, what he asks me to do for him? Answer, by Isis! Answer, for the truth's sake!"

"Oh!" she began, "he is—"

"A Roman, meaning that I, a Jew, must not determine dues from me to him by any measure of dues from him to me; being a Jew, I must forgive him my winnings because he is a Roman. If you have more to tell me, daughter of Balthasar, speak quickly, quickly; for by the Lord God of Israel, when this heat of blood attains its highest, I may not be able longer to see that you are a woman and beautiful! I may see but the spy of a master the more hateful because he is a Roman. Say on, and quickly."

She threw his hand off and stepped back into the full light, with all the evil of her nature collected in her eyes and voice.

"Thou drinker of lees, feeder upon husks! To think I could love thee, having seen Messala! Such as thou were born to serve him. He would have been satisfied with release of the six talents; but I say to the six thou shalt add twenty—twenty, dost thou hear? The kissings of my little finger which thou hast taken from him, though with my consent, shall be paid for; and that I have followed thee with affectation of sympathy, and endured thee so long, enter into the account not less because I was serving him. The merchant here is thy keeper of moneys. If by to-morrow at noon he has not thy order acted upon in favor of my Messala for six-and-twenty talents—mark the sum!—thou shalt settle with the Lord Sejanus. Be wise and—farewell."

As she was going to the door, he put himself in her way. "The old Egypt lives in you," he said. "Whether you see Messala tomorrow or the next day, here or in Rome, give him this message: Tell him I have back the money, even the six talents, he robbed me of by robbing my father's estate; tell him I survived the galleys to which he had me sent, and in my strength rejoice in his beggary and dishonor; tell him I think the affliction of body which he has from my hand is the curse of our Lord God of Israel upon him more fit than death for his crimes against the helpless, tell him my mother and sister whom he had sent to a cell in Antonia that they might die of leprosy, are alive and well, thanks to the power of the Nazarene whom you so despise; tell him that, to fill my measure of happiness, they are restored to me, and that I will go hence to their love, and find in it more than compensation for the impure passions which you leave me to take to him; tell him—this for your comfort, O cunning incarnate, as much as his—tell him that when the Lord Sejanus comes to despoil me he will find nothing; for the inheritance I had from the duumvir, including the villa by Misenum, has been sold, and the money from the sale is out of reach, afloat in the marts of the world as bills of exchange; and that this house and the goods and merchandise and the ships and caravans with which Simonides plies his commerce with such princely profits are covered by imperial safeguards—a wise head having found the price of the favor, and the Lord Sejanus preferring a reasonable gain in the way of gift to much gain fished from pools of blood and wrong; tell him if all this were not so, if the money and property were all mine, yet should he not have the least part of it, for when he finds our Jewish bills, and forces them to give up their values there is yet another resort left to me—a deed of gift to Cæsar—so much, O Egypt, I found out in the atria of the great capital; tell him that along with my defiance I do not send him a curse in words, but, as better expression of my undying hate, I send him one who will prove to him the sum of all curses; and when he looks at you repeating this my message, daughter of Balthasar, his Roman shrewdness will tell him all I mean. Go now—and I will go."

He conducted her to the door, and, with ceremonious politeness, held back the curtain while she passed out.

"Peace to you," he said as she disappeared.

## CHAPTER VII.

THE STREETS were filled with people going and coming, grouped about the fires roasting meat, and feasting and singing, and happy. The odor of scorching flesh mixed with the odor of cedar-wood aflame and smoking loaded the air; and as this was the occasion when every son of Israel was full brother to every other son of Israel, Ben-Hur was saluted at every step, while the groups by the fires insisted, "Stay and partake with us. We are brethren in the love of the Lord." But with thanks to them he hurried on, intending to take horse at the khan and return to the tents on the Cedron.

To make the place, it was necessary for him to cross the thoroughfare so soon to receive sorrowful Christian perpetuation. There also the pious celebration was at its height. Looking up the street, he noticed the flames of torches streaming out like pennons; then he observed that the singing ceased where the torches came. His wonder rose to its highest, how-

ever, when he became certain that amidst the smoke and dancing sparks he saw the keener sparkling of burnished speartips, arguing the presence of Roman soldiers. What were they, the scoffing legionaries, doing in a Jewish religious procession? The circumstance was unheard of, and he stayed on.

As if the moon and the torches, and the fires in the street, and the rays streaming from windows and open doors were not enough to make the way clear, some of the processionists carried lighted lanterns; and fancying he discovered a special purpose in the use of such equipment, Ben-Hur stepped into the street close to the line of march. The torches and the lanterns were borne by servants, each of whom was armed with a bludgeon or a sharpened stave. Their duty seemed to be to pick out the smoothest places among the rocks in the street for certain dignitaries among them—elders and priests; rabbis with long beards, heavy brows, and beaked noses; men of the class potential in the councils of Caiaphas and Hannas. Where could they be going? Not to the Temple, certainly, for the route to the sacred house from Zion was by the Zystus. And their business—if peaceful, why the soldiers?

As the procession began to go by Ben-Hur, his attention was particularly called to three persons walking together. They were well towards the front, and the servants who went before them with lanterns appeared unusually careful in the service. In the person moving on the left of this group he recognized a chief policeman of the Temple; the one on the right was a priest; the middle man was not at first so easily placed, as he walked leaning heavily upon the arms of the others, and carried his head so low upon his breast as to hide his face. His appearance was that of a prisoner not yet recovered from the fright of arrest, or being taken to something dreadful—to torture or death. The dignitaries helping him on the right and left, and the attention they gave him, made it clear that if he were not himself the object moving the party, he was at least in some way connected with the object—a witness or a guide, possibly an informer. So if it could be found who he was the business in hand might be guessed. With great assurance, Ben-Hur fell in on the right of the priest, and walked along with him. Now if the man would lift his head! And presently he did so, letting the light of the lanterns strike full in his face, pale, dazed, pinched with dread; the beard roughed; the eyes filmy, sunken, and despairing. In following the Nazarene, Ben-Hur had come to know his disciples as well as the Master; and now, at sight of the dismal countenance, he cried out,

"The 'Scariot!"

Slowly the head of the man turned until his eyes settled

upon Ben-Hur, and his lips moved as if he were about to speak; but the priest interfered.

"Who are thou? Begone!" he said to Ben-Hur, pushing him away.

The young man took the push good-naturedly, and, waiting an opportunity, fell into the procession again. Thus he was carried passively along down the street, through the crowded lowlands between the hill Bezetha and the Castle of Antonia, and on to the Sheep Gate.

It being Passover night, the doors of the Gate stood open. The keepers were off feasting. In front of the procession as it passed out unchallenged was the deep gorge of the Cedron, with Olivet beyond, its cedar and olive trees dark against the moonlight silvering the heavens. Two roads met and merged into the street at the gate—one from the northeast, the other from Bethany. Ben-Hur, caught up in the crowd, was led off down into the gorge. And still no hint of the purpose of the midnight march.

Down the gorge and over the bridge at the bottom of it. There was a clatter on the floor as the straggling rabble passed over beating and pounding with their clubs and staves. A little farther, they turned off to the left in the direction of an olive orchard enclosed by a stone wall in view from the road. Ben-Hur knew there was nothing in the place but old gnarled trees, the grass, and a trough hewn out of a rock for the treading of oil after the fashion of the country. While he was wondering what could bring such a company at such an hour to so lonesome a quarter they were all brought to a standstill. Voices called out excitedly in front; there was a rapid falling-back, and a blind stumbling over each other. The soldiers alone kept their order.

Ben-Hur disengaged himself from the mob and run forward. There at an opening in the stone wall, he halted to take in the scene.

A man in white clothes and bareheaded was standing outside the entrance, his hands crossed before him—a slender, stooping figure, with long hair and thin face—in an attitude of resignation and waiting. It was the Nazarene.

Behind him, next the gateway, were the disciples in a group; they were excited, but no man was ever calmer than he. The torchlight beat redly upon him, yet the expression of the countenance was as usual all gentleness and pity.

Opposite this most unmartial figure stood the rabble, gaping, silent, awed, cowering—ready at a sign of anger from him to break and run. And from him to them—then at Judas, conspicuous in their midst—Ben-Hur looked—one quick glance, and the object of the visit lay open to his understanding. Here was the betrayer, there the betrayed; and these with the clubs and staves, and the legionaries, were brought to take him.

A man may not always tell what he will do until the trial is upon him. This was the emergency for which Ben-Hur had been for years preparing. The man to whose security he had devoted himself, and upon whose life he had been building so largely, was in personal peril; yet he stood still. The very calmness with which the mysterious person confronted the mob held him in restraint by suggesting the possession of a power in reserve more than sufficient for the peril. Peace and good-will, and love and non-resistance, had been the burden of the Nazarene's teaching; would he put his preaching into practice? He was master of life; he could restore it when lost; he could take it at pleasure. What use would he make of the power now? Defend himself? And how? A word —a breath—a thought were sufficient. That there would be some signal exhibition of astonishing force beyond the natural Ben-Hur believed and in that faith waited. And in all this he was still measuring the Nazarene by himself—by the human standard.

Presently the clear voice of the Christ arose. "Whom seek ye?"

"Jesus of Nazareth," the priest replied.

"I am he."

At these simplest of words, spoken without passion or alarm, the assailants fell back several steps, the timid among them cowering to the ground; and they might have let him alone and gone away had not Judas walked over to him.

"Hail, master!"

With this friendly speech, he kissed him.

"Judas," said the Nazarene, mildly, "betrayest thou the Son of man with a kiss? Wherefore art thou come?"

Receiving no reply, the Master spoke to the crowd again.

"Whom seek ye?"

"Jesus of Nazareth."

"I have told you that I am he. If, therefore, you seek me, let these go their way."

At these words of entreaty the rabbis advanced upon him; and, seeing their intent, some of the disciples for whom he interceded drew nearer; one of them cut off a man's ear, but without saving the Master from being taken. And yet Ben-Hur stood still. And while the officers were making ready with their ropes, the Nazarene was doing his greatest charity —not the greatest in deed, but the greatest in forbearance, so far surpassing that of men.

"Suffer ye thus far," he said to the wounded man, and healed him with a touch.

Both friends and enemies were confounded—one that he

could do such a thing, the other that he would do it under those circumstances.

"Surely he will not allow them to bind him!" thought Ben-Hur.

"Put up thy sword into the sheath; the cup which my Father hath given me, shall I not drink it?" From the offending follower, the Nazarene turned to his captors. "Are you come out as against a thief, with swords and staves to take me? I was daily with you in the Temple, and you took me not; but this is your hour, and the power of darkness."

The posse plucked up courage and closed about him; and when Ben-Hur looked for the faithful they were gone—not one of them remained.

The crowd about the deserted man seemed busy, with voice, hand, and foot. Over their heads, between the torchsticks, through the smoke, sometimes in openings between the restless men, Ben-Hur caught momentary glimpses of the prisoner. Never had anything struck him as so piteous, so unfriended, so forsaken! Yet, he thought, the man could have defended himself—he could have slain his enemies with a breath, but he would not. What was the cup his father had given him to drink? And who was the father to be so obeyed?

Now the mob started to return to the city, the soldiers in the lead. Ben-Hur became anxious; he was not satisfied with himself. Where the torches were in the midst of the rabble he knew the Nazarene was to be found. Suddenly he resolved to see him again. He would ask him one question.

Taking off his long outer garment and the handkerchief from his head, he threw them upon the orchard wall, and started after the posse, which he boldly joined. Through the stragglers he made way, and at length reached the man who carried the ends of the rope with which the prisoner was bound.

The Nazarene was walking slowly, his head down, his hands bound behind him; the hair fell thickly over his face, and he stooped more than usual; apparently he was oblivious to all going on around him. In advance a few steps were priests and elders talking and occasionally looking back. When, at length, they were all near the bridge in the gorge, Ben-Hur took the rope from the servant who had it, and stepped past him.

"Master, master!" he said, hurriedly, speaking close to the Nazarene's ear. "Dost thou hear, master? A word—one word. Tell me—"

The fellow from whom he had taken the rope now claimed it.

"Tell me," Ben-Hur continued, "goest thou with these of thine own accord?"

The people were come up now, and in his own ears asking angrily, "Who art thou, man?"

"O master," Ben-Hur made haste to say, his voice sharp with anxiety, "I am thy friend. Tell me, I pray thee, if I bring rescue, wilt thou accept it?"

The Nazarene never so much as looked up or allowed the slightest sign of recognition; yet something seemed to say, "Let him alone. He has been abandoned by his friends; the world has denied him; in bitterness of spirit, he has taken farewell of men; he is going he knows not where, and he cares not. Let him alone."

And now a dozen hands were upon Ben-Hur, and from all sides there was shouting, "He is one of them. Bring him along; club him—kill him!"

With a gust of passion which gave him many times his ordinary force, Ben-Hur raised himself, turned once about with his arms outstretched, shook the hands off, and rushed through the circle which was fast hemming him in. The hands snatching at him as he passed tore his garments from his back, so he ran off the road naked; and the gorge, darker there than elsewhere, received him safe.

Reclaiming his handkerchief and outer garments from the orchard wall, he followed back to the city gate; thence he went to the khan, and on the good horse rode to the tents of his people out by the Tombs of the Kings.

As he rode, he promised himself to see the Nazarene on the morrow.

The heart the young man carried to his couch beat so heavily he could not sleep; for now clearly his renewed Judean kingdom resolved itself into what it was—only a dream. It is bad enough to see our castles overthrown one after another with an interval between to recover, but when they go altogether —go as ships sink, as houses tumble in earthquakes—the spirits which endure it calmly are made of stuffs sterner than common, and Ben-Hur's was not of them. Through vistas in the future, he began to catch glimpses of a life serenely beautiful, with a home instead of a palace of state, and Esther its mistress. Again and again through the leaden-footed hours of the night he saw the villa by Misenum, and with his little countrywoman strolled through the garden, and rested in the panelled atrium; overhead the Neapolitan sky, at their feet the sunniest of sun-lands and the bluest of bays.

# Chapter VIII.

Next morning, about the second hour, two men rode full speed to the doors of Ben-Hur's tents, and, dismounting, asked to see him. He was not yet risen, but gave directions for their admission.

"Peace to you, brethren," he said, for they were of his Galileans, and trusted officers. "Will you be seated?"

"Nay," the senior replied, bluntly, "to sit and be at ease is to let the Nazarene die. Rise, son of Judah, and go with us. The judgment has been given. The tree of the cross is already at Golgotha."

Ben-Hur stared at them. "The cross?"

"They took him last night, and tried him," the man continued. "At dawn they led him before Pilate. Twice the Roman denied his guilt; twice he refused to give him over. At last he washed his hands, and said, 'Be it upon you then'; and they answered—"

"Who answered?"

"They—the priests and people—'His blood be upon us and our children.'"

"Holy father Abraham!" cried Ben-Hur; "a Roman kinder to an Israelite than his own kin! And if—ah, if he should indeed be the son of God, what shall ever wash his blood from their children? It must not be—'tis time to fight!"

He clapped his hands. "The horses—and quickly!" he said to the Arab who answered the signal. "And bid Amrah send me fresh garments, and bring my sword! It is time to die for Israel, my friends."

He ate a crust, drank a cup of wine, and was soon upon the road.

"Whither would you go first?" asked the Galilean.

"To collect the legions."

"Alas!" the man replied, throwing up his hands. "Master" —he spoke with shame—"I and my friend here are all that are faithful. The rest follow the priests."

"Seeking what?" Ben-Hur drew rein.

"To kill the Nazarene."

Ben-Hur looked slowly from one man to the other. He was hearing again the question of the night before: "The cup my Father hath given me, shall I not drink it?" In the ear of the Nazarene he was putting his own question, "If I bring thee rescue, wilt thou accept it?" He was saying to himself, "This death may not be averted. The man has been travelling towards it with full knowledge from the day he began his mission: it is imposed by a will higher than his; whose but the

Lord's? If he is consenting, if he goes to it voluntarily, what shall another do?" Nor less did Ben-Hur see the failure of the scheme he had built upon the fidelity of the Galileans; their desertion, in fact, left nothing more of it. But how singular it should happen that morning of all others! A dread seized him. It was possible his scheming, and labor, and expenditure of treasure might have been but blasphemous contention with God. When he picked up the reins and said, "Let us go, brethren," all before him was uncertainty.

"Let us go, brethren; let us to Golgotha."

They passed through excited crowds of people going south, like themselves. All the country north of the city seemed aroused and in motion.

Hearing that the procession with the condemned might be met somewhere near the great white towers left by Herod, the three friends rode thither, passing round southeast of Akra. In the valley progress against the multitude became impossible, and they were compelled to dismount and take shelter behind the corner of a house and wait.

The waiting was as if they were on a river bank, watching a flood go by, for such the people seemed.

An hour the flood surged by Ben-Hur and his companions, within arm's reach, incessant, undiminished. At the end of that time he could have said, "I have seen all the castes of Jerusalem, all the sects of Judea, all the tribes of Israel, and all the nationalities of earth represented by them." The Libyan Jew went by, and the Jew of Egypt, and the Jew from the Rhine; they went by on foot, on horseback, on camels, in litters and chariots, and with an infinite variety of costumes, speaking all known tongues, they went by in haste—eager, anxious, crowding—all to behold one poor Nazarene die, a felon between felons.

These were the many, but they were not all.

Borne along with the stream were thousands not Jews— thousands despising them—Greeks, Romans, Arabs, Syrians, Africans, Egyptians. So that, studying the mass, it seemed the whole world was to be present at the crucifixion.

The going was singularly quiet. A hoof-stroke upon a rock, the glide and rattle of revolving wheels, voices in conversation, and now and then a calling voice, were all the sounds heard above the rustle of the mighty movement. Yet was there upon every countenance the look with which men make haste to see some dreadful sight, some sudden wreck, or ruin, or calamity of war. And by such signs Ben-Hur judged that these were the strangers in the city come up to the Passover, who had had no part in the trial of the Nazarene, and might be his friends.

At length, from the direction of the great towers, Ben-Hur

heard, at first faint in the distance, a shouting of many men.

"Hark! they are coming now," said one of his friends.

The people in the street halted to hear; but as the cry rang on over their heads, they looked at each other, and in shuddering silence moved along.

The shouting drew nearer each moment; and the air was already full of it when Ben-Hur saw the servants of Simonides coming with their master in his chair, and Esther walking by his side; a covered litter was next behind them.

"Peace to you, O Simonides—and to you, Esther," said Ben-Hur, meeting them. "If you are for Golgotha, stay until the procession passes; I will then go with you. There is room to turn in by the house here."

The merchant's large head rested heavily upon his breast; rousing himself, he answered, "Speak to Balthasar; his pleasure will be mine. He is in the litter."

Ben-Hur hastened to draw aside the curtain. The Egyptian was lying within, his wan face so pinched as to appear like a dead man's.

"Can we see him?" he inquired, faintly.

"The Nazarene? yes; he must pass within a few feet of us."

"Dear Lord!" the old man cried, fervently. "Once more, once more! Oh, it is a dreadful day for the world!"

Shortly the whole party were in waiting under shelter of the house. They said but little, afraid, probably, to trust their thoughts to each other; everything was uncertain, and nothing so much so as opinions. Balthasar drew himself feebly from the litter, and stood supported by a servant. Esther and Ben-Hur kept Simonides company.

Meantime the human flood poured along, and the shouting came nearer, shrill, and cruel. At last the procession was up.

"See!" said Ben-Hur bitterly, "that which cometh now is Jerusalem."

The advance was in possession of an army of boys, hooting and screaming, "The King of the Jews! Room, room for the King of the Jews!"

Simonides watched them as they whirled and danced along, like a cloud of summer insects, and said, gravely, "When these come to their inheritance, son of Hur, alas for the city of Solomon!"

A band of legionaries fully armed followed next, marching in sturdy indifference, the glory of burnished brass about them the while.

Then came the Nazarene!

He was nearly dead. Every few steps he staggered as if he would fall. A stained badly torn gown hung from his shoulders. His bare feet left red splotches upon the stones. An inscription on a board was tied to his neck. A crown of thorns had been crushed hard down upon his head, making cruel wounds from which streams of blood, now dry and blackened, had run over his face and neck. The long hair, tangled in the thorns, was clotted thick. The skin, where it could be seen, was ghastly white. His hands were tied before him. Back somewhere in the city he had fallen exhausted under the transverse beam of his cross, which, as a condemned person, custom required him to bear to the place of execution; now a countryman carried the burden in his stead. Four soldiers went with him as a guard against the mob, who sometimes, nevertheless, broke through, and struck him with sticks, and spit upon him. Yet no sound escaped him, neither remonstrance nor groan; nor did he look up until he was nearly in front of the house sheltering Ben-Hur and his friends, all of whom were moved with quick compassion. Esther clung to her father; and he, strong of will as he was, trembled. Balthasar fell down speechless. Even Ben-Hur cried out, "O my God! my God!" Then, as if he divined their feelings or heard the exclamation, the Nazarene turned his wan face towards the party, and looked at them each one, so they carried the look in memory through life. They could see he was thinking of them, not himself, and the dying eyes gave them the blessing he was not permitted to speak.

"Where are thy legions, son of Hur?" asked Simonides.

"Hannas can tell thee better than I."

"What, faithless?"

"All but these two."

"Then all is lost, and this good man must die!"

The face of the merchant knit convulsively as he spoke, and his head sank upon his breast. He had borne his part in Ben-Hur's labors well, and he had been inspired by the same hopes, now blown out never to be rekindled.

Two other men succeeded the Nazarene bearing cross beams.

"Who are these?" Ben-Hur asked of the Galileans.

"Thieves appointed to die with the Nazarene," they replied.

Next in the procession stalked a mitred figure clad all in the golden vestments of the high-priest. Policemen from the Temple curtained him round about; and after him, in order, strode the sanhedrim, and a long array of priests, the latter in their plain white garments overwrapped by abnets of many folds and gorgeous colors.

"The son-in-law of Hannas," said Ben-Hur, in a low voice.

"Caiphas! I have seen him," Simonides replied, adding, after a pause during which he thoughtfully watched the haughty pontiff, "And now I am convinced. With absolute assurance—

now know I that he who first goes yonder with the inscription about his neck is what the inscription proclaims him—King of the Jews. A common man, an imposter, a felon, was never thus waited upon. For look! Here are the nations—Jerusalem, Israel. Here is the ephod, here the blue robe with its fringe, and purple pomegranates, and golden bells, not seen in the street since the day Jaddua went out to meet the Macedonian —proofs all that this Nazarene is King. Would I could rise and go after him!"

Ben-Hur listened surprised; and directly, as if himself awakening to his unusual display of feeling, Simonides said, impatiently,

"Speak to Balthasar, I pray you, and let us begone. The vomit of Jerusalem is coming."

Then Esther spoke. "I see some women there, and they are weeping. Who are they?"

Following her hand, the party beheld four women in tears; one of them leaned upon the arm of a man of aspect not unlike the Nazarene's. Presently Ben-Hur answered, "The man is the disciple whom the Nazarene loves the best of all; she who leans upon his arm is Mary, the Master's mother; the others are friendly women of Galilee."

Esther pursued the mourners with glistening eyes until the multitude received them out of sight.

The demonstration was fanatical and bloodthirsty; it boiled and raved, and was made up of many elements—servants, camel-drivers, marketmen, gate-keepers, gardeners, dealers in fruits and wines, proselytes, and foreigners not proselytes, watchmen and menials from the Temple, thieves, robbers, and the myriad who, on such occasions, appeared no one could say whence, hungry and smelling of caves and old tombs— bareheaded wretches with naked arms and legs, hair and beard in uncombed mats, and each with one garment the color of clay; beasts with abysmal mouths, in outcry effective as lions calling each other across desert spaces. Some of them had swords; a greater number flourished spears and javelins; though the weapons of the many were staves and knotted clubs, and slings, for which stones were stored in sacks improvised from the foreskirts of their dirty tunics. Among the mass here and there appeared persons of high degree—scribes, elders, rabbis, Pharisees with broad fringing, Sadducees in fine cloaks—serving for the time as prompters and directors. If a throat tired of one cry, they invented another for it; if brassy lungs showed signs of collapse, they set them going again; and yet the clamor, loud and continuous as it was, could have been reduced to a few syllables—King of the Jews!—Room for the King of the Jews!—Defiler of the Temple!—Blasphemer of God!—Crucify him, crucify him! And of these

269

cries the last one seemed in greatest favor, because, doubtless, it was more directly expressive of the wish of the mob, and helped to better articulate its hatred of the Nazarene.

"Come," said Simonides, when Balthasar was ready to proceed, "Come, let us forward."

Ben-Hur did not hear the call. The appearance of the part of the procession then passing, its brutality and hunger for life, were reminding him of the Nazarene—his gentleness, and the many charities he had seen him do for suffering men. Suggestions beget suggestions; so he remembered suddenly his own great indebtedness to the man; the time he himself was in the hands of a Roman guard going, as was supposed, to a death as certain and almost as terrible as this one of the cross; the cooling drink he had at the well by Nazareth, and the divine expression of the face of him who gave it; the later goodness, the miracle of Palm-Sunday; and with these recollections, the thought of his present powerlessness to give back help for help or make return in kind stung him keenly, and he accused himself. He had not done all he might; he could have watched with the Galileans, and kept them true and ready; and this—ah! this was the moment to strike! A blow well given now would not merely disperse the mob and set the Nazarene free; it would be a trumpet-call to Israel, and precipitate the long-dreamt-of war for freedom. But the opportunity was going; the minutes were bearing it away. Was there nothing to be done?

That instant a party of Galileans caught his eye. He rushed through the press and overtook them. "Follow me," he said.

The men obeyed, and when they were under shelter of the house, he spoke again:

"You are of those who took my swords, and agreed with me to strike for freedom and the King who was coming. You have the swords now, and now is the time to strike with them. Find our breathren, and tell them to meet me at the tree of the cross making ready for the Nazarene. Haste all of you! Nay, stand not so! The Nazarene is the King, and freedom dies with him."

They did not move.

"Hear you?" he asked.

Then one of them replied, "Son of Judah, it is you who are deceived, not we or our brethren who have your swords. The Nazarene is not the King; neither has he the spirit of a king. We were with him when he came into Jerusalem; we saw him in the Temple; he failed himself, and us, and Israel; at the Gate Beautiful he turned his back upon God and refused the throne of David. He is not King, and Galilee is not with him. He shall die the death. But hear you, son of Judah. We have your swords, and we are ready now to draw them

270

and strike for freedom and we will meet you at the tree of the cross."

The sovereign moment of his life was upon Ben-Hur. Could he have taken the offer and said the word, history might have been other than it is; but a confusion fell upon him; he knew not how, though afterwards he attributed it to the Nazarene; for when the Nazarene was risen, he understood the death was necessary to faith in the resurrection. Without the faculty of decision he stood helpless. Covering his face with his hand, he shook with the conflict between his wish, which was what he would have ordered, and the power that was upon him.

"Come; we are waiting for you," said Simonides, the fourth time.

He walked mechanically after the chair and the litter. Esther walked with him.

## CHAPTER IX.

WHEN THE party—Balthasar, Simonides, Ben-Hur, Esther, and the two faithful Galileans—reached the place of crucifixion, Ben-Hur was in advance leading them. He had walked in total unconsciousness, neither hearing nor seeing and without a thought of where he was going, or the semblance of a purpose in his mind. In such condition a little child could have done as much as he to prevent the awful crime he was about to witness.

Ben-Hur came to a stop; those following him also stopped. As a curtain rises before an audience, the spell holding him broke, and he saw with a clear understanding.

There was a space upon the top of a low knoll rounded like a skull, and dry, dusty, without vegetation except some scrubby hyssop. The boundary of the space was a living wall of men, with men behind struggling, some to look over, others to look through it. An inner wall of Roman soldiery held the dense outer wall rigidly to its place. A centurion kept eye upon the soldiers. Up to the very line so vigilantly guarded Ben-Hur had been led; at the line he now stood, his face to the northwest. The knoll was the old Aramaic Golgotha, Calvary; translated, The Skull.

On its slopes, in the low places, on the swells and higher hills, he saw only thousands of eyes in ruddy faces; off a little way in the perspective only ruddy faces; off a little farther only a broad, broad circle, which the nearer view instructed him was also of faces. And this was the vast multitude; under it hearts throbbed with passionate interest in what was taking place upon the knoll; indifferent as to the thieves, caring only for the Nazarene, and only as he was an object of hate or fear or curiosity—he who loved them all, and was about to die for them.

Up on the knoll, and visible over the heads of notables, conspicuous because of his mitre and vestments and his haughty air, stood the high-priest. Still higher, near the round summit, was the Nazarene, stooped and suffering, but silent. The wit among the guard had complemented the crown upon his head by putting a reed in his hand for a sceptre. Laughter, execrations, sometimes both together blew upon him like blasts.

All eyes were fixed upon the Nazarene. It may have been pity with which he was moved; whatever the cause, Ben-Hur was conscious of a change in his feelings. A conception of something better than the best of this life—something so much better that it could serve a weak man with strength to endure agonies of spirit as well as of body; perhaps the spirit-life which Balthasar held to so fast, began to dawn upon his mind, bringing to him a certain sense that, after all, the mission of the Nazarene was that of guide across the boundary to where his kingdom was set up and waiting for him. Then, as something borne through the air out of the almost forgotten, he heard again, or seemed to hear, the saying of the Nazarene, "I am the resurrection and the life."

And the words repeated themselves over and over, and took form, and the dawn touched them with its light, and filled them with a new meaning. Instantly he was sensible of a peace such as he had never known—the peace which is the end of doubt and mystery, and the beginning of faith and love and clear understanding.

From this state Ben-Hur was aroused by the sound of hammering. On the summit of the knoll he observed then what had escaped him before—some soldiers and workmen preparing the crosses. The holes for planting the trees were ready, and now the transverse beams were being fitted to their places.

"Bid the men make haste," said the high-priest to the centurion. "These"—and he pointed to the Nazarene—"must be dead by the going-down of the sun, and buried that the land may not be defiled. Such is the Law."

A soldier went to the Nazarene and offered him something to drink, but he refused the cup. Then another went to him and took from his neck the board with the inscription upon it, which he nailed to the tree of the cross—and the preparation was complete.

"The crosses are ready," said the centurion to the pontiff, who received the report with a wave of the hand and the reply,

"Let the blasphemer go first. The Son of God should be able to save himself. We will see."

The people who had assailed the hill with incessant cries of impatience, permitted a lull which became a universal hush. The men were to be nailed to their crosses. When the soldiers laid their hands upon the Nazarene first, a shudder passed through the great concourse. Afterwards there were those who said the air suddenly chilled and made them shiver.

"How very still it is!" Esther said, as she put her arm about her father's neck.

And remembering the torture he himself had suffered, he drew her face down upon his breast, and sat trembling.

"Avoid it, Esther, avoid it!" he said. "I know not but all who stand and see it—the innocent as well as the guilty—may be cursed from this hour."

Balthasar sank upon his knees.

"Son of Hur," said Simonides, with increasing excitement, "son of Hur, if Jehovah stretch not forth his hand, and quickly, Israel is lost—and we are lost."

Ben-Hur answered, calmly, "I have been in a dream, Simonides, and heard in it why all this should be, and why it should go on. It is the will of the Nazarene—it is God's will. Let us do as the Egyptian here—let us hold our peace and pray."

As he looked up on the knoll again, the words were wafted to him through the awful stillness: "I am the resurrection and the life."

He bowed reverently as to a person speaking.

Up on the summit the work went on. The guard took the Nazarene's clothes from him, so that he stood before the crowd naked. The stripes of the scourging he had received in the early morning were still bloody upon his back; yet he was laid pitilessly down, and stretched upon the cross—first, the arms upon the transverse beam; the spikes were sharp—a few blows, and they were driven through the tender palms; next, they drew his knees up until the soles of the feet rested flat upon the tree; then they placed one foot upon the other, and one spike fixed both of them fast. The dulled sound of the hammering was heard outside the guarded space; and such as could not hear, yet saw the hammer as it fell, shivered with fear. And withal not a groan, or cry, or word of remonstrance from the sufferer: nothing at which an enemy could laugh; nothing a worshipper could regret.

"Which way wilt thou have him faced?" asked a soldier.

"Towards the Temple," the pontiff replied. "In dying I would have him see the holy house hath not suffered by him."

The workmen put their hands to the cross, and carried it, burden and all, to the place of planting. They dropped

273

the tree into the hole; and the body of the Nazarene also dropped heavily, and hung by the bleeding hands. Still no cry of pain—only the words: "Father, forgive them, for they know not what they do."

The cross, standing singly out against the sky, was greeted with a burst of delight; and all who could see and read the writing upon the board over the Nazarene's head made haste to decipher it, and presently the whole mighty concourse was ringing the salutation from side to side, and repeating it with laughter and groans,

"King of the Jews! Hail, King of the Jews!"

The pontiff, with a clearer idea of the import of the inscription, protested against it, but in vain; and the titled King, looking from the knoll with dying eyes, must have seen the city of his fathers at rest below him.

Suddenly a dimness began to fill the sky—at first no more than a scarce perceptible fading of the day; a twilight out of time; an evening gliding in upon the splendors of noon. But it deepened, and directly drew attention; whereat the noise of the shouting and laughter fell off, and men, doubting their senses, gazed at each other curiously: then they looked to the sun again; then at the mountains, getting farther away; at the sky and the near landscape, sinking in shadow; at the hill upon which the tragedy was enacting; and from all these they gazed at each other again, and turned pale, and held their peace.

"It is only a mist or passing cloud," Simonides said soothingly to Esther, who was alarmed. "It will brighten presently."

"It is not a mist or a cloud," Ben-Hur said. "The spirits who live in the air—the prophets and saints—are at work in mercy. I say to you, O Simonides, truly as God lives, he who hangs yonder is the Son of God."

And leaving Simonides, he went where Balthasar was kneeling near by, and laid his hand upon the good man's shoulder.

"O wise Egyptian, hearken! Thou alone wert right—the Nazarene is indeed the Son of God."

Balthasar drew him down to him, and replied feebly, "I saw him a child in the manger; it is not strange that I knew him sooner than thou; but oh that I should live to see this day! Would I had died with my brethren!"

"Comfort thee!" said Ben-Hur. "Doubtless they too are here."

The dimness went on deepening into obscurity, and that into positive darkness, but without deterring the bolder spirits upon the knoll. One after the other the thieves were raised on their crosses, and the crosses planted. The guard was then withdrawn, and the people closed in upon the height, and surged up it like a converging wave. A man might take a look, when a new-comer would push him on, and take his place, to be in turn pushed on—and there were laughter and ribaldry and revilements, all for the Nazarene.

"Ha, ha! If thou be King of the Jews, save thyself," a soldier shouted.

"Ay," said a priest, "if he will come down to us now, we will believe in him."

Others wagged their heads wisely, saying, "He would destroy the Temple, and rebuild it in three days, but cannot save himself."

Others still: "He called himself the Son of God; let us see if God will have him."

What all there is in prejudice no one has ever said. The Nazarene had never harmed the people; far the greater part of them had never seen him except in this his hour of calamity; yet they loaded him with their curses, and gave their sympathy to the thieves.

The supernatural night, dropping from the heavens, affected Esther as it began to affect thousands of others braver and stronger.

"Let us go home," she prayed, saying, "It is the frown of God, father. What other dreadful things may happen, who can tell? I am afraid."

Simonides was obstinate. He said little, but was plainly under great excitement. Observing, about the end of the first hour, that the violence of the crowding up on the knoll was somewhat abated, at his suggestion the party advanced nearer the crosses. Ben-Hur gave his arm to Balthasar; yet the Egyptian made the ascent with difficulty. From their new stand, the Nazarene was imperfectly visible, appearing to them not more than a dark suspended figure. They could hear him, however—hear his sighing, which showed an endurance or exhaustion greater than that of his fellow-sufferers; for they filled every lull in the noises with their groans and entreaties.

The second hour after the suspension passed like the first one. To the Nazarene they were hours of insult, provocation, and slow dying. He spoke but once in the time. Some women came and knelt at the foot of his cross. Among them he recognized his mother with the beloved disciple.

"Woman," he said, raising his voice, "behold thy son!" And to the disciple, "Behold thy mother!"

The third hour came, and still the people surged round the hill, held to it by some strange attraction, with which, in probability, the night in midday had much to do. They were quieter than in the preceding hour; yet at intervals they could be heard off in the darkness shouting to each other. It was noticeable, also, that coming now to the Nazarene, they approached his cross in silence, took the look in silence, and so departed. This change extended even to the guard, who so shortly before had cast lots for the clothes of the crucified; they stood with their officers a little apart, more watchful of the one convict than of the throngs coming and going. If he but breathed heavily, or tossed his head in a paroxysm of pain, they were instantly on the alert. Most marvellous of all, however, was the altered behavior of the high-priest and his following, the wise men who had assisted him in the trial in the night, and kept place by him with zealous approval. When the darkness began to fall, they began to lose their confidence. In their secret hearts they associated it with the Nazarene, and yielded to an alarm which the long continuance of the phenomenon steadily increased. In their place behind the soldiers, they noted every word and motion of the Nazarene, and hung with fear upon his sighs, and talked in whispers. The man might be the Messiah, and then— But they would wait and see!

In the meantime perfect peace abode with Ben-Hur. He prayed simply that the end might be hastened. He knew the condition of Simonides' mind—that he was hesitating on the verge of belief. He could see the massive face weighed down by solemn reflection. He noticed him casting inquiring glances at the sun, as seeking the cause of the darkness. Nor did he fail to notice the solicitude with which Esther clung to him, smothering her fears to accommodate his wishes.

When the third hour was about half gone, some wretches from the tombs about the city came and stopped in front of the centre cross.

"This is he, the new King of the Jews," laughed one of them.

"If thou be King of the Jews, or Son of God, come down," they said loudly.

At this, one of the thieves quit groaning, and called to the Nazarene, "Yes, if thou be Christ, save thyself and us."

The people laughed and applauded; then, while they were listening for a reply, the other felon was heard to say to the first one, "Dost thou not fear God? We receive the due rewards of our deeds; but this man hath done nothing amiss."

The bystanders were astonished; in the midst of the hush which ensued, the second felon spoke again, but this time to the Nazarene:

"Lord," he said, "remember me when thou comest into thy kingdom."

Simonides gave a great start. "When thou comest into thy kingdom!" It was the very point of doubt in his mind; the point he had so often debated with Balthasar.

"Didst thou hear?" said Ben-Hur to him. "The kingdom cannot be of this world. Yon witness saith the King is but going to his kingdom; and, in effect, I heard the same in my dream."

"Hush!" said Simonides. "Hush, I pray thee! If the Nazarene should answer—"

And as he spoke the Nazarene did answer in a clear voice, full of confidence: "Verily I say unto thee, To-day shalt thou be with me in Paradise!"

Simonides waited to hear if that were all; then he folded his hands and said, "No more, no more, Lord! The darkness is gone; I see with other eyes—even as Balthasar, I see with eyes of true faith."

The faithful servant had at last his fitting reward. His broken body might never be restored; nor was there riddance of the recollection of his sufferings, or of the years embittered by them; but suddenly a new life was shown him and its name was Paradise. There he would find the Kingdom of which he had been dreaming, and the King. Peace fell upon him.

Over the way, in front of the cross, however, there were surprise and consternation. The cunning casuists there put the assumption underlying the question and the admission underlying the answer together. For saying through the land that he was the Messiah, they had brought the Nazarene to the cross; and, lo! on the cross, more confidently than ever, he had not only reasserted himself, but promised enjoyment of his Paradise to a malefactor. They trembled at what they were doing. The pontiff, with all his pride, was afraid. Where got the man his confidence except from Truth? And what should the Truth be but God? A very little now would put them all to flight.

The breathing of the Nazarene grew harder; his sighs became great gasps. Only three hours upon the cross, and he was dying!

The intelligence was carried from man to man, until every one knew it; and then the breeze faltered and died; a stifling vapor loaded the air; heat was superadded to darkness; nor might any one unknowing the fact have thought that there were three millions of people waiting awe-struck what should happen next—they were so still!

Then there went out through the gloom, to those within hearing of the dying man, a cry of despair, if not reproach: "My God! my God! why hast thou forsaken me?"

The voice startled all who heard it. One it touched uncontrollably.

The soldiers in coming had brought with them a vessel of wine and water, and set it down a little way from Ben-Hur. With a sponge dipped into the liquor, and put on the end of a stick, they could moisten the tongue of a sufferer at their pleasure. Ben-Hur thought of the draught he had had at the well near Nazareth; an impulse seized him; catching up the sponge, he dipped it into the vessel and started for the cross.

"Let him be!" the people in the way shouted angrily.

Without minding them, he ran on, and put the sponge to the Nazarene's lips.

The face then plainly seen by Ben-Hur, bruised and black with blood and dust as it was, lighted nevertheless with a sudden glow; the eyes opened wide, and fixed upon some one visible to them alone in the far heavens; and there were content and relief, even triumph, in the shout the victim gave.

"It is finished! It is finished!"

The light in the eyes went out; slowly the crowned head sank upon the laboring breast. Ben-Hur thought the struggle over; but the fainting soul recollected itself, so that he and those around him caught the last words, spoken in a low voice: "Father, into thy hands I commend my spirit."

A tremor shook the tortured body; there was a scream of fiercest anguish, and the mission and the earthly life were over at once.

Ben-Hur went back to his friends, saying, "It is over; he is dead."

In a space incredibly short the multitude was informed. No one repeated it aloud; there was a murmur which spread from the knoll in every direction, "He is dead! he is dead!" and that was all. The people had their wish; the Nazarene was dead; yet they stared at each other aghast. His blood was upon them! And while they stood staring at each other, the ground commenced to shake; each man took hold of his neighbor to support himself; in a twinkle the darkness disappeared, and the sun came out; and everybody, as with the same glance, beheld the crosses upon the hill; but the one in the centre alone seemed to extend itself upwards, and lift its burden against the blue of the sky.

When the sunlight broke upon the crucifixion, the mother of the Nazarene, the disciple, and the faithful women of Galilee, the centurion and his soldiers, and Ben-Hur and his party, were all who remained upon the hill.

"Seat thyself here," said Ben-Hur to Esther, making a place for her at her father's feet. "Now cover thine eyes, and look not up; but put thy trust in God, and the spirit of yon just man so foully slain."

"Nay," said Simonides, reverently, "let us henceforth speak of him as the Christ."

"Be it so," said Ben-Hur.

Presently Ben-Hur looked at Balthasar and beheld him prostrate and still. He ran to him and called—there was no reply.

Then Ben-Hur remembered he had heard a cry in answer, it seemed, to the scream of the Nazarene in his last moment; but he had not looked to see from whom it had proceeded; and ever after he believed the spirit of the Egyptian accompanied that of his Master.

The servants of Balthasar had deserted their master; but when all was over, the two Galileans bore the old man in his litter back to the city.

It was a sorrowful procession that entered the south gate of the palace of the Hurs about sunset that memorable day. About the same hour the body of the Christ was taken down from the cross.

The remains of Balthasar were carried to the guest-chamber.

Ben-Hur would not trust a servant to inform Iras what had befallen her father. He went himself to see her and bring her to the body. He imagined her grief; she would now be alone in the world; it was a time to forgive and pity her. He remembered he had not asked why she was not of the party in the morning, or where she was; he remembered he had not thought of her; and, from shame, he was ready to make amends, the more so as he was about to plunge her into such acute grief.

He shook the curtains to her door; and though he heard the ringing of the little bells echoing within, he had no response; he called her name, and again he called—still no answer. He drew the curtain aside and went into the room; she was not there. He ascended hastily to the roof in search of her; nor was she there. He questioned the servants; none of them had seen her during the day. After a long quest everywhere through the house, Ben-Hur returned to the guest-chamber, and took the place by the dead which should have been hers; and he bethought him there how merciful the Christ had been to his aged servant.

When the gloom of the burial was nigh gone, on the ninth day after the healing, the law being fulfilled, Ben-Hur brought his mother and Tirzah home.


About five years after the crucifixion, Esther, the wife of Ben-Hur, sat in her room in the beautiful villa by Misenum. It was noon, with a warm Italian sun making summer for the roses and vines outside. Everything in the apartment was Roman, except that Esther wore the garments of a Jewish matron. Tirzah and two children at play upon a lion's skin on the floor were her companions; and one had only to observe how carefully she watched them to know that the little ones were hers.

A servant appeared in the doorway, and spoke to her. "A woman in the atrium to speak with the mistress."

"Let her come. I will receive her here."

Presently the stranger entered. At sight of her the Jewess arose, and was about to speak; then she hesitated, changed color, and finally drew back, saying, "I have known you, good woman. You are—"

"I was Iras, the daughter of Balthasar."

Esther bade the servant bring a seat.

"No," said Iras coldly. "I will retire directly."

The tall figure remained with some of its grace; but the face was coarse; the large eyes red and pursed beneath the lower lids; there was no color in her cheeks. The lips were cynical and hard, and general neglect was leading rapidly to premature old age. Her attire was ill chosen and draggled. The mud of the road clung to her sandals. Iras broke the painful silence.

"These are thy children?"

Esther looked at them, and smiled. "Yes. Will you not speak to them?"

"I would scare them," Iras replied. Then she drew closer to Esther, and, seeing her shrink, said, "Be not afraid. Give thy husband a message for me. Tell him his enemy is dead, and that for the much misery he brought me I slew him."

"His enemy?"

"The Messala. Further, tell thy husband that for the harm I sought to do him I have been punished until even he would pity me."

Tears arose in Esther's eyes, and she was about to speak.

"Nay," said Iras, "I do not want pity or tears. Tell him, finally, I have found that to be a Roman is to be a brute."

She moved to go. Esther followed her.

"Stay, and see my husband. He has no feeling against you. He sought for you everywhere. He will be your friend. I will be your friend. We are Christians."

The other was firm.

"No; I am what I am of choice. It will be over shortly."

"But"—Esther hesitated—"have we nothing you would wish; nothing to—to—"

The countenance of the Egyptian softened; something like a smile played about her lips. She looked at the children upon the floor.

"There is something," she said.

Esther followed her eyes, and with quick perception answered, "It is yours."

Iras went to them, and knelt on the lion's skin, and kissed them both. Rising slowly, she looked at them; then passed to the door and out of it without a parting word. She walked rapidly, and was gone before Esther could decide what to do.

Ben-Hur, told of the visit, set out immediately and hunted for her vainly; they never saw her more, or heard of her. The blue bay, with all its laughing under the sun, held close its dark secrets.

Simonides lived to be a very old man. In the tenth year of Nero's reign, he gave up the business so long centered in the warehouse at Antioch. To the last he kept a clear head and a good heart.

One evening, in the year named, he sat in his arm-chair on the terrace of the warehouse. Ben-Hur and Esther, and their three children, were with him. The last of the ships swung at mooring in the current of the river; all the rest had been sold. In the long interval between this and the day of the crucifixion but one sorrow had befallen them: that was when the mother of Ben-Hur died; and then and now their grief would have been greater but for their faith.

The ship spoken of had arrived only the day before, bringing intelligence of the persecution of Christians begun by Nero in Rome, and the party on the terrace were talking of the news when Malluch approached and delivered a package to Ben-Hur.

"Who brings this?" the latter asked, after reading.

"An Arab."

"Listen," said Ben-Hur to Simonides. He read then the following letter:

Know, O friend of my father's, how my father loved you. Read what is herewith sent, and you will know. His will is my will; therefore what he gave is thine.

All the Parthians took from him in the great battle in which they slew him I have retaken—this writing, with other things, and vengeance, and all the brood of that Mira who in his time was mother of so many stars.

Peace be to you and all yours.

This voice out of the desert is the voice of

ILDERIM *Sheik.*

Ben-Hur next unrolled a scrap of papyrus yellow as a withered mulberry leaf. Proceeding, he read:

Ilderim surnamed the Generous, sheik of the tribe of Ilderim, to the son who succeeds me.

All I have, O son, shall be thine in the day of thy succession, except that property by Antioch known as the Orchard of Palms; and it shall be to the son of Hur who brought us such glory in the Circus—to him and his forever.

Dishonor not thy father.

ILDERIM THE GENEROUS, *Sheik.*

"What say you?" asked Ben-Hur of Simonides.

Esther took the papers pleased, and read them to herself. Simonides remained silent. His eyes were upon the ship; but he was thinking. At length he spoke.

"Son of Hur," he said, gravely, "the Lord has been good to you in these later years. You have much to be thankful for. Is it not time to decide finally the meaning of the gift of the great fortune now all in your hand, and growing?"

"I decided that long ago. The fortune was meant for the service of the Giver; not a part, Simonides, but all of it. The question with me has been, How can I make it most useful in his cause? And of that tell me, I pray you."

Simonides answered,

"The great sums you have given to the Church here in Antioch, I am witness to. Now, instantly almost with this gift of the generous sheik's comes the news of the persecution of the brethren in Rome. It is the opening of a new field. The light must not go out in the capital."

"Tell me how I can keep it alive."

"I will tell you. The Romans, even this Nero, hold two things sacred—I know of no others they so hold—they are the ashes of the dead and all places of burial. If you can not build temples for worship above ground, then build them below the ground; and to keep them from profanation, carry to them the bodies of all who die in the faith."

Ben-Hur arose excitedly. "It is a great idea," he said. "Time forbids waiting. The ship that brought the news of the suffering of our brethren shall take me to Rome. I will sail to-morrow."

He turned to Malluch. "Get the ship ready, Malluch, and be ready to go with me."

"It is well," said Simonides.

"And thou, Esther, what sayest thou?" asked Ben-Hur.

Esther came to his side, and put her hand on his arm, and answered, "O my husband, let me not hinder, but go with thee and help."

Today, the Catacomb of San Calixto, more ancient than that of San Sebastiano, bears testimony as to what became of the fortune of Ben-Hur. Out of that vast tomb Christianity issued to supersede the Cæsars.